His eyes raked the raised deck in front of the bridge, passed over a black object and then returned. His heart leaped into his throat as eyes and brain coordinated to pick up the clear outline of a Browning automatic pistol. It must have been flung there by one of the sailors as his shattered body jerked and jumped with the impact of the Chinese bullets.

Turnbull's body arced as he flung himself from the cover of the starboard side on to the roof of the cabin, his hands reaching for the weapon. He had no thought now of survival by running. He was a primitive animal, a man attacked who was determined to fight back. To kill or be killed.

JAMES ADAMS

TAKING THE TUNNEL

A SIGNET BOOK

SIGNET

Published by the Penguin Group
Penguin Books Ltd, 27 Wrights Lane, London W8 5TZ, England
Penguin Books USA Inc., 375 Hudson Street, New York, New York 10014, USA
Penguin Books Australia Ltd, Ringwood, Victoria, Australia
Penguin Books Canada Ltd, 10 Alcorn Avenue, Toronto, Ontario,
Canada M4V 3B2
Penguin Books (NZ) Ltd, 182–190 Wairau Road, Auckland 10, New Zealand

Penguin Books Ltd, Registered Offices: Harmondsworth, Middlesex, England

First published by Michael Joseph 1993
Published in Signet 1994
1 3 5 7 9 10 8 6 4 2

Printed in England by Clays Ltd, St Ives plc

To Daniel

AUTHOR'S NOTE

Readers should know that the Tunnel in this book is intended to be a convincing but not identical recreation of the Channel Tunnel.

They should be reassured that this book could not be used as a blueprint for a terrorist operation. Significant changes have deliberately been made to the details of the Tunnel and the terrorist operation in the novel, so that if any criminal or terrorist tried to benefit from the ideas outlined in this book, he or she would be unsuccessful.

ACKNOWLEDGEMENTS

I am grateful to Christopher Bennett who helped me with some early research.

For an understanding of the Triads I recommend *Triad Societies in Hong Kong* by W. P. Morgan (Government Press, Hong Kong, 1960) and *Secret Societies in China in the 19th and 20th Centuries* by Jean Chesneaux (Heinemann, London, 1971).

In Hong Kong, I am grateful to Maggie and Rob Herries for their hospitality and advice; to Mark Pinkstone in the Hong Kong Government Office and to the captain and crew of HMS *Plover*.

In Britain, Captain Jeremy de Halpert and the officers and crew of HMS *Campbeltown* took me to sea and allowed me to explore the ship and understand its capabilities. Hugh Colver, formerly the Chief of Public Relations at the Ministry of Defence, was his usual helpful self. Captain Peter Voute, formerly DPR (RN), allowed me access to the Navy and I am grateful for his assistance and advice. Liam Clarke, *The Sunday Times*'s Ireland Correspondent, shared with me his detailed knowledge of the IRA. I am also grateful to Mike for his knowledge of explosives and detection systems, to another Mike for his knowledge of special forces and underwater warfare, to Kevin for his help with intelligence methods in Northern Ireland, to Richard and David for their guidance.

My editor, Richenda Todd, helped me improve

this book immeasurably and I am grateful for her wise counsel.

Finally, my wife René patiently read the different drafts of the script. Her encouragement kept me going and her imagination, good humour and love helped make it all work.

GLOSSARY

AD	Action Directe
BBC	British Broadcasting Corporation
Box	Slang for the Security Service
BR	British Rail
CHOPS (M)	Chief Petty Officer Operations (Missiles)
CINCFLEET	Commander in Chief Fleet
CLF	Commander Land Forces
COBRA	Cabinet Office Briefing Room
DIS	Defence Intelligence Staff
DSRV	Deep Submergence Rescue Vehicle
DST	Direction de la Surveillance du Territoire
EW	Electronic Warfare
FCO	Foreign and Commonwealth Office
GOC	General Officer Commanding
G-PODS	General Purpose Electro-Optical Directors
IRA	Irish Republican Army
JIC	Joint Intelligence Committee
JOC	Joint Operations Centre
Met	Metropolitan Police
MI5	The Security Service
MI6	The Secret Intelligence Service (SIS)
NIO	Northern Ireland Office
PIRA	Provisional Irish Republican Army

PIS	Passenger Identification System
PRC	People's Republic of China
PSA	Property Services Agency
PUS	Permanent Under-Secretary
PWO	Principal Warfare Officer
RAF	Red Army Faction, Royal Air Force
SAS	Special Air Service
SB	Special Branch
SBS	Special Boat Service
SIS	The Secret Intelligence Service (MI6)
SPU	Special Patrol Unit
TCG	Task Coordination Group

PROLOGUE

THE RUBBER OF the silent patrol boat squeaked softly as the craft bobbed in the ocean swell. The five men sat, stood or squatted in the position each favoured to absorb the shock of instant action. Jonny Turnbull hunched over a narrow metal bar that connected the control cables from the coxswain's station to the twin 250 Mercury outboards that seemed to dwarf the stern of the small boat. His hands gripped the frayed piece of cord that circled the bar; he felt like a rodeo rider with an unbroken horse between his legs suspended in the short half-life that exists between mounting the steed and the moment the wooden gate opens on the vast arena.

The two sailors to his left appeared relaxed – bored even – by their vigil, which over the past few days had become something of a routine. The Chinese sailor sitting to his right had said nothing since they had boarded two hours earlier, his presence only revealed by the glow of a carefully cupped cigarette. Turnbull glanced ahead to the reassuring bulk of the coxswain, a Royal Marine nicknamed Geordie.

He felt an affinity for the large man: not just the bonding of two men bound by a shared danger, but a clear similarity in their backgrounds. Both came from Newcastle, although Geordie's Benwell accent was more obvious than Jonny's longer Jesmond vowels. They had both sought service far from the grime and poverty of the north-east in an attempt to shake off the constraints of their narrow upbringing. But there the common bond ended. The Marine was in his mid-forties; tall, broad-shouldered and dark, with the strong chin and scrawny neck of the runner. Jonny had always thought of himself as a throwback to the Norsemen who had colonized the north-east of England, leaving behind their accent and their blue eyes and blond hair. The looks had mostly died out, but Jonny, a fit man in his early thirties, could in height and colouring have stepped from a longboat on to the beach at Whitley Bay. He wished he had inherited the other attributes. He hated and feared the sea and all this bobbing about was making him feel sick.

They had taken up station two hours earlier in the Tolo Channel in the New Territories. Two miles to the east, the mother ship, HMS *Plover*, a 690-ton Peacock class patrol boat, waited at anchor. Turnbull had been ferried from Hong Kong to the vessel in a small rubber dinghy and then they had sailed north-east into the dusk for three hours before anchoring at the mouth of the channel. He recalled the tiny bridge, the ballets that officers and crew performed as they tried to work around each other. The briefing the captain had given before they left the security of the mother ship had been short.

'We sit here at the mouth of the hole while we send you down as ferrets to flush out the rabbits,' he explained. 'We have a Kelvin Hughes radar and a thermal imager we borrowed from a Challenger tank. Between the two we can see anything moving out there.'

The radar showed both the outline of the surrounding hills and any surface movement. Jonny looked through the binoculars of the thermal imager and could see the green shimmer of the town of Tai Po ahead and half a dozen slow-moving green hot spots, junks plying their normal business.

'The smugglers use thirty-foot fast boats with four Mercury outboards on the back. Even loaded with tele-

2

visions, videos or the odd Mercedes for the party élite over there' – he gestured to his right towards China – 'they can barrel along at around seventy knots, which is about what we can manage, so the chase is usually a close-run thing.

'As I understand it, you expect the Ma brothers to try and make a break for the mainland tonight?'

'That's what we hear,' Jonny replied. 'But these two are smart, so who knows? What's certain is that they are not going to make us welcome so your men will have to be ready to fight if necessary.'

It was difficult for Jonny to keep the excitement and the nervousness out of his voice. For six months he had been hunting White Powder Ma, the controller of the 14K Triad, and his younger brother, Golden Ma, so named because of his lavish lifestyle and generosity with tips.

The Ma brothers had emigrated to Hong Kong from China in the early 1960s and with the help of the Taiwanese government had graduated from being street sellers of drugs to control of the most powerful Triad in the colony. An early trip to the Golden Triangle by White Powder Ma and a fortuitous meeting with General Li, the leader of the Chinese Nationalist army in Laos, had convinced the general that Ma was worth helping. Supplies of opium from Li were subsidized by the nationalist government in Taiwan who paid him with cash and guns. In return, as Ma's power grew so did the scale of the intelligence he gathered for Taiwan. Eventually, he controlled thousands of people and had the best spy network in the region as well as the most effective system for distributing heroin.

Of course, financial success gave the Mas the social acceptance these two illiterate men had always craved. White Powder Ma bought Chung Fat Pak, the colony's most famous horse racetrack, and became a prominent member of the Royal Hong Kong Jockey Club. Golden

Ma was on the board of a number of worthy local charities and helped run the Hong Kong Boy Scouts.

Jonny's investigation of the Ma brothers was exciting, frightening and the most challenging operation of his career. Normally, the Mas would have remained immune from the Hong Kong justice system, which was modelled on Britain's but had evolved into a bastardized version where the rich were untouched and the poor were offered as sacrificial pawns to make the arrest records look impressive. But the Mas had misjudged a deal and a traitor had appeared who talked not to the police but to the press, and the resulting scandal meant an investigation.

After only a few years in the colony, Jonny had not yet been corrupted and pursued the case with a vigour lacking in his older colleagues, who either knew such cases never made careers or who were already in the pockets of the Triads. There had been the usual threats made against Turnbull and his family, but he was just inexperienced enough to ignore them and carry on regardless. It had all paid off and two days earlier they had been about to raid the Mas' offices in the heart of Hong Kong, known as Central, when the brothers vanished.

It was money paid to an informant that had put Jonny in the boat that night. The informant reported that the Mas would head for the mainland by boat and so Jonny had been elected ferret.

As he absorbed the technology, Turnbull tried to understand the flow of acronyms that washed over him: the smuggler's ship was an FMT (fast-moving target); his rubber dinghy (how offended the Navy would be if they knew he thought of their boat in such terms) was an FPC or fast-pursuit craft; it chased 'trade' or smugglers towards HMS *Plover*, 'Mother'.

Their chance to intercept the smugglers was brief, as the journey from the New Territories to the Chinese mainland took only thirty minutes, of which around ten

4

were in China's territorial waters. The fact that the traffic in televisions, videos and cars was currently worth around $500 million a year showed that the Navy's efforts were pretty ineffectual; a few arrests, the occasional craft sunk, a reasonable price for the smugglers to pay.

Geordie suddenly clamped his left hand to his headphone and leaned forward, the red glow from the instruments giving his face an unearthly appearance. Turnbull hurriedly pulled his headphones from around his neck and pushed them over his ears.

'. . . Vector 110.'

The reply was drowned out as Geordie punched the twin throttles forward and the Mercury outboards responded instantly. Within seconds the craft had accelerated up from nothing to fifty knots, the force lifting Turnbull off his seat and trying to propel him back in a somersault off the stern. He gripped the rope between his hands, muttered a silent prayer and felt his mouth pushed open by the force of the wind so he appeared to be laughing.

The darkness was absolute. The roar of the engines assaulted his senses yet even their thunder was diminished by the speed which whipped the sound away behind them. To complete his disorientation, there was no horizon and no sign of the surface of the sea. He half shut his eyes to keep the tears from completely obscuring his vision, but he could still see nothing so each wave came as a surprise and each plunge into a trough was a jolting, jarring crash that seemed to compress his spine into his hips. Determined to be professional among the professionals, he was surprised to find himself muttering over and over again, 'Christ Almighty, Christ Almighty,' as exhilaration battled with raw terror.

Both the coxswain and the leader of the three-man assault force were wearing portable thermal imagers which produced a greenish haze for around four hundred yards. The two were shouting to each other, seeking the

5

target, knowing that at a combined intersecting speed of around 160 knots, Geordie would have just seconds to see, identify it and then change course to avoid a collision.

Suddenly, a hand shot out to Turnbull's left. The hunter had found his quarry. The boat heeled to starboard for a few moments and then in a sickening lurch came back on its former course. Peering ahead, Turnbull thought he could dimly discern an intermittent flash of white which rapidly hardened into the wake of a speeding boat. They were coming in at an angle and aiming to hit the smuggler amidships. Already his imagination had pictured the moment of impact: the bow of their boat carving through the other vessel's centre, a moment of panic and then both boats locked in a fatal embrace and sinking beneath the waves, dragging pursuers and pursued – himself among them – beneath the surface.

Geordie flicked a switch at his right hand and a white light lanced through the darkness to illuminate the smugglers' boat and its startled occupants. Turnbull took in the boxes piled high in the centre of the boat, the three men who appeared transfixed by the beam, the four huge outboards at the stern, the impossibly large wake and the sudden movement of the helmsman.

There was a microsecond to register the beam and then Turnbull's retina contracted and his world dissolved into a single sheet of intense whiteness, so bright it was both blinding and painful.

'The bastards,' Geordie shouted, his body tensing as he hunched over the throttles trying to peer through the wall of light as the two beams fought for supremacy of the night. With a stubbornness bordering on the reckless, Geordie kept the boat on course. He could see nothing, was relying instead on instinct and experience. Turnbull felt the deck lift slightly. To him, that meant impact was imminent, but to Geordie the proximity of the other boat's wake was the signal to turn the helm slightly to port and bring himself on to a parallel course.

Now Turnbull could see through the whiteness the outline of the other ship as they moved underneath the cone of the bow-mounted searchlight. A shuffling of feet, the cocking of SA80 rifles and the crew were ready. The Chinese crewman shouted through the loudhailer, urging the smugglers to heave to. The response from the helmsman was to drive the throttles forward, trying to urge another knot or two from the boat in a last desperate effort to reach the safety of Chinese territorial waters.

'Prepare to board,' Geordie shouted.

The three crew moved to the starboard side, SA80s slung across their backs. A slight flick of the helm and the two boats were racing side by side, the wakes soaring out in two huge, white arcs to either side. Turnbull noticed a moment of calm as Geordie cut the craft inside the smuggler's wake and then for a fraction of time the two hulls caressed. At that instant, the three men sprang over the side. The moment their feet left the deck, Geordie swung the boat back through the wake so that once again the light shone on them directly – and they were blinded.

Then the smugglers' light died and in the undisturbed illumination of their own searchlight they could see the three Chinese crew standing with hands in the air.

'Piece of cake,' said Geordie, turning with an open smile, determined to maintain the image of the unflappable Royal Marine in front of the civilian outsider.

But it was Jonny who heard the noise first, the distant burble that in a moment became a throbbing roar. From their left a piercing white light cut behind their own, pinning the two men down. Geordie's smile turned to a snarl, and then the shooting began. In clearly distinct moments of time Jonny registered the red and orange flashes of a gun barrel firing, heard the ripping explosion of bullets over the engine and then saw the splashes as the gunman marched the rounds up the beam of light.

He felt completely impotent, the attack was so fast, the

bullets suddenly so close that he had no time to move. The first rounds struck the stern of their boat, snatching huge chunks out of the rubber and spitting them into the sea. The bullets marched onward and into the smugglers' boat, this time scarring the smooth aluminium into huge jagged tears. Then it was people and not objects and the shots were cutting indiscriminately into prisoner and captor. Each body reacted differently. One seemed simply to fold over and die without any visible sign of injury, another lost an arm and a leg and teetered for a moment, blood fountaining from its side before falling sideways below Jonny's line of sight.

The blood and the imminence of death shocked Geordie out of his lethargy. He slammed the throttles forward and the Mercurys responded with a roar of power. At the same time, he swivelled the light away from their captive and towards their attacker. As they pulled away from the smugglers' boat, Jonny followed the beam and saw in its brightness the low, lean shape of a Riva powerboat. Instead of the vanity pennant at the stern there was a mounted machine-gun with a man hunched over it. In the well of the boat, two men sat, calmly, apparently almost indifferent to the carnage being caused by the man behind them. Jonny recognized the squat, toadlike form of Golden Ma sitting next the thin, ascetic White Powder Ma, the Laurel and Hardy of the drugs business.

'It's the Mas,' Jonny shouted over the noise of the engine. 'It's a trap. We've walked right into a fucking trap.'

'Pick up a gun and start shooting,' Geordie replied.

Jonny unclipped an SA80 from the side of the tiny wheelhouse. He brought it up to his shoulder, flicked off the safety catch and started firing astern in groups of three. But the boat was bucking and rearing in the waves and he didn't even have the half-satisfaction of seeing his rounds hit the water. Instead they simply disappeared.

8

Fifty yards astern there was a roar and a huge, jagged curtain of orange flame as the fuel tanks of the smugglers' vessel exploded. In the beam of the Mas' searchlight, Jonny's retina retained the image of the boat for a moment before it was replaced by the thousands of pieces of aluminium metal and flesh cascading into the night sky.

The image went dark as the Riva shifted its aim and began the chase, its light probing the sea ahead. Geordie was talking urgently into his throat mike, summoning help from Mother. He finished speaking, turned off the light and heeled sharply to port for ten seconds and then began a zig-zag course away from the scene. Behind them, the Riva's light swept the darkness, sniffing for their scent. It only needed a glimpse of their wake and they would be dead.

'A chopper's on its way,' Geordie shouted.

Just then one of the outboards coughed, spluttered and died. Geordie moved to correct the sudden imbalance on the helm but the loss cut their power dramatically and the Riva appeared out of the darkness, its light sweeping over them, past them, and returning to fix the boat and the two men in its bright, relentless gaze. Jonny fired down the light, the gun recoiling into his shoulder. There were no tracer rounds in the magazine and for all the good he did he might as well have been firing straight up into the sky.

There was no such uncertainty in the machine-gunner's aim. With the sea as a guide, he once again directed his fire towards them. Geordie was jinking frantically now, left then right then left, then further left, all the time trying to throw the gunner off his aim. But there were too many bullets chasing them through the night and too little speed left in the one engine for them to hide from the deadly combination of light and gun.

With the experience bred of knowledge, Geordie weighed the odds and found them unacceptable.

'Jump,' he shouted. 'Get out of here.' One hand reached out and grabbed Jonny's shoulder, lifting him from his seat and propelling him towards the side away from the approaching craft. Half pushed and half driven by his own instinct for survival, Jonny fell over the side, thrusting against the rubber to force himself outside the embrace of the chopping propeller.

The sea was warm and seemed instantly welcoming after the exposure of seconds earlier. Floating on his back, he turned to look at the scene he had left behind. The two vessels were still tied together by the cord of light and bullets were shredding the port side of the dinghy as the gunner found his aim and the gap between the boats closed. Ignoring his own advice, Geordie was still at the helm and Jonny saw that he was urgently trying to lash a rope around the throttle and the helm to keep the boat on course after he, too, jumped overboard. Then he jerked upright as the first bullet struck. Held erect by the bullets travelling up his body, the Marine began to shake in a grotesque parody of a dancer. It lasted only moments and then the gunman moved on, his human target destroyed, to remove all evidence of their passing. His aim shifted to the stern of the boat and the fuel tanks. His fire fractured the tanks and then the sparks of the bullets bouncing off the engines ignited the vapour. The shock wave from the explosion seemed to reach out and push Jonny's head beneath the surface. He emerged gasping for air, his mouth filled with water from the wave that had been driven out from the boat by the blast.

By the time his eyes had cleared and his breathing was back to normal, the Mas had given back the night. Bobbing alone in the sea, legs kicking and arms windmilling to stay afloat, there was only darkness. Disorientated, he could not even tell where Geordie had died, could only try to recover from the sudden and terrifying brush with death.

It took thirty minutes for the Lynx helicopter to reach the area and pinpoint the search so that the tiny light on his lifejacket was visible to the winchman peering out through the open belly of the aircraft. Once again his horizon narrowed in the white beam of a searchlight but this time it was to illuminate the collar and harness being lowered slowly down from the helicopter. He pulled the ring over his head and under his armpits and tightened the cinch. There was a moment of terror as he was sucked out of the security of the sea and became a spinning, weightless, powerless body. Then the Lynx lifted up and to the left as the winch reeled him in. Moments later arms reached around his waist and pulled him backwards into the helicopter.

Fifteen minutes later the helicopter landed in the shadow of the Prince of Wales barracks at HMS *Tamar*, the military headquarters of both the Army and Navy in Hong Kong. Ducking underneath the whirling blades, Jonny ran towards a small knot of people who were waiting for him. He had changed from his soaking jeans and sweater into a Navy jumpsuit. It was the solemn face of Harry Keating, his deputy, that first rang the warning bells. He had expected a sober greeting – after all, they had just lost their quarry and several people had died. But there was something about the stillness of Keating's face, the rigidity of his jaw muscles, that suggested personal pain rather than professional anguish.

After the ritual congratulations on his narrow escape, the small group moved as if on command to leave Jonny and Keating alone on the tarmac.

'I'm afraid I've got some bad news, Jonny,' Keating began tentatively.

Jonny had used those exact words three months earlier when he had visited the wife of one of his men who had been killed in a car accident. She, like him, had instantly understood that behind the mild façade lurked a world of horror. With a numbness gripping his heart he asked the inevitable question.

'It's Lisu? She's dead?'

'No, Jonny, your wife's fine,' Keating replied. 'I think you'd better let me take you home.'

They spent the five-minute drive to his apartment just off Po Hing Fong Road in silence. Reassured about Lisu, Jonny's concern had immediately focused on Sam, their two-year-old son. But he couldn't bring himself to ask the question, so instead he suffered as his imagination cast forward to the small apartment in Central; his wife and their child inside; Sam crippled, Sam dying, Sam dead. Each image more terrible than the last, he could feel his stomach compressing into a tight ball of anxiety, his heart thumping against his chest wall, as if trying to fly from this horror.

Too quickly, the driver pulled up at the small, grey apartment block. Keating got out first and held the door for Jonny. Reluctantly, Jonny led the way up the two flights of stone stairs to the wooden door of number eight. As he put the key into the lock, he could hear the first cry of what would become a lingering lament.

He followed the sound down the hallway, past the policewoman and into the second door on the left, Sam's bedroom. He saw Lisu, prostrate at the bottom of the bed, her shoulders heaving. Then his eyes moved to the cot and he almost cried out with relief. His son was lying on his bed, his tiny frame wrapped in a shirt covered with little dinosaurs, his hips bulging unnaturally with the nappy. He looked as he had looked all those other nights when they had come in to peer at their gift before going to bed: his face at rest, his breathing so quiet it was almost impossible to detect. Jonny did now what he always did, leaned over to pick up the tiny reassuring flutter of air from his nose.

But this time there was no little gust of wind, just an awful stillness. Then he saw the small red stain in the middle of the green dinosaur on Sam's chest. His finger reached out to touch it and came away as if charged with a jolt of electricity, the sticky texture of blood unmistakable.

He felt Lisu's hand touch his and then curl into the embrace of his palm. It was a moment so redolent of the touch of Sam's tiny hand that he wanted to scream. Instead, he reached down and brought Lisu into his arms. He felt her tears soaking into his shirt and felt his own tears pricking his eyes. He held her close, trying to smother the grief with his arms and her closeness.

'It was a stiletto, we think.' Keating spoke softly, trying to paper over the suffering with facts. 'He died immediately. There was no pain.'

Jonny turned around, his face contorted, blue eyes made dark with anger. 'No pain? No pain? How the hell do you know?' He paused, seeking some way out of the nightmare. Then his mind focused on action and revenge. 'Who did this?'

'The answer is simple enough,' Keating replied. 'Doing something about it is going to be more difficult. We found this in Sam's hand.' He reached into his jacket pocket and produced a small circular ring. It was a beautiful object made out of green jade and looked like a small napkin ring. Called a thumb ring, it is used by Chinese archers to help draw the string of a bow smoothly back. Down the centuries, thumb rings have become a valuable part of the Chinese artistic heritage. Jonny immediately understood what it meant.

'Dai Choi?' Jonny asked. Keating's nod confirmed it.

Jonny took the ring and turned it over in his hand. It was beautifully carved with tiny rabbits chasing each other endlessly around the circle, an image that would appeal to a child. This was Dai Choi's signature all right, the message from the 14K quite clear. Jonny had ignored their warnings. Now he had paid the terrible price.

Dai Choi, known to the Chinese as The Archer, was the Triad's chief enforcer. Such was the power of the gangs in Hong Kong that the police had never been able

13

to get any witnesses to his many murders. Indeed, he was so confident that he always left the same trademark on the body of his victims. Jonny supposed he should have been flattered. The humble peasant gunned down in an alley merited only a brass thumb ring. This was jade. But it wasn't flattery he wanted. It was Dal Chol.

PART ONE

THE PLAN

CHAPTER 1

IN HONG KONG, there is a delicate power structure that
allows Oriental and Westerner to live side by side, the
latter officially ruling the former in the certain knowledge
that both sides understand that in reality the roles are
actually reversed. To those who appreciate such subtleties, the attention Stanley Kung received was a clear
signal that this man had power. It was not just the
perfectly cut suit from Cheng and Chang or the distinctive
striped pattern of the Ascot Chang shirt – based on the
Turnbull and Asser original – but the way the staff
reacted.

Bowing so that his upper body was at an angle of
ninety degrees to his legs, the doorman, an enormous
Negro dressed in a peacock-blue shantung silk frock
coat, opened the car door and helped Kung out on to the
carpet leading to the entrance of the Lotus Casino.

Officially illegal, the gambling at the Lotus was tolerated in part because of the substantial sums in bribes –
known as squeeze – paid to the police and government
officials and in part because the authorities preferred to
know the location of the gambling dens, the identity of
the gamblers and above all the headquarters of the White
Lotus Triad.

As Kung made his progress through the disco the
staff responded with servility mixed with fear. A low bow
was balanced by the shifting of eyes to left and right,

17

anywhere in fact that Kung might not be looking, in case eye contact could provoke attention.

Kung, apparently oblivious to these undercurrents, moved straight through the lobby to a small doorway without a visible handle or a lock. Reaching into his trouser pocket he drew out a thin metal rod with hundreds of tiny serrations embedded in the shaft. He inserted the rod into a small hole in the side of the door and a half-turn to the left opened the entrance to the lift.

Twenty minutes later and three floors above the noise of the disco, Kung stepped into another world a different man. The elegant Western clothing had been replaced by a simple red cotton shift that hung to mid calf. The shift was secured by a white belt. White is the colour of mourning and the wearing of the girdle commemorates the dead founders of the first Triad. Around his head, Kung had tied a red silk scarf knotted in five places as a gesture of respect to the Five Ancestors whom all Triad members revere. On his left arm was a white circle containing the Chinese character Kin or Heaven. On the right arm the character Kwan, Earth, was drawn inside a similar circle. On the left breast, an octagonal shape, the Pat Kwa or Eight Diagrams, represented the eight groups of broken and unbroken lines from which Chinese script is said to have originated. In the centre of the octagon a white circle contained a rough representation of the relationship between Yin and Yang on which much Chinese philosophical thought is based. On his feet he wore one ordinary black shoe and one grass sandal which to the initiate recalls the story of a pair of magic sandals that had helped an early group of Triad members walk on water to escape their pursuers. Both sandals had been lost and only one recovered.

It was this uniform, little changed over hundreds of years, that gave Kung his real power. Only he was allowed to wear the red shift with the potent symbols that announced he was the Leader. As he entered the room, he remained upright but moved his left hand, knuckles out, across the front of his body. His thumb and little finger pointed up and down and his middle finger pointed directly away from the body. This is the personal sign of a Shan Chu or Leader. The other ten men in the room all replied with different hand signals which indicated their place in the Triad.

The origin of the Triads is lost in the folklore of the organizations but is thought to have begun sometime in the seventeenth century. Its members were bound by oaths of blood brotherhood and all were pledged to overthrow the foreign conquerors of China and restore the ancient ruling house to the throne. Down the centuries, the Triads evolved, moving their headquarters from China to Hong Kong, where they became more akin to a trade union. Each Lodge of a Triad fought for the rights of members and jealously guarded jobs. Only in the last hundred years have they taken on their current role of criminal gangs. Today the Triads are the largest criminal organization in the world, managing over half the world's heroin traffic and controlling the majority of the business in counterfeit money and documents.

What has not changed down the centuries is the secrecy, the bonding of initiates to the group, the reverence for history and awareness that the group is more powerful than any individual.

Stanley Kung had called this meeting of the ruling clique of the Triad to mete out justice to one of their own. Like everything else in the Triad, there was an order and a ritual to punishment as there was to promotion.

The room was rectangular, about thirty feet long by twenty wide, with plain white walls adorned with red and yellow flags, each with a single Chinese character symbolizing the five first ancestors of the Triad and the different branches of the White Lotus Lodge.

Kung walked past two guards armed with the

wide-bladed ceremonial swords, past the three bamboo arches symbolizing the entrances to the first Triad castle, past the heaven and earth circle of stones, the fiery pit which was in fact a small burning brazier, past the stepping stones which the magic sandals had once trod, past a line of black-robed officials, to stand on the left of the altar facing the room. Amongst the stones, rocks and flags that are all redolent of Triad history, the sheet of clear plastic stretched across the floor at the foot of the altar was starkly incongruous.

At the right-hand side of the altar stood the white-robed figure of the Heung Chu or Incense Master, the master of ceremonies within the Triad.

Lighting a joss stick, the Incense Master held it high.

After joining the Lotus family, remain loyal and faithful. The wicked and treacherous will perish like this stick.

He threw the joss stick to the ground where in a tiny burst of sparks it extinguished, a small blue tendril of smoke marking its passage.

With one voice, the dozen other men in the room intoned the traditional response.

The foolish one has done wrong.
He brought havoc to our brethren.
His death is not a matter of regret.
Let joss paper be his coffin.

As the last tones of the chant faded away, Kung spoke for the first time. 'Bring forward the Cho Hai,' he commanded.

Two men moved from behind the line of officials on the left of the Leader and brought towards the altar the Cho Hai, a man in his early thirties dressed in the uniform of a Grass Sandal, or messenger official, who is responsible for liaising between different lodges and mediating disputes between Triads. This man had been discovered passing information about White Lotus interests in the heroin traffic on the island to the rival Kam Lan Kwan Triad. The matter had been investigated, the Cho Hai found guilty and now it was for the Leader to see the sentence carried out.

The two guards forced the Cho Hai to kneel in front of the altar and then stood, heads bowed on either side. The Incense Master reached behind the altar and brought out a cockerel from inside a wooden cage. Grasping it by the body, he held it in front of him as another official stepped forward holding an ornately inscribed silver bowl. Drawing a short sword from a sheath at his waist, the Incense Master held the blade aloft.

The silver blade brings blood from the cock.
Do not reveal secrets to others.
If any secrets are disclosed,
Blood will be shed from the five holes of your body.

As he finished speaking, the sword descended in a single smooth motion and the severed head of the cock dropped to the floor with a slight plop, the one eye still open looking up at its executioner, startled by the suddenness of its end. Blood flowed into the cup as the cock's heart pumped out the last vestiges of life.

The assistant passed the cup first to the Incense Master and then to the Leader. Both drank deeply, the blood leaving a thin moustache of red on their upper lips. Stanley Kung picked up a white towel from the table, passed it over a bowl of water and delicately dabbed a corner of it across his lips to remove the smear of blood. He intoned the final, ritual sentence.

The white cloud covers the sea and sky.
When the floating cloud is removed the bright sky is seen.
Then can be perceived who are loyal and righteous.
Those who are deceitful and unfaithful will perish immediately.

The two assistants on either side of the kneeling Cho

Hai grasped him by each arm and forced his head down. Stanley Kung gestured to his left and a man dressed in the robes of the senior Hung Kwan or Red Pole stepped forward. He reached underneath the black robe with the red and white ribbon which showed he was the leader of the Triad's fighting section, and brought out a Browning 9 mm pistol. Standing slightly to one side, he placed the barrel against the kneeling man's left ear and gently squeezed the trigger. The sound of the shot was startlingly loud in the quiet of the Triad temple. The head jerked to one side under the impact and the bullet pushed through the ear drum into the cranium and exited the other side, carrying in its wake blood and brains that scattered in an arc, splashing over the assistant and the plastic sheet that carefully protected the floor.

Already dead, the body of the Cho Hai slumped, supported only by the two assistants. Kung moved around to the other side to fire a second shot into the right ear. This was followed by a third and fourth through the eyes and a fifth through the mouth. Only then did the assistants allow the body, its head now a pulpy unrecognizable mass, to slump to the floor. The ritual had been carried out and the body would be dumped in the back streets of Kowloon to serve as a warning to anyone thinking of betraying the White Lotus Triad.

The ceremony over, Kung walked down the room between the rows of his bowing acolytes. Once outside the temple, he turned left, walked down a richly carpeted passage and into a second, more comfortable room. Here, beneath paintings commemorating scenes from Triad folklore, Kung took off his robe and in a few swift movements was transformed back into a prosperous local businessman.

He paused in front of the mirror to check on his parting, his right hand delicately touching a few strands of dark, brilliantined hair back into place. He adjusted the knot in his tie, smoothed his jacket and shot the cuffs on his shirt, small gestures that reassured him that the transformation was complete. A swift glance at either cheek to make sure it was clear of blemishes and blood, then Kung pulled open another door and moved into the quiet of a comfortable, European-style dining room. At the simple mahogany dining table, a legacy of Britain's Imperial involvement in the colony, there were only two places set. Bowing, Kung advanced to greet the person at the head of the table. Now Kung, who only minutes earlier had been the ruler, was the supplicant, clearly anxious to please and impress.

'Stanley. Come in, sit down.' There was no affection in the greeting or the clear, commanding tone.

Kung was handed a computer printout and his eyes flickered over the figures, his experienced financial brain assimilating the columns and totals and assessing their significance. His brow furrowed as his host began speaking.

'This is a dismal performance. For the first time ever profits are down. Drugs, pornography, smuggling to the mainland; all the mainstays of our business are being hit by the Chinese.

'They hit us again in Guangdong last night and wiped out the Lam Wing Chui Lodge. What the mainland does, the police here imitate and we can expect further trouble soon. This cannot go on. I am not prepared to see all that we have worked for be destroyed as the Chinese try and prepare the ground for their takeover in 1997.'

'But there is little we can do,' Kung interrupted. 'We have tried bribes. We have tried intimidation. But the Chinese are determined to come in with their own agenda. You know as well as I do that the Communists in Beijing see Hong Kong as the Golden Child, the source of enough wealth to keep their lunatic policies alive. Whatever we say or do, they won't want us around taking any of the cash they think should be theirs by right.'

'No solution is not an answer, Kung,' his commander

replied. 'I will not sit here and watch our business fall apart and then have the Chinese come in and take over everything. We must think about this problem more aggressively.

'What we need is a new home, somewhere we can continue to work and to build on what we already have. We have been expanding all our operations in Europe, particularly in the new Eastern European countries. That is our future and we need to be in a position to exploit it properly. That means moving from Hong Kong to Europe – but to do that we need passports, passports which the British have refused to provide.'

Despite Hong Kong's colonial status, the British had refused to give residents British passports. Typically, the British Foreign Office had produced a classic bureaucrat's compromise which satisfied no one. Under a quota system, several thousand residents were allowed to get British passports each year while the very rich could automatically qualify. In fact, until five years before the Chinese takeover, the quotas had not even been taken up since the Hong Kong residents, entrepreneurs to a man and woman, hoped to continue making money. Then, as insecurity replaced greed, the quotas became rapidly oversubscribed. Demonstrations ensued, which had deteriorated into riots as the local people tried to force the British to honour past promises of citizenship to all.

Kung listened attentively as his controller's voice continued.

'We have tried persuasion. We have hired PR people to lobby Parliament. We have threatened. But the British are too frightened of Beijing to do anything to annoy the Communists. Without the passports our whole existence is threatened. We must have them.

'So, if the only thing they understand is fear, then that is what we shall give them.'

A piece of paper came fluttering down the table to rest in front of Kung. He recognized the front page of the

South China Morning Post. The article circled in red ink was headlined 'IRA bomb defused in Whitehall'.

A bomb containing 5 lbs of Semtex explosive was defused by police bomb-disposal experts in Whitehall yesterday.

The bomb, which had been left underneath a car parked outside the Royal Horseguards Hotel, would have caused serious damage to the hotel and the nearby Ministry of Defence. However, Scotland Yard confirmed last night that the IRA had issued a warning in time for the bomb to be defused.

The attack is believed to have been carried out by an IRA unit which has been operating in Britain for the past five years.

'You need to be more creative, Stanley,' the voice mocked. 'The British have been fighting the IRA for years and will no doubt be still doing so long after we are gone. The politicians and the public accept that terrorism is a part of life and they have adjusted their lives accordingly – although there is a universal hatred of the IRA which we can exploit. When you have a nation that has learned to live with terrorism you have a government that understands the subtleties of compromise.

'Go away and think about that, Kung. Come back to me with a plan that will drive the English to us. And remember what Sun Tzu says: "All warfare is based on deception. So attack the enemy when he is unprepared. Let your plans be dark and impenetrable as night, and when you move, fall like a thunderbolt."'

CHAPTER 2

EVEN AFTER TEN years, Jonny was surprised at the energy that seemed to flow off the pavements and into the people. Everywhere people hurried, the taller profile of the Europeans seeming to lope at a slower pace which actually carried them faster than the smaller Chinese. When he had first arrived in the city, this energy had been transferred and he had got caught up in the pace and the excitement.

Now there were too many memories. Where the tourists saw the magnificent façade of the Furama Kempinski hotel, Turnbull remembered the killing of a German businessman who had failed to meet his debts to the Triads. One of his hands had been skinned and the skin stuffed in his mouth with a single dollar bill. It was crude and brutal, but the message would have spread throughout the international crime syndicates: you don't mess with the boys or you pay. As usual, he had solved the case and as usual he was sure that the two hoods who had confessed to the crime actually had nothing to do with it. They had been offered up by the Triad concerned and the two had volunteered for jail in return for a commitment from the Triads to look after their wives and extended families generously. It was a form of social welfare which had worked well in Hong Kong for generations and to the Chinese it seemed eminently satisfactory: a man had been punished, police honour was restored and everyone had benefited – except for the dead man.

But such crimes were the exception. Mostly the Triads did their work away from the tourists' gaze, where any fallout would do nothing to damage the business on which they all depended.

The scene changed from the obvious, grasping glitter of the fashion boutiques and tax-free gold shops of Central as Queens Road passed Pottinger Street and the car moved towards the stalls selling bolts of cloth next to others selling live chickens, snakes and pigs. This is the Triad heartland on the edges of Central, the traditional bastion of the organizations that really run the colony.

Turnbull's car pulled up on the edge of a small crowd, the tourists outnumbering the locals, who have learned it is better to keep away from trouble, particularly police trouble. Turnbull pushed his way through the crowd, his tall, broad-shouldered body overpowering local and visitor alike. At the front of the crowd, a small knot of police were gathered with the lights, cameras and tapes that mark both a film set and a scene-of-crime unit. The subject of their interest was huddled in the doorway of the Aw Boon Tailor. Turnbull knelt down to look up into the face of the victim without touching the body. There was little left of the head, which had been blown to fragments, but the body told Turnbull all he needed to know. One arm was folded over the bloodied chest, its posture unnatural against the sprawling limpness of the rest of the body. On the thumb a single brass ring rested. Jonny peered at it closely, his lips tightening in disgust as the flies that already covered the wounds scattered. The ring was covered with tiny carvings of donkeys, each nose sniffing the next animal's tail, a message that used to represent the archer's method of getting to battle. But The Archer had adapted it to send a message, the donkey's universal image for stupidity perfectly clear.

He straightened and turned to the sergeant standing next to him. 'This is one of The Archer's men,' he said, the sergeant's nod confirming his own analysis. 'By the

27

look and number of bullet wounds, he has executed one of their own. Probably a Grass Sandal. But why here? They normally bury their men.'

'It's a message to the Kam Lan Kwan,' the sergeant said. 'The building over there is one of theirs and this is their turf.' He pointed to the Win Sun Porcelain Co. shop on the other side of the street, the modern shopfront contrasting with the overhanging wooden apartments above, from which laundry, pots, pans and clotheslines hung. 'This guy must have been working for them and he's been dumped here as a warning.'

Turnbull let out a small grunt, part agreement and part anger. The sergeant continued: 'It's one thing for them to settle their arguments among themselves but it's quite another when they start dropping bodies around the place and upsetting the visitors.'

The lines were well rehearsed, a litany that Turnbull had come to know well over the years. He had learned that another of the colony's compromises with crime was that a blind eye was frequently turned on Chinese killing Chinese, on protection rackets within the Chinese community, and on other illegal acts as long as they did not disturb the civilized tenor of society as a whole. It had proved a fatally flawed method of law enforcement, because the Triads had developed an independent police and judicial system which made the legitimate police and the courts largely irrelevant. That in turn meant that crime had grown almost unchecked. While Turnbull understood the game, he had never really played it according to the rules the government and the governed had established. There was often little to be done but when it was personal he could still find the energy to go on the attack. And the thumb ring made this personal.

'I think it's time we paid someone a visit,' he said to his sergeant.

If all the glitz in Hong Kong is London, Paris and New

York taken to Oriental excess, then the Mandarin is the hotel that is the ultimate in luxury. Its magnificent opulence, where ancient and genuine Chinese sculptures decorate the walls and each step inside its gilded doors is attended by a servant eager to anticipate the guest's wishes, attracts the Westerner. The hotel's proximity to the Star Ferry complex, which connects Hong Kong to Kowloon and the mainland, makes it a convenient meeting point. That, and its excellent pastries, made the hotel The Archer's favourite place to hold court.

Dai Choi was now the senior Hung Kwan or Red Pole – Enforcer – of the White Lotus Triad. Unlike his Mafia counterpart in New York, Dai Choi was no simple thug but a well-respected member of a feared organization responsible for the training and supervision of some five hundred men who provide the guards, street toughs and army for the White Lotus. The exiling of the Ma brothers had seen the eclipse of the 14K Triad and, as White Lotus gained in influence, they had recruited the best talent from 14K. Dai Choi had been one of the first to cross over, his prowess as an Enforcer already legendary.

He had earned his nickname in the Tai A Chau refugee camp shortly after he arrived from China with his sister eleven years earlier. One of the Gurkha guards had molested his sister who had later contracted typhus and died. Grief and frustration at his own impotence in the face of his sister's illness had focused Dai Choi's enmity on the guard and he had determined on revenge. Using wood cut from the walls of one of the huts for the arrow, a cross spring from a bed-frame for the bow and the guts from a camp cat for the string, he made a powerful weapon. The single shot had struck the guard in the neck, severing the artery, and he had died minutes later, his life leaking out on to the filth of the beaten earth of the camp compound.

The camp inmates were united in their hatred of their guards and the later investigation produced no leads and no suspects. But the incident had made Dai Choi famous as a man who had repaid dishonour with courage and regained some control of his own fate in a camp that was specifically designed to remove any freedom of spirit or action. Word of The Archer's success had naturally reached the ears of the Triad recruiters who drew their men and women from the ranks of refugees.

Squeeze and a set of new papers got him outside the wire and into the secure embrace of the 14K. The violence that had helped propel Dai Choi out of the camp became a way of life, and he had developed a new, darker personality. After eleven years, killing was an accepted part of his work, one that gave him status, money and the chance to enjoy the kind of lifestyle he had dreamed of in China.

Soon after he joined the White Lotus, Stanley Kung had sought him out. It was a time when the Triad was becoming established as a major force, and there was plenty of work for the right muscle and opportunities for advancement for those with the brains to seize them. As White Lotus had advanced so had Stanley and Choi, the one acting as the right hand of the Commander and the other rising to the coveted position of Red Pole, the blunt instrument available to enforce his master's wishes.

Now, with the struggle to survive far behind them, the two men had consolidated their positions as key figures of power in Hong Kong. Kung attended the Jockey Club races, was photographed at the right society dinners where fluttering European women sought his views and his charity donations and gossiped among themselves at the rumours that surrounded him. Dai did not have such access, but in the highly stratified Hong Kong society occupied the next rung in the social ladder: a dinner here and there but no pictures, and he only gave to Chinese charities. He was a successful international criminal, who had graduated from enforcer to entrepreneur.

Still only 35, he had long ago shucked his Chinese origins and dressed in the Hugo Boss suits, Sulka shirts and Nicole Miller ties of the smarter Western boardrooms in town. In the last couple of years he had taken to working out in the gym in the Mandarin in the mornings and then holding court in the coffee room overlooking the lobby immediately afterwards. He liked the after-exercise rush combined with the feeling of power that the Mandarin gave; a regular reminder of his roots and how far he had come.

He was a good-looking man. Life outside the camps had filled out the hollow cheeks and softened the jawline, although he still retained the thin features so common to the Chinese peasant, which in old age would make his face wither like a prune. His bushy eyebrows, strong dark hair and rather full lips set him aside from many of his friends and made his features attractive to those Chinese who admire hair as a sign of Western culture. To Westerners, he was appealing because he looked more like them.

It was all a sham, of course. But the Orientals greeted him with the deference he had come to expect while the foreigners saw only a fashionably dressed young man who blended perfectly into his cosmopolitan surroundings.

Turnbull found him at his usual table sipping a dark espresso and taking small bites from a Florentine while listening carefully to what his guest, another dark-suited Chinese, was saying. He looked up as Turnbull's shadow blocked out the view of the harbour.

'Inspector, what a pleasant surprise.' The smile was wide, the affection apparently genuine. Turnbull caught the order in rapid Chinese to the guest, who immediately left without a backward glance. Turnbull felt his hand gripped in a firm but perfunctory pump and then he was facing Dai Choi, who looked up expectantly.

'We found one of your men in Central this morning,' Jonny began, his normally soft voice made hard by anger. 'A Triad execution. He had been dumped on Kam

Lan Kwan territory. So that's your department.' He waited expectantly.

Dai took a sip of his coffee and dabbed the corner of his mouth twice with his napkin. 'My department, Inspector?' The tone of injury was a little overdone, carefully calculated to let Turnbull know that both sides understood the little game that was being acted out. 'I'm afraid that kind of thing is not my style. As I'm sure you know, my business takes up all my time. I stay well clear of any violence. Us former street kids value our freedom too much to put it at risk.'

As Dai moved to bring the cup to his mouth once again, Jonny's hand reached out to grip his wrist, the massed blond hairs on Jonny's arm contrasting with the smooth brown Chinese skin. Jonny squeezed but there was no give in the wrist and no reaction in the face.

'The body we are currently carting off to the morgue had your hands all over it,' Jonny continued. 'One of your thumb rings was on the body. Your signature, your body, your murder.'

Dai Choi smiled slightly, his teeth hardly visible, and used his left hand to free his right wrist. He began to twirl the ring on his right thumb with the fingers of his left hand. It was the beautiful deep rich green of the finest Chinese jade, the intricate carving of hawks made with a delicacy found only in pieces from the seventeenth century. The gesture was a calculated insult, a reminder of their relationship and its origins.

Since that day when The Archer had destroyed his family, Jonny had followed Dai Choi's career with the focus of the obsessive. As he had watched the killer prosper, his need for revenge was matched only by his inability to find any way of exacting it. There were always alibis; other, lesser, hoods offered up as sacrifice; always that superior smart-ass look of the man who is aware that in Hong Kong knowledge of guilt means nothing without the power to act. And Jonny had come to understand that he had no real power. But the struggle had become a part of his life and his determination to succeed was the single reason why he remained in the colony.

Now, as Dai Choi twirled his thumb ring, all the frustrations of the wasted years spent hunting this man returned. Turnbull extended a hand in front of Dai Choi's face and began ticking off the fingers.

'One, you don't execute people and dump them on my patch. Two, I expect to charge somebody with murder within the next twenty-four hours and I don't just want one of your penny-ante street thugs. Three, you deliver for me and I may – just may – not go and see Stanley to complain about you. And four, you're a cheap little hood despite the fancy clothes.' He contemptuously flicked the collar of Dai's dark green linen suit.

Dai Choi leaned forward, eyes narrowed, The Archer supplanting the artificial cosmopolitan. Turnbull could smell the chocolate on his breath. 'Don't you presume to tell me what I can or can't do in this town, Mr Turnbull. You're just a visitor here. This is my town and these are my people. What I do for, with and to my people is my business and my people's business. Not yours.

'And don't threaten me. You work here because we allow you to. You get your little victories because we give them to you. Because it suits us to do so. When you fail, you fail because we have decided that you should. We own you as much as we own this town. So go peddle your sanctimonious bullshit to your own kind on the Peak. You'll find people there who actually believe in that ridiculous uniform you wear.'

Turnbull looked at the clever, polished gangster. He knew that what he said was true. He would do anything to make it not so.

CHAPTER 3

THE UNSEASONAL ENGLISH summer fog lay close to the
ground, masking the sound of their footsteps. The damp,
grey morning would soon give way to a glorious August
day but for now even the birds were silent. The quiet
suited the two men, who, despite the darkness and the
embrace of the fog, shuffled along close to the verge, toes
pointing, seeking the twig or leaf that might betray them.

Young Marty didn't like it. Inexperience heightened
his natural nervousness and the silence compounded his
fear, making the absence of sound rather than noise itself
appear a threat. Sean Thomas reached out to touch the
younger man's arm, the brief gesture intended to reassure
as the moment approached.

It was odd, he thought, how the old always had to
reassure the young. There was never anyone to give him
the comfort and guidance his tight stomach and sweaty
armpits indicated he needed. Sean knew he was living on
borrowed time. He had been active in the Movement for
ten years, although for the last five he had officially been
dead and buried in a clearly marked grave in the church-
yard of St Mary's at Castleblayney on the banks of
Lough Muckno in the Republic of Ireland. A new identity
and a move to England had kept him one step ahead of
the security forces, but he knew that freedom was now
measured in luck not time.

The two men crept along the hedgerow, the wayward

stems of the ancient yew dripping small spots of dew on to their dark green jerseys. If the Boys had done their work properly, the gap in the hedge should come up in about fifteen feet. Then a turn to the left, a twenty-five-yard slow walk along the grass verge of the gravel drive and the house would appear. The second window on the left should be the kitchen and – if the information was correct and the man was keeping to his routine – the family would be at breakfast, a brief meal together before the car arrived to take him up to the Ministry of Defence.

Each man carried a 7.62 mm AKMS Kalashnikov assault rifle with a thirty-round banana magazine. The weapons were part of the shipments sent over by Colonel Gaddafi to Ireland ten years earlier. Since then the weapons had been moved from the Republic to Britain where they had remained buried in one of several caches dotted around the British countryside. The IRA maintained a logistics team on the mainland whose sole job was secreting arms and explosives in safe sites. These two weapons had been dug up from Crab Wood, a little-visited Conservation Woodland near Winchester. The two men had stripped and cleaned the weapons of their protective grease but the wet early morning air had given the dull barrels a slight sheen.

This was the third attack Sean Thomas's Active Service Unit from the Provisional Irish Republican Army had tried in the past two weeks. So far, they had been unsuccessful, which was why Sean himself had decided to lead this strike, to make sure they scored one. The first attack had been easy enough: fire bombs to be planted at the Prince of Wales Theatre in London's West End where *Les Misérables* had been playing for years. This was the simplest form of terrorist attack. The devices could be planted and the terrorist well on his way before they detonated. There had in fact been five small incendiary bombs in a clear plastic box the size of a man's wallet, with enough power to burn down the building. Unfortunately, the theatre had chosen that evening to try a new security system and everyone was being thoroughly searched. The girl with the bombs had panicked and instead of placing them in the theatre had gone to the Cross Keys pub in nearby Panton Street. To compound the incompetence, only one of the bombs had gone off, destroying the whole top floor of the pub. The police had recovered the rest and Sean knew that to the forensic experts each bomb was a filing cabinet filled with priceless reference material. They would know where the explosives had come from, if the bombs had been made up recently and even who had done the engineering. So he knew they knew that they were using old explosives from a cache buried five years previously. In the subtle interplay of terrorist and counter-terrorist, this was an important psychological edge for the Brits. They now understood that the ASU was being forced to use old equipment and inexperienced people so they were gaining some advantages after months of frustration.

The second attack four days ago had been aimed at an Army Recruiting Office in Nottingham. In the past five years while Sean had been running the mainland campaign, there had been forty-five attacks of which eight had been on recruiting offices. They were 'soft' targets in that they were rarely properly defended, and yet they hit the military so they had real value to the Movement. This time something had gone wrong and the two-man team had been taken. There had been the usual crowing in the media and plenty of references to brilliant detective work but no clear details on what had happened. The ASU's intelligence section suggested that the recruiting centre attack had been foiled because of a major undercover police operation code-named Neon. They based the assessment on a single reference to Neon in the *Daily Mirror*. A similar reference in the *Sun* two years earlier had betrayed Operation Octavian, which had been set up to protect individuals thought to be likely targets of assassination by the IRA. The planners back in Dublin were convinced that Octavian had been abandoned as too costly in police manpower and cash and so the instructions had gone out for Sean's men to hit a high-value target to make up for the bungled attack. He had personally chosen Bill Royce, an Assistant Secretary at the Ministry of Defence. Royce was not on anyone's list that he knew of but Sean had marked him because of his involvement five years before in coordinating security policy in Northern Ireland. For the past six months, the reconnaissance unit had been gathering information on the routine of the Royce family. The dossier had been passed to Sean the previous week, complete with points of vulnerability ready marked. The file was one of two dozen that he had. Each one carried information and no instructions. There were no orders of whom to attack or when, so there could be no betrayals.

No words passed between the two men. They had gone over the simple plan one last time in their rented Ford Orion, which was parked in a layby half a mile away. Their weapons were cocked, a round already chambered, and the safety catches were off. There would be no tell-tale snick to betray their approach.

Turning into the drive, the two men padded softly up the verge, each step leaving a distinctive impression of a dark foot against the lighter wet grass. The house emerged as a vague outline in the mist and then swiftly clarified into the shape of a large red Victorian building with the distinctive arrow-shaped attic windows pointing into the dawn. To the left of the square shape of the garage there was a door and then the diffused yellow light of a window. Their pace quickened, their steps coming faster, the impact greater in the earth as experience and caution became sublimated by the urge to convert caution into action.

The gravel strip in front of the window was a brief

obstacle, pebbles rattled underfoot and then Sean was at the window, Marty by his side, breath coming in short pants of fear. A swift, embracing glance through the window took in an older man – Sean recognized the face from the pictures painstakingly cut from newspapers and magazines over the years – a middle-aged woman – his wife perhaps? – two younger people, a man and woman – children? guests? Sean even registered the slumbering form of a golden retriever spread out in front of the Aga cooker.

There was no time now for selection, for accurate fire, for mercy. All were targets, all reduced to participants in a war he was determined to win. As one, the two men moved their rifles up and directed the barrels through the window into the bright homeliness of the interior. Even as he squeezed the trigger and the distinctive staccato of the Kalashnikov crackled through the still dawn air, Sean's honed survival instincts sensed danger. The very noise he and Marty had tried to avoid, the snick of a safety catch coming off, reached his brain and sounded the alarm.

As the first burst of gunfire splintered the glass of the window and sprayed into the room, he began to turn away from his target, searching behind him for the source of the noise. Marty, less experienced, had heard nothing and continued to hose the room, the banana clip of his rifle emptying in under three seconds. Marty was still at the stage in his terrorist career where he got a voyeur's thrill from the killing. He saw the plates on the breakfast table disintegrate, scattering cereal, milk and marmalade to splatter the four people who only now were beginning to express the first moments of terror in the face of certain death.

The bullets followed the china as the recoil lifted the barrel of Marty's gun so that they marched across the table, splintering the wood, until with a soft splatting sound they began to hit their real targets. The older woman was lifted up and flung backwards across the room. Marty corrected his aim, swivelling the gun to his left and then holding it as bullet after bullet made contact. Bill Royce literally fell apart, one bullet tearing off a forearm and flinging it dismissively to one side, leaving a bloody trail in its wake. Another punched a hole in his stomach, making him bend at the waist as if to genuflect before those who had planned his execution so skilfully. Already dying, Royce was hit twice more in the chest, the first round tearing away half his ribcage and the second driving through his left breast. Marty paused, inspired and overwhelmed at the carnage his weapon had caused. His vanity was to kill him.

While Marty completed the mission, Sean spun round, gun barrel thrust before him sniffing out the sound that had warned him. To the side of the path, just feet away from where they had walked, a patch of earth beside a rhododendron bush was moving, pushed into the air by a pair of hands that had emerged at the edge.

Sean realized it was a trap, that Octavian was still going on. They had walked right past the cops in the lair, the noise too slight to wake the dozy watchers. He had lived for many years with the expectation that his time would come like this: trapped in some obscure place far from home on a mission few knew about, his only epitaph a few lines in *Republican News*. He had no coherent thought of survival, no time to plan a solution. Instead, years of living on the edge propelled his body in response to the subconscious will to fight.

As the head of the first cop emerged from the hide and the stubby barrel of a Heckler and Koch machine-pistol peeped over the edge of the hole, Sean loosed off a short burst and then dived left, rolling on the gravel, tearing knuckles and knees. The few bullets did no damage but were a brief distraction. Prone, a low profile to the enemy who were now aiming on his level, Sean brought his rifle up to squeeze off another burst which shredded the bush above the hide, raining leaves and branches on the two men below.

There was no shouted warning to give up, no opportunity to surrender. Instead, both police ignored Sean, recognizing that firing on a flat trajectory is difficult in the calm of a range and virtually impossible in the heat of combat. Their guns turned towards Marty, who had been alerted to his danger too late. As he turned towards his partner, the first beginning of an imploring sound, half cry, half imprecation, emerging from his mouth, the two cops opened fire – but not with a 'double tap', the two carefully aimed shots that well-trained marksmen are supposed to use to dispatch killers. This was life, not fantasy. Their aim was not to execute but to destroy. The guns erupted with a ripping roar and Marty danced the tune of a mad marionette before slumping against the wall of the house, the bright red of the blood from his torn body mingling with the softer colours of the brick.

The distraction was all Sean needed. He continued to roll, turning over and over as he strove for the cover of a large oak tree in the garden. Behind its trunk, he jumped to his feet and began to run, keeping the tree between himself and his pursuers. The first few seconds were vital, he knew. He had left behind a colleague and a friend, but Sean was focused on his own survival, the sanctuary of the safe house that awaited him.

Three hours later, the old-fashioned black Bakelite telephone perched on the end of the long, polished wooden bar of The Felons rang. Brian Murray, who had been seated nursing his first beer of the day while idly chatting with his companion, levered himself up, walked across to the bar and picked up the receiver. He glanced in the ornate Victorian mirror over the bar, a vain man seeking reassurance. He saw a tough and confidently handsome man, and grimaced, smiling at his reflection to reveal briefly a set of strikingly white false teeth. His vanity was justified only in a long-lost youth; the face others saw already showed the dissipation of a man ten years older, the veins around his nose just beginning to show the reddish tinge of too much drink, and the small, tight eyes the suspicion and darkness of a man hardened to too long a life as a missionary among the unbelievers.

Murray's nickname was Spike, after his preference for kneecapping hoodlums and IRA malcontents by hammering a metal spike through the crown of the knee. Kneecapping is one of the IRA's hallmarks. It is a painful punishment and the limping men and women in the province are a constant reminder to others of the fate that can await them. The normal method is to blow the kneecap to bits with a bullet, but using a Black and Decker drill is also popular. This grotesque and brutal method has given rise to a new term in the Irish language: 'to be Decked'. But in the rather peculiar code that has evolved among IRA men, while kneecapping with a gun or even with a Black and Decker drill is considered socially acceptable, Spike's predilection was thought very strange. However, he was in charge of the Northern Command of the IRA and so any criticisms about his personal habits were muted.

The message was short and apparently meaningless.

'Hello, Brian,' a woman's voice with a soft Southern Irish accent began. 'You remember that meeting we were talking about? It went well but I'm afraid your cousin has caught food poisoning. Your brother is fine.'

Murray merely grunted and hung up the phone. The conversation had lasted no more than fifteen seconds, which the IRA believed made it impossible for the British to trace. In fact, technology was no longer dependent on time but on location. On this occasion, since the call had been made from a public call box, it would be three days before the computers at GCHQ, which record all conversations across the Irish Sea, would scroll through the database pending tray and bring the message on to the screen for the analysts watching for any link between the mainland teams and their masters in Ireland.

There was a lightness in Murray's normally heavy tread as he moved back to the table, sat down, leaned forward and placed his mouth next to Adams's ear before speaking. 'That was from across the water. Royce is dead and Thomas is OK. Marty is dead.'

Brian noticed a brief tightening around Adams's eyes, the only sign of distress from the Movement's leader at the loss of one of their youngest recruits. But the image was fleeting, overlaid by the same satisfaction that Brian himself felt of a mission successfully completed and the continued survival of their most experienced operator.

Adams's head turned until his mouth almost covered Brian's ear. A brief look of distaste – invisible to Murray – crossed Adams's face as he was forced to put his mouth next to his comrade's unwashed locks.

Gerry Adams was the one man who could tell Murray what to do and how to do it. As the President of Sinn Fein, the IRA's political wing, Adams is the establishment figure in the Movement, a savvy politician who perfectly understands the utility of covert terrorism and overt moderation. Adams was born in the Catholic heartland of West Belfast in 1948, joined the IRA's old D company in 1965 and became one of the founders of the Provisionals when they split from the Officials in 1969. A period in jail in the early 1970s ended with his release to take part in the abortive negotiations with Home Secretary William Whitelaw. The talks were a formative experience for Adams who still believes that the British will be forced to the table again.

In 1977, when Adams became Chief of Staff of the IRA, he organized a complete reform of the Movement to restore sagging morale and an ineffective military structure. He introduced a new cell structure which, with some refinements, remains in place today. This means that the British have found it very difficult to penetrate

the IRA with agents, relying instead o̶
keep them abreast of the game.

At the same time Adams began to cultiv̶
as a calm thinker, even a voice of mode
voice was heard frequently on television in
United States explaining radical revolution in a reasonable and reasoned manner that won the Movement many
supporters. The beard and the ever-present pipe enhanced
the thinking, professorial image. Like many habitual
pipe smokers, Adams's teeth had suffered from years
of chewing on the wooden stem. His lower teeth had
retreated into his mouth while his two front teeth
protruded, making him look rather like Bugs Bunny.

After years of practice, he has come to see himself as
Renaissance man: warrior in the morning, critic in the
afternoon and politician in the evening. To others in the
Movement he is known simply as Condor, a nickname
derived from the tobacco he smokes and the North
American vulture, combining a dig at his pretentious
ways with a grudging recognition of his ruthlessness.

In the 1980s support for Sinn Fein steadily declined in
the face of a consistent British policy of improving the
conditions of Catholics in the province and reducing the
profile of the Army. In the 1992 general election, Adams
lost his seat as a Westminster MP, a blow to his pride
and to the prestige of the IRA. The result was greater
pressure on Adams to push for a military solution. Under
pressure from the hawks, Adams had authorized a new
round of attacks in England.

Now Adams is in charge of an organization of no
more than around 200 men and women prepared to pull
a trigger or press a detonator; another 1,000 willing to
carry their bags or provide safe houses; and about 10,000
sympathizers who will gather intelligence and act as low-
level informants. Gone are the days when 5,000 people
turned out for a funeral of one of the Boys who had died
on active duty. These days they were lucky to get a

of hundred. The days when the Brit patrols down Falls Road would be greeted with a rolling cacophony of dustbin lids banged together by angry housewives have gone, along with the slums they used to live in. The orchestra has given way to a few soloists who understand the need for a performance but have largely forgotten the music.

It was hardly surprising then that Adams, ever the realist, had come to understand that a subtle change in the relationship between politics and terrorism was required. He knew that terrorism was no longer going to force the Brits to the table. Instead, terrorism helped keep his troops loyal by giving them an outlet for the violence, a way of keeping the romantic flame of Republicanism alive in the Provisional heartlands of South Armagh, West Belfast and Londonderry. Adams knew that it was political realities which would bring the Brits round in the same way that it had forced the Israelis reluctantly to talk to the Palestinians. He knew, too, there would never be a deal that would result in a united Ireland led by an IRA-dominated government. That was a 1970s dream which had faded in the apathy of the 1980s. The 1990s required the pragmatism of a politician, and he was the only man with the vision and the intelligence to deliver even a part of the Republican dream.

The latest mainland campaign had two goals. The Movement had always believed that if they could cause the Brits enough pain on their home ground then the people would force the politicians to compromise. Over the years, the headlines detailing bombs in Oxford Street and killings in Wiltshire had served to reinforce that conviction, which was, in fact, based on a fundamental misunderstanding. The news reports bore no relation to political process; while the British public and most of their politicians would like Northern Ireland to sink into the Atlantic Ocean, there was no stomach for a deal. On the contrary, the Brits had grown used to the security checks and the bomb warnings. Even the few directly threatened had learned to live with daily checks under their cars and changing their route to work each day. Just as the IRA had a hard core of supporters who would always be ready to die for the cause, so the Brits were tough enough to resist any temptation to compromise produced by even the worst atrocity. It was an equal match.

Over the years Adams had developed a healthy respect for the enemy. He knew that he was followed everywhere by people and microphones. He assumed that every conversation he had was later dissected by British intelligence, and he knew that every person he met was photographed, a file opened on every contact, however innocent. That was why he was meeting his odious lieutenant in a drinking club in the Catholic heartland and leaning close to his revoltingly dirty ear to carry on a conversation.

'At last. Sean Thomas is a bloody genius.' The praise was obligatory but Adams was already thinking ahead. 'We'll put out a statement saying the attack was one of ours, and let's put in a line about the campaign being for the people and against the military.' He paused and then added, 'Oh, and we'd better get there before the Brits so make sure Royce's Ministry of Defence work is emphasized. We don't want them telling the media he was some innocent working in the accounts department.'

Spike turned his head to reply. 'What about Sean? He's going to need help and we've no one over there to fill the gap.'

'Send someone in from the South. One of the ghosts who's clean.' Adams was referring to the small group who had been formed in the last twenty years for active service. Each of them was officially dead and buried, some from accidents, some from natural causes. But in each case the coffins were full of stones and the grieving families were supporters of the cause. Now, with false identities in the Republic, they could travel on their old, genuine papers, and pass through all the normal computer checks. It was a simple and very effective method of infiltration. The single difficulty was that the ghosts, although prized assets, lacked the experience to cope with a life on the run in England and so they were often caught.

'We want him to last but above all we don't want him to do anything that will betray Thomas. He's our single best asset in this campaign and at last we're beginning to cause the Brits some pain. Let's keep up the pressure and move to another target.

'At the same time get the intelligence boys to find out what happened to Marty. We don't want to make the same mistake again.'

'What do you want to hit this time?' Spike asked.

'People. We must keep at the people,' Adams replied. 'For every one we hit, there will be a hundred who have to check their cars each morning, a thousand who worry if they might be on our list. That's pressure and that's pain and that's what we want.'

Adams stood up, put his pipe in his pocket and gestured to the two men standing at the bar. They drained their glasses and moved to flank him. As Adams turned to leave, he suddenly stopped and leaned over Spike's ear.

'And tell Sean he's a bloody hero.'

Nico's was one of those expense account restaurants which had flourished in Thatcher's eighties and suffered in the more austere nineties. Douglas Hurd, the British Foreign Secretary, was one of the few who could still afford to eat there regularly. He defended the large bills by arguing that it was a restaurant where the tables were set far enough apart to allow discreet conversation. Hurd was one of the handful of civilized men left in John Major's cabinet. After the 1992 election Major had cleared away the last vestiges of the Thatcher inheritance and many of the old guard had been fired to make way for a more egalitarian – some would say bland – group who were more in the image of their leader.

Hurd was the exception. An Eton and Cambridge man, he had been Foreign Secretary in Thatcher's government and had hung on through the change of power to become one of the few left with international experience. Hurd had cut his teeth in the Gulf War and had since become one of the strong hands controlling international policy against Iraq and arms proliferation. His hoarse, gravelly voice, which sounded as if he was being permanently strangled, was widely imitated by comedians and his unruly bouffant silver hair was a cartoonists' dream. Although a figure of fun, he was respected as a man with a good brain and a sensible approach to foreign policy, which tempered a realistic assessment of Britain's current position in the world with a developed sense of what was morally defensible. In other words, he was the perfect apparatchik for the Foreign Office where pragmatism was always the preferred policy.

Between mouthfuls of hazelnut bread liberally spread with butter, Hurd was rehearsing arguments he had voiced many times before.

'But it is the practicalities of the thing, you see. We simply cannot be expected to play host to four million people from Hong Kong. The country wouldn't stand for it, not when we've already got three million unemployed of our own.'

'As you know perfectly well, that is not the point,' his guest replied. 'The issue is not whether the country would like it or not. That is a political problem. The issue is, Did the British government promise passports to those people or not? They did, and the British should keep their word, something that I would not even have had to mention fifty years ago.'

The rebuttal was familiar, the conversation a dance

where both knew the steps and the music. Dame Mary Cheong was the acceptable voice of Hong Kong, a spokesman for the local people and an articulate interlocutor between the British and the Chinese community.

Unusually for the highly stratified Hong Kong society, she was not a local at all but a refugee from the Chinese who had fled the Communist regime twenty years earlier. Looking at her now – poised, carefully coiffed dark hair, Yves St Laurent suit, expensive jewellery – Hurd found it hard to believe. She was one of the very few who had turned sanctuary into success.

She was the main bridge between the Western and the Oriental communities in Hong Kong. As the head of one of the most successful businesses in the colony, importing clothes, plastics and gold and exporting toys, jewellery and china, she employed hundreds. A member of LegCo, the Legislative Council that runs Hong Kong under the British Governor, on the board of the Chinese General Chamber of Commerce and prominent in the Jockey Club, she had the connections and the political influence to matter. Ever since the British had agreed to hand the colony over she had been trying to force Britain to fight the Chinese – and had failed.

Now Hurd tried once again to convince her that the British government were honest.

'It's easy for you to argue that we must do this or have to do that. But I have a responsibility to Parliament and the people and I can assure you neither would tolerate an influx of refugees on the scale you're talking about. We didn't allow it in Kenya or Uganda. We have tough laws to stop it happening in India and Pakistan. And they're all former colonies, just like Hong Kong.'

'But Hong Kong is different,' Mary insisted. 'You promised the people that they would get British passports. Most of us who came from China are anti-Communist. When you hand Hong Kong over, the Chinese are not going to sit around allowing us to continue with

with business as usual. Half my friends will be in jail and the other half will be dead.'

Hurd responded with the British distaste for drama and the scepticism of someone who has never had to fight to survive. 'I have never accepted that argument. We have assurances from the Chinese that they will leave well alone.' He was interrupted by a grunt of disagreement from Mary. 'And anyway, it will not be in China's interests to do anything that will disturb the status quo. They see Hong Kong as their point of access to the capitalist world. It will be something they inherit so they can bridge the philosophical gap between Communism and Capitalism.'

There was a pause while the first courses were served. After the first mouthful Mary took up the cudgels again.

'I don't think you have ever really understood just what it means to be a refugee from China. Perhaps if I explain how I arrived in Hong Kong you might begin to appreciate why we feel so strongly about the British betrayal.'

It had been her brother Lui who really wanted to make the journey. She was seventeen at the time, he was twenty, and with all the anger of the young he wanted a better life. He had seen their father grow old working the fields, still living in the same one-roomed shack in the same village surrounded by the same people. The Mao revolution had largely passed them by and so had the liberalization of the new regime. Their lives were set, and Lui could not bear it; the confinement, the hopelessness.

For years the family listened to travellers telling stories of this fabulous place where even the humblest peasant could own his own home; where Chinese people were welcome and the opportunities were there for all to take. It was a vision for them, something to believe in outside the prison of the village.

Then one spring, just after the first planting, Lui told

Mary that he had decided to leave and that he wanted her to join him. He had always looked after her, defended her from the other children or lied to protect her from her parents' anger. She had grown used to following his lead. It seemed only natural to her that she should join him on what promised to be a great adventure.

The family all contributed cash for their father to exchange in Guangzhoushi for two gold ingots, the currency of the border traders. They had a cousin in Shenzhenshi near the border and they hoped he could be relied on to help them across.

In those days, there were two ways of getting into Hong Kong: south to the peninsula at Shekou and then an eight-mile swim to the New Territories; or overland. Mary couldn't swim and, anyway, the sharks and the currents took care of most of the people who went that way, so the land route was the only option.

After five days of travelling by night they reached Shenzhenshi, the first big city either had ever seen. They could see it shining for two nights before they arrived, the huge buildings shimmering on the skyline. But when they actually arrived, they discovered it was all a sham. The buildings were mostly empty, the lights placed in windows to make it seem the city was alive, so the Hong Kong people just over the border would understand that China, too, had thriving cities with all the best technology. It was all just an exercise in face.

Their cousin passed them along the network to a man who said he would guide them through the patrols to the British fence that ran along the border. He promised to show them how to get through the fence. They would be met on the other side by another guide who would give them papers and new clothes and take them into Hong Kong. Giving up their gold, they set off for the border in the middle of the night.

There is a border curfew after midnight so there was nothing moving, just dogs barking and the occasional startled goose. The first barrier to cross was the Sham Chun river, which runs about half a mile from the border. It takes all the sewage from the city down to the sea, so was full of eels and so thick it was almost possible to walk across it. Their guide placed them in tyre inner tubes and they floated downstream for two miles in the filth past a couple of guard posts, and then paddled to the other bank where they collapsed stinking, wet and frozen.

On the south side of the river, local people have made dozens of ponds for breeding ducks so there are water, high earth banks with narrow paths and birds everywhere, ready to quack at the slightest noise. It was a terrifying journey of only a few hundred yards that seemed to go on for ever.

After about three hours, they reached the fence, worried that the sun would be up and the curfew over before they crossed the border.

There is a cleared track on the Chinese side of the border and then a seventeen-foot-high wire fence that runs for more than thirty kilometres along the border, covered with sensors and patrolled by Gurkhas. When the fence was cut or climbed, an alarm went off. Also, the British had sensors buried in the ground on the Chinese side that could hear somebody walking before they even reached the fence.

Their guide took them to a small stream, about three feet across. It wasn't water exactly, more like a deep sludge, the outflow from a pig farm on the Hong Kong side of the border. They slid into the ooze so that their bodies were covered, put on nose clips and used bamboo shoots so that they could put their heads under the sludge and breathe through the bamboo. It was terrifying. The mud was everywhere, sticking to them, sliding along their bodies, into ears, between toes, legs, everywhere. Mary knew that if she panicked the mud would come into her mouth. With each breath she imagined that black slime pouring down her throat.

Mary was leading, sliding along on her back, feet first, propelling herself forward with her hands. For forty-five minutes she had to push her hands into the slime, and after a hundred yards she was convinced that monsters lived in that ooze. She wanted to scream but couldn't open her mouth. She wanted to feel air on her face but couldn't take the risk of being seen by one of the patrols. Then her feet ran into the barrier, which was the posts supporting the fence above. She brought her head out of the mud and looked around. Above was the narrow bridge that formed part of the patrol road. Under its cover, the guide came up with the lorry jack he had been carrying for the past four hours. He placed the jack between two of the struts and started pumping. Gradually the struts were forced apart until there was just room to squeeze through.

It was beginning to get light and the guide was desperate to get out, but didn't want to leave his jack behind. Mary slid under the mud again and gripping the two steel bars used them to pull herself forward and under the jack. It was a tight fit but after some flexing and squeezing, she was through. The worst moment was when she had to get completely under the jack. She was forced to take the bamboo out of her mouth, slide it under the jack and then put it back in on the other side. To breathe again, she had to blow out the mud from the tube and then suck back in. She would carry the memory of the foul-tasting black slime for the rest of her life.

When Mary surfaced, she could hear the alarm bells ringing along the fence and knew they had only a few minutes before the first of the Gurkha patrol arrived on their bicycles. Lui was next. The guide urged him on from behind while Mary encouraged from the front and he slid into the mud. Mary followed his progress with the bamboo shoot which cut through the ooze like a little periscope.

Lui made slow but steady progress until he came

under the jack. The bamboo vanished into the mud as he pushed his head under the jack. There was a brief disturbance of the water and then the jack disappeared beneath the surface. Without the pressure the metal struts collapsed and the gap closed. Lui now had the weight of the jack and the smaller space pressing in on him and no way to draw breath. The guide and Mary moved to help but they were both more than ten feet away. Mary could see the mud heaving as Lui struggled to free himself, and tried to drive herself forward through the cloying filth which gripped her legs like treacle. She could almost feel her brother's panic, the sheer terror of being trapped. She reached him and pushed her hands into the mud. She could feel the jack and tried to lift it off his chest. The guide's hands met hers and together they pushed and pulled for what seemed like hours, but was probably only minutes. The jack moved from left to right but they couldn't get enough purchase to lift it. Mary could feel her brother's chest heaving and pushing as he struggled to get free. Then a huge, single, bubble of air burst on the surface of the mud and Mary knew it was over.

She had lived with the horror of that moment ever since, imagining that last breath of mud, the final seconds of knowing that death was certain. Sometimes, she could even feel the choking filth as it slid down her throat.

Hurd could see the tears in her eyes as she finished her tale and his British distaste for such displays of emotion fought with the sympathy evoked by the story. When he spoke, his voice was softer, the old debater's instincts sublimated behind a more humane façade.

'What did you do next?' he asked.

'The guide bolted leaving his precious jack behind and I never saw him again. I heard the Gurkhas coming along the path. By then I was crying with frustration. I wanted to stay with my brother, but we had come so far together, he would have wanted me to go on – or at least that is how I rationalized it later. Anyway, just before the guards arrived, I found myself running along the bank of the stream. Within a couple of hundred yards I was in the foothills and the Gurkhas had found Lui's body, which kept them busy while I made my escape.

'After that I made my way to Kowloon, found some relations and managed to find a niche. Money got me my papers and my passport and access to opportunity. Now, of course, people think I have power, but, as you so ably point out, I am your conscience not your controller.' She took a sip of wine. 'So now you know why I feel so strongly about this whole problem. It's all right for me. I have a passport and money. I could easily buy a place to go. But there are thousands of others who fled a brutal regime, hoping to find sanctuary with the British, who are now being thrown back into poverty and oppression, all because the British won't keep their word.'

The story and the digs at his credibility had offended Hurd's sense of doing what was right. But when honour fights with political reality it is generally not principle that wins the struggle.

'I can understand how you feel. I can even understand now why you fight so hard for your people. But I can assure you this is a futile struggle. It is an argument you should have had with me ten years ago when the negotiations were going on with the Chinese. But that was before my time and who knows if I would have acted any differently? The point is, Mary, the deed is done. No government is going to go back on the deal and all the public commitments that have been made without a very good reason. And your personal story is simply not reason enough. I'm sorry.'

They both sat back in their chairs, two fighters pausing to draw breath, their differences no longer ironed out by the atmosphere and good manners. Mary's eyes were almost black in the candlelight. She saw Hurd with absolute clarity for the calculating politician he was, whose social graces were a veneer to disguise the pragmatism of experience. And, now that he understood her background, Hurd saw not an elegant establishment figure from Hong Kong society but the tough self-made woman who had watched her brother die and was determined to avenge his death by defending the lives of all the other Chinese in Hong Kong. The gulf between them would never be bridged.

CHAPTER 4

ON THE PREMISE that the more public the place the less suspicious the meeting, Dai Choi had arranged to see the cutout at the café on the ground floor of the Etap Marmara Hotel in the fashionable Taksim suburb of Istanbul. The café is where those who wish to flaunt their European taste after a day shopping on Siraseliler Caddesi, the city's Bond Street which starts just 100 yards away from the hotel, assemble. The cutout would set up the arrangements for a meet with Selim, the leader of the Spiders, the gang which had a stranglehold on the Turkish drug-smuggling business and was responsible for the purchase and distribution of White Lotus heroin in Turkey and other parts of Europe.

The woman who sat down at his table blended perfectly into the cultured environment of Taksim. Dai Choi registered the elegant clothes, the Italian leather pumps, the perfectly coiffed long brown hair, and he caught a whiff of understated perfume as she stretched a hand out in that languid way that continental women have which offers a touch rather than a handshake. Her hands were soft.

'Mr Dai Choi? My name is Eleanor Swift. I believe we have some mutual friends. They have asked me to look after you during your stay with us.'

To the other parties – almost all the leaders of Istanbul's society of gossips – they looked like an intriguing new couple just arrived in town. And in fact their conversation was just the right kind of small talk with no hint of Dai's more deadly purpose.

Dai Choi had flown in the previous night via Paris after setting up the meeting through the contacts his organization had developed with the drug distributors of Turkey's underworld. The underground economy works very like its more open counterpart where people in the same line of work tend to help each other out, provided it's not bad for business. Dai Choi had sent a coded fax to Selim, and his request for assistance was answered the same day with a message to go to the Etap Marmara Hotel where he would be met. Dai Choi assumed that over the years Selim had done exactly what he would have done, which was to build up a detailed dossier on all his contacts which would include his own photograph. There would be no need for complicated codes or carnations in buttonholes.

'If you come to Valentino's bar tonight you might find what you want,' Eleanor suggested. As she spoke, her fingers reached out and touched Dai Choi's forearm, the *double entendre* clear in the message. Dai enjoyed both the touch and the anticipation of an evening in the company of this fascinating woman.

That night Dai Choi walked the four hundred yards from his hotel down the pedestrian precinct of Siraselviler Caddesi. Just past the Hermès outlet he turned down an alleyway and saw the small red flashing sign for Valentino's. The bar was just like any other bar in any prosperous Western city. A few steps down to the basement, past a bouncer and he was inside the club itself. He looked around, taking in the large room, the small tables laid with white linen, the dark red walls decorated with art from the Ottoman empire, all of which appeared to focus on women and their consorts in various stages of undress.

But there was neither the smell nor the atmosphere of

many clubs he had been to in Hong Kong, London or New York. This was a sophisticated international clientele who appeared remarkably quiet. Each of the guests was watching the small stage and it was clear the performance was about to begin. A strikingly pretty dark-haired woman dressed in the bodice and flowing trousers of the Turkish dancer escorted him to a table next to the stage. As he sat down, another waitress appeared, to place a fluted glass of pink champagne in front of him. Clearly he was expected, his Chinese features distinctive amid the uniformly swarthy men at the other tables.

He looked up at the stage as a single high fluting note echoed around the room, stilling the hum of conversation. As the sound died away a woman glided on to the stage. Dressed in the pantaloons and bodice that appeared to be the club uniform, she seemed to float, her steps taking her back and forth across the stage. It was both elegant and erotic, the movements suggestive of earthy delights hidden beneath the diaphanous clothing and the almost transparent veil.

The pipe was now accompanied by a single kettle drum which picked up the rhythm of the undulating body. Dai Choi had seen plenty of strip shows – indeed he employed plenty of strippers – but this was different. As the woman moved so the crowd moved with her. There was none of the tawdry atmosphere associated with such events. This was sensual, delightful, arousing.

With a delicate gesture that moved her right hand across her face, the veil was undone and fluttered to the floor. Dai Choi leaned forward in surprise as he recognized the elegant and sophisticated Eleanor Swift. But it was a woman transformed. To his surprise Dai Choi felt the beginnings of an erection as his mind strung together the touch of the woman in the café that afternoon with the one being revealed now.

'You should always look at the throat and the wrists, my friend,' said a voice at his elbow.

Dai Choi turned and saw that a short, round man had slipped into the spare chair at the table. He had a tall glass of raki, the aniseed drink popular in Turkey, and he took a deep draught before continuing.

'Look carefully. The woman you are admiring so much is a man; one of our population of transsexuals. You can always tell by the Adam's apple and the thicker wrists. Surgery and hormones can do nothing to disguise that. It is a curious fact that in our country where manhood is a fetish to be worshipped, these sexual deviants are welcome. In fact, Stamboul has become something of a Mecca for them. The lovely Eleanor is really John Rakestraw. He comes from Seattle in Washington.'

Although a liberal man, Dai Choi was upset that he had been so nearly seduced and that his companion had seen his excitement. It wasn't so much the homosexuality that offended him but that he had nearly been ridiculed. He moved his chair slightly so that he faced towards the stranger, who now offered his hand.

'My name is Selim. You must be Mr Dai Choi. Welcome to Istanbul, my friend.'

Dai Choi dispensed with further preliminaries. He wanted to do business and leave. 'I understand you may be able to arrange the delivery of some special equipment to Britain.'

Selim nodded. 'Exactly what do you have in mind and when do you need it?'

Dai Choi handed over two sheets of closely typed white paper. Selim glanced down the list, nodding occasionally as he mentally compared arms, ammunition and explosives with what he had in his warehouses off the Ragip Gumus road by the Galata Bridge.

'There are one or two items here that might be a little difficult,' he said. 'That type of phosphorus is not that common but I can probably find some. The weapons are easy and so is the ammunition. The explosive might be tough. I'll probably have to send out for that and the same with the detonators. But we have people in Bulgaria and we have a shipment of other goods going through Sofia next week, so we should be able to bring out what you want on the return trip.'

'What about cost and delivery?' Dai Choi asked.

'Delivery first. We have a good distribution system already in place in Europe and we should be able to use it for this. The only problem is bulk so some of our normal methods won't work. But we have been experimenting with a sea-delivery system which the Colombians pioneered and we haven't had a failure yet.

'Get to Britain and buy a small yacht or motor cruiser big enough to take the cargo. Just make sure it carries a Grundig echo sounder on board which you will need to modify so that it can send a signal on a precise frequency. When you get back let me have some secure numbers and I'll call you with the final arrangements.

'As far as cost is concerned, you'll have to let me work it out. This is quite a list you have here and I don't have the figures in my head. I would say you're looking at around $750,000 including delivery but that may be off plus or minus twenty per cent.'

Seeing the surprise on Dai Choi's face, Selim hurried to reassure him.

'Look, my friend. You're going to be getting the best quality and guaranteed delivery and that doesn't come cheap. But I'm not going to cheat you. We do too much business together. Be assured, you are safe in my hands.'

'There is just one other small matter,' Dai Choi interrupted, his hand reaching inside his jacket pocket to produce a single sheet of neatly folded paper.

Selim unfolded the sheet and his eyebrows rose. 'For this, my friend, you are talking serious money and serious trouble.'

'I know the risks and I am prepared to pay the price,' said Dai Choi. 'The question is, can you deliver?'

Selim's lips pursed as he thought through the problem.

'There have been rumours for months that some of these are coming on the market,' he replied. 'But I think many of them have been started by the CIA and other intelligence agencies trying to trap people like me. But for the right money, it just might be possible. We have some good contacts with the Russian Mafia and they may have a source in the right place. I'll see what we can do.'

Their business concluded, Dai Choi briefly shook Selim's hand and rose to leave. As he walked towards the door, sliding between the tables, he could not resist a final look at the stage. Eleanor was now naked and Dai Choi's eyes took in the pair of small breasts with what appeared to be long, dark brown nipples. Below the waist, the imagined pubic mound was revealed as a man's penis and testicles. He smiled ruefully. It had been a close call.

The trilling of the telephone interrupted Turnbull's restless pre-dawn sleep. Like most policemen used to having his rest disturbed, his brain clicked in before his body was fully awake and he immediately recognized the softly sing-song voice of his Chinese deputy.

'We may have a break on the Triad murder,' the sergeant said. 'An eyewitness. He claims he saw a red Mercedes sports car at the scene and got a good look at the driver.'

It was all the carrot Jonny needed to kick off the sheets and push himself out of bed towards his uniform. 'I'm on my way,' he said, hanging up the telephone and reaching for his shirt.

On the other side of the bed Lisu mewed softly in her sleep, too used to the nightly interruptions to wake up, too used to the drama even to inquire the cause of the call.

Jonny knew that the red Mercedes could only belong to Dai Choi. Like the thumb rings, it was another of his trademarks. Another symbol of the difference between the two men that had rankled all these years. Jonny could feel the excitement in his chest, the first time since his meeting with the killer at the Mandarin that he had felt anything other than anger and frustration. Perhaps this time, he thought, they would get the evidence they needed.

There was a car waiting outside his apartment block to take him on the ten-minute journey to police headquarters. No. 1 Arsenal is a magnificent site on which the police have constructed one of the ugliest buildings in Hong Kong, a city which prides itself on its wonderful modern architecture. On the outside, a nineteen-storey white vertical rectangle; inside, it is like police headquarters all over the world: scuffed corridors with linoleum on the floor and pastel colours on the wall. Each office is cramped, the thin doors barely shielding passersby from the shouts of anger or excitement from their occupants. There is also the all-pervading smell of stale cigarette smoke and old coffee, proof that whatever the health concerns of the outside world they have not penetrated the traditional hearts of the police.

Jonny's office was on the twelfth floor, which had been taken over by the Organized Crime Unit three years earlier. It had a large picture window looking over not the harbour but the apartment buildings that now surrounded what had once been a deserted part of the Hong Kong waterfront. The main building on the right had opened only a month before and in one of their regular demonstrations of power, the Triads had sent along their people to get the coveted allocations for a flat. In theory, it was first come, first served. In reality, all the Triad members arrived wearing a single white glove as an identifying mark. Anyone not conforming to the dress code either left the queue or was encouraged to do so, leaving the Triads in control of yet another apartment block. It was just one more visible manifestation of the impotence of the police to deal with the Triad problem.

Jonny sat down behind his desk and rocked back in the armchair, waiting for the knock on the door. He knew that the efficient office bush telegraph would have alerted the staff to his arrival. Two minutes later there was a firm knock on the door and, without waiting for an answer, Sergeant Gordon Fung Siu Yuen walked in, a buff folder in one hand.

'Two bits of good news, sir,' he began. 'You remember that the body was found outside Aw Boon's tailor shop?' Jonny nodded. 'Well, it seems the body was dumped just before dawn as Aw Boon himself was coming to work. He had just turned the corner into the street when two cars came in from the other direction, one some kind of estate car and the other the Mercedes. Our man is a cautious fellow and smelled trouble, so he retreated into a doorway and watched as they got the body out of the back of the car. Then the man in the Mercedes got out and bent over the body before both cars drove past him and away.'

As the sergeant's tale unfolded, Jonny's right hand began to pull at his ear lobe, a clear sign to his subordinate of the nervous tension his little speech had provoked. When Jonny had first arrived in the colony, his fair hair and fair skin had made him the butt of many jokes. His single-minded enthusiasm for the job and his colouring in the hot Hong Kong weather had gained him the nickname Cheong Wui or Red Spear. But acclimatization, the death of Sam and a respect for his work combined to produce a more sympathetic response to his foibles among the Chinese in police headquarters. Inside No. 1 Arsenal, he was now simply known as Tan Yee or Single Ear, because of his nervous habit.

'Christ, that's great, Gordon,' Jonny exclaimed. 'What have we done with the observant Mr Aw Boon?'

'He's still down at his shop,' the sergeant replied. 'We tried to get him to come in but he says he's got orders to fill and refuses to move.'

'Well, we'd better get down there right now and persuade him that he won't be making any more suits once Dai Choi finds out what he knows.'

Jonny got up from the desk and headed for the door.

'There's more, sir,' the sergeant said, putting a hand on Jonny's arm to restrain him. 'We've picked Dai Choi up on PIS and if you think Aw Boon's evidence stands up, there's a chance to pull him in before he knows what we've got.'

Jonny opened the folder his sergeant handed him and took out the single sheet which contained a simple three-line message: *Dai Choi, Hong Kong Citizen. Travelling on Thai Airways Flight No. TA 625, Depart Istanbul 14.30 Arrive Hong Kong 10.50.*

Terrorist attacks on aircraft have led to a new generation of computers designed not just to provide passengers with boarding passes but also to forward those details to the country of destination so that any names or suspicious characteristics can be matched with the police and immigration database. Known as the Passenger Identification System, which had generated the unfortunate acronym PIS, the data had proved an invaluable weapon not just in countering terrorism. Police forces and intelligence agencies were now able to match passenger information against watch lists for drug-traffickers, money-launderers or just simple criminals. In the international business that crime has become it is a step in the inevitable development of a computerized intelligence response that truly straddles the globe.

As PIS had coughed out Dai Choi's name, so the Hong Kong police computer had matched his name with the identical name in their watch file and flagged it for the computer operator. From there, it was a short step to Jonny's desk.

'Istanbul. That's outside his usual haunts,' he thought out loud. There was a pause while he mulled over the possibilities. 'OK. Two things. Get a pic of Dai wired to the Istanbul police and see if they have anything on him. Second, let's get to Aw Boon and see what he has. If it's as good as you say, then we can go pay our friend Dai Choi a visit.'

Aw Boon was everything a Chinese tailor should be, Jonny thought: small, old, wizened, shoulders bowed after so many years hunched over the cutting table. But his eyes were bright and his anger still real after the insult of having a body dumped outside his shop. After years of selling his suits, skirts and shirts to American and British tourists, his English was good enough to allow Jonny the luxury of not having to practise his fractured Mandarin.

'I saw the man in the Mercedes quite clearly, Inspector,' he said, confirming Jonny's optimism. Jonny held out a black and white photograph of Dai Choi, taken at a recent Jockey Club ball.

'Yes, yes. That's him. Although he wasn't wearing a dinner jacket at the time. He had on one of those baggy suits the young people wear these days.' He gave a faint shudder of disapproval.

Aw Boon was the perfect witness for a case like this and Jonny was determined not to let him go. He had no immediate family, was law-abiding and found the activities of the Triads deeply offensive. Adding in the insult of the body on his doorstep, the tailor was angry enough to set the law to work. It took ten minutes of persuasion to convince Aw Boon that he would be safer with the police than in his shop. Without police protection, Jonny told him, it was certain that Dai Choi would come after him. With police protection, he could continue making suits and then have a new identity.

'Gordon, you take Mr Aw Boon back to the Arsenal and I'll go to Kai Tak and call on Dai Choi,' he told his sergeant.

The journey from Central on Hong Kong Island to

Kai Tak airport on Kowloon can take over an hour in what seems to be a never-ending rush hour. But this time the lights were with them and there were no accidents in the Cross Harbour Tunnel, which links the island with the mainland. Jonny had a twenty-minute wait until the Thai Airways jet banked in over the city for the landing that all international pilots dreaded. Five minutes after touchdown the aircraft was at the gate. As Dai Choi stepped out of first class and on to the walkway he was greeted by the familiar sight of Jonny Turnbull.

'Inspector Turnbull. You shouldn't have taken the trouble,' he began with a small smile. 'I can find my own way home, thank you all the same.'

Jonny signalled to the two airport policemen who gripped Dai Choi just above the elbows and swung him away from the crowd and in through an unmarked door. Inside was a simple interrogation room. Dai Choi sat down without being asked and lit a Gauloise Jeune, exhaling blue smoke in a calculated insult as the tendrils wound their way across the room and into Jonny's face.

'Whatever you want, Inspector, if it is mine to give, you may have it,' Dai Choi began. 'Money? Take what's in my wallet. An apartment? We have a wide choice available and I am sure we can offer you the rates which many of your colleagues find so attractive. A bank account abroad? Just ask and I'll open one for you with a healthy starting balance.'

It was a serious offer which Dai knew would not be accepted. But it was also an offer made by a calculating man who believed in taking and holding the initiative. The gambit usually worked, but this time – for the first, wonderful time – Jonny felt in control.

'As usual, you are generous with your offers, Dai Choi,' Jonny replied, a slight smile on his face. 'This time, I too have an offer, or perhaps I should say an invitation – for you to come down to headquarters for a little chat.'

'Oh, and just what do we have to talk about, Inspector?'

'The matter of the murder of the Grass Sandal. You will recall we discussed that at the Mandarin and you claimed to know nothing about it, despite the fact that your trademark was on the body,' said Jonny, gesturing to Dai Choi's thumb ring. 'I knew then as I know now that you killed that man. What is different today is that this time you have been very careless. There is an eye-witness, a man who saw you with the body, who can clearly identify you. What is more, he is one of the few people you and your henchmen haven't reached. He is prepared to testify.'

'Impossible.' The rebuttal was harsh, underlined by the grinding of the cigarette in the ashtray as Dai Choi stood to leave. 'The witness is a liar. I was nowhere near wherever it was the murder happened and I'll produce twenty witnesses who will say so.'

For the first time in their long relationship, Jonny had managed to induce in Dai Choi just a fraction of the fear he routinely induced in others. It was a moment he had wanted for a long time and he was pleased the gangster's confident veneer was so easily scratched.

'Cuff him,' he ordered the constable. 'We'll caution him at the Arsenal.'

He turned to leave the office. As he reached for the handle, the door opened. He recognized Inspector Richard Dearlove of the airport police and saw, too, the anxious look. He followed him out into the corridor, shutting the door behind him.

'I'm afraid it's bad news, Jonny,' Dearlove began. 'Your sergeant was taking a witness to the Arsenal this morning?'

Jonny nodded, his stomach already knotting with the foreknowledge of disaster.

'Their car drove into an ambush just off Pottinger Street. Two cars, four guys with machine-guns. They didn't stand a chance. The driver and the witness are both dead; your sergeant is pretty badly injured and may not make it. I'm sorry.'

Grief mixed with anger and frustration had a taste so familiar that Turnbull's senses were overwhelmed for an instant. Then the thoughts came rushing in. 'So near. I was so bloody close to getting the bastard,' he muttered. But once again he had been trumped by the corruption that riddled the Arsenal from top to bottom. Christ, it didn't even require Dai Choi to be around to issue the orders. His finks knew what he wanted and simply passed on what they thought he needed to know and then his lieutenants acted.

He pushed his hand through his hair, took a deep breath and then walked back into the interrogation room. 'I've received some new information and for the moment you're free to go,' he told Dai Choi, gesturing to the constable to remove the handcuffs.

'Your witness get cold feet, Inspector? Or perhaps he got some concrete feet?' Dai Choi chuckled lightly, all his old confidence restored.

'By the way, Dai Choi, how was Istanbul?' asked Jonny, seeking to salvage something from the wreckage of the morning.

The Chinese lit another cigarette and exhaled noisily. 'I was in Istanbul to sample some of that new Caspian caviar they have started importing from the Republics. Capitalism has done wonders for the business: quality is up and prices are down. You should make sure you try some next time you're over there.'

Dai Choi pushed past Jonny, opened the door and strolled out into the corridor, leaving the door open behind him. Jonny watched the broad back until it vanished around the corner, wishing that just once he could bury his principles and shoot until the back was blood and the body was on the floor in front of him.

*

The headquarters of the Emniyet Mudurlugu, Turkey's Security Police, is a crumbling brown building in the Fatih suburb of Istanbul. Were it not for such a shoddy edifice, its location would make it the most prized police headquarters in the world with the magnificent Topkapi palace towering behind and the blue of the Sea of Marmara in front. The decayed state of the building is an indication of the low esteem in which the police are held in Turkey. But bad pay and poor conditions have not stopped the import of technology essential in the face of the increasing sophistication of the drug-smugglers and international arms dealers who call Istanbul home. The fax of Dai Choi's photograph had been received that morning at the fourth-floor international liaison centre and fed into the computer data bank which matches picture to picture in the same way as other systems can match voices or fingerprints.

Two years earlier, the son of an American congressman on a summer tour of Europe had arrived in Istanbul to get a brief taste of Eastern culture. He had wandered into the Taksim district, been picked up by a gorgeously dressed and extremely attractive woman and taken to Valentino's nightclub. When a hand wandered up the woman's thigh and discovered bulges where there should have been soft curves, a fight had broken out and the young man had been knifed. Although the wound was not fatal, it was enough to cause the congressman to call the US ambassador who in turn complained to the Minister of Interior who passed the buck to the police with a demand that something be done about the lawlessness in the Taksim area which was hurting the tourist industry.

Police patrols were stepped up and cars now regularly cruise through the pedestrian precinct to reassure tourists and warn the crooks. But action stopped short of going inside Valentino's, which would have been seen as an unnecessary provocation to the many pillars of the

Istanbul community who pass through the doors each week. Instead, a surveillance camera was inserted in the sign advertising the Bilsak Jazz Club on the opposite side of the road. All those going in or out of the club were photographed and the pictures dumped in the police data base.

Within an hour of the fax arriving in Istanbul, the image had been matched with a photograph of Dai Choi taken two days earlier. There was regular contact between the police and the club's owner who cooperated with them in return for tolerance of some of the club's more unusual activities. The owner confirmed that the Chinese had met with a well-known drug dealer and arms supplier called Selim; their waiter had heard little of the conversation: England was mentioned, there was talk of sailing.

Five hours after Jonny had sent his original message and only two hours after he returned to the office following his trip to the airport, the reply from the Turkish police was on his desk complete with a brief biography of Selim and the Spiders, showing their influence in the international drugs business.

The conclusion seemed clear: Dai Choi was trying to expand the influence of the White Lotus Triad with the help of Turkish drug-dealers. Turnbull assumed that Dai Choi was setting up a major drug deal and that the goods would arrive by boat in Britain. The information appeared to be confirmed when British Airways alerted the police that Dai Choi had booked a ticket to Britain for the following week.

That night Jonny arrived back at the apartment in time for supper. He was in a foul mood, the news about Dai Choi's travel plans had done nothing to relieve the depression of a truly awful day. After the débâcle at the airport, he had returned to Hong Kong and gone to the hospital to see Gordon. He wasn't allowed into the intensive care unit and could only peer anxiously through the square of glass in the door. The doctors had removed ten bullets from Gordon's body and he had lost a leg. He would live but it was the end of his career.

As he looked across the table at Lisu he no longer saw the waif he had fallen in love with, the young Chinese girl whose innocence had captured his heart. The vulnerability which had provoked his love had vanished. He had come to loathe the hurt he could see in her eyes, and hate himself too, for it was his fault. Before Sam had died, they had been so happy, the relationship as perfect as a mixed marriage can be in a country where such events are commonplace.

They had met when he had interrogated her after a riot in the refugee camp had resulted in two stabbings. Such incidents were common enough but killings were actually quite unusual. Both the guards and the camp inmates knew that certain social boundaries were essential if order was to be maintained in the overcrowded camp and so murder was out of bounds. But this time the camp stewards had been unable to hold the gangs back.

She had appeared before him, haggard, dirty and defensive. The interrogation had been brief; pointless really. She had told him nothing, obeying the unwritten camp rule of non-cooperation with the British officials. But there had been something about her; her huge, black eyes in the emaciated face had stared at him in fascination and fear, but her answers had been determined, exposing the strength of character under the dirt. He had been intrigued and returned the next day to see her again.

This time, there had been real fear in her eyes. She was the only one of the women to be called back again and she was certain that a second meeting meant trouble.

She spoke no English and he no Chinese, either Mandarin or dialect, and so they had to work through an interpreter, a painful and lengthy business, where the emotion of a sentence became a dry string of words that often lost much of their meaning.

He never really understood what drove him on after
that second meeting. Perhaps he was simply lonely in a
foreign country; perhaps her vulnerability appealed to
him; perhaps it was a subconscious fantasy to have a
Chinese woman. But whatever the reasons, he came back
the next day and this time he ordered the camp supervisor
to make her presentable and he dismissed the interpreter.

The difference was astonishing. The dark hair that had
been lank and streaked with the brown of dust and dirt
was a lustrous black, falling to her shoulders. Her face
had the flat features of people from the Eastern provinces
with almost no eyebrows and tiny eyelashes. (He would
discover later that the rest of her body was also practically
hairless, which he found very exciting.)

When he stood up to greet her, he saw how small she
was, her tiny frame only just coming up to his shoulder.
But the camp organizers had loaned her a pale blue silk
shift and a pair of baggy peasant's trousers. He could see
that she had a tiny waist, small, tight buttocks and small
breasts that he tried and failed to discern through the
shift.

That day and for two weeks afterwards, they struggled
to communicate, the language barrier creating an enforced intimacy as he touched her to point to an object,
or they shared the laughter at a mistake in interpretation
or understanding. It was her laugh that he first fell in
love with. She would throw her head back, stretching her
neck and opening her mouth wide to expose teeth that
had not rotted or fallen out like those of so many of
her contemporaries. She was so filled with vitality and
good humour that he wanted to catch her enthusiasm in
the hope that some would rub off on him.

Those were the days when refugees were allowed to
stay in Hong Kong after the bureaucracy had processed
them. He knew that for her and perhaps for her relatives
inside the camp he represented a ticket to freedom. But
he never thought her pleasure in his company was faked.

Instead, they really did like each other and he believed she had grown to love him.

Once she was free of the camp, she had come to live with him, at first as mistress and then as wife. The promise of those first few days had been fully realized. As she became fluent in English and he in Mandarin, they were able to talk and share thoughts and ambitions. She had proved remarkably experienced at sex but she had refused to talk about her past life at all and so he had never learned where or with whom she had gained her knowledge.

When Sam was born, their life together reached new heights, especially as his professional life was going well. Joining the Organized Crime Unit seemed like a sound career move and the threats against him and his family were little more than routine – everybody suffered them. But what Jonny didn't realize was that behind the macho bravado, everyone else paid attention and made the compromises necessary to survive and prosper.

It was natural that he had blamed himself for Sam's death. After the grief had lessened, Lisu tried to persuade him to try for another child but he couldn't persuade himself to take the risk. He couldn't bear the responsibility of bringing another child into the world who might die because of him.

Lisu suggested they head back to England but he refused, his obsession with Dai Choi still fresh and the idea of revenge a real goal that he was sure could be achieved. His guilt and rejection of her had driven a wedge between them that gradually became a chasm. Now they had settled into a routine where familiarity sustained a marriage that was little more than a convenience.

He had arrived in Hong Kong fresh from the police force in Newcastle-upon-Tyne. The opportunity of a few years in the Far East had seemed exotic and exciting, offering opportunities that he would never have policing the slums of Benwell and Blaydon. He had happily left the city he loved, for it had been butchered by the social engineering ideas of planners with no understanding of community, and he had been made to feel welcome in an environment where the European policemen, whatever their background, formed an élite club, an Us-and-Them society based not on education and accent but on race. The local police, however well qualified, were always sergeants, and the Europeans always officers. It had been that way since the last century and each side had grown comfortable with the tradition.

The Europeans, with the patronizing certainty of the colonialist, failed to learn Chinese, had little understanding of the community they were supposed to control and relied on their subordinates to interpret both the language and the crime. The result was that on the surface Hong Kong was a respectable, relatively crime-free country – or at least the Europeans weren't burgled, mugged or shot. The criminals soon understood that the Europeans were largely irrelevant to their need for a secure and profitable working environment. A few well-placed bribes among the local force and eyes were turned the other way, false reports filed, the innocent found guilty on behalf of the guilty and the statistics consistently made to appear as if crime did not pay.

For the first few weeks, Jonny had been happy to spend his days in the Police Officers' Club which looked out on to Causeway Bay and was within a comfortable ten-minute walk of the Arsenal. There was sailing every weekend, the police junk available for barbecues and parties and the challenge of finding his way in a new community and a new job. Then he had moved into their flat in Central, a few minutes from the office and in the heart of downtown. Then it had been a coup to get a place so close to the office. Now he was the only person he knew who lived in the area. All his colleagues had moved up the hill either to the mid-levels or on to the

Peak itself. In the stratified society of Hong Kong, social status was measured by how far up the mountain that overlooked Central you lived. At the bottom of the hill, Jonny was well below the social salt.

After Sam had died, he had pursued Dai Choi with a single-minded fury that left him exhausted. He followed every lead, interviewed every possible source, questioned his colleagues and pored over the files. It all led nowhere. By the time he had finally run out of steam, he was no nearer getting Dai Choi in the dock than when he started. The disillusion had seeped into his bones like the winter fog that blankets so much of Hong Kong for month after month.

His resentment evident, he had been taken aside by one of the senior officers. 'Look, Jonny,' he had been told, 'you did a good job with the Mas and I understand how you feel about Sam's death, but beating yourself over the head with a cricket bat every day is not going to bring him back and it's not going to put Dai Choi behind bars. You have to understand the country you are dealing with. You have good cops working here; some of them are very good indeed. But in the end the cash equation tells. A sergeant earns maybe $10,000 Hong Kong a year, an inspector $25,000. Then the Triads come along with an offer of $100,000 or $200,000 to look the other way just once. It's easy, painless and it happens. That's the reality of life here. It's not like working back home and if you are going to survive then you have to adjust to it.

'Don't forget, the gangsters help run this place. Their investments helped build Central. Half the apartment blocks on the Peak are owned by apparently respectable people who got their start in crime. Most people who make it here have done something crooked – beginning with the old European families who made their money in the opium business. So, lighten up and lower your sights.'

He had tried to take the advice. He had settled into the routine of ordinary police work. The difference between him and his fellow officers was his visible determination to remain uncorrupted. At first, it had been sheer bloody-mindedness that had kept him clean, a reluctance to become tainted by the same blood money that had paid for Sam's death. Then he began to take pride in his stand, and independence became a point of principle. However, although Dai Choi had taken second place to day-to-day policing, everyone knew his interest and so he was fed a constant diet of information about the man and his associates. He had taken over Sam's room in the apartment as a study and along one wall he had built a filing system and card index to keep track of Dai Choi. He hadn't given up.

CHAPTER 5

ORDER, STRUCTURE, A pattern, anything that will give them a lever, he thought to himself. That's what they want and that's what I'm not going to give them.

Even as he drove himself forward, Sean Thomas knew that the challenge was becoming impossible. He knew that in London, Manchester, Newcastle and every other police centre in England and Scotland, the cops would be poring over every detail of every action; every report that might, just might, be linked to IRA activities on the mainland. Each scrap of information would be analysed, each piece of data fed into the giant HOLMES computer system to see if a pattern could be discerned that might direct them to people, places or targets.

After a while the idea of so many people focusing on you became an almost impossible burden to bear. Over the months Thomas could see the visible changes. He no longer liked to look in the mirror as his physical deterioration depressed him. Two years ago he had had a full head of wavy black hair and an unlined, lightly tanned face. A stranger might have thought him a successful businessman who spent time abroad, or perhaps a farmer. The money he had brought with him allowed him to live well, buy decent clothes and eat at smart restaurants so that his face and body looked healthy. Now, his hair had started to grey and was much thinner. Each morning when he brushed it clumps came away in his hand. He no longer looked healthy either. The clear grey-blue eyes which he had always thought of as one of his better features were now bloodshot from too little sleep filled with nightmares. The money had run out after three months and he was forced to draw on the caches that had been hidden around the country. That sounded fine from the security of Dublin or Belfast, but the reality was that living on the run was bloody expensive. He had to husband his cash so the clothes started to look threadbare and the diet was so bad that he had lost two stone in the last year. He had lost his tan after spending so many months peering from behind the curtains of different safe houses.

There were other, less visible, changes too. He had been unable to stop his natural watchfulness from becoming acute paranoia. His normal concern for security had developed to a clawing of the fingers as he reached for the gun under his sweater at the first imagined threat from an innocent passer-by.

Now he could almost feel the concentration and the enmity flowing in his direction, could imagine the final moments when his skills proved unequal to the task and he either betrayed himself or was betrayed.

But in a strange way, the challenge was what it was all about. He had started all those years ago with the idealism fostered by tales told on his grandpa's knee about the Easter Rising and the bravery of the Few against the Brits, the former always romantic, the latter cruel. It was hardly surprising that he had turned to the Movement for sanctuary. The Boys had given him the family he had needed after the loneliness of his childhood after his grandpa died and father left on the back of another drunken fighting match with his mother.

What set him apart was his cunning, a skill that he had developed almost as an instinct to keep his father's big hands from bringing the strap to his small body, and had channelled into killing. Only when the Brits had begun to

78

get too close in South Armagh did he disappear to die in the Republic.

He realized that he had allowed this struggle to become too personal. He was still the clever killer he had been for years but he had allowed his emotion to rule his head and that was dangerous. Even though he could rarely see· his enemy, he could imagine them all around him. Day after day he put himself in their place. He watched John Witherow, the head of SO13, Scotland Yard's anti-terrorist squad, on the news waffling about 'leads' and issuing solemn warnings. None of it meant much but the detective's red-veined, overweight face had given the threat a personality. He felt as if they were almost old friends, or at the least jousting partners who knew each other well.

At the same time, the Irish in him liked the idea of the lone hero pitted against the forces of evil. It fitted his romantic notions of the Republican struggle, with which so many of the Movement bolstered their courage. He knew, too, that it was that very romanticism which killed people, which led to stupid mistakes, like grandstanding in a shoot-out when a quiet retreat was the order of the day.

He struggled to keep his personality in balance and to exploit the weaknesses of his enemy as well as playing on his own strengths. Now after months in the field it was hard. He knew he should pull out but he was too proud, too locked into a course of confrontation to want to withdraw without victory. He laughed cynically to himself. Victory used to mean getting the Brits out of Ireland. Today, he wasn't sure what it meant. But each strike was a personal victory and he was determined to do a few more before calling it a day.

It was this compelling need to keep the initiative and to avoid a pattern that found him driving a Ford Fiesta down the Stockbridge Road towards Winchester station. The car had been provided the night before from a support cell in Bristol and he had travelled up the previous night to stay in a bed and breakfast in Andover where he used the name Peters and practised the West Country burr he had developed to overwhelm his Irish accent.

Winchester Station was one of the targets prepared by the reconnaissance cell over the previous three years. Housewives, students and ordinary workers had travelled through the station at different times, noting security, potential targets and methods of getting in and out of the area. It had always fitted the requirements of a good soft target and it seemed to Thomas that now was the ideal time: in the immediate aftermath of the Royce killings, the police would be focused on forensics and safe houses where he might be hiding. That was their pattern and they believed his pattern would be to lie low for a while and then strike somewhere far away from the first hit. So he would attack again immediately and close to the last strike. Always break the pattern.

Stuck in the slow-moving traffic, he could see the red brick of the station ahead of him. The closer he got, the more he could feel the tension, the reflexive licking of the lips caused by the dry throat; the slight trembling of his right knee as the pressure on the accelerator was augmented by the involuntary tensing of his leg muscles. It made no difference that this was supposed to be a soft target, an easy kill with no security and no threat. Too often in the past, he had seen people die through such complacency. It only needed one hero or a police car on routine patrol in the wrong place to make a smooth operation fall apart.

It was this moment he always hated the most, this and the long nights that followed a killing. It was the suspension of time between the planning and the execution. The few minutes when the goal was in sight and both time and the target seemed to telescope so that every moment dragged and the target never got closer. Then suddenly he was there. A right turn immediately after the roundabout and a two-hundred-yard slow drive to the end of the car park and he stopped in the spot reserved for the handicapped just by the short ramp leading to the platform where passengers for the 8.05 Intercity for London would be waiting.

He got out of the car, leaving the engine running and the door open, as if he had just gone on to the platform to help some ageing relative catch the train. As he walked up the ramp, his right hand reached under his long, light brown raincoat to feel the butt of the 9 mm Star automatic pistol in the pocket of his jacket. He had found the gun in a cache in nearby Crab Wood the previous evening. It was one of several hundred that had originally been bought from the Spanish government by an Arab arms dealer, Monzer Al Kassar, who is also known in the trade as The Prince of Darkness. He sold them to Colonel Gaddafi who shipped them to Ireland in the early 1980s.

There was no guard on the gate to the platform and Thomas simply walked through and turned left. He wanted to start at the end of the platform near the first-class carriage to hit the higher value targets first and then work his way down the passengers towards his escape route. This was a Thomas killing: careful, well planned and ruthless. There would be no panic or scattered shots fired for dramatic effect. He intended each round in the fifteen-shot magazine to hit its target.

Resisting the impulse to increase his pace, he moved sinuously through the crowd, polite and inoffensive. He knew that afterwards it would be the shocking image of the gunman that would be remembered and described to the police and not the real picture of the quiet man passing through the commuters. It was that distortion which would help keep him free and alive.

Thomas was pleased to see that for once the reconnaissance had got it right. The platform was crowded, mostly with middle-aged males dressed in conservative dark suits. These were the ones who could afford the exorbitant price for British Rail's uncomfortable, hot and invariably late commuter service. These people were the legitimate targets he sought. It was men like this who bolstered the Brits in their policy towards Northern Ireland.

Turning, Thomas faced back the way he had come, his eyes flickering over the passengers, selecting both targets and a path through the crowd. Satisfied, his hand locked around the butt of his weapon, drawing it from his pocket. There was a brief pause and, for anyone with good enough hearing, a snick as his thumb depressed the safety catch. He drew a deep breath to fill his lungs and pump an extra gasp of oxygen to his brain. Then with a single fluid motion the gun came from under the coat and up level with his face. Turning slightly, his left hand clasped his right as the sights on the gun's stubby barrel found the first target. His right forefinger tightened around the trigger taking up the first pressure. A slight squeeze and there was a flat crack as the hammer hit the first cartridge to explode the bullet out from the barrel at 380 metres a second.

The single round struck the first man in the centre of his face just above his upper lip. For a brief, almost imagined, fraction of a second, Thomas could see the hole as the bullet forced its way into the flesh. Then, as the man's body was lifted from the ground by the force of the impact, the bullet, pushing an arrow of air ahead of it, drove up through the skull. The nose and bottom half of the forehead shattered and imploded and then the bullet exploded out of the back of his skull. Bright red blood, the light brown of brain and the white of bone formed separate trails in a long crescent that arced into the open space between the two platforms. The man's body followed, falling away from the platform on to the rails. As his body touched the electrified line there was a sizzling and the carcase jumped back into the air, muscles contracting with the shock, to bow the now lifeless form before it collapsed back on to the line. Later, it would be the sickly sweet smell of burning flesh that the commuters would most remember.

Before the body had even left the platform, Thomas had begun moving, his pistol sniffing the air to left and right. The first shot was followed by a moment of complete silence as the commuters looked on stunned, each immobilized by total shock.

The spell was broken by the delicate tinkling of the spent cartridge case falling to the concrete floor. Then Thomas fired again, this time to his right, and a man collapsed without a sound against the woman next to him. As the gun moved to the left and Thomas continued his forward march, the screaming began. The crowd parted before him as the people shrank away seeking the few feet or inches that perhaps could provide the safety barrier between life and death, between bullet and target.

His trigger finger was jerking again and again, the barrel kicking up with the recoil and the sound of each shot merging into what seemed to be a continuous crack that echoed and re-echoed off the concave roof covering the platform. Each bullet found a mark, but the devastation was more than just the hitting of targets. Each bullet not only killed or maimed but sprayed blood and bone around the platform covering the victims and the fortunate alike. There were few who were on the platform that day who did not have a physical reminder of the mental trauma.

As Thomas advanced, dead and wounded lay sprawled behind him, the cries of the dying and the terrified adding to the panic among the passengers.

With ten bullets gone, it was time to ensure his escape. Three final shots and then he was at the exit, running now to vault over the ramp to his car. A few steps around the bonnet, into the driving seat, a spurt of gravel and he was away. The parking lot was a blur, his concentration focused entirely on the exit. He turned left out of the station and back on to the Stockbridge Road.

He reckoned he had around four minutes before the exits from Winchester would be sealed by the police. By that time he would have turned off the A272, be through the tiny village of Sparsholt and heading at a sedate pace along the back roads to Southampton and the sanctuary of another safe house.

He allowed himself a swift glance in his rear-view mirror. There was no sign of pursuit. The eyes that looked back at him held no reflection of the horror he had just left. For now, there was only the satisfaction of a tough job done well.

Fifty-nine miles away in the west London suburb of Ealing there is a small enclave bounded to the west by Boston Road, to the north by Uxbridge, to the east by South Ealing Road and the south by the M4 motorway. This geographic box bounded by such prominent arteries for London's traffic has helped create a small outpost of London's Chinese community which is headquartered in Soho.

It had begun predictably enough when Hung Sun Lu opened the North China restaurant on Uxbridge Road. He needed staff to work the long hours demanded by every Chinese restaurant owner and they took lodgings nearby. Two other restaurants opened soon afterwards to take advantage of the expense account traffic from the BBC TV studios nearby. Then in the 1980s, the influx of Chinese from Hong Kong who arrived before the British tightened the rules meant that Chinatown became over-crowded. Hong Kong entrepreneurs bought up sites in the area as fast as they came on the market but still there was not enough accommodation to meet the demand for shops, restaurants and cinemas catering to the ethnic community. So there was an emigration west to Ealing where the new immigrants found a small group of people who at least spoke their own language. Now there are several thousand living in a small patch of London which shows no real sign of their presence, so unobtrusive are they.

The architecture of the area is typical of many parts of London's suburbia: Victorian terrace houses built on two, three and occasionally four storeys. Attractive when cleaned up and modernized, they simply look old and tired in most parts of Ealing. But the streets have a sameness to them, big and little, tall or squat they look what they were: home to thousands of bank clerks, shopkeepers and artisans who formed the middle class in London at the turn of the century and who used Ealing as a dormitory before their commute to the West End and the City each day. That sameness made it attractive to White Lotus and particularly to those who sought the anonymity of the few among the many.

It was here that the real work of the Triad went on. Goods were moved in and out, deals done, rules enforced while the police concentrated their efforts ten miles away in Soho. The police had simply no understanding of the way the Triads worked and the contained Chinese community had made it virtually impossible for them to gather any hard information with which to counter the growing influence of the criminals.

This was Michael Leung's patch. As the Hung Kwan, Leung was responsible for the muscle in the Third Lodge of the White Lotus Triad. The term Hung Kwan literally translates as 'strong arm' and it was his job to make sure that those who broke the Triad's laws were punished. It was also his job to train and keep disciplined the Triad's four fighting sections of twenty men each. It was a job rich in status and honour and placed him number three in the British hierarchy of the Triad.

Model Cottages was actually a small dead-end street tucked between Occupation and Loveday Roads. The northern end of the street faced on to a small common known locally as The Hop after some long-lost tradition of holding a dance there every summer. Sometime in the

1950s three of the cottages at that end of the row had been knocked down after the effects of a near miss by the Luftwaffe finally took their toll. In their place had been built three double garages; Michael Leung owned the two closest to The Hop, or rather White Lotus owned them in the name of the AI Repairs company. This was where the local Chinese community brought their cars for repair. They were guaranteed a decent job at a fair price and they also knew that if the insurance company was difficult AI Repairs would change the odd sum here or a description there.

For the past week, AI Repairs had been turning away business. Indeed no bookings had been taken for the next three weeks and, as he walked through the door, Leung could see why. Around him was ordered chaos. There was the crash of hammer on metal, the whine of a drill, and to one side the deep red glow of a furnace made the men working by it appear dark and sinister. He supposed this might be what people meant by the fires of hell.

To his left a British Leyland Sherpa van had been stripped. Without the covering of side panels, doors, roof and bonnet, the van looked strangely primeval. It was as if some professor a hundred years ago had devised a mechanical beast without any consideration for aesthetics. The vehicle was all angles and joints, bare metal and rust.

To the right a VW Kamper had its tailgate up while a mechanic worked on the engine. The car's main battery and its spare (the Kamper has an auxiliary battery fitted to run the electrics) were lying on a bench. One of the batteries had been taken apart so that plastic container, lead mounts and the central container for both the water and the acid were exposed.

In the centre, a standard black Ford Granada sat alone. There was nothing mechanical to do to this car aside from a check of the engine to make sure it ran on the day.

Michael Leung walked over to an older Chinese dressed in the oily blue coveralls that are the uniform of mechanics all over the world. 'Are we on schedule?' he asked.

The mechanic nodded. 'The Ford is in good shape. We bought it last week. Only 5,000 miles on the clock, so there should be no trouble.

'Your idea for the VW was clever. We can make the electrics all work off the one battery and so the second will appear part of the system when in fact it will do nothing. The second battery seems pretty pointless to me.' He sniffed derisively. 'Some bright idea of the sales people probably. Anyway, it will do what you want.'

'And what about the Sherpa?' Leung asked.

'Well, the van itself is fine. And the respray is just a standard job.' They paused by a plastic-lined booth down which streaks of paint had dried. The mechanic picked up a panel that would fit the side of the truck. He pointed to the lettering: 'Security' and, underneath, 'Brussels, Par' stencilled in black on a white background.

'Good. That seems fine.'

'Well, that's all the basic stuff. The real tricky bit is what you want to go inside. We have had to construct a small furnace and a couple of moulds over here.'

They went over to the corner of the garage and, as they approached, Leung could feel the fierce glow from the furnace which was heating what appeared to be a vat of oil.

'In there is the lead,' the mechanic said, pointing to the oil. 'We can pour it out using the hoist and it will then go into the moulds over here.' Leung saw the square moulds which were in three different sizes, each one designed to fit inside the other. 'It's been difficult getting the lead to the right temperature but we cast one this morning and it seems to have cooled all right, so maybe we've solved the problem.'

'Good. So you'll be ready on time?' Leung asked.

The mechanic nodded, determined not to give this man any reason to doubt his professional ability or his commitment to the White Lotus. Michael Leung's reputation was enough to ensure both loyalty and devoted labour.

Only twenty-five, he was part of the young guard who had risen on the back of the influx of new blood from Hong Kong in the previous ten years. Unusually for a senior official in the organization, he had been born where he now lived in Ealing. But he had broken through the natural bias towards Hong Kong immigrants by the application of ambition and initiative in equal measure.

In 1989, Chinatown had been racked by gang warfare as the White Lotus attempted to fight off an attack by the Sap Kau Yau, or Nineteen Brothers Triad from Taiwan. Waiting in the wings were the 14K Triad from Hong Kong who hoped to emerge from the strife between the other two undamaged and dominant.

It was a struggle that went on unobserved by the British police. The Chinese were used to looking after their own affairs. The Triads were judge and jury for the local community and there was no appeal to an outsider whether the verdict was fair or not. So the dead were quietly buried or thrown into the river, the injured tended by Chinese doctors and the innocent were looked after by whichever Triad exacted tribute each week.

At the time Michael Leung was leader of a fighting section that defended the network of restaurants and shops along Gerrard Street from any interloper trying to take over the protection rackets or the food distribution, both of which were run by White Lotus. There is a traditional, even ritualistic, way of fighting these turf battles where both sides use chains, machetes and daggers, but on this occasion, Michael Leung sought out the Hung Kwan of the Nineteen Brothers in his house in Hampstead. He broke in with his team, killed the guards and captured the Hung Kwan. He was strung up naked from his Nordiflex exercise machine in the basement so that arms and legs were stretched out in the form of a cross. Leung then proceeded to beat him, not with a whip or a chain but with a long length of bamboo cane which he had carefully cut at the end. Each time the cane sang through the air to strike the flesh, the separate lengths of the cane parted until they came together with the impact. With each blow, a long portion of flesh was pinched by the bamboo and then as he drew back for another swing, the flesh stretched and broke. After ten blows the Hung Kwan's back was a mass of blood. After fifty, his back was red meat with strings of white flesh hanging loose.

A blow from a chopper, the traditional Triad weapon which is similar to a machete, severed the man's neck from his body. When he left the house, Michael Leung left behind the red and green flag of the 14K as a message to the Nineteen Brothers. The result was a retaliatory strike against the 14K who then became part of the struggle. There was now likely to be no benefit to any of those involved without a great deal of bloodshed. The Nineteen Brothers sued for peace and the earlier status quo prevailed.

Michael Leung had acted with great courage and his use of the bamboo torture had showed a suitable respect for Triad history, a respect unusual in one not born in the East. Promotion followed and with it the power he sought.

Leung was no intellectual but he was clever, with an intuitive understanding of the strengths and weaknesses of his fellow man. He was not sadistic but saw force as a tool to apply in measures equal to the circumstances. He believed that one day he could rise to the very top of the organization that had given him the status he now enjoyed. To his followers, men and women alike, he was a chilling leader. His ruthlessness was respected, even admired, as they all knew that as he rose so would they.

But they had all seen how he treated others and worried that one day they might merit the same. To them all, he was known as Chui Kan or The Red Club, a traditional Triad symbol of punishment.

When the word had come from Hong Kong that a big operation was planned, it had fallen to him to coordinate the British end. He had called a meeting of his four deputies and delegated the research tasks. One group had gone to the British newspaper library at Colindale, another had hit the phones to talk to journalists and academics. One enterprising young woman was given a card which described her as a reporter for the Xinhua News Agency and she was given access to the cuttings files of *The Times* and the *Independent*. The British were so trusting.

The result was a surprising amount of detailed information on the target selected by Stanley Kung and Dai Choi. They had drawings; the safety precautions against fire and flooding. There was even a remarkable amount of detail about the security systems that were going to be installed.

For a week, Leung and his team had pored over the plans, dissected the maps and toyed with different ideas until finally a plan of attack evolved. With a few minor modifications it had been approved by the Leader in Hong Kong and now they were almost ready to go.

CHAPTER 6

JONNY ALWAYS FOUND eating with Lin Yung a truly disgusting experience. Lin Yung had the Chinese habit of leaning over and almost into his food and then using the chopsticks to shovel rice, noodles or fish directly into his mouth. It wasn't so much the shovelling that was so offensive but the accompanying slurping noises. Also, every time Lin Yung broke off to talk, he did so with a mouth full of half-chewed food. It was a ridiculous prejudice to retain after so many years of living in the East but somehow he could never shake off his mother's voice echoing down the decades exhorting him not to talk with his mouth full.

'You spend too much time on this Dai Choi, Jonny. There are bigger fish swimming in the waters of Hong Kong. Why go for the minnow when you can catch sharks like Stanley Kung?' Lin Yung asked.

'That's easy for you to say,' Jonny replied. 'You may not have to worry about the law, but I do. Kung is too big, too well-connected and too rich for me. I reckon that when you come in and I'm back pounding the pavement in England you'll just pick Kung up and stick him in jail. We can't do that and for the moment I aim where I think my shots will hit.'

The two men were old sparring partners, one charged with upholding the law in Hong Kong, the other doing his best to weaken the hold of the British in preparation for the Chinese takeover. Lin Yung was the head of the Guojia anquanbu or Chinese Ministry of State Security in Hong Kong. Officially, he was the Chinese representative on the Hong Kong and Macao Workers Committee, but in the hall of mirrors that is Hong Kong, everyone who needed to knew what his real job was.

There were in fact two branches of Chinese intelligence operating in Hong Kong. The Gonganbu, or Ministry of Public Security, was the traditional intelligence gathering unit of the Chinese Foreign Ministry. It is run by Li Chuwen, whose official job is deputy director of the Xinhua News Agency in the colony. Li Chuwen, a former clergyman in his late sixties, comes from Shanghai and speaks fluent Cantonese, French and English and has become a familiar figure on the social circuit, even appearing in the society pages chatting to British officials.

Lin Yung is a different breed, part of the 'Chaozhou Mafia', the group of Young Turks from a small region south of Canton who in recent years have gained so much influence in the second tier of government in Beijing. The Guojia anquanbu was formed by Deng Xiaoping in June 1983 to gather intelligence abroad and carry out repression at home. By forming the new organization Deng wanted to create a rival for the old spy network and introduce some young radicals into the new group to make Chinese intelligence more effective.

By 1983 Lin Yung had already carved out a career in intelligence and would probably have stayed in the Gonganbu. But he had come to Deng's attention after a spectacular outcome to one of his operations.

Many years previously, soon after he had been recruited into the Gonganbu, he had been given the normally mundane task of watching diplomats in Beijing, which included the file on Bernard Boursicot, a French diplomat working in the Embassy's archive section. Lin noticed his admiration for opera and arranged for him to be introduced to Shi Pei-pu, a well-known Chinese singer.

As Lin hoped, the two fell in love but prospects for a match were dashed when the young diplomat was posted to Saudi Arabia. Lin encouraged Shi Pei-pu to write a letter to her lover saying that she had given birth to a boy and that he was the father. Boursicot arrived back in Beijing in the middle of the cultural revolution, found his lover and tried to flee the country when they were arrested. Lin then offered the diplomat the choice of leaving the country with his family and spying for China or being expelled, leaving his wife and child to rot in jail.

Boursicot spied for China for nearly fifteen years until he was arrested in 1982 along with his wife. Under interrogation, the French were astonished to discover that his 'wife' was in fact a man who had somehow managed to fool his husband for fifteen years. Embarrassed, the French tried to cover up the scandal but Lin arranged for the story to be leaked to a friendly correspondent at *Le Monde*. This *coup de théâtre* and espionage triumph appealed to Deng. Not only had the young Lin Yung managed to recruit a spy who had proved a valuable asset but he had also managed to ridicule a feared and respected foreign intelligence service.

On Deng's orders, Lin Yung was transferred to the Guojia anquanbu specifically to get the technology to make the spy network competitive. Lin Yung travelled all over Europe and America and at every stop found people eager to sell him the equipment he wanted. He bought tape recorders in Switzerland and encryption devices in Britain, but the greatest coup came in the United States. There Lin dangled before the US National Security Agency the chance of building a listening post at Lop Nor in the Xinjiang Uygur region on the border with the Soviet Union. From there, the NSA could listen to Soviet military communications and monitor missile launches. This carrot was enough to encourage the CIA and the NSA to bypass restrictions on transfers of high technology systems to China and a steady flow of modern computers, software and other high-tech equipment followed.

Ironically, it was this equipment that allowed Lin Yung to do such an effective job in putting down the rebels in the aftermath of the massacre at Tiananmen Square in June 1989.

In many ways Lin Yung and Turnbull were the original odd couple. But they had a secret relationship born out of necessity which had been nurtured on the back of successes each could bring back to their respective masters. Jonny enjoyed feeling he was on the inside track, having access to information, and Lin Yung saw Jonny as a source, an agent to be run. In a classic intelligence exchange, both saw the other as the spy.

Now Jonny was probing for information on Dai Choi's trip to Britain that Lin Yung might have picked up from his extensive network operating in the colony and particularly within the Triads.

'I want Dai Choi and so do you. This trip to England may be the chance I have been waiting for. And for you it is an opportunity to stop an expansion of the Triads into Europe,' said Jonny. 'The last thing you want is the Triads with a new outlet, with new opportunities for making money – money which they will plough back here and then into China, subverting the last bastion of Communism with their Mercedes cars and videos.'

Jonny knew the buttons to press and he was pushing them all. The Triads were the single largest source of Western goods in China. In the last decade, whole regions had become marketing opportunities, and the corruption had spread outwards from Guangdong province across the border from the New Territories north to Shanghai and Beijing like some horrible weed covering the clear waters of a spring-fed lake. Few were immune; most party officials now drove Mercedes limousines, none in Lin Yung's generation were without television and many had acquired a coveted satellite dish and access to Western television programmes.

It was an insidious process, which the senior party officials watched with alarm. They had seen how Western television had raised the expectations of the people in Poland, East Germany and Czechoslovakia and contributed to the collapse of Soviet-style Communism. They were now grappling with the problem by allowing the élite to get some of the perks of leadership but preventing those perks trickling down to the masses to undermine the very system that created the opportunities in the first place. It was a fine line that saw Lin Yung being chauffeured in his own Mercedes in Hong Kong and enjoying his lunch with Turnbull at the Yung Kee restaurant, once rated by Fortune magazine as one of the world's fifteen best restaurants. At the same time he was doing his utmost to control the expansion of the Triads whose corrupting influence threatened them all.

'You may be right,' he responded, inserting another helping of fish into his already bulging mouth. 'But my people have picked up nothing about any activity by Dai Choi or the White Lotus in Europe. As far as I know, that territory has been left to the Italians and more recently the Columbians. I would have thought our friend Stanley may be getting a little over-ambitious. Anyway, even if it's true, I'm not sure what I can do.'

'Oh, come on, Lin,' Jonny interrupted. 'You and I both know that you have an extensive network in Britain. If what I hear is right, it's one of your main sources of economic intelligence and you use it as a gateway to and from America. If you get some of your assets working on the problem, you'll come up with something.'

Lin Yung nodded, acknowledging the accuracy of Jonny's description. 'That's as may be, but you're asking me to expose my people for something that might or might not be true and might or might not have any advantage to me. Why should I go to the trouble?'

'First because it is in your interests to try and break the White Lotus. If we get Dai Choi then we may also get Stanley Kung and that would be a kick in the balls for your friend Li Chuwen and the Gonganbu. If this works out, you might even have your position secured here after the handover.'

'That's fine if it works,' Lin Yung replied sceptically. 'But what if I expose my people and Dai Choi is actually going to Britain on holiday and there's no drug shipment? Then British intelligence will have seen some of what we have and it could blow whole networks there. Then where will my career be? In the shit.

'I need something now if I'm to take the kind of risk you want.'

Jonny hated this part of the deal; the trade where he had to decide the value of one operation against the price of compromising another. Lin Yung always demanded a price and Jonny had come prepared. He justified the reality of betrayal as 'operational necessity'. He found this cynicism in himself vaguely disgusting, but the price would be worth it if he could break that bastard Dai Choi.

'You know the Triads have been infiltrating the Chek Lap Kok project?' he asked. Lin Yung nodded, aware that since the start of building work for the new airport in 1992, the Triads had got involved in everything from supplying the cement to the security guards at the site off Lantau Island. 'Well, we've learned that they have developed an interesting new wrinkle on the old suitcase scam. Instead of bribing a baggage loader to select the expensive cases and siphon them off so that their contents can be stolen, the White Lotus have gone high-tech. The X-ray machines that all the airlines use are being duplicated by the Triads with one of their own which works like a mass spectrometer and is able to distinguish between different heavy metals and composites. So any suitcase with some decent gold jewellery in it can be siphoned off for examination.'

'I'm sure that's a scandal, Jonny, but it's your problem not mine. I can't see its relevance to China.'

'Ah. Well, that's where they've been really smart. The intention is not just to steal on the way out but to smuggle on the way in as well. So they'll extract goods on the Hong Kong side and then insert goods for extraction on the Chinese side. I reckon they'll have a handy business in cash, gold, diamonds and information. Of course, it will all change from your point of view after the handover but between now and then you're going to have a big problem on your hands.'

Jonny was ashamed to note that he had to sit back now that the information had been passed. He had leaned forward across the food as if betrayal were diminished by the distance the words had to travel.

Lin Yung's swift mind was already questing for the hidden advantage behind the obvious benefits. Now he realized that where the Hong Kong police saw smuggling that they would probably be unable to control, he could see an opportunity. If his people could infiltrate and control the Chinese end of the operation then it would be their information going out, their information being dispersed while the British and their American allies thought it was only the crooked Triads. And even when they discovered the truth the Guojia anquanbu would see the compromise and know that they knew. Therein lay the real advantage in the mirrored world in which he lived.

'Again, that's not of much interest to me,' he lied. 'But I'm sure that my colleagues will be grateful for the information.' He smiled slightly. 'Perhaps I will be able to gain something from this.'

Lin Yung dabbed gently at the corners of his mouth, the delicacy of the movement contrasting with the ill-mannered performance of a few minutes earlier.

'Very well, Jonny. Let us agree a way forward. I will speak to my people in London and see if they can provide any information that will shed some light on Dai Choi's plans. How shall we keep in touch?'

'That may not be so easy,' Jonny replied. 'I think I will be better placed going to England myself. I'm not sure the Brits are really equipped to deal with the likes of Dai Choi and I would prefer to be on the spot.

'Anyway, it's time I went back. Once you lot come in here, my time will be up. Unlike my richer colleagues up on the Peak, I don't have a little thatched cottage to return to and I'd better start making some plans. I can take my wife and we'll see if there's anything left of the England I remember.'

'Let me know where you'll be staying and I'll see if we have anyone over there who could liaise with you,' offered Lin Yung.

Five minutes away from the Yung Kee restaurant is another part of Hong Kong; this one hidden from the tourists and beyond the reach of all but a very few of the residents. The China Club was founded in 1990 by David Tang, the grandson of one of Hong Kong's greatest merchants.

Tang would be what the Blacks in America describe as an Oreo, after the biscuit, which is black on the outside and white on the inside. Always immaculately turned out in his London suit and Harvie & Hudson shirts, he has one of those braying, fruity English voices which used to be common among chinless members of the British upper classes in the 1930s. Today, only rich colonialists with a public school education or very rich heirs to a colonial fortune like David Tang can afford such an affectation.

To emulate the privilege of Brooks's or Boodle's in St James's in London, Tang had decided to create his own exclusive men's club in Hong Kong. It was to be, he decreed, a haven for all civilized Hong Kong men (and occasionally women) to go for gossip and the odd bit of very discreet business.

He had found the perfect spot on the thirteenth floor of the old Bank of China building in Bank Street. The building had been constructed in the 1920s and had a view of the Hong Kong and Shanghai Bank headquarters across the road. This stunning building, designed by the British architect Norman Foster, looks like a series of giant coat hangers piled one on top of the other to hang enormous plates of glass reaching to the heavens. For those members who value their history, the club and the building opposite are a ready reminder of the colony's rich past, its prosperous present and its uncertain future.

In recent months, the China Club had become the focus for the anxieties of the Chinese community in the colony. With common fears, the Chinese aristocracy found a ready audience with each other, their voices becoming an echo of the paranoia that was beginning to infect the colony as the Chinese dragon loomed. Today, they could almost feel its hot breath.

Today, too, there was none of the mad optimism that seemed to drive the Hong Kong business community whatever else might be happening in the world. Over the years, the small community had developed an insular view of life. The few did business with the few and, in an orderly existence where the rules were clearly understood, there was ample profit for all. Even at the beginning of the 1990s there had been no lessening of the rush to destroy, develop and build as the local rule of thumb that a profit on any development could be made inside ten years still left enough time to make the money and run before the Chinese arrived.

Now those recent days seemed a distant and prosperous memory. Building work had virtually ceased; no developer was prepared to risk cash when the future was uncertain and the profits problematic. The collapse of building, for generations a mainstay of the economy, had caused a colony-wide depression. Unemployment was up from under one per cent to seven per cent, an unheard-of level for the country. There had been demonstrations which had been dealt with by the police without recourse to the British Army but everyone knew that it was only a matter of time before things turned very ugly.

Today the talk at the club (in English, of course) was the same as it had been for months: the collapse of the economy and the imminent arrival of the Chinese. Above all, the talk was of escape.

The first table on the left of the dining room is the power table and it was here that Dame Mary Cheong was reporting back the results of her recent trip to Britain. Her failure to move Douglas Hurd made an already gloomy gathering deeply depressed.

'Doesn't the bloody man understand that everything is going to hell here?' asked Chung Shang Hot, the owner of a conglomerate that included the colony's most important quarry. He also had a monopoly on the import of dynamite, a licence which rumour suggested he had expanded to include arms which were smuggled to China, a business which would be ended by the arrival of the Chinese.

'It's not as simple as that, I'm afraid, CS,' said Mary. 'From Hurd's point of view he has nothing left to bargain. The Chinese have pushed them into a corner and they gave away whatever hope they had of moving them along in 1984 when they agreed to hand us over in '97.

'Anyway,' she continued. 'The argument is different now. The Chinese are coming and there's nothing we can do about it. What matters is getting passports and somewhere to live for all our people who have served the British so faithfully all these years.'

'Faith. Faith. They don't know the meaning of the word,' interrupted Stanley Kung. A pillar in the financial community, he was a regular at the club. Like many other members, his financial clout and not his business dealings were what mattered. Everyone around the table had some secret and so they all maintained the fiction that they were who they pretended to be – successful, honest businessmen.

'If the British had any decency, any principles at all, then they would give our people passports and offer them a home. As it is they don't even bother with promises any more. They've abandoned us and we just have to live with the consequences.'

A huge fat man sitting facing Mary Cheong interrupted. Despite his bulk, he had a high, almost girlish voice which rose even higher when he was excited and had given him the nickname Sing Sing. The name was an in-joke appreciated only by the few. His real name was Lai Ching Heen and his grandfather had indeed spent some time in Sing Sing in the 1920s. Now Lai Ching Heen was the eminently respectable chairman of Hong Kong Enterprises. His sideline in the import of young boys for those of a similar sexual inclination as himself was never mentioned. Neither was his role as Shan Chu or Leader of the Green Pang Triad which controlled the lives of some 100,000 Shanghainese exiles in Hong Kong.

'I have heard that Vancouver is now known as Little Hong Kong, so many of our people have found sanctuary there.' There were a few smiles around the table but no laughter. 'I have heard too that some of the people are planning a mass exodus. They will take boats and head south for Australia. It will be a migration just like the eighties when the Vietnamese came here. It will be a humiliation for the British and for the Chinese and many of our people will die or be homeless.'

Sing Sing spoke the language of concern, but the subtext of this conversation and many others like it in town that day was really about business. To those around the table a passport and somewhere to live was not a problem. Under the British quota system they were rich enough to buy a passport and find a home abroad. But without their employees all would be faced with starting again. They would have to find people they could trust, men and women who would not reveal the secret world in which they all lived, who understood the value of loyalty and the price of betrayal.

Mary Cheong sipped slowly at her cup of Yin Yan, a traditional drink which was half tea and half coffee, usually served to coolies in China to give them the caffeine they needed to keep going. She still drank it in preference to the fine wines and Scotch that sat in front of the other guests. The harsh, bitter taste was a ready reminder of her roots and her loyalties. The difference was that today the drink came not in a chipped china bowl but in a glass cup resting in a silver container.

'It's still too soon to say that we have lost the political fight,' she corrected Sing Sing. 'Until now the British have paid no real price for their treachery. Each time we push them the Chinese push a little harder and it has been more expedient for the Foreign Office to bend Beijing's way. It may be that as the deadline draws closer and the British begin to suffer some pain here in Hong Kong they might change their view.'

'But by the time people really begin to panic it will be too late,' protested Sing Sing. 'We need time to get our people out and to start up elsewhere. If there are riots when the Chinese are just about to come over the border it won't help. By that time, the British will have written the problem off.'

'So the key is to try and make sure the pressure comes early enough to make the British change their position,' replied Mary.

It was a discussion they had had many times before over the past few months. Each time 'pressure' and 'movement' were the words that everybody agreed on. And each time the conversation ended with agreement in principle but no plan. To the other guests, this meeting was no different from all those that had gone before. Stanley Kung, however, knew that this time, it was going to be different.

CHAPTER 7

IT WAS THE darkness Rita always remembered most. It would sweep over her, an enormous enveloping cloud that would reach from her toes to the top of her head; dark, rich and so comforting. As she allowed its embrace to smother her she knew that again there was to be a respite from the pain, the cramps and, above all, the hunger that turned her stomach to knots, the acid eating into her very heart and the ache of her bones as they too cried out for succour.

In the darkness there were always the dreams. They were an ache, a reaching out for the solace of a youth that was filled with family, opportunity and hope for the future. Strangely, the scenes of her childhood in Greencastle outside Belfast, the picnics along the banks of the River Lagan, were always accompanied by music; not the rock of her childhood but the soaring thrill of orchestras. She later learned the music was Sibelius's *Finlandia*, and although she never understood how her mind could recall notes so clearly when she could never remember hearing them, from then on she would always weep when the music played.

As reality and weight vanished in equal measure, she began to imagine her body as something almost infinitely pliable. As the fantasies consumed her she became certain that some malevolent being – a being with definite substance but no coherent form – had a tight grip of the flesh in the centre of her back and was pulling her inexorably to a hole in the floor of her cell. She knew that with just one final tug her body would be sucked downwards, her wasted frame collapsing inwards so that feet and arms would vanish together. She would fight against the nightmare and drag herself back from the brink of oblivion to wake with screams echoing through her head. Her will was still strong enough to hold on to what was left of her life but she was no longer able to give voice to her fears.

But when she awoke, he was there, offering a sip of water and words of comfort. He had first come a week after the hunger strike had begun; a small, rather rumpled man who favoured brown suits and the kind of nubby woollen ties you could buy at the mill shops on the west coast. He was a Brit, of course. He hadn't tried to disguise the fact, hadn't even pretended to the soft Irish brogue that the Brits learned at the training school at Ashford but which always marked them out as a spy.

This one spoke with the long vowels and shortened consonants of a man from the Yorkshire Dales. He said his name was Kevin. Later, when they knew each other better, he would tell her that he actually came from Hampshire and his name was Bryan with a Y. He had adopted his northern persona as he thought it more classless and therefore less likely to offend. He didn't say then but she understood now that from the beginning he was planning, scheming to draw her into his little circle. But by the time she had realized what was afoot, it was too late.

The strike had begun on the morning of December 1, 1980 and she had been selected with Mairead Nugent and Mairead Farrell, the officer commanding the IRA volunteers in Armagh women's prison. The decision marked the culmination of almost a year of protest which had begun with a refusal to cooperate with the prison authorities and escalated through a 'no wash' phase where they refused to bathe and smeared the walls of their cells with excrement. The protests were designed to force the authorities to recognize the political status of IRA prisoners and the women were acting in sympathy with the men who were carrying out their own protests at Long Kesh.

For the first day of the strike they had been allowed to stay together. This was a mistake on the part of the authorities because they had drawn comfort from each other and gained strength from ridiculing their captors. They had all agreed they would take water and began taking salt tablets. To wear down their resistance, the prison guards brought in mounded plates of hot food – bacon, eggs, sausage and tomatoes for breakfast, fish and chips for dinner – so that the pungent smell would waft round the cell. Their bodies reacted automatically to the smell and they had been appalled to find themselves sitting on their cots actually watching the drool fall from their mouths to the floor. Then they had laughed and it had been all right again.

But once they had been separated each woman had had to deal with her terrors alone. There were no visitors, no shared moments to unite Us against Them. Only hour after hour of loneliness that swiftly degenerated into horror as death approached.

Then Bryan was there with his water and honeyed words. At first she had been suspicious, frightened that he would make her betray her comrades and the strike. But he never tried to talk her into eating, never reproached her for the killings or the bombings. Instead he listened and he talked. Oh, how he talked in those first few days. There seemed no logic in any of it to her. He told her of days spent fishing in Yorkshire, walks along the coast, a cottage he had in Robin Hood's Bay. He talked of comradeship. How much he valued friends, how lucky he felt to have parents he loved and who loved him.

It was all a lie, of course. He never fished, had seen a postcard of Robin Hood's Bay but never visited it, his parents were dead. And he never mentioned the wife and two children because that would have ruined the image he was creating, an image carefully designed to fit the psychological profile put together by the shrinks back at Lisburn.

Captain Bryan Dickens had been in Military Intelligence for ten years, five of them spent in Northern Ireland. He was part of the new breed of intelligence officers brought in after the disasters of the early seventies when the Army seemed to think it was still fighting in the jungle in Malaya. Belfast was not somewhere where you could simply shoot people you didn't like after torturing others to find them.

He had joined the Devon and Dorsets as a simple infantryman but found the routine boring and asked for a transfer. The Intelligence Corps was actually second choice (he wanted the Army Air Corps but failed the eye exam) but he found he had an aptitude for the duplicity and secrecy that is meat and drink to the better spies. He had to suffer the barbs of former colleagues who refer to the Corps as the 'green slime', a reference to the bright green of their berets and the generally low opinion soldiers have of those who work in intelligence.

It wasn't that Dickens was dishonest, or even that he thought lying an acceptable pastime, rather that he was clear about his loyalties and equally clear that if wars were to be won they needed people like him who used their minds not their muscle so that when the shooting started the bullets hit the right target. The Corps motto of *Manui Dat Cognitio Vires* (Knowledge gives Force to the Arm) summed it up well.

His looks, too, were a help, or at least they were when he first went into intelligence. He had a round face with the rosy cheeks of a farmer, which made him look friendly, and the blue eyes which vanished in the crinkles when he smiled were topped with bushy black eyebrows and straight black hair brushed off his forehead in the style of some thirties matinée idol. His wife told him he was good-looking but he wasn't vain enough to give it much thought. The important thing was that people warmed to him and trusted him. Trust was a commodity of real value when you dealt in lies.

The Rita Cloghan file had been passed to him along with those of the other two women the day the hunger strike began. The file, in its customary buff folder with the purple diagonal stripe across the top right-hand corner marking its 'Secret' status, told a familiar story of terrorism and capture, interrogation and jail. But what made Rita different from the others was the psychiatric report at the back which suggested that there might be an opportunity. It had all seemed very glib to Dickens, their talk of a father figure and substitution and dependency. But intelligence was attractive because it was a game of the mind, a pitting of wills, a delicate balance between the hunter and the hunted.

He had read the file but it was not until he began prising out her story in that filthy and depressing cell that he really began to understand her. It had taken three days of him talking and her listening before she began to reveal herself.

'I joined the Movement in '78,' she began. Her voice was low and husky, the vocal chords dry and contracted after months of talking in whispers to avoid being overheard by the screws and the microphones that all the prisoners were certain were everywhere. Dickens was surprised that he found her voice, if not her emaciated body, sexy.

'Looking back, it's hard to remember just why I did it. I'd heard stories from other women about brothers killed, houses searched and the brutality of the Prods or the Brits, but they were just stories to me, things that had happened to other people. I grew up in Greencastle, just north of the city.'

Dickens knew all of this, of course, but he nodded encouragingly as if it was all news to him.

'By what I saw of other kids' parents, we were quite well off. Not rich, just comfortable. Dad was one of the few Catholics to get a job at Harland and Wolff but even there he worked in the drawing office and so didn't get such a hard time from the Prods on the shop floor. He drew up the electrics for those big container ships that Wolffs used to build. He loved drawing, reading. He was such a gentle man.'

'You were close to your father then?' he asked.

She grimaced with what he thought was a shallow attempt at a smile that recalled happier times. 'I was an only child and they always say that daughters are closer to their fathers. Well, it was certainly true in my case. Mam was happy at home, happy if Dad was happy. But he 'was different. We used to go down to Loughshore Park and picnic on the edge of Belfast Lough: ham sandwiches, crisps and a bottle of pop. He would walk on the edge of the water and tell me about the revolution that would come one day.' Seeing the question in Dickens's eyes, she gave a low laugh. 'No. No. You think I'm the heir to an IRA legacy. Not at all. He thought the Boys were just a bunch of pansies, that they didn't understand the inevitability of political revolution. He was a true Marxist, born out of the Depression and hardened on the sacrifices of the war.

'Our little house was filled with books – Marx, Engels, Bakunin – he must have been the best-read draughtsman in Belfast. Before the war he had been certain that revolution was inevitable but it never happened. He became a dreamer, always hoping for the call to arms which never came. It must have been very lonely for him. Mam didn't understand. I was his audience, someone he could explain everything to.'

In fact the assessment Dickens had seen in Peter Cloghan's file, which had been gathered from interviews with his manager at Harland and Wolff and with family friends, had produced a different picture of a man who drank too much, who lived in the past and had no prospects for the future. The books that Rita saw as a sign of sophistication in fact marked both the development of his political thought and the disintegration of his political hopes. By the time baby Rita was old enough to understand, all he had left was the lit flame of revolution which he was determined to pass on to his daughter.

'I never bought into all that Communist stuff. It seemed so irrelevant to me, to my life in Belfast. God, I was just a kid and he wanted me to carry his torch. I may not have cared about what he said but it mattered that he was saying it to me. We would spend hours with him talking to me or we might just read together.

'I suppose I was just lonely and he was a good friend. I . . . I . . .' She stumbled and Dickens reached out.

'So what happened?' he prompted.

'I was thirteen. He was walking from Wolffs to catch the bus. I was at home and we had agreed to go down to the lough for a walk that evening. Then a policeman came to the door and I heard my Mam crying. A brick had fallen on him from a building site. So stupid. Such a waste.

'I felt so alone. I had depended on him for so much – friendship, love, somebody to turn to. I had nowhere to go and nobody to tell me what was happening to my life.'

She turned her face to the chipped grey wall of the cell, but Dickens had seen the tears forming and running off the bridge of her nose on to the wool blanket. He reached into his pocket and drew out a pristine folded white square of handkerchief, shook it out of its folds and then gently dabbed away the tears. It was a brief moment of intimacy that established a bond between them: she was grateful for the sympathy and he satisfied that she had given enough of herself to cry in front of him.

'So what happened then?'

'Oh, I lost it for a while. Started running with a fast crowd. Hanging around the city centre; going to discos and pubs. We all thought it was great fun, boosting cars, drinking too much, some drugs. Our favourite pastime would be to get stoned on beer and dope and then con our way into the Europe Hotel and vomit. You scored five for the toilet and ten for any public room. It was pathetic really; our way of sticking one to the rich businessmen and the Brits who stayed there.

'I pretty much dropped out of school. Went out with a few boys and that came to nothing too. By the end of the seventies, Belfast was a dump and the counties a hopeless place to make a life. But I had nowhere to go and no job I wanted to do.

'The Movement then was doing pretty well. They were doing fine in the elections, they were opening advice centres across town, helping people with their social security and housing, stuff like that. Sure there was terrorism, too, but it didn't seem too bad, you know? More like they were a popular social service. It was the Brits and the Prods who were hopeless, doing nothing for the community, beating up women and children.

'Anyway, I didn't become a card-carrying fanatic or anything like that. I'd read the old guys, the people my father was brought up on, but I'd also read Marighella and I even remember him giving me a copy of Gaddafi's Green Book – no wonder the Boys couldn't stand him.

'But back then the Movement was a refuge for people like me. They wanted locals and their security was hopeless. They wanted numbers and weren't fussed about the quality. There was still the legacy of the early seventies when IRA stood for I Ran Away because there were so few of them and they were so badly armed. So they wanted bodies on the ground and there was no trouble about joining. Friends who'd signed up said it was great, like being part of an élite, separate somehow but one of a group. So I volunteered.'

Dickens remembered it differently. In the early days the IRA had relied on Second and even First World War weapons which had been buried under floorboards or hidden in hedgerows. They were just a bunch of enthusiastic amateurs – but then so were the British. Northern Ireland had been a cushy posting for second-rate officers who hunted, shot and fished and played the part of landed gentry, which is what the locals seemed to expect. When the Troubles began, the army had no idea how to respond, while all the police understood was beating up Catholics, something they had been doing for generations. Then reinforcements had arrived, some fresh from the ruthlessness of the Malaya campaign. But their tactics were not right for an urban environment and nor were they right for Britain, and losses had been high on both sides. However, there had been a steep learning curve and by the time Rita joined the ranks, the IRA was beginning to look like a reasonably professional terrorist organization.

Of course, Rita was an ideal recruit: no family connections to the Republican cause and no record.

'Did they send you to that training camp south of Sligo? The Ox Mountains?'

A momentary hesitation showed Dickens that he had surprised her with his knowledge. But he wanted to make himself part of her story and not just a bystander. He wanted to draw her closer to him.

'Sure. We drove there one night. It was a small camp with tents and shacks and for two weeks me and one other woman and eight blokes learned about guns and explosives. It was all pretty basic stuff: field stripping an Armalite, planting a culvert bomb, firing a command wire, that kind of thing.

'All that was easy enough and I quite enjoyed it. But God it was a beautiful place: the hills, the dawn swims in Lough Easky, the rain, the mist. We'd sit for hours around a fire in the evening talking about the Movement, about politics, about anything really. We all had views. We were all part of something and that brought us together. I knew more about politics than anyone there and I think they were amazed that anyone, let alone a woman, could know more than they did.

'The instructors told us tales of The Big Fellow, of Pearse, Connolly and the others. We learned about the brutality of the Brits, Bloody Sunday and the rest. But what made it for me was the belonging, feeling a part of something. In a strange way I thought I'd found a home.'

Dickens broke off the confession. It had been a good beginning. She had spoken for the first time and clearly wanted to say more. But the essence of the agent runner–spy relationship was subtlety and care. He had read once that the Apache, perhaps the greatest hunters in the world, hunted through the soles of their feet and through their noses. Their feet were so sensitive they could pick up the slightest vibration and their noses could smell their quarry. They would stalk their prey for hours, moving back a little, advancing a little on their nervous target. Recruiting an agent was a bit like that. You needed all the skills of a hunter and a delicate touch to avoid scaring the skittish prey. So now he wanted to give her time to rest, to think about him and to allow her subconscious to mull over what she had said.

The next day, he returned in the afternoon when he thought her morale would be at a low ebb and she would be grateful for some attention and some company. He took up the conversation where they had left off.

'So, after you'd done your training, they must have wanted to get you bloodied. An operation tends to cement the ties that bind,' he added helpfully.

'Ah. Well. That is where it all went badly wrong.'

She was still lying down – there were no pillows as the prison regime had banned them after an inmate had used the down to start a fire. But he felt a small thrill of satisfaction as he saw that she had used some of her water to wash the worst of the grime from her face. He noted absently that under all that mess there might be an attractive woman.

'We were briefed one night by the Commander of the Belfast Brigade. It was a grand title but he was not much older than me and his nerves were shot to pieces. He smoked so much that every sentence ended with a cough. You could practically see the nicotine dripping from his yellow fingers.

'Anyway, there were four of us. Three men and me and I was to do the snipe. The target was the Ladybrook RUC station and we would shoot from the cemetery at the junction of Suffolk Road and Stewartstown Road. There was nothing smart about it. I would just hit the first RUC man out of the station with a couple of rounds from the Armalite and then we'd all run like hell.'

They had got into position, creeping along the edge of the wall, bodies doubled over, fear and inexperience causing them to mutter curses as one or other of them stumbled in the darkness. From where she was hidden, it was an easy open shot to the door of the police station and she hunkered down, blackened face peering over the edge of the wall, rifle questing ahead.

The shout when it came had broken the night with such force that she had literally felt her skin jump. It had been a British ambush.

'God, I was terrified. I heard the shout. For a second I didn't know what to do. I heard one of the guys curse, another started crying and messed himself with the fear. Then I stood up. I meant to leave the gun but I was just in a panic and clung on to it. As I came above the wall and the soldiers could see me, they started firing. I saw the flashes and wanted to shout at them I give up, I surrender, anything to make it stop. Then this huge fist hit me in the chest and I was literally lifted up and punched over the wall and into the street. I must have

113

blacked out for a few seconds. When I came round it was suddenly bright as day, brighter even. The cops had turned on a searchlight and I was pinned down. I heard more shouting from the station. The cops wanted me to move towards them and I tried to stand up. But I'd taken another bullet in the leg and couldn't walk so I had to shuffle the fifty yards on my bum. There was no pain really. I just remember feeling so humiliated at having to do this ridiculous shuffle across the road.

'Then there were these guns pointing at my head, men shouting orders I couldn't understand. The pain started and I remember hearing this screaming and thinking God, what a noise and then realizing that it was me.

'A soldier gave me some morphine but I think he was as frightened as me because the needle broke off in my arm. One of the Pigs came and I was dumped in the back. Some of the soldiers were really angry, shouting at me, spitting in my face, stuff like that. But then this young Brit came and squatted on all fours over me on the floor of the Pigs. He was shouting at the others, telling them I was wounded, protecting me with his body. I was lying there looking up into his face and thinking that this was the oddest position I had ever been in. Then I passed out.'

'How badly were you injured?' Dickens asked.

'It could have been worse, much worse. One bullet went straight through but took a fair bit with it. They had to take out one kidney and I've got a few feet less intestine. The other bullet they took out of my thigh and the bone seems to have knitted back together although I'll always walk with a slight roll. People say I walk like a sailor just home from a long sea voyage.'

Dickens had laughed gently at the image. The conversation was easier now; a gentle seduction, the candlelight replaced by the harsh fluorescence of the single ceiling light and the bouquet of a fine burgundy replaced by the stench of faeces and stale sweat.

Over the next week he called in every day, at first in the afternoons and then twice a day and then three times, so that he was the last person she saw at night and the first she saw in the morning. Through it all she became weaker, her body collapsing in on itself like a balloon with a leak. All the time he worked away, listening to her talk of herself and her hopes. He told her what he thought she might like to hear about the persona he had created. At the same time, he worked on her loyalty.

The IRA had made it easy for him. Although they had welcomed her as an increase in their numbers, women were still seen as a sub species. When the men began their hunger strike, the women were not allowed to join at first. When the men had begun the blanket protest and refused to wash, the IRA high command refused to let the women take part. It was three months before Mairead could get the reason: the men thought the women would be embarrassed when they got their periods. Of course, the women were as strong as the men – stronger in some cases – and their protests carried more weight.

But it was the attack where she had been shot that Dickens went back to again and again.

'All I can say, Rita, is if you'd been a member of my family, I would never have sent you out that night,' he would explain. 'No training, no reconnaissance, no one of any experience leading. They were sending you out to get killed. And that is not the way any member of my family would behave.'

When the leadership called off the hunger strike, the bond had been forged. Between them Rita and Bryan had seen it through together. For Dickens the difficulty was to build on the trust that had been established without alerting the other members of the IRA. The hospital stay was easy to fix and extend and it was six months before Rita was finally out of the doctor's hands, and by then parole was an option.

They had never discussed spying but they had discussed

peace and in a strange way had evolved boundaries to their relationship. She had begun by passing fragments of information, small details that he said just helped to fill in a few gaps. In fact, for two years there had been nothing of value. But gradually, as she moved up the IRA hierarchy, she knew more and the information became more significant. Always she talked of plans and never of people. Always she talked of likely targets but never of timing. This way lives were saved but her own loyalties to the Movement were not fatally compromised.

She had come to think of the spying as a way of carrying her father's torch. This was not the revolution they had talked about but she believed that he would approve of her fighting in her own way for change. He was a loner and she, too, had taken an independent road but she was convinced that her course was more likely to succeed than his.

She and Bryan had become lovers, of course. It was both inevitable and essential. Bryan had taken her to bed one night in a safe house on Galwally Avenue in Newtownbreda overlooking the Belvoir Park Golf Course. He had expected a sordid evening but had, in fact, been charmed by her innocence and captivated by her body. She had filled out by then but there was still no real fat. Her breasts were small and tight against her chest, her stomach flat, thighs firm and strong. Her pubis was covered in thick, dark hair and the folds within were constantly, unaccountably, wet, which he found tremendously stimulating. He was a kind, careful lover and for a time he forgot the microphones and the cameras that recorded the words and the action.

It seemed to seal their bargain and they had been lovers ever since. As they had grown closer, he had let some of his own barriers down, bringing out the pipe he preferred. She now called him Bryan. In their own way they were like a married couple, comfortable with a familiar relationship that gave both sides what they wanted.

He had called her using the code of two rings and then hanging up so that she knew to meet at their rendezvous in four hours time. They had met in a Val's Video in Sydenham, across the river from Greencastle where she still lived. The IRA had recently diversified into video hire stores but then so had Army Intelligence. It gave them unparalleled access to the local community and, by careful analysis, it was possible to discover who was home when by what videos were rented. It also had its virtues as a place to meet because the Army could control the opening and closing of the shop, so Rita would arrive just before lunch and immediately she came through the door, the 'Closed For Lunch' sign was posted.

Bryan kissed her on the lips and her hand slipped into his as they sat together on a sofa in the room behind the store.

His eyes seldom smiled now although the crinkles had deepened to continue to give the impression of good humour. Northern Ireland more than anything else had changed his personality. He had first arrived at the end of the 1980s at the end of Tom King's turn as Secretary of State. There was talk of progress then, a widely held belief that Catholics and Protestants were weary of the struggle, that compromise might be possible. Then Peter Brooke had arrived with his strangled upper-class vowels, his Farmer Giles manner and his brilliant diplomacy, which had managed to move the stone up the hill a few feet.

The rock rolled down again when the Nelson case surfaced. Brian Nelson was the intelligence officer for the Ulster Defence Association, the Protestant terrorist group, who had been recruited by Dickens in 1987. For nearly three years he had filed over 700 reports producing a stunning amount of timely and accurate intelligence. The Nelson files had allowed the Army to stop the sectarian murders that had plagued Northern Ireland and prevented the assassination of a number of prominent politicians.

Then John Stevens, the Chief Constable of Cambridge-shire, had been appointed by the government to investigate collusion between the security forces and the Loyalists. Before the Army were aware of what was happening, Nelson had been questioned and arrested by Stevens. For Dickens, the arrest meant the end of what had been perhaps his most successful intelligence operation. That was bad enough, but then Stevens insisted that Nelson be tried for his involvement in murder. Despite intensive lobbying, Stevens refused to make an exception, showing what Dickens considered to be extraordinary ignorance of the compromises that were necessary in the fight against terrorism.

Nelson was tried and convicted. Dickens was allowed to make a plea for leniency behind the cloak of anonymity in the court. But it was no use. Nelson, a man who had exhibited enormous courage in fighting terrorism on the government's behalf and whose information had saved perhaps 200 lives, was jailed for life. The travesty of such a miscarriage of justice convinced Dickens that there was little he could do to alter the course of Ireland's painful history.

In the aftermath of the Nelson case he watched as the murders mounted – forty-one tit-for-tat killings in the six months after his arrest compared with none in the preceding six. With the deaths, the political climate changed and both sides once again withdrew to their previous positions which even the affable Peter Brooke was unable to change before he, too, was moved on.

Dickens had lowered his sights now to try and prevent some of the killings. Like so many who tried to solve the Northern Ireland problem, Dickens had been broken by the complexity of the issues and the sheer stubborn bloody-mindedness of the people who insisted that every discussion in the 1990s had a relevance to events that happened four hundred years earlier. He no longer believed that he could provide a solution. His goal, like so many Brits, was containment. He was determined to limit the damage done by both sides so that the majority could live something approaching a normal life. That, too, was a goal which many shared but few had achieved. It was with this limited idea in mind that he had called Rita to the meeting.

'You've heard about the latest attack in England?' She nodded. 'Well, that was ten innocent civilians dead. And I am not interested in the Adams argument that they were government people engaged in the war. You and I both know that's just crap for the media and even if they buy it, I certainly don't.'

'Well, why don't you catch whoever it is that's doing it?' she asked. 'You must have enough people on the trail by now. Surely the Boys aren't that good?'

The sarcasm annoyed Dickens but he bit back the sharp retort. Instead he said, 'You know it's not that easy. Since the reorganization at the end of the eighties the cells are virtually impossible to penetrate. To be honest, we haven't a lead worth bothering with. We either need luck or hard intelligence. We've clearly run out of the former so I'm coming to you for the latter.'

'I haven't been involved in this operation. These days I'm running liaison between Danny and the leadership, keeping lines clear. I'm just a messenger and I don't get involved in the planning.'

'I know all that,' Dickens replied. 'But there must be something – anything – that will give us an indication of just who the people are and where they plan to strike next.'

He saw Rita shake her head slightly and when he spoke again there was a note of impatience in his voice. 'Look, we know that even Adams and Murray are getting nervous about the killings. Too many civilians. It's bad for PR at home and abroad and Adams can't afford that right now.'

'Well, you know more than me,' she responded.

'I doubt it.' He paused, taking a few moments to tamp down the tobacco in his pipe. 'What about your friend Morrison? Aren't you due for a visit soon?'

Since her release from jail she had moved into the IRA's organizational structure, first working for *An Phoblacht*, the Republican newspaper, then for *Iris*, the monthly Provo magazine, and then joined Danny Morrison's staff as deputy head of public affairs for the Movement. Like so many positions in the IRA, this had a dual purpose. On the one hand public affairs meant dealing with the media and on the other it meant advising Adams and others on the General Council about tactics and their effect on public perceptions.

Morrison is one of the Movement's key strategists. At the Sinn Fein annual convention in Dublin in 1981 he had first articulated what became known as 'the bullet and the ballot box' strategy: 'Will anyone here object if, with a ballot paper in this hand and an Armalite in this hand, we take power in Ireland?'

Since then, the IRA had fought elections in the north and south while encouraging terrorism. But with the loss of Gerry Adams's seat in West Belfast in the 1992 election, the political wing of the IRA gave way to those who favoured a military solution. This suited Morrison, who in recent years had fallen out with Adams; he thought Adams was too willing to compromise with the British.

A short, slim, feisty figure, Morrison is known to his friends in the Movement as Bangers, IRA slang for nerves. It is a perfect description of the man who chain-smokes Benson and Hedges cigarettes and drinks large amounts of Guinness with a Jameson whiskey chaser, known to locals as a Wee One. There are plenty of people who smoke and drink in Northern Ireland; what sets Morrison apart is his apparently inexhaustible energy. Adams once described Morrison as a 'Duracell Drummer', referring to a TV advertisement that showed a soldier marching in endless circles beating a tin drum. Morrison has a similar habit of pacing and smoking while talking, which everyone in the Movement finds very unsettling. In fact, Morrison's nerves are no worse than anyone else's. He is just less able to disguise the fact.

As the flag carrier for the militants, the end of the 1980s saw a rise in his prestige which was sharply curtailed after he was arrested for falsely imprisoning Sandy Lynch, a police informer who was about to be executed by the IRA. It was a stupid mistake by a normally careful man which could have removed him from the scene altogether. But, certain he would end up in jail, he laid his plans carefully.

All high-risk IRA prisoners are held in Long Kesh prison eight miles from Belfast, where there is different access for the families of prisoners than for ordinary prison visitors. Divorced from his first wife, Sandra, Morrison saw an opportunity to keep up contact with the outside world and looked for a willing member of the Movement to marry. Rita was volunteered – much to the fury of his then girlfriend who worked for the BBC in Belfast. It had been truly a marriage of convenience. Rita did not even like Morrison – she found his smarmy way with women and his sexist jokes repugnant. Certainly they had never slept together, although she had been obliged to get used to an enforced intimacy which she hated.

But the arrangement had worked well and Morrison was able to maintain his influence in the Movement through Rita and the complex network of IRA terrorists who use their families to pass messages in and out of the jail. This link had made Rita even more valuable because, as the conduit, she was able to intercept both sides of any correspondence. Thus Bryan had a reasonable hope that she might produce some useful intelligence from the forthcoming visit.

'I'm going out to the Kesh this afternoon,' she said.

'I'm to see Gerry first so I suppose there'll be a message in and maybe Danny will have one for me to pass on.'

'Well, we'd like to know if there is anything relating to England.' He held up his hand to ward off the protest he saw forming on her lips. 'I know I know. Look, we've known each other long enough. I understand how far you can go and you understand what I want. I'm not asking you to betray your people. I'm not even asking for details on a bombing of an Army barracks. What I want is to save any more civilians from being killed. It was innocent businessmen last time. It could be innocent women and children the next.'

He paused to allow her to protest, to argue with his interpretation, but she said nothing. He reached out a hand to touch hers, hoping the brief intimacy might help bridge the gap between hope and reality.

'I know you'll do what is right,' he said and was relieved to see Rita give a slight nod.

CHAPTER 8

SEAN THOUGHT IT funny that he should have ended up in Waterloo Road, a Southampton street named to commemorate one of the great British victories. He hoped it was not an omen.

He had arrived two days earlier, two hours after the success at Winchester. He had dropped the car behind the railway station, just next to the Spitfire Museum, hoping that the police might think he had taken the train out of the area. Actually, he doubted that they fell for such an obvious ruse these days but you used every opportunity there was available.

Then he had walked north up Hill Lane towards the football club, following the memorized directions that had been given to him over the telephone just after he had left the previous safe house on his way to Winchester. After twenty minutes he had turned left into one of those 1930s British housing estates built for the working classes that have become quite fashionable in London but remain stubbornly lower middle class elsewhere in the country.

Waterloo Road was identical to Inkerman Place which was identical to Omdurman Road. It was this sameness that gave Sean the anonymity he needed. There was nothing to distinguish No. 23 from the rest of the road. But when he walked up the small front path with the pansies and the last of the daffodils sealing the peaceful suburban atmosphere he knew that once more he had come home – or what he had come to accept as home, which in reality was simply another place to sleep and to hide. But when he thought about it, he always referred to these places as 'home', which he supposed was his subconscious trying to hold on to some semblance of stability in the increasingly fractured world where he struggled to survive.

When he turned up at the safe houses he never knew what to expect. Sometimes it might be an old-guard Republican, some lonely old man reliving the memories of youthful Republican activism. These days, such people were rare because the planners in Belfast and Dublin believed that most of them were on some British list somewhere, and also old age had taken its inevitable toll. Instead, they were more like the occupants of No. 23, innocents who had at some time pledged allegiance to the cause and now after years of inactivity had been summoned to the flag.

Like the sleeper agents planted by the former Soviet Union, the reaction of the people to the call to serve was mixed. Sometimes they were thrilled at finally having their chance to do something. Others were reluctant participants, too frightened to refuse but regretting a promise made in a flush of romantic enthusiasm years before. Sean had learned to judge just where he stood and for the first couple of hours he tried to decide between further flight or trust.

He had been told to ask for Judith Peters and it was she who answered the door. He was her cousin from Bath, travelling the country looking for work as a steeplejack, a profession that had fallen on hard times recently. It was thin but it would be enough. The British public rarely asked questions and only showed enough interest to cover the unavoidable social pleasantries. So it was with Tony Peters, a round, sociable man who worked in the Monkey House at the nearby zoo.

It was Judith who knew his real identity. She had

originally come from Ireland just before the Second World War as Irish Prime Minister Eamon De Valera launched a purge against the Movement in a gesture designed to appease the British and ensure Ireland's neutrality in the forthcoming conflict. She had married Tony soon after the war, her Irish heritage subsumed by English suburbia. But she was one of those who had never forgotten, and when a stranger from the logistics cell came to her home three months earlier, she'd had no hesitation in accepting the challenge.

Sean lay watching the curl of smoke from his first cigarette of the morning waft towards the ceiling to fragment into a thousand tendrils. The two days had done him some good, but already this home was looking dangerous. The problem was neither Tony nor Judith but their young daughter. As a general rule, he stayed clear of women while on active service. They were nothing but a damn nuisance. Either you got attached to them or they to you. Either way the road led to mistakes and betrayal and he could afford neither.

It had been a long time but this was not the moment to break his enforced celibacy. He had known from the instant he had met Sally that she was trouble. Small, with short dark hair and enormous brown eyes, her face was almost perfectly round with a pair of lips that had not yet decided whether to form a bad-tempered pout or a sensual Monroe moue. She had been wearing the uniform of the young: baggy jeans, T-shirt and a blouson jacket that effectively disguised her figure. He had examined her not as a woman but as a potential threat and then quickly dismissed her. Although he had noticed her eyeing him speculatively, he had dismissed the question in her gaze.

He had asked Judith about her that afternoon as they walked along the banks of the Itchen. Sally had been an afterthought, explained Judith, a very late arrival after they had both given up all thought of having children.

The story that unfolded was a familiar one of older parents struggling to bridge a generation gap that was even wider than normal, and a child/woman of sixteen with knowledge she couldn't understand and parents who no longer had the words to help her.

The damage was done when they all sat watching *News at Ten* that first evening. The lead item was the shooting at Winchester station. Sean was used to hearing about himself and was sure he showed no reaction. For Judith, the graphic account and the footage of grieving families and the blood-stained platform were horrifying. She could not resist looking at Sean to see if the results of his work that day produced some sign of emotion. She saw none, but Sally noticed the look, registered its intensity. Her mother had never made any secret of her sympathies for the Republican Movement but Sally had never had any reason to believe that sympathy would be translated into action. Then Sean had arrived, a cousin she had never heard of who seemed to do nothing much for a man supposed to be looking for work. In one of those intuitive leaps, Sally made the link between the on-screen drama and Sean's appearance.

Of course, in any other household the coincidence of a stranger's arrival and a news item might have led simply to a harmless excursion for the girl and a flattering diversion for the older man. But Sean could afford none of that. He did not want the emotional entanglement and he especially did not want this girl to learn anything about him. So he had been careful to keep the contact to a minimum.

Life since puberty had been an endless string of frustrations for Sally. The fumbling and groping that passed for seduction in her circle were unsatisfying. Her parents seemed to have no understanding of her problems or her dreams: her father was so boring she could hardly bring herself to speak to him and Mum, well, she liked to talk but her world just seemed so far away from all the new

126

things Sally had experienced. Sean's arrival had brought some excitement into Sally's life. At first she had fantasized about him, his hard body against hers, those strong hands on her skin. Then when she thought she had discovered his secret, he became not just a sexual fantasy but a man who was actually living life. With the innocence of youth, she sublimated the killings and concentrated on the romance. This was someone who was fighting for what he believed, who had kept the best of the British police at bay, who needed help. This was a real man.

There was a knock at the door and before Sean had a chance to get out of bed it had opened and Sally came in, a tray perched on one arm.

'I brought you some breakfast,' she said. He almost laughed at the banality of it but restrained himself, afraid that her attraction would turn to offence and then betrayal.

'Sure. That's kind of you. If you put it down over there, I'll get to it when I get up.'

Instead of doing what he said, she came towards him and placed the tray on the bedside table. She sat on the bed and he noticed idly that this morning she had shucked off her teenage clothes and was wearing a skirt and blouse. There was even eye shadow, so the plot was obvious, but he was determined to avoid its execution.

'I know who you really are, Sean,' she began.

'Oh, really, and just who is that?' he asked.

'You're the terrorist who killed those people at Winchester station. You're here because you're hiding out.' She stopped, almost breathless with her own effrontery.

'You have a fine imagination, Sally,' Sean replied. 'I'm a simple steeplejack in town looking for work. I was nowhere near Winchester that day and I'm certainly no terrorist. Why not ask your mum, she'll tell you.'

'I have asked her and she says you're her cousin from Bath. Well, I've never heard of a cousin in Bath and I don't believe either of you.'

127

Casually, she reached her hand out to touch his thigh. Startled at the overt nature of the act, he tried to move away. But Sally moved closer, her bottom sliding along the bed until his length was against the wall and she was established beside him.

'It must be horrible for you being on the run all the time. All that violence and then nowhere to go. I want to help.'

'I'm afraid you've got the wrong man, Sally. And even if you hadn't, do you think a terrorist could afford to take up with someone like you? Christ, you're just a child.'

'Is that so?' she replied. 'Do children you know do this?' She moved her hand up his thigh to grip the bulge in the sheet that was his penis. 'Or this?' She leaned forward, her other hand sliding around his neck, and brought her lips down on his, her tongue searching, probing.

The movement was so sudden, the action so brazen that he was taken by surprise. He was unused to women taking the initiative in sex and had no experience of girls so young acting so aggressively.

He wanted to push her away but her tongue was darting between his teeth; her right hand was squeezing through the bedclothes, arousing him. Their tongues met and passed, each searching for the heart of the other. Her tongue flicked along his teeth, first the top and then the bottom and then was inside, darting, caressing, touching the roof of his mouth. God, he could feel himself being swept along, losing his will to struggle.

She felt his penis start to harden under her hand and knew that she had won. Her tongue moved from his mouth, her lips dabbing short, urgent kisses on his face before sliding to his ear and once again her tongue was darting inside, her mouth breathing fire into him. Her mouth left his face and started questing down his chest, her left hand pushing back the bedclothes to give her

128

access to his body. He was lying back now, head against the pillows, caution gone in the face of her attack. Eyes closed, he felt her fingers and then her mouth exploring his penis and balls. Her right hand cupped him and seemed to push him forward into her mouth. He imagined those wonderful lips circling the crown and then he drowned in the hot, smooth sensation as her mouth inhaled his length.

Her left hand fluttered across his stomach, pausing at each nipple to caress it. He was surprised to feel that those, too, were getting hard with the stimulation. They felt intensely sensitive and he pulled back, but already her hand had moved on to slide down his ribcage and then to his buttocks to squeeze and push as he slid back and forth inside her mouth.

A groan escaped his lips, his need as urgent as hers. But he wanted to give as well as take and reached out to draw her head back from him. He brought her up alongside him. They were both panting, urgent and frustrated by the confinement of her clothes. His hands moved under her skirt and found nothing. As her blouse fell apart he saw she had not troubled to put on a bra either. He found her brazen role of seductress intensely erotic.

Her breasts were tiny, but the nipples were huge, extending fully half an inch in their aroused state. He put first one and then the other between his teeth, sucking them deep inside his mouth, tongue flicking over the tip and then circling around the aureolae. She sighed, her head hanging back, her throat stretched tight.

'Yes, like that. Take them, bite them. They're for you. My breasts, my body. Take it. It's yours.'

The words came out in short pants, each one punctuated by a moan of excitement as his mouth or hands found another sensitive spot.

He slid down the bed, wanting to taste her, to savour again that intense flavour. Her legs parted and he saw for the first time her thick, dark bush of pubic hair. He kissed the insides of her thighs, running his tongue from knee to groin. He could feel the flutter of her muscles just below the surface of the skin, each one quivering as his lips touched. Then he was parting her lips, his tongue moving through the jungle of her hair.

Suddenly he felt less driven. Unwanted, an image – more a sensation – came over him of the exact moment before he had begun shooting two days earlier. That brief hiatus between preparation and action. His mouth moved slower, his lips gathering Sally's hair between his lips and tugging gently, his pursed lips kissing softly on the top of the pubic bone and working down to the small mount surrounding the clitoris. He circled it gently, pecking, caressing until she was groaning with frustration. Then he moved his head slowly back and forth, drawing it in and out of his mouth. Her thighs had locked around his head, drowning out sound and all sensation other than what he could feel and smell. His senses felt overwhelmed by her, by the powerful smell of her.

Impatient again, he moved up her body, his penis thrusting the air, questing for more. Her hands circled him, her legs opened and he slid in one smooth motion deep inside her.

At the bottom of the stroke he could feel her cervix and she cried out at the shock of it. But there was no holding back, no time for thought, conscious or subconscious. They were both riding on instinct now, touching each other, hands running down back, gripping thigh and buttocks. Sensing that he might be about to come she pushed against him, panting out her request. 'Let me turn over. Come in from behind and then we'll both come together.'

He slid out and back on to his haunches as she turned around and pulled a pillow under her stomach. She pushed her buttocks at him and he moved back in to her, laying his body along her back, elbows on either side of her neck. He saw that one of her hands had slid underneath and then he felt the vibration as she began to stimulate her clitoris.

He was moving deep inside her now, each thrust met by one of hers as they both raced towards a climax.

'Talk to me,' she ordered. 'Tell me how it feels.'

Cry echoed cry and obscenity, obscenity until they both went to that separate place where all lovers go just before orgasm. With a final thrust and a cry that was half pure agony and half ultimate pleasure he came, spurting passion, pain and months of frustration inside her. His orgasm triggered hers and as he began to come down, she cried out, pushing herself against him, opening herself so that by some miracle he seemed to go even further inside her.

He fell forward against her neck, kissing the beads of sweat that had gathered from them both.

The aftermath of passion, which is supposed to bring two lovers close together, was a luxury he could never afford. That brief moment of depression that some lovers experience was magnified for him. He knew that he had just made a terrible mistake. He should kill her now and then kill her parents and leave.

But there was an unwritten rule that you never did anything to harm the keepers of the houses for fear of closing the door at the next one. He knew they should die, but he couldn't do it. He couldn't just snuff out the lives of these people. Unlike the others, they really were innocents in his war. Even as his hands reached under her body to feel her breasts again, his training and his experience told him he was being a fool.

The battered green minibus pulled up outside the Sinn Fein Advice Centre at 51, Falls Road. A depressing building with wire shutters on the windows and an air of decay, the building was the headquarters of Sinn Fein in the city. Rita had just spent twenty minutes with Adams receiving the message he wanted passed on to Morrison.

She boarded the bus, paid her fifty pence and made her way to the back to find a bench seat where she perched for the eight-mile journey to the jail. She loathed these trips. They seemed to symbolize the depressing futility of the struggle.

The bus was packed with relatives of the men and women in the jail: wives visiting husbands; husbands seeing wives; children on their monthly trip to see one or perhaps both of their parents. The bus always smelled of vomit. Today another child, excited by the trip and overfed on Smarties and Mars Bars, brought up the half-digested mess on to the floor of the bus. Across the aisle from Rita, one young girl who couldn't have been more than sixteen was breast-feeding her child. Both mother and child looked unkempt and dirty, their spirits drained by the dehumanizing business of eking out a life on welfare while the breadwinner was in jail.

The bus joined the M1 motorway heading south and then after a few minutes took the Hillsborough exit and then the Baliris Cemetery Road. It had always struck Rita as ironic that a monument to Protestant dead should lie in the shadow of the prison that housed the most violent of Catholic terrorists.

The bus turned on to Halftown Road and for a short distance drove alongside the forbidding wire fence that was the first line of defence around the jail. A left turn and the bus parked. There was an immediate rush for the door as the visitors struggled to be first in the queue for the security checks.

Rita walked across the asphalt to a turnstile in the close-meshed wire fence and pushed her way through. She walked a few steps to a small complex of Portakabins. Inside, she was confronted with the first step in a bureaucracy filled with petty refinements, designed both to demean and discourage any attempt at smuggling weapons, drugs or other contraband into the jail. The trouble was, many of the prison warders had actually worked at the jail for longer than most of the inmates had been sentenced. The identity of all the warders was well known on the outside and each one knew that their continued wellbeing depended on the goodwill of the terrorists. They were as much prisoners of the system they were enforcing as the terrorists themselves.

So, there was a routine to the process but it was a well practised one where both sides knew the limits and rarely stepped beyond them.

After handing over her chit, known as a 'visit out', which showed that Morrison had asked her to come, Rita passed through to the search area. She entered a small cubicle which had a mirror on the floor so that the searcher could look up her skirt and make sure there was nothing concealed. A woman warder entered and Rita began emptying her pockets. As the woman approached, Rita raised her hands to adopt the search position so that she looked rather like a penguin about to take off. The hands pressed and kneaded, feeling the underwire of her bra, pushing deep up inside her thighs, checking between her buttocks.

She moved towards the next Portakabin and into the waiting room. Uncomfortable grey plastic chairs and plain camouflage grey walls reinforced the institutional flavour. In some ways this was the part she loathed the most. Here Protestant and Catholic sat side by side, both factions of the sectarian divide usually present because someone from their immediate family was inside Long Kesh as a terrorist. It was common for verbal abuse, even fights, to punctuate the coughing, hawking and snuffling that are the hallmarks of waiting rooms everywhere.

This time, Rita waited only four minutes before her name was called with half a dozen others and she went out of a door in the far wall into another minibus. Now she was about to enter the heart of the complex and the van with its hard benches, its blackened windows and the bullet-proof glass between passenger and driver reflected that. They drove for some minutes over a series of ramps and then high-pitched warning bleeps told her they were approaching the first set of fifteen-foot-high iron gates. Although she couldn't see it, she knew that the gates opened outwards, allowing the van to pass into a holding pen. The back door of the van opened and two prison officers came out of the Tally Lodge to the left. Rita could see two prison officers entering the Lodge, handing over their outside passes and receiving the special coded pass that allowed them access to the jail itself.

The two warders counted the passengers, compared the numbers to a list and then the door was closed and locked again. The warning beeps started as the inner gates opened and the van moved forward again along a Tarmac road, past well-kept lawns and flower beds, to pull up by yet another turnstile in another wire fence. Rita stepped out, stretched and looked around, her eyes taking in the fence topped with lethal razor wire. Behind her was the twenty-foot-high wall of the main prison, topped by a three-foot circular tube which she had read somewhere was coated with a substance that prevented grappling irons or fingers getting a grip.

She passed through the turnstile and into yet another Portakabin. Beyond it was the infamous H-Block which housed the most dangerous terrorists. There was discrimination now between wives and other visitors. She moved to the left to the cabin with small booths where spouses could have some private conversation away from the other visiting area where one large room accommodated everyone.

Another short wait and she heard a van draw up. Then a warder entered, followed by Danny Morrison. The warder carried the red book which showed that Morrison was a high category prisoner. The book travelled everywhere with him and was always carried by a warder.

For years, the IRA terrorists in the jail had kept in

touch through Comms, their shorthand for a unique brand of communication. Terrorists inside or IRA people outside would write messages on paper from the inside of cigarette packets. These would be rolled to the size of a small fingernail and then wrapped in cling film and stored in the cheek. In the family room some kissing was allowed and so messages could be passed back and forth.

The system was known but nothing was done because of the unspoken deal that existed between the warders and the inmates. Then a planned breakout was discovered in 1992. Inside one of the IRA terrorists' cell a cache of messages was found that spelled out how the terrorists were going to be met outside the wire and where the safe houses were in case the cars were caught. The result was a spate of searches which uncovered a series of messages. At the same time, the rules were tightened so that only wives and husbands were allowed to kiss and the screws began random searches of people's mouths.

A new Comms had to be devised which had involved Rita going to the dentist. There one of her back teeth had been drilled out and a false crown fitted. Without any cement to bind it to the stump, Rita could flick it off with her tongue. Inside the hollowed-out centre was hidden the message, which she had not had time or opportunity to read since it was inserted in the Falls Road.

Now Morrison moved towards her, hands out-stretched. 'Rita, me darlin', *a chara*.'

Danny had flourished in prison. He had lost the un-healthy jowls of too much booze and homemade spa-ghetti. Unlike some terrorists who exist on tranquillizers, Morrison had elected to join the prison fitness club. Now he was well muscled, his shirt filled by his expanded chest. Rita found it repulsive. Outside she knew him as a smart-assed and ruthless killer who relished violence. Whenever she had visited his home he was either drunk or listening to Bruce Springsteen or both. But he was

135

no buffoon. He was a cold and calculating strategist who was not afraid of dirtying his hands in the bloody end of the terrorist business.

He hated the Brits with an almost mindless passion, which had made for some odd family gatherings, as his two sisters are married to British soldiers. Inside jail he had changed, channelling the violence into clever stratagems and body-building. Jail had hardened him both mentally and physically. Before, he was prepared to accept the compromises that Adams often suggested. Now, he was impatient with the lack of success. He spent his time dreaming of ways he could cause the British more pain. Thomas's recent successes on the mainland had convinced him that with a little more pressure they could be on the brink of a significant victory. He was the undisputed flag-bearer of the militants, the group who now were squeezing Adams, forcing him to commit more men to the armed struggle at the expense of the political movement.

He was still a smart-ass, with his trademark cocky walk and high laugh. But now he almost glowed with power, exuding a strength that made him appear even more menacing. Rita steeled herself.

His mouth met hers, tongue thrusting between her parted lips, wet and slimy. She almost recoiled but then met him, her tongue flicking back against her tooth. After a moment of panic when nothing happened the tooth came loose and she felt the tiny packet in her mouth. His tongue slithered around her mouth one final time and then took the packet and stored it in his cheek.

They parted and for the next twenty minutes engaged in the strained small talk of partners who should have separated years ago. They had nothing in common and Morrison's tales of the petty squabbles and victories of prison life held no interest for her. He was eager for news of the campaign in England, happy that there had been another successful strike. But she knew little more than he had seen on the television and certainly nothing that she could tell him in this room where every gesture and every word was recorded for later analysis.

When the warder signalled that it was time for her to go, she stood up and once again they embraced. This time his tongue pushed a package into her mouth and, as they clung together, her tongue eased it into the tooth and pushed the tooth back on to its stump. An operation that took seconds now had taken her many minutes the first time she had tried it. When they parted, there was no hint that her mouth contained anything other than tongue and teeth.

With a casual '*Slán*', or goodbye, they parted.

She had arranged to meet Adams at his house in Norfolk Drive in Andersonstown, an easy ten-minute walk from where she was dropped off by the bus. The Falls Road was one of the last unchanged bastions of Catholic Belfast and Rita always found travelling along it a depressing reminder of the failures of the Movement really to change things. Over the years the British had gradually knocked down and replaced most of the Catholic slums and so had given many of the people who would have supported the IRA a stake in their future. It was a sensible tactic in a long war that was paying off. It was no coincidence then that the slums around the Falls Road remained an IRA stronghold.

Half a mile from the Sinn Fein headquarters, Rita walked down some steps and into the ladies' lavatory, a dirty, graffiti-marked Victorian public convenience that smelled of urine and stale sweat. She went into one of the cubicles and sat down, her tongue already working on the tooth. The tiny plastic-wrapped pouch dropped on to her palm and her fingers wrestled with the plastic film. She knew she had only minutes because Gerry would know the time the bus was due and the time it took to walk to his house. A few minutes was explicable but any more and she was in trouble.

Her nails prised apart the film and set it to one side and then, careful not to tear the fragile sheet, she gradually opened out the rectangle of cigarette-packet paper. She peered at the tiny writing, struggling for a moment to decipher the minute letters. She stretched back, her head leaning against the wall, and groaned. That bastard Danny had written his message in code. The jumble of numbers meant nothing to her, the whole operation had been a complete waste of time.

Fifteen minutes later she pressed the doorbell of Gerry's home in Norfolk Drive. A simple terraced house, the security camera panning the front path and doorway, combined with the mesh screens on all the windows facing the street to deflect a bomb blast or a thrown grenade, showed that this was the home of a politician or a terrorist – or, in Adams's case, both.

Rita sensed hidden eyes on her and then the door opened and she saw Gerry's wife, Colette.

'Rita, come along in. The boys are in the back.' She gestured with a flour-stained hand towards the rear of the house. Colette was in many ways the perfect antithesis to her husband. She rarely spoke about politics, instead she concerned herself with providing her husband with a comfortable sanctuary and bringing up their son, Gerald. Her efforts had counted for little in recent years as Gerry never spent more than two nights at a time in Norfolk Drive to avoid attack by Protestant terrorists and to keep British Intelligence on the hop.

Rita walked along the passage, passing an open door to her left where Eamon McCaughley, one of Gerry's two bodyguards, sat in front of the TV monitors. Past the stairs, which were protected by another steel cage in case of a night attack, Rita turned right into the room Gerry had recently finished constructing. This was the room he called The Safe, where most sensitive conversations took place hidden from the prying eyes and ears of the British.

Until recently these talks had happened in the parlour, a room at the back of the house which also acted as Gerry's study. But then he had read in one of those helpful articles published by the newspapers that the Brits had developed a new laser microphone that could pick up the tiniest vibrations from window curtains and make out every word spoken in the room. Adams had brought in an IRA contractor to build a new room in the centre of the house. This one was shielded by lead panels and as an additional defence had hollow-foam soundproofing lining all the walls.

In meetings with the faithful, Adams can quote from memory the bad poetry written by inmates from H-block, the saccharine ballads of the Movement that commemorated feats of heroism or martyrdom, and the writings of the great Republican thinkers. But in private he is different; he has a broad intellect and wide tastes, in particular a fondness for classical music and the more traditional English writers like Trollope and Thackeray. As Rita walked into The Safe, she heard the final movement from Mendelssohn's Scottish Symphony, its dark and dramatic cadences somehow appropriate for the place and the time.

Adams had been in power for so long that his normally sensitive political antennae had become dulled. He didn't understand that this love for intellectual pursuits, which in any other man or organization might have been considered an attribute, was a cause for concern among the Boys. They saw a lack of political certitude, an ambivalence to his heritage that some thought suggested deeper doubts about the Movement.

Now he rose from his comfortable leather armchair to welcome Rita. 'A Rita, *a chara*,' he said, kissing her on both cheeks. She knew that the greeting had almost exhausted his grasp of the Irish language, another source of complaint from the traditionalists.

Adams drew her over to the table in the centre of the

room and gestured to the one free seat. As she sat down she looked around and saw that she had interrupted a meeting. To her left was Spike Murray, the familiar glass of Guinness half empty in front of him. He seemed more flushed than usual and she assumed they had been arguing just before she arrived.

To her right, Gerry Kelly, Danny Morrison's replacement inside the IRA hierarchy outside the Kesh, looked at her impassively. In a group of complex individuals, she found Kelly one of the most confusing. As a woman, she found him very attractive. He was a shade over six feet, with a thin face and high cheekbones, light blue eyes and dark hair which he swept back from his forehead. Unlike most of the Boys, he favoured smart clothes and invested large sums in keeping up with fashion. Today he was wearing a dark green double-breasted baggy suit, a pale grey silk shirt and a tie which had champagne corks, bubbles and bottles dotted all over it. His steel-rimmed glasses magnified his eyes, making them appear almost luminescent. If it weren't for his record of ruthlessness and courage, he might have been considered a gadfly. As it was, no one crossed Gerry Kelly.

He had risen to prominence after he had escaped from the Maze prison in 1983. He fled to Europe from where he had successfully organized IRA operations on the Continent. He had planted explosives and killed British soldiers with great success until he was arrested at Amsterdam docks with the raw materials for a bomb in a container. Rather than go through the expense and risk of a trial, the Dutch authorities had extradited Kelly to Belfast where he completed his sentence. It is one of the peculiarities of the British system of justice in Northern Ireland that although both the police and the intelligence organizations had plenty of evidence about Kelly's terrorist acts in Europe, they could not produce that evidence in a Belfast court and expect to get a conviction. So, Kelly walked out a free man to assume a position at the top of the IRA Army Council, the organization's policy-making body.

Now he was the heir to Morrison's mantle. He was the hard man who wanted to attack and attack again until the Brits were driven from Northern Ireland.

'So, Rita, what have you brought us from Danny boy?' he asked, leaning forward expectantly.

Once again her tongue poked out of her mouth and she lifted off the tiny plastic-coated ball and handed it to Adams. He carefully unwrapped it and then unfolded the paper on the wooden table in front of him. The code was obviously no problem to him and he reached behind him to the bookshelf and brought down a paperback copy of his own autobiography, *Falls Memories*. She had read it and, although she admired the man, she had found his self-indulgent romanticism about his childhood in Belfast almost impossible to swallow. She knew the reality of poverty and the slums was far removed from the friendly, help-my-neighbour pastiche that he had painted. But then she supposed the book was fodder for the unquestioning faithful or propaganda for the uncommitted, particularly in America.

Adams looked up, seeing the surprise she was careful to paint on to her face. 'Since the Brits cracked down on the old Comms we devised a more secure method. It's always in code and it works on a combination of the day of the month and a page from a different book each month. That way only Danny and I know the codes and even if the British find the message, they'd never be able to crack it.'

He was scribbling as he wrote, his familiarity with the system making him fluent in the transcription. But as he wrote his brow furrowed and then a flush spread into his cheeks from his beard making it look as if a small fire had started in the undergrowth.

'Christ Almighty,' he exclaimed. 'The stupid bugger wants us to launch a new phase on the mainland. Hit civilians, the royal family, anyone we can get at. The man's mad. The Kesh has scrambled his brains.'

'What's so mad about it?' The question was put softly by Kelly, and made all the more forceful by its quiet delivery 'After all, we're doing well. Two strikes and we're still intact in England. The politicians are calling for our blood and so are the media. We've even had a couple of editorials in the Tory press that have questioned the military commitment to the North. We've had nothing like that for years. Maybe now's the time to turn the screw tighter, to squeeze and squeeze until they pop.'

'Don't be so fucking stupid.' Adams glared across at Kelly, furious that he should be so openly challenged by his own creation. 'Sean fucking Thomas has gone off the deep end. The killing of Royce's wife and kids was bad enough but then to knock those people off at Winchester was just plain dumb.' He raised a hand to silence Kelly's protests. 'You just don't bloody well understand. We think it's a triumph. We say it's a strike against the British establishment. Fine. And so it is. Down the Falls Road they raise their glasses to our man. But they're the converted. We know we have them, come what may. What matters is England. We have to convince the British public that Northern Ireland is too high a price so they tell that to their politicians. Well, for every innocent we kill, the Brits have another propaganda weapon to shoot us with.'

'But they weren't innocent,' protested Kelly.

'Oh for God's sake, Gerry. You know that. I know that. But that is not the point. What matters is what the British public think and I'm telling you that they'll believe what the Tory press publish and they're saying we've let a madman loose in Britain and that we're a bunch of heartless terrorists who should be strung from the nearest lamppost.

'And now you want us to increase the violence! We've gone that route before. The Brits will never concede to military action. It has to be done by Sinn Fein to give them a political escape. Fight with guns alone and we're all dead men.'

'Ah, Gerry, that's crap and you know it,' Kelly replied. 'Look where ten years of politics has got you.' He began to tick off his fingers. 'The hunger strikers dead, some of our best men gone for nothing; the Anglo-Irish agreement in place and we didn't even get a chance to put our views; we no longer even have an MP at Westminster; political support is so far down in north and south as to be almost off the measuring scale.' He breathed heavily, the exhalation somewhere between a snort of disgust and a sigh of exasperation. 'We're becoming a political laughing stock. The only thing we have left is the gun and now is the time to use it.'

To buy time, Adams began thumbing Condor into his pipe bowl. The tamping finished, he struck a match and started puffing. The airless room quickly filled with the sweet-smelling smoke, making Rita desperate for a glass of water. But the scene was too tense, the byplay of personalities too dramatic to risk an interruption.

'Look, Gerry,' Adams began. 'If we give up the political struggle now, then we have lost everything we have fought for all these years. You and I both know that we cannot win militarily, that the Brits will never concede a victory to us. It would bring down their government.

'And if we do what Bangers wants and escalate the military campaign, kill more civilians, we'll lose what little support we have left. We'll be nothing, just a few people trying to keep the flame of Republicanism alive in the face of public indifference.'

Adams was voicing a fear that had been central to his thinking for many years. Above everything, he dreaded the obscurity of indifference. He had grown used to the media attention, to the adulation that leadership bestows. Personally he could not face banishment to the exile of failure. But it was politics and not the armed struggle that gave him his credibility. For him to survive, the political struggle had to go on.

'The trouble is that you have failed to deliver the ballot half of the strategy,' Kelly told Adams, his voice cold and hard. 'You promised all of us success at the polls and we've seen nothing but fewer votes year after year. I don't believe that you can deliver what we need. We have only two choices: give up or escalate the armed struggle. And I for one am not prepared to give up. I vote we go with Danny.'

'And I forbid it. Such a decision would have to be ratified by a full meeting of the Council and they will never support such a change in policy,' Adams said.

Until now Spike Murray had held his peace. He had chosen his moment well.

'I will vote with the others,' he told Adams. 'If you push this one, you might lose at the Council. It's a different world now. There's no mood for compromise. There will be no return to the old days when you told us the Brits would sit down and talk terms. If you fight this one, Gerry, if you take it to the Council, you could lose everything.'

Adams had always been able to conceal his feelings behind his beard. But such open rebellion forced his lips to compress and whiten with anger, his eyes to narrow in calculation. As a politician he had lost this round. As a tactician he also knew that he was about to set the Movement on a course to destruction. But he could see no way to stop them.

CHAPTER 9

DAI CHOI CURSED as the boat ploughed into another swell that appeared to come rolling from nowhere. Visibility was down to fifty yards or so now and as he peered forward the mist began to take on swirling shapes, first a huge, snarling dog, then a house, then a rock. It was a series of terrifying visions that disorientated him and sapped his confidence.

Each plunge down the back of a wave ended in a jarring crump that seemed to push every bone in his body together in one long and painful crack. Much longer and he believed that his brain would be shaken loose from its mountings to rattle around inside his head. He grunted once more as the boat slammed down into a trough, sending a jolt of pain up his arms which were braced on a supporting handrail in front of him. Each climb through a wave pushed him up against the supporting rail and then flicked his head back as the boat paused at the top of the arc before plunging down to begin the whole painful process again.

'How much longer, for God's sake?' he asked the helmsman, a tall, thin, unshaven Englishman he knew only as George.

It was the third time he had asked the question and Dai Choi despised himself for showing such weakness. He sensed rather than saw the white of the man's teeth as he laughed into the darkness before giving the same reply as before. 'We're nearly there. Just a few more minutes.'

For the fiftieth time Dai Choi cursed his arrogance, furious that he had not listened to the Turk and bought a cabin cruiser. Instead of plodding stealth he had opted for flashy speed and bought a boat that suited his flamboyant personality. Nestling at the quayside he had thought the sleek craft was so graceful, forty feet of raw power. Dark blue with a single white stripe down either side, the *Fire-Eater* had six huge Evinrude outboards at the stern which the skipper told him could punch out 1,200 horsepower, enough to push them along at over a hundred m.p.h. – if the passengers could stand the crashing, bucking and rolling that would result.

This was exactly what Dai Choi had asked for when he arrived in England four days earlier. It was something familiar in a foreign land; the same kind of boat he had used in Hong Kong for the smuggling run to China. He had told Vincent Sum that he wanted something fast and smart that would defeat any British patrols and his English associate had duly obliged.

Sum was a third generation Englishman whose family had originally arrived from Guangdong province at the turn of the century. Now, the thirty-year-old lived the dual life of many of London's Chinese. He ran a vast underground empire on behalf of White Lotus in London's Chinatown next to Soho, an area that appeared impoverished but which actually disguised great wealth. By night he lived in Chigwell in Essex, north of the city, a fashionable haunt for the *nouveaux riches*, who had often made their money by illegal or questionable methods. His house was a white-and-black marble palace complete with indoor swimming pool, gold taps and a private cinema.

He had been honoured and flattered when Dai Choi had called and asked for his help. Visits from Hong Kong were rare and when they came it was an opportunity to shine. Together the fashionably dressed Dai Choi and Vincent Sum looked like two sons of some rich Far

East merchant. But the Issy Miyake suits and Valentino ties covered raw, ruthless power which both men had used to rise and stay at the top of their chosen profession.

Finding the boat for Dai Choi had not been a problem. Powerboating is a popular sport in Britain and he wanted one of the most powerful boats around – a Cigarette boat. Named after the company that created the original design, it has become synonymous with drug-smuggling off Florida because of its high speed and low radar signature. The most important person on a large powerboat is the throttleman who handles the levers that control the acceleration of the boat. He needs the touch of an artist to lift the boat off the crest of a wave at precisely the right angle where an inexperienced man would hit it wrong and capsize. It is a highly skilled job which seems to attract a particular type, seduced by the macho image and the glamour associated with the big boats. Among such men there are always those who drink or do drugs to excess and Vincent Sum had found Dave Abbott in Manchester. He had run up a large debt to the local branch of White Lotus to feed his growing cocaine habit. The local club where he bought the drug appeared to be owned by whites but was actually a front for White Lotus. Abbott had insisted on bringing George and once they had seen the boat there had been no complaints. The prospect of a fast night trip in such a vessel far outweighed any concerns they may have had about smuggling contraband.

Following Dai Choi's careful instructions, Vincent Sum had installed a Marconi VHF radiotelephone. This was a standard piece of ship's equipment available off the shelf. But Sum had also bought the morse adaptor which allowed for a preprogrammed signal to be sent out in a series of dots and dashes rather than voice. In addition, he had procured through Dave Tomkins, an arms dealer contact who works out of his home in Old Basing,

Hampshire, a TC-182 wide band direction-finding system which came in a small suitcase and was completely portable.

The trip had begun with an almost festive mood among passengers and crew. They had joined the boat at South-wold, a tiny picturesque fishing village on the Suffolk coast. The sight of such a boat was unusual but not so strange as to excite too much comment. Many power-boats came up the coast for races and the locals had got used to seeing the wakes carving across the horizon of the North Sea. To the curious onlookers, Dave Abbott had explained that he was taking *Fire-Eater* and her sponsors to put the boat through her paces out at sea. They would return further north up the coast, perhaps at Gorleston or Caister-on-Sea. Dai Choi had been amazed at the lack of interest shown in them. There were no inquisitive police launches, no Customs men asking about cargo and destination, just a bunch of kids admiring the massive engines and swift lines.

Heading north and east away from the brightness of the setting sun, they were looking for a grid reference, a dot on the map, supplied by the Turk. It seemed to lie north of Leman Bank and inside the arc created by the two Viking buoys in water that shallowed to twenty-five metres. It was a journey of around fifty kilometres and at a steady and bearable pace should have taken just over an hour.

The rapid fall in temperature after sunset had brought the fog swirling in to engulf them so that their pace had slowed and the noise of their engines had boomed back at them out of the grey darkness.

Fifteen minutes earlier, Dai Choi had turned the radio on and begun sending a ten-second pulse of morse into the darkness. At the same time he brought out the suitcase containing the DF equipment, turned it on and tuned it to 950 FM.

From the beginning of the trip, Dai Choi had refused

to tell Sum what its purpose was. Instead he had been told the equipment required and what to do with it. Now he felt it was time to know more. 'So, what happens now?' he asked Dai Choi, shouting to make his voice heard above the engines.

'The Turk's people came through here a few days ago and dropped off our cargo in a container that should be resting on the bottom at the coordinates we have been given.'

'That's great,' said Sum sarcastically. 'I hope you don't expect me to dive down and fetch it.'

'No. It's a little easier than that,' Dai replied. 'Right now the radio is sending out a coded signal which will be picked up by an aerial that is floating on the surface above the container. As soon as the signal is detected, it goes down the wire and trips a relay switch in the container which in turn fires off a small explosives charge. That will release the valve on the oxygen cylinder which will pump in air to the floats on either side of the container and bring it to the surface.

'Once it hits the air, a radio will start a continuous transmission which should be picked up by the DF equipment. We just follow the trail and pick up the cargo. Simple.'

'That's pretty smart,' said Sum. 'I've heard of the Columbians doing stuff like that but I never thought I'd see it in action.'

There was no indication that the morse pulse had reached its target but the dial in the centre of the DF console was suddenly illuminated with a three-digit number and an arrow pointing on the compass rose.

'There. We've got it,' Dai Choi exclaimed. 'Turn on to that heading and keep on it.'

It took another fifteen minutes of circling in the fog before the large grey cylinder, coddled by two orange bags, appeared out of the mist. Dave Abbott carefully brought *Fire-Eater* alongside and eager hands reached over to bring the cargo aboard.

*

Two miles astern, Jonny Turnbull perched in the wheel-house of Her Majesty's Customs ship *Venturous* as she nosed through the fog, sniffing *Fire-Eater*'s trail. They had been following her ever since she left Southwold, closing up once the sun set but staying out of what they believed was the other boat's radar range.

The *Venturous* was a ten-year-old boat designed for inshore work, intercepting fishermen breaching the twelve-mile limit. She had a maximum speed of twenty-two knots, at which she started to shudder in an alarming way, so the captain tended not to exceed eighteen knots and preferred to cruise at a steady fifteen. British Customs tended to carry out the light work and leave the interception of arms-dealers and drug-runners to the Royal Navy. But there had been no time to find a frigate and all the Navy's fishery protection patrol were in the Irish Sea or off the north of Scotland. So *Venturous* had been delegated the task of following Dai Choi.

The Customs boat had a crew of eight. The skipper was a thirty-year-old Yorkshireman, Peter Cole, on his first command and his first drug bust. The inexperience of the captain and crew made Jonny nervous but then he had little direct knowledge of arrests at sea either. He only had instinct and that told him they needed more people, more muscle, more everything if they were going to take on Dai Choi.

As he had promised, Jonny had followed Dai Choi to Britain. For once the liaison arrangements between the colony and New Scotland Yard had worked properly. He had shared his intelligence with Commander Roy Penrose, the head of SO9, the Regional Crime Squad, who was responsible for combating drugs in the city. He in turn had passed him to Customs. Between the two groups Dai Choi had been kept under surveillance and the telephone in his room at Dukes Hotel in St James's Place had been tapped. The transcripts had produced little of interest but the Chinese had made the mistake of requesting a window table at Rue St Jacques, one of Charlotte Street's better restaurants.

A laser microphone in a Ford Transit van on the opposite side of the road had picked up the window vibrations from Dai Choi's conversation. The dinner with another young Chinese with a London accent had been conducted entirely in Cantonese. SO9 had no Cantonese speakers but could draw on translators when required. Two days later and five hours before the *Fire-Eater* left Southwold, Commander Penrose had the translation and so did Jonny.

Technology, Jonny thought, occasionally delivered the goods. On this occasion, Dai Choi had spelled out where he and his lunch companion would be meeting their boat and that they expected to rendezvous at sea. From there it had been simple to lie in wait and pick up the boat as she headed out to sea. Exactly what she was meeting and what cargo Dai Choi would pick up remained a mystery.

'She's stopped, sir.' The radar operator looked up, his face bathed in a sickly green glow from his screen.

'Bearing? Range?' asked Cole.

'Bearing 280 degrees. Range 1,000 yards.'

'Cox'n, bring us round to 280. Full speed. Call the men to action stations. Prepare boarding party.'

The instructions were familiar from a hundred films, and their familiarity was somehow reassuring to Jonny, as was the professional way the crew set about their preparations for boarding. Three men stood on the port side with boathooks and ropes, ready to jump the gap between the two ships when they came alongside. Jonny was alarmed to notice that none of the men were armed. He turned to the captain. 'Don't you have any weapons? Your men should be armed.'

'I hardly think that's necessary. Our orders are not to carry weapons unless we know that we are going to be attacked. That's not the case here.'

'Christ, captain, you just don't understand what's

going on here.' His voice rose above the note of the engines so that the boarding party turned to listen in eagerly. 'You are about to try and board a boat owned by one of Hong Kong's toughest gangsters. He's probably killed more people than you've even met. He's also probably got the biggest load of drugs you've ever seen and you think he's just going to give up and come along quietly on your say so? You're fucking crazy! If you've got some guns, get them. If you haven't, let's go back and wait for them to come ashore.'

Jonny saw the younger man hesitate, weighing up the risks associated with breaking out the weapons against the penalty for disobeying orders. Jonny was sure that the prospect of action and a successful bust – almost regardless of the risk – would drive Cole onward.

'OK. We'll play it your way. But there'll be no shooting without my direct order and safety catches will be on. Understood?' He looked around the cramped bridge and then out the port door to the boarding party, taking in the nods of each man.

He turned and, reaching into his jacket pocket, produced a key which he inserted in the door on the aft bulkhead of the bridge. He pulled the door open and Jonny saw two rifles – they looked like standard Army issue SA80s – and four handguns, again the regulation Browning 9 mm automatic pistol.

'None for you, I'm afraid,' he said over his shoulder. 'Regulations strictly forbid handing weapons to civilians. Anyway, I'm sure this is an unnecessary precaution.'

For someone used to going on operations armed with a pistol and sub-machine-gun and supported by men with automatic weapons, gas and grenades, the armoury appeared pathetically inadequate.

The captain passed round the weapons and there was the snick and slap of magazines being jammed home while the radar operator was calling out the range. When he reached the 200-metre mark, the coxswain snapped on the searchlight mounted on the top of the cabin. Its beam pierced the darkness but failed to penetrate the wall of fog. Instead, the white light broke apart, carried like an opening curtain on the tendrils of white fog to be reflected back at the Customs men. In an instant their night sight was destroyed and no one could see anything.

'Turn it off,' Cole hissed, and instantly darkness, thicker than before, descended.

Then out of the black appeared a soft white glow, so faint as to be almost imagined. The cox's right hand left the helm and pointed forward. The captain saw the glimmer through the fog and immediately ordered slow ahead.

Jonny moved out to the starboard side and walked forward so that he could see ahead. The light was brighter now, steady about ten degrees off the port bow. Then, in an instant, the curtain parted and they burst through the fog.

The boredom of the past few hours vanished with sudden and shocking action. Each step of the unfolding drama appeared to Jonny to be encapsulated in its own separate compartment. For months afterwards, he was able to play the action back scene by scene like a single-lens-reflex camera in autodrive with an infinite amount of film.

The image before him was startlingly clear, illuminated by the lights on the long, slender, dangerous boat ahead of them. The *Venturous* lost way as the cox shifted the gears to bring the boat alongside. Jonny registered their sizes – the difference not in length but in height, one built for speed and performance, the other for reliability and heavy weather.

The tableau before them froze for a moment as each face looked around. Two people, Chinese – Dai Choi? – were hunched over a long grey cylinder that glistened in the light. A door to the container was open and the men seemed to be transferring the cargo into their own vessel.

Of the two other men, one, bearded and tall, had his mouth open in shock; the other, smaller, broader, was still hunched over the throttles, looking back over his shoulders, his eyes staring white without pupils in the strange light

'British Customs. Heave to. We are coming aboard.' Cole's voice over the loudspeaker sounded so British, Turnbull thought. It was as if his lines had been rehearsed for a play where all the actors knew their parts. But Jonny knew that Dai Choi would never play to some British idea of right and wrong, fair or unfair.

Cole's voice broke the mirrored surface of the scene, fracturing it into a thousand pieces. The two Chinese seemed to move as one, their hands emerging from the crate with the stubby and distinctive shape of machine-guns in their hands.

Jonny's mouth framed a shout but it was already too late. The first ripping tear of bullets leaped the narrow divide between the boats. Each man emptied a full thirty-round magazine into the Customs boat. The noise, which was somehow contained and amplified by the fog, added to the terrifying suddenness of the attack.

Each bullet found a target and Jonny was showered with splinters from the wooden deck and then by pieces of flesh, blood and bone as the bullets struck and destroyed the bodies of the boarding party. One moment they were young men preparing to do what they had routinely practised many times. The next they were dead.

Jonny could feel blood running down his face, whether his own or other people's he had no idea. His nostrils were filled with the sickly, creamy, cloying smell and he felt his stomach heave as both mind and nerves rejected the invasion of his senses.

He saw that the Chinese had shucked their empty magazines and were fitting two new rectangles underneath the barrels. He had only seconds, fractions of seconds to do something, anything, to live. His eyes darted around the deck, shutting out the sounds of war: the splash of bodies and parts of bodies hitting the water; the curses from the captain and the screams from the coxswain who must have taken a hit.

His eyes raked the raised deck in front of the bridge, passed over a black object and then returned. His heart leaped into his throat as eyes and brain coordinated to pick up the clear outline of a Browning automatic pistol. It must have been flung there by one of the sailors as his shattered body jerked and jumped with the impact of the Chinese bullets.

Turnbull's body arced as he flung himself from the cover of the starboard side on to the roof of the cabin, his hands reaching for the weapon. He had no thought now of survival by running. He was a primitive animal, a man attacked who was determined to fight back. To kill or be killed.

As the fingers of his right hand closed around the butt of the gun, his left hand smacked into the palm of his right, squeezing the butt in a classic double-handed grip. His left thumb flicked the safety catch upwards and his arms were pushing the pistol out ahead of him as his eyes began to search and focus on a target.

He heard again that terrible tearing sound as one of the Chinese fired another clip at the boat. But the angle was wrong, the height of the Customs boat making him fire upwards. The bullets raced along the edge of the cabin roof and then into the bridge. The screaming he had heard was abruptly cut off.

As Jonny brought the pistol up to aim, he saw the froth begin to churn at the stern of the boat as the throttleman punched the levers against the forward stops. Jonny was firing now, his forefinger jerking back against the trigger guard again and again. He saw the back of the tall bearded man at the helm suddenly turn dark and he appeared to levitate before slumping forward over the wheel. But the boat was moving fast now, the roar of its engines deafening him, drowning out all other sound, all thought. He saw the second Chinese raise his weapon as if to fire, but the gap was too wide now, the range too great. Instead he stood erect, looking astern as his colleague reached forward and with one push shoved the helmsman overboard before taking control.

For a brief moment before the fog swallowed the speedboat, Jonny met the man's eyes. There was instant recognition and Dai Choi raised a hand in salutation and farewell.

CHAPTER 10

BRYAN DICKENS HAD come to hate London because it represented so many of the failures in his professional life. When he was younger, a rotation into the Ministry of Defence in Whitehall was considered an essential part of the job, an opportunity to make contacts outside the regiment and the enclosed world of intelligence. Such contacts were essential to the informal network which made the vast bureaucracy of the MoD actually work. It helped when promotion came around to know the man on the board, perhaps to have smoothed the path of a particular memo or found a way to get the job done faster than the system would normally have allowed.

But today London seemed to be the home for all that was wrong with his business. Like so many others involved in intelligence in Northern Ireland he found that his good ideas had been broken on the back of entrenched interests and a process that was unwilling to countenance change. The dead hand of the Northern Ireland Office, where civil servants had successfully managed a career out of not solving the problems of the province, was the worst example of the rot that had set in.

He knew that frustration was pretty much universal but it did not make it any easier to take. Now, the politicians were suffering one of their periodic spasms of indignation when they wanted something – anything – done to appease the cries of outrage from their

157

constituents and the editorial writers of the *Sun* and *The Times*. As usual, he would be expected to pull some rabbit out of the intelligence hat so that the House of Commons could resound with platitudes about 'winning the war against the IRA' and how Britain 'will never give in to terrorism'.

The truth was that Britain had given in to the fact of terrorism years ago. There had been an acceptance by the Army, the police and, above all, by the politicians that a certain level of violence was acceptable. The result was a decision by default to contain rather than eliminate the problem. Despite twenty-five years of warfare, there was still no strategy to deal with the terrorists, just a whole series of micro-managed tactics designed by people like himself which tinkered with the problem rather than tackled it head on.

Now he had been summoned from Belfast to a meeting in the Home Office where he knew everyone present understood the real issues but where they all would simply try and find a crumb to throw back to the political table to keep their masters quiet. It was not a happy prospect.

He came out of St James's Park underground station on to Tothill Street, turned right and then crossed the road and headed through the revolving doors into the Home Office. The building, he thought sourly, was like so many of the people inside: born in the 1960s, developed in the 1970s and beginning to show signs of age in the 1990s. For a building close to Parliament Square and looking on to St James's Park, the planners of the 1960s bore considerable responsibility for defacing the landscape with such a boring building as the Home Office headquarters. It is a rectangle of glass and pale grey concrete almost entirely devoid of personality. It is a standing joke to those inside that the architect actually thought he was designing a new prison for the Home Office and to save money it was made into their London headquarters instead.

Taking the lift to the seventh floor, Bryan turned right and walked around the east side of the square to the corner leading to the north side. Strategically placed with a stunning view of St James's Park is the office of Sir Clive Whitmore, the Permanent Under-Secretary at the Home Office. The senior civil servant in the Department, Whitmore is responsible for the police and for the Security Service, also known as MI5. Dickens had come across Whitmore some years earlier when they were both working in the MoD, Dickens with the Defence Intelligence Service and Whitmore as PUS. Then as now, Whitmore sat on the Joint Intelligence Committee which oversees all British intelligence.

The JIC is not, as is popularly thought, simply a meeting of the heads of different branches of intelligence. Instead, it is the JIC that produces the assessments on which ministerial decisions are based. For the past two years, the vast amount of JIC work had focused on the problems posed by the former Soviet Union as well as helping formulate a future role for British intelligence both at home and abroad.

The day-to-day activities of the IRA in England are not of interest to the JIC but devolve to the department responsible, which in Northern Ireland is the Northern Ireland Office and in England the Home Office. Hence, Whitmore's involvement in a meeting to discuss terrorism was not that unusual.

He is a silver-haired man of almost exquisite politeness who appears soft and sometimes diffident. But he is a legendary political infighter who mastered the intricacies of Whitehall through service in the Cabinet Office under Thatcher during the Falklands war and then in the MoD under Michael Heseltine during the shambles of the Westland business which brought Heseltine's resignation.

He is now in his late fifties, but is still young enough to have a son who plays in a punk rock band. So in discussion he can be relied upon to take a fairly liberal stand as long as it does not conflict with his first loyalty to his colleagues in the civil service or his second loyalty to the Secretary of State.

The summons had come that morning and Dickens had caught the nine a m shuttle to make the noon meeting. As he entered the private secretary's office he looked around to see if he was flying solo or if this was a group effort. One of the private secretaries waved him straight through and he entered Whitmore's personal office.

Like most of the Home Office, it was furnished in fading Habitat with none of the fine antiques that the government's Property Services Agency seemed to supply so liberally to the Foreign Office. Instead Whitmore has a plain blue carpet, a pastel suite of sofa and armchairs to one side and a light oak conference table at the other. The Victorian watercolours on the wall were yet another example of the bad taste that seemed to be a requirement for employment at the PSA. Whitmore stood up and moved towards Dickens, hand outstretched.

'Colonel Dickens, how nice to meet you again,' he said. 'Come along in and take a seat.'

Dickens saw that all but one of the six seats were taken and so he sat down between Stella Rimington, the Director General of MI5, and John Witherow, the newly appointed head of SO13, the counter-terrorist unit from New Scotland Yard.

Whitmore resumed his seat at the top of the oval. 'Let me introduce you, Colonel,' he began, and gestured to his right. 'This is Stuart Purnell, my private secretary; on his right David Bickford, the Security Service legal adviser; Stella you know; John you know; and Mike Williams, head of Met Special Branch, you also probably know.'

Dickens looked around, marking the people and judging the atmosphere. This meeting spelled trouble. There were too many leaders from too many agencies for it to be anything but a crisis. Bryan's hand reached into his jacket pocket for the solace of his pipe but as he brought it to his lips he saw the disapproval in Rimington's face and set it aside.

As always in the Home Office, his thoughts were backed by the air conditioning which seemed to give off a perpetual hiss. It was as if a hidden audience was permanently showing its displeasure at the goings on inside the building.

Dickens immediately dismissed Purnell. He would take notes and stay silent, his job simply to record his master's voice and make sure that a politically correct version of events went into the files. Apart from Whitmore, the most important player in the room was Stella Rimington, whose public claim to fame was her appointment as Box's first female DG. Bryan had come across her in Northern Ireland when she headed G Branch, which handles counter-terrorism for the service. Back then, it had looked as if her career was going nowhere. Indeed, rumour had it that she had applied to be headmistress of Roedean, the girls' public school. Not surprisingly she had been turned down, as a life in intelligence may teach many things but experience of real life and particularly teenage girls is not one of them.

Then Margaret Thatcher had appointed Sir Antony Duff to reform MI5 and he had brought Stella in to be one of the five directors. When Patrick Walker took over as DG, he determined to elect Stella as his successor to keep the appointment inside the organization.

Dickens had always found her a formidable operator. She had a quick mind and, like many intelligent people, had little patience with those of lesser intellect or who presented weak arguments. When Bryan had last met her, she had seemed younger than her fifty-five years, her hair cut in a pageboy style, her jewellery Victorian cameo and her skirts and blouses sensible Liberty prints. But the years of additional responsibility had aged her. Now just short of her sixtieth birthday, she looked it. The hair was still dark but the streaks of grey were more noticeable and the lines around her neck and wrists were deeper. Her dark eyes had drawn back so that her face appeared even more impenetrable.

It was interesting that she had chosen to come to the meeting with David Bickford, who was a largely unknown but very powerful figure in the intelligence world. He was the conscience of MI5, the man who made sure that everything the organization did was strictly legal. His appointment was in part a response to the criticism made by Peter Wright and others that MI5 was a loose cannon on the deck of English politics. While Wright had exaggerated wildly, there had been too many occasions in the past when decisions had been taken without due regard to the law. Today, like its counterpart in America, MI5 is so constrained by bureaucracy and legalities it is difficult to get anything done.

In his late forties, Bickford had been brought in from the Foreign Office where he had done some pioneering work on devising ways to stop the laundering of drug money. He favoured well-cut suits, striped shirts and had a habit of sucking his lip between his teeth while he thought of answers to difficult questions. Dickens had met him once in Belfast and in searching for some common ground had been surprised to discover that he collected original scores from Gilbert and Sullivan operas. His full laugh, which he used often, was a poor disguise for a tough and at times ruthless mind. But he was a highly moral man and would always side with the law and principle.

Mike Williams, the head of the Metropolitan Police's Special Branch, was a man who three years ago would have had real power. But today he was a bit player in the intelligence game and he knew it. The importance of SB had declined dramatically when a hundred years of tradition had been reversed by Kenneth Clarke, the Home

Secretary, and MI5 was put in charge of countering IRA terrorism on the mainland. The change had been dressed up in plenty of weasel language but the truth was that SB was no longer up to the job and the change reflected a view that had been widely held for years.

Dickens looked at Williams, remembering how he had once gone down to the police training college at Bramshill to lecture to the commanders' course on counter-terrorism techniques. These were the high fliers in SB, the fast-track inspectors who were certain to rise to the top. It had been like talking to the wallpaper: no feedback, and when the questions came they displayed such ignorance that he had never again taken the organization seriously.

For Mike Williams, the changeover had been particularly galling. He had been promoted to what would undoubtedly be the pinnacle of his career, only to have his power chopped from under him. He had fought a fierce rearguard action and lost. His drawn face had the yellowish tinge of a man who smokes too much, giving him a pinched and bitter look. He was clearly here to save face rather than make a serious contribution.

Witherow was a different matter. He had inherited SO13 from George Churchill-Coleman who had run the organization through much of the 1980s and into the 1990s. George, who looked rather like Farmer Giles but favoured better suits, had received a lot of the brickbats for the failure to catch the IRA teams operating in England. Much of this criticism was unfair as SO13's job is to act on intelligence and not to gather it, to catch the criminals rather than prepare the ground for their capture. Even so, as the pressure mounted, George had tended to see his world in terms of SO13 rather than as part of a huge team. He distrusted Box, Six, the Army, everyone in fact except his own coppers. He had been glad to get shot of the lot of them and move on to a quieter life.

Witherow was a different man. In Dickens's experience police officers tended to fit into two categories. The first was the overweight, beer-drinking 'copper's copper and proud of it'; the kind of man who touched the side of his nose with his forefinger and muttered about 'instinct' when asked what makes a good policeman. The second was the younger, serious man who came out of the training courses in the seventies and who talked a great deal about the social relevance of community policing and the importance of bridging the cultural divide with the Anglo-African community. It seemed to him that both groups were just as out of touch with the real world. Above all, he felt that people so singularly lacking in humour would never be good at anything. Fun was a vital part of the human condition.

But Witherow at least seemed to laugh at life and himself occasionally, so Dickens tended to treat him as more of an equal. Such an attitude to the tall, rather shambling figure was common and may have accounted for Witherow's thriving in the fast-track graduate programme. He was in fact one of the very few to have survived and prospered. Every other man of his intake – and most of those who followed – had left in disgust at the backward, entrenched attitudes that still prevailed in the police. Unlike any other branch of government, or even any other business, the police still believed that an officer had to be promoted through the ranks. A good copper had to have worked a beat. It was nonsense but no government was prepared to tackle such prejudices and be criticized for undermining law and order.

Since taking up his post, Witherow had done what he could to bridge the barriers that existed between Box, the police and the Army and he had had some success. The regular Thursday morning meetings on the fifth floor at New Scotland Yard were no longer the cat fights between different branches of the counter-terrorist effort determined to protect their turf.

'Thank you all very much for coming here at such short notice,' Whitmore began. 'The Minister is concerned about the IRA problem. We have questions in the House on Thursday and he's going to get a rough ride. I had a meeting with him last night and he asked me to get together with all those involved to get a sense of where we're going with this one.'

Bryan stifled a smile. There was a certain type of civil servant who spoke in a particularly strangulated version of the British upper-class accent and Whitmore was one of them. All the Os came out in elongated form so 'involved' became 'invoalved'. Whitmore's enemies, of whom there were many, said that it was an overcompensation for an education at Sutton Grammar School which he tried to disguise. The truth was that Whitmore was a Cambridge classics graduate and it is a mark of that university that Latin is always taught with the O pronounced long. For those in the know, it was a mark of a man with the right stuff. For the vast majority who didn't understand the intricacies of the British class system, it merely sounded affected.

'We seem to be in an accelerating pattern of violence. First the attack on Royce and now that dreadful business in Winchester. The violence is reaching levels where even the steadfast British public are getting restless. The Minister wants action and I have promised him some. And it is up to us to come up with some solutions. So all suggestions are welcome. Stella?' His gold-rimmed spectacles caught the light as he turned towards her, giving a brief impression of a spotlight.

As always, Stella had prepared her ground methodically and presented an ordered résumé of Box's position. 'You will recall, Clive, that we were only given control of the mainland problem recently and it takes time to put the necessary people in place to get the kind of information we want. What we have done is bring those people in, so that a structure is now in place and information –

good information – is beginning to flow back. But I would stress that it is early days and if you are looking for instant answers from my department you're not going to get them today.'

'Is there really nothing?' replied Whitmore. 'No crumbs for me to pass on to Secretary of State? No houses under surveillance, no suspects that could be arrested?'

'You know we don't discuss operational matters, Clive. We do, of course, have a number of operations ongoing but they are not about to come good. As far as arrests are concerned, I'm afraid that the days when arrests would happen just after an attack are long gone. Too many long-term surveillance operations were ruined and sources compromised because of that kind of stupidity. And we never managed to get evidence that held up in court. So no deal there either.'

Good for you, Bryan thought to himself. The police habit of lifting a bunch of 'suspects' immediately after a bombing or a killing was the worst possible example of knee-jerk counter-terrorism. It gave the cops something to crow about and fed a few scraps to the politicians. But the suspects were invariably released when the fuss had died down, everyone got back to business as usual and nothing was gained in the long term.

Both Mike Williams and Witherow appeared visibly to bristle under Rimington's thinly veiled attack. It was Williams, a man who now had little to lose, who responded. 'That's not quite accurate, PUS,' he said, using Whitmore's formal title. 'We have two operations ongoing, one in Manchester and one in North London, which are ready to be wrapped up. My men could deliver you the arrests this afternoon and they could be charged tonight, in time for Question Time tomorrow.'

The brazen nature of the offer and Williams's willingness to sacrifice operational requirements for political needs infuriated Dickens. It was behaviour like this that had made sure that the fight against terrorism marked time for twenty-five years instead of moving inexorably towards the IRA's defeat. He found himself talking, anger overcoming his usual caution, years of cynicism finally finding a voice.

'It's exactly that kind of rubbish that got us to this meeting today,' he began. 'Years of policemen bending the rules to suit the political agenda. Decades of the politicians doing nothing unless the newspaper headlines and the evening news demanded it.

'And just where has it got us? Every single terrorist jailed for the campaign in the 1970s freed as heroes because the police faked the evidence. No significant convictions of IRA terrorists in Britain in the 1980s and in the 1990s the police have such a rotten reputation that the courts no longer believe the evidence even when you have some that's worth presenting.'

Whitmore tried to speak but Bryan rode over the interruption.

'You and the dreaded Northern Ireland Office are as much to blame, Clive. You set the agenda in the seventies for a policy of containment and so we've been happy basically to do nothing. We have so many different organizations combating the IRA it's impossible to keep track, while they are one group and bloody good at what they do. The only thing that gives us an edge is our technology – the Army's technology – and without that we'd get damn all either from forensics or signals.

'And while they develop their strategy and improve their tactics we scrabble around looking for a few quick headlines to keep the politicians off our backs. Not one of us sitting around this table knows what the British strategy for dealing with the IRA actually is. And the reason for that is we don't have one.

'Christ, if the great British public only knew what a pathetic bunch we are they'd rise up and deal with the terrorists themselves.'

There was a slow ironic handclap from Stella

Rimington. 'Thank you for your support, Bryan, but I can manage quite well on my own, thank you. As Bryan so rightly says, we have made a number of mistakes in the past and my intention is that these will not be repeated. I am familiar with the operations to which Mike refers but it is my recommendation that these remain in place until I decide on the basis of information from G Branch just when we should make a move.

'I would remind everyone here that the responsibility for countering terrorism in England now belongs to the Security Service. If any of you want to argue with my decision then you can take it up with Secretary of State.'

By invoking the authority of the Secretary of State Rimington had essentially trumped all the other cards on the table. No civil servant and certainly no policeman would dare to challenge such authority and risk a rebuff without very good cause. It was clear to everyone that this was not the occasion to push for change on such a fundamental issue.

'Well, now that we have all taken up our positions, perhaps we can get back to the issue in hand,' Whitmore said. 'As you seem to feel so strongly about all this, Bryan, perhaps you have something to offer us.'

Rita had passed on the contents of the conversation between Adams and Kelly so there was information available. The question for Bryan was how much to pass on. In principle he was all for sharing intelligence but information was power in this game and he needed all the help he could get. Also, he did not want Rita to become another Brian Nelson, charged with terrorism and sent to jail, when in fact she was a priceless source who had saved many British lives.

'We have received some information recently that suggests there is a disagreement between Adams and the militants on the Army Council.'

'Huh, that's nothing new,' Witherow muttered.

'True enough, but the difference is that this time

Adams is losing the battle. Kelly and those close to him think that the campaign in England is really beginning to make a difference while Adams thinks the killing of civilians is counter-productive. He wants to rein in the team that's here but Kelly wants to escalate. Adams lost, so we're in for some big trouble.'

'You seem remarkably well informed,' said Rimington. 'How good is your source on this?'

'I'm satisfied that the information is accurate,' Bryan replied.

'Well, if it's that good, perhaps you could tell us something about the people operating here,' Williams suggested.

'The name of the team leader is Sean Thomas. But where he is or what he looks like I can't tell you.'

In any other group, the revelation of the name of the man they had all been hunting for so long might have produced whoops of joy or at least a passing expression of enthusiasm. But this was a political meeting and advantage was never conceded willingly. So the response was muted although every pencil moved along the white pads in front of each of the other participants as the name was faithfully recorded for later investigation.

It was Bickford the lawyer who followed up. 'If we get this Thomas, will your source stand up for us?'

'There is no way I'm going to sacrifice another of my people to the clods in the judicial process,' Bryan replied, the bitterness at the loss of Nelson bubbling to the surface. 'Anything you get on Thomas you'll have to prove for yourselves, but my betting is you'll be very lucky to get him as far as the courts. This one was born to die.'

For Whitmore the meeting had been almost a total waste of time. He had nothing to offer his master and Question Time would be a bruising business. But he could have a private word just before battle was joined to hint that something was in the wind. That might straighten his spine, he thought.

For the others, a name meant a new dimension to the hunt. Data bases could be scanned, phone taps gone over, computers programmed to trigger on the new words. At last the hunters had a scent.

CHAPTER 11

ALL THE BOOKS and all the training told you that you were supposed to know when you were being followed. An atavistic response sent the shiver down the spine and aroused the tingles between the shoulder blades. If properly trained and fully aware even he should be able to pick the face from the crowd, identify the stranger whose eyes suddenly moved aside to avoid contact, who stayed too long looking in a window that had no display.

But Jonny had enough experience of undercover operations to know it was rarely that simple. To follow one man took a minimum of twenty-four people working in shifts. You needed enough transport to make sure no car, van or motorbike was in the frame too long; enough men and women to confuse the watched; and enough clothes to keep ringing the wardrobe changes. It was also a logistical nightmare, keeping everyone on track, in touch with base and with each other and making sure that every avenue of escape was predicted and covered. For the real artists of the watching game, discovery was rare, and if the person under surveillance was untrained, it was virtually impossible.

But for all that, he was sure that there were people on his tail. There was no hard evidence, no recurring face or car, just a subconscious registering of a regular cycle in an irregular pattern of his own life.

He hardly thought it likely that he could be followed

all this way from his home turf. But since the horror of the North Sea, the hunt for Dai Choi had taken on a different pace. He had been driven by the man for so long, the hunt had become a concrete part of his life, and now the old pain of Sam's death had been stoked to fresh life by the attack on his sergeant and the confrontation in the North Sea. He had relived the horror of that clash over and over again. Like someone bested in a conversation he thought again and again how he could have done it differently; how if only he had fired faster, sooner; how the bullets would have looked as they entered Dai Choi's flesh. But this time he felt different. The frustrations had become focused. This time Dai Choi had chosen to fight outside his own territory and, for the first time, Jonny felt it might be an equal match.

When he first felt he was being watched, he dismissed it as paranoia engendered by the shootings. He had just returned from the endless debriefings that had followed the attack. The boarding party had all been killed, the coxswain had lost a leg and most of his right jaw and Captain Cole had still been in shock when he had left.

He had planned to stay to help the police but he had been made to feel unwanted, a foreign interloper interfering with the practised routine of a manhunt. Once they had Jonny's evidence of Dai Choi's involvement, the secret drug investigation became an open murder inquiry. With the whole panoply of the British police forces in action, he realized there was little to be done and, rather than remain on the outside, he decided to head to the flat he currently called home. At least there was the familiarity and the comfort of Lisu.

His suggestion of a liaison mission with the British had been readily agreed to at headquarters. His obsession with Dai Choi was no secret and he knew there had been an element of indulgence in the deal, as if by getting him out of the way life could return to a more normal pace.

'Look, Jonny, get yourself over there, see old friends,

make some new contacts,' the Chief Inspector told him. 'From what I hear, they need all the help they can get with the Triads. You'll be able to give them some good advice on that. If your ideas on Dai Choi work out, that will be an added bonus for them and us.'

Pay rates in Hong Kong are high to take account of the exorbitant cost of housing. That, combined with the generous overseas allowance, had enabled him to take a decent flat in a service block off Sloane Square. The rates were low because of the absence of the annual migration of Americans who had been put off by the exchange rate.

The trip was supposed to have been a time of renewal and opportunity for them both and it had begun well enough. It was Lisu's first trip to London and his first visit for many years, so they were both strangers in a foreign land. His parents were dead, his family scattered and he found little common ground with those he had once considered friends. They had done the touristy things – the Tower, Madame Tussaud's, a trip on the Thames – and it had been fun. They had recovered some of their old spark and even their lovemaking was a pleasure rather than the duty it had become.

But still the trip seemed to make him depressed. Subconsciously he had endowed England and London with a glow that did not exist. He was shocked by the dirt, the traffic and the general air of decay; and the scale of the place made him feel intimidated. How on earth could he make a life in a city so vast among a people he didn't know and who wouldn't care whether he lived or died?

He proposed a trip to recapture his roots in Newcastle. 'Let's take a couple of days. We can go on the Flying Scotsman, if it still exists, see the countryside and I'll take you to all my old haunts.' He could feel his heart lightening at the prospect and she responded enthusiastically.

They both needed to get away from the city but for different reasons. They had talked over dinner in their

Sloane Avenue flat about their impressions of Britain just before Jonny left for the North Sea. It should have been a conversation about hopes and prospects but it became an argument about futility.

'It's easy for you,' Lisu said. 'You were born here. You lived here. You speak the language and you're accepted. This is a foreign country to me. I may speak the language but I'm still a foreigner and Chinese too. You see the way the people look at us when we're together. I can see the men stripping me with their eyes. And the women just think I'm your whore.'

'Oh, come on, Lisu. That's unfair,' Jonny protested. 'You're just feeling vulnerable because it's all so different. Think about it. I could get a job here away from all that corruption and frustration in the colony. I might even get a job where I'd have some prospects instead of marking time and spending all my energy fighting the system.'

'Well, that would be fine for you. But what about me? If we move here, I will be coming to a place where everybody is going to see me as some kind of being from outer space. It's not like Hong Kong where the Chinese community is used to *gweilos*. You would not be welcome among my people here and vice versa.

'And as for living in this city, we could only afford a small flat in the suburbs somewhere and by the time we could buy anything decent we'd be too old to enjoy it. Anyway, I hate it. It's just too big. I'm lonely and now you're going away to leave me here with no one to talk to, nothing to do and nowhere to go.'

Jonny saw the tears spring to the corners of her eyes. Before he would have reacted with solicitous words, but Lisu's passivity now angered him, partly because she was expressing some of his own doubts. He did not want a dream he had lived with for so long to be so easily destroyed.

'This was never going to be easy,' he replied. 'I made my life in a foreign country. I married you and we became accepted in a community with its fair share of backward traditions, but you know we have nothing to look forward to in Hong Kong. Already younger men are moving past me on the promotion ladder and others get richer while we mark time. We'll have to move to make a new life and Britain is the only place I know –'

'Well, that may be so for you but it isn't for me,' Lisu interrupted. 'If you weren't so bloody stubborn we could have as much money as our friends. We would be up on the Peak by now, and if we were going to come to England we could buy a decent house somewhere nice instead of lowering our standards even further.'

The bitterness in her voice shocked him. For the first time he understood that while he had been holding to principles he believed in, Lisu had resented every dinner and every cocktail party that allowed others to flaunt their wealth. As the gap between them and their friends had widened, so had the gulf between him and Lisu.

'You always told me that you supported the way I dealt with my work.'

'That's not the issue.' Her voice sounded tired, too tired to reflect the anger she felt at so many wasted years. 'Of course I support you. But you have been trapped in the past for too long. This obsession with Dai Choi is madness. Everyone on the force thinks you're crazy and in all your time on the force you've got nowhere. And now here we are thousands of miles from home chasing another fantasy with Dai Choi. It's time to let Sam die so that we can get on with the rest of our lives.'

Lisu watched Jonny fold his arms. His mouth seemed to draw in on itself, making his lips flatter and narrower, signals that he was drawing a mental line. She realized that further argument would be futile.

'Look, Jonny, you go off on your trip and maybe that will produce some answers. All I am asking is for you to think of me, think of *us* for a change, and see if we can't work something out.'

Surprised by her sudden conciliatory tone, Jonny also backed off. 'I understand how you feel. Dai Choi is only part of it. Ever since Sam died I've felt responsible for his death. If I'd been more careful, listened to the warnings, been there. Since he died, knowing who killed him and knowing I could do nothing has taken over everything. This time I really think I might be able to get the man. And after that, maybe we can make a new life for ourselves over here.'

It was then that he thought of the north-east. Perhaps it could be the middle ground they both needed if they were to have a future together.

They had taken the Flying Scotsman from King's Cross. Instead of taking five hours, as he remembered, the journey had taken three, and the Central Station in Newcastle was almost unrecognizable, all red plastic and chrome in place of the stone and cold, echoing hallways thronged with people.

In the city, Jonny found that in his absence his roots had withered and died. The place had been transformed. Whole suburbs, once the slums he patrolled, had disappeared, to be replaced by modern housing estates. Newcastle itself, which used to be a small, fairly pleasant city, appeared to have folded in on itself. Whole blocks had been destroyed to make way for a spaghetti of huge roads containing little traffic. Getting across town, which used to take twenty minutes, now took five. But Jonny could see little advantage to the change if at the same time the heart of the city had been sucked out.

It reminded him of the children's story of the Little Engine That Could. The city had thought itself bigger and better for so long that it had finally developed the infrastructure for a place three or four times its size.

It may have been the feeling of being watched or it may just have been a result of feeling so apart from his roots that left Jonny feeling depressed. A trip that should have opened up new opportunities for them both had, in fact, closed them off.

It was Lisu who suggested a visit to the Metrocentre before they caught the train home. Everywhere they had gone in the city, this had been held up to them as an example of the new north-east, a place which led Europe in both style and substance. The half-mile-long complex in unfashionable Gateshead housed shops, estate agents, solicitors and banks, as well as Metroland, an indoor amusement park and a string of restaurants. In the past two years, a mock Mediterranean village had been added so that Geordies could be transported to the Costa del Sol without the cost of actually going there.

Jonny drove south over the new Redheugh Bridge that crosses the Tyne and then followed the signs west off the A1 to the Metrocentre. He entered a complicated one-way system that circled the vast concrete structure containing the centre. It was surrounded by what looked like thousands of cars – bees around a honey pot, Jonny thought. Each point of the compass was given a different colour so that shoppers could orientate themselves and find their way out of the maze. Jonny parked their Ford Orion in the yellow zone.

They walked the fifty yards through the car park and up the ramp and through the automatic red sliding doors. The smell hit them first and then they took in the two-storey McDonald's on the right. Stretching ahead was a spine leading to the central walkway of the complex. They strolled idly forward, the crowd of people jostling them.

'This is pretty impressive,' Jonny remarked to Lisu.

'Sure is. But I bet there's nothing here we don't have in Central and you don't have to drive miles to get there.'

It was true, of course, but Jonny resented the reminder. Before he had time to reply, he heard the first scream behind him.

He turned in time to see the automatic glass doors begin to open and the bonnet of a car plunge into the narrow gap. He watched as both doors exploded off their

177

rails in a shower of glass. He heard a man shout 'Ram raider' next to him, the latest in the spate of attacks on jewellery and hi-fi shops that Jonny had read were fashionable in the north-east. Thieves would steal a car and then ram a shopfront, seize the goods in the window and make their escape in a second car. It was a bold system that worked very well as the police were rarely able to respond to the incident fast enough to catch the robbers.

All this flashed across his mind as he grabbed Lisu by the arm and propelled them both to the right towards a shop called Knobs and Knockers. Looking back, he could see the crowd parting. Squeezed against the shopfront, Jonny felt strangely remote from the event. He did not feel under threat, more like an observer at an incident which didn't involve him. He watched with interest as shopping bags were crushed or brushed aside. He almost laughed as a Big Mac caught the nearside wing and was propelled into the air, bun, hamburger, lettuce and tomato forming a parabola over the shoppers.

Then, instead of driving past them or veering into a shop window, the car drew up with a squeal of brakes. At the same instant as the passenger door opened, Jonny saw the driver's face. The slanting eyes, round face and smooth hair translated into danger.

Christ, it's me, he thought, a groan of fear escaping as his eyes darted around. I was right. I was right. That little shit Dai Choi. The words were discarded as he tried to focus on escape. He could feel his stomach heaving and his bowels loosening. The revolting mess that had been the boarding party was still fresh in his mind and, unbidden, his subconscious was recalling the horror of that moment, only this time it was he who was lying broken on the ground.

He caught hold of Lisu's arm. 'Run. Run, for God's sake. It's us they're after.'

He pushed her away from him down the hallway, his eyes searching for a weapon, for anything to defend himself against imminent death. He could see that the man getting out of the car had a gun, its stubby twin barrels swinging in his direction. The back door of the car was opening now.

'Fucking hell. More of the bastards.'

But he couldn't just allow himself to be sacrificed. Frantic now, he turned, his head swivelling back and forth, his vision tunnelled towards the threat, the crowd now a distant echo, his mind watching and assessing as the barrel moved towards him.

'A Lupo.' The name sprang into his mind from some long-forgotten course on weapons: a shotgun with the barrel sawn off. In the thirties it had been a favourite weapon of the Mafia, hence its Italian nickname, the Wolf. At close quarters it could blow a man almost in half.

The barrel looked cavernous, an enormous hole pointing directly at him. He could almost feel the man's finger squeezing the trigger, could imagine the striker hitting the cartridge, the explosion, the cloud of lead pellets pouring out of the barrel and into his body, shredding him.

Instinct forced him to move and he sank to the ground, sprawled limply in front of the window as the gun roared. Immediately he was showered with glass as the shop window exploded above him. Doorknobs and knockers cascaded down from the display. Scrabbling for a handhold, his fingers fell on a rounded doorknob and seized it as a weapon. His arm levered it forward in a bastardized version of an overarm bowl. It missed, skimming past the gunman's ear. The Chinese had clearly not been expecting any return fire and he ducked just as he fired the second shot.

The second man was up now, another Lupo in his hand as he stood on tiptoe to bring the gun to bear over the roof of the car and on to Jonny lying on the floor in front of him.

179

The first gunman's right hand moved in a swift pumping motion as he chambered another cartridge. There was no emotion on the face of either man, just a certainty that they would complete their mission. He saw the driver's mouth opening, his face contorting as he shouted something at them, driving them on. But Jonny could hear nothing, his ears ringing with the gunfire and his concentration absolute on the next shot.

The second man brought his gun to bear. Jonny's hands were searching among the glass for more weapons. He was throwing things, anything, feeling the wetness on his hands as the glass sliced through skin. But his feeble attempts were having no effect. This time he knew that he was going to die.

Then into his consciousness came a sharp, light crack and he saw a white streak appear on the roof of the car. An instant later, the face of the first gunman appeared to flatten and then disintegrate in a flash of red. Another crack and the second gunman's face turned away from Jonny, a look of consternation and then alarm flashing across his face.

'Gunshots,' Jonny prayed to himself. 'Gunshots.'

Then he felt a hand on his arm, pulling him. He looked up and then shrank back as the slim figure in a baseball cap and dark sweater brought a pistol up.

Seeing the fear in his eyes, the newcomer shouted at him, screaming to make the voice penetrate the fog of fear. 'No. I'm not with them. I'm here to help. Come. You must come. Now.' The newcomer jerked, dragging him for a few inches along the floor. As the glass began to tear his legs, the pain helped focus his mind. He was still alive. He had not been shot by the newcomer. He began to help himself. He levered himself up, driving from the floor like a sprinter pushing from starting blocks, and then headed straight at the crowd. He could see the terrified face of Lisu just ahead of him and he reached out, grabbing her arm and dragging her alongside him down the passage.

The newcomer fired twice more, the sharp cracks of a small pistol, and then was running alongside them, heading down the corridor towards Marks and Spencer and the T-junction with the main corridor. There was a boom behind and Jonny felt Lisu stagger, a small scream escaping from her lips.

But there was no time to stop, no time for anything other than escape. He could hear the racing of the car's engine behind them.

'They're coming after us,' he shouted unnecessarily.

They ran on, fear lending speed and causing Jonny's throat to contract so that he could hardly breathe. Much more and he would be finished.

They were at the junction now. Their companion turned on one knee, brought up the pistol and fired twice more. 'Fuck. Missed.'

The figure turned and pushed them to the left towards the purple car park. It was a race now between the three of them and the car behind. Jonny could imagine the driver powering through the crowd, determined to finish off the job his comrades had handled so badly. His eyes would only see their backs drawing closer and closer to the bonnet of his car. Then they were out of the doors and clattering down the stairs. A crash and the car was through, the doors no barrier.

But the purple car park has a ramp for wheelchairs at the side and the steps down the centre leading to the doors were an unexpected obstacle. The front wheels hit the top step, bounced and hit the fourth with a crash that Jonny could feel in his feet as he ran off to one side.

They had seconds now, time to run, time to hide, time even to escape. They stopped at a blue Nissan Sunny and Jonny helped Lisu into the back and got in alongside her. With a squeal of tyres they were off, heading for the exit. Within two minutes they were on the A1 heading south. There was no sign of pursuit.

*

An hour later he was sitting in the Nissan with his rescuer. Lisu was in surgery in the casualty department at Durham Hospital, having dozens of shotgun pellets removed from her right arm and back. Fortunately, the effective range of a Lupo is short and so by the time she was struck the pellets had spent much of their force. Even so, she had lost blood and the removal of the pellets required a general anaesthetic.

The fifteen-minute drive to Durham had been a frantic business. They were all still high on adrenalin and fear, shaking with the aftershock of the attack. Jonny had been astonished to discover that his rescuer was a woman whose long dark hair emerged from underneath a New York Giants baseball cap.

Aside from a muttered introduction ('My name's Julie Cohen. I was asked to look after you.'), he had learned nothing. She had refused to come in to the hospital, insisting instead that Jonny rejoin her in the car.

He had called the police and they were on their way.

'So who the hell are you? How come you turned up there?' Jonny asked.

'I'm a friend of Lin Yung's. He asked me to keep an eye on you over here, just in case anything happened.'

'Well, I'm very grateful for the attention of Chinese intelligence,' Jonny replied. 'But what do you have to do with them?'

She paused, debating how much to tell him. There were advantages to confidences and Jonny's face encouraged them. Each feature seemed slightly out of proportion – bushy dark eyebrows below straight blond hair, the aquiline nose contrasting with a full-lipped, large mouth – but the overall effect was somehow pleasing. His blue eyes met hers directly and she decided to tell him enough to forge an alliance. If she told him too much her work could be compromised; too little and he might insist she stayed for the police to interview her.

'Did you ever hear of Morris "Two Gun" Cohen?' she

asked. As Jonny shook his head she continued: 'He was a Jew from the East End of London. For reasons too complicated to go into, he became a close ally of Sun Yat Sen and Chiang Kai-shek and helped found the modern Chinese secret service. He was in China before the war and he took a Chinese mistress, whom he kept in Beijing, where he had two sons and a daughter. His elder son married a Chinese woman and, by some genetic quirk, I was the result.'

She opened her arms as if asking Jonny to confirm her explanation. But in the dark, curly hair, fair skin and strong nose there was no hint of her Chinese ancestry. On the contrary, she looked middle European or Jewish, her strong yet sensitive face softened by pale brown, rather than the more common dark eyes.

She laughed at his obvious appraisal, showing strong white teeth behind thin lips. 'As you can see, you would never know I was from Beijing. This made me a pretty attractive asset so from childhood I was set up for a life in intelligence. When my grandfather moved back to London in 1966, my parents and I came with him. He died in 1975 when I was nine.

'I went to school here and then went on a scholarship to the Beijing Institute of Contemporary International Relations. As you probably know, it's a training ground for Chinese intelligence and it was there I was taught the truth about my grandfather. It was all very flattering: a man whom they all respected had played a key part in the Revolution and I was being asked to carry on the family tradition.

'Anyway, once I graduated, I was recruited almost immediately by Lin Yung into the Guojia anquanbu. I moved back to London and set up as a translator from my flat in Highgate. I went back to my roots among the Jews.' She smiled.

'So how did you find us up here?' Jonny asked.

'Lin Yung sent me a message a week ago that you

were on your way and asked if I would keep an eye on you. He's coming over himself but he was anxious that you should stick around until he appears to explain things to you himself.

'I have to confess this kind of thing is not really my style. I've done all the courses, but I haven't had to do much action stuff. I managed to put a trace on your car the first night you came north and that made life a bit easier.

'I'd followed you into that shopping centre and then everything went wrong. I'm afraid I've never used a gun in anger before. If it hadn't been for the ricochet off the car roof, I probably wouldn't have hit that man at all. As it was, I didn't do much to slow up the car.'

'Well, I can assure you that if you hadn't come along, I'd have been a dead man.'

'Look, Jonny. I have a favour to ask,' she continued. 'I want to keep out of the way of the police here. It would blow my cover and I want to go on helping you get Dai Choi. So when the police come, put them off. Say you were pulled out by some person with a gun who drove you here and then pushed off. You can tell them you tried to persuade me to stay but I insisted on leaving. Say I was from a local gang, anything you like. Will you do that?'

It was the kind of deal that Jonny would have done with Lin Yung. The kind of arrangement that was necessary in the fight against organized crime. Anyway, he owed this woman his life and it was good to talk to someone again who spoke his language.

CHAPTER 12

DESPITE THE MASSIVE manhunt, it had been remarkably simple for both Dai Choi and Vincent Sum to keep ahead of the police. They had brought the *Fire-Eater* into Kessingland Beach north of Southwold and unloaded the cargo directly on to a truck for the three-hour drive back to London. Both Dai Choi and Vincent Sum had taken separate cars, the former to stay the night at the Angel Inn at Stoke-by-Nayland in Suffolk and the latter to return to London and oversee the safe storage of the cargo.

Dai Choi had made the mistake of telling Vincent Sum that Jonny Turnbull was a 'problem that needed to be solved'. By the time Dai Choi had arrived back in London the hounds had already been set on the trail. It had seemed then that a simple execution in a city far away might indeed solve the problem. He had not realized that the branch of White Lotus in the north-east was inexperienced in dealing with such matters. They were in fact just petty hoods, used to small-time robberies, some thuggery and a little protection; not at all the sophisticated gangsters with strong leadership that Dai Choi was used to.

He had heard about the shambles at the Metrocentre at about the same time as Stanley Kung had read about it in the *South China Morning Post*, where the attack on a local cop on assignment in England was front-page news. The message from Kung that he was on his way to

England had arrived soon afterwards. No doubt the Shan Chu wanted to make sure the rest of the operation was running as planned. No doubt, too, he would want to make his views known about the progress so far. Dai Choi was not looking forward to the meeting.

They had arranged to meet at Model Cottages. In a few days the garages had been transformed. The fires were out, the cauldron stilled. There was no drilling, none of the noise that is associated with a mechanic's workshop. Instead, an almost antiseptic stillness had settled over the building. The few men who were left appeared to be walking so softly as to be on tiptoe. The silence accompanied by the movement gave the garage a surreal quality, as if the sound had been turned off in a film.

'They are all terrified that the slightest mistake will blow us all up,' Leung said with a laugh, turning to Dai Choi and Vincent Sum. 'They have no understanding of modern explosives. All they know is that there's enough stuff to blow up the terrace and most of the streets around here.'

'Well it's better that they take care than that we have an accident,' Dai Choi said.

'Oh, there's no worry about that,' Leung replied with the carelessness of the man who knows just enough to be dangerously confident. 'Look, I'll show you.'

He went over to two cardboard boxes and came back with a thin sheet of material half an inch thick, ten inches wide and twenty-four inches long. It was a slate-grey colour, completely malleable, flopping in Leung's hand rather like uncooked pizza dough. As he approached Dai Choi, he flicked the sheet in his direction and the Chinese reached out with both hands to catch it, the fright clear in his face.

'Don't worry, this stuff is the best. The days when you had to worry about handling explosives or be concerned about them going off prematurely are long gone. This is

Demex 200, made by Royal Ordnance in Britain, sold to Turkey, their loyal Nato allies, and then passed on to us. Each one of these sheets has enough power to blow up this whole street. About a hundred times more powerful than C4 and ten times more powerful than Semtex,' Leung said with the pride of ownership. 'It's fitting that we should be using their own explosive against them, don't you think?'

Dai Choi merely nodded, uncomfortable with his burden.

Leung reached over and took the sheet back. 'Come over here and I'll show you just how safe this stuff is.'

They approached a bench where one of the soft-footed workers was cutting the sheets into strips with a Stanley knife.

'You see, this can be cut, thrown around, shaped into anything we want. And if you come over here' – gesturing towards the Kamper – 'you will see that the type we have fits perfectly.'

Dai Choi looked inside the van. He saw that the roof lining had been taken out and was being replaced with strips of the explosive by the simple method of stripping off a paper backing on each sheet and exposing an adhesive surface. Another man was waiting at one side with a portable paint sprayer to make sure the new lining blended in perfectly.

'Over there,' Leung said, pointing to a man at a table against the far wall, 'we are using an iron to join together and then flatten out strips into floor mats for the cars. Those, too, will be spray-painted black to match the material we're replacing.'

Leung then hefted the tube in his other hand. 'This may look like bathroom sealant but actually it's a tube of Demex 400. Same manufacturer, same source. Except you can squeeze this stuff out in precise amounts.' He squeezed the trigger device on the base of the tube and a small grey blob appeared, to sit innocently in the palm of his hand. Leung put the tube down and then proceeded to mould the blob, squeezing it between his palms and rolling it out like a strip of Plasticine until he had a long snake. 'We can take all the door and window sealers out and substitute this in each car. A bit of paint and you'd never know the difference.'

'Very impressive,' Dai Choi acknowledged. 'What about detonators and weapons?'

'We've solved that problem too. You remember we insisted on a VW Kamper?' Dai Choi nodded. 'Well, we've taken out the second battery, rewired some of the electrics and used the second battery as a safe for the detonators. I'm confident detection is impossible. As far as the weapons are concerned, you'll find the answer over here.'

They walked over to the van which was now resprayed and in one piece. Dai Choi looked inside and saw three large lead containers bolted to the floor. Stepping inside the van he saw that each of the containers was hollow.

'There's enough room for all of this?' He pointed towards the wall where the remainder of the equipment he had brought back from the North Sea was stacked. MAC10 sub-machine-guns, automatic pistols, stun and phosphorus grenades, night-vision devices, ammunition and even a broken down Steyr Aug rifle with an image-intensifying sight. It was a formidable armoury that under normal circumstances even the most basic security system would have no trouble detecting.

'I can assure you that on the tests we have run, unless we are very unlucky, there will be no problem.'

'And what about our little surprise package?' Dai Choi gestured to the far corner where a wooden packing case lay in isolation.

Leung gave a small chuckle. 'Ah, now that is the real reason this place is like a morgue. All the men are terrified of it.'

'They're not the only ones,' Dai Choi replied. He gave a small shudder. 'When I think what that can do and how easily, I would prefer to be somewhere a long way away.'

The small side door to the left of the large wooden doors opened and Stanley Kung ducked his head and strode into the garages dressed for a day at the Happy Valley racecourse. He was wearing a perfectly cut pale grey suit with the distinctive slight sheen of silk. A pale yellow shirt with wide blue stripes that spoke of Jermyn Street and his brightly patterned Hermès tie were framed by the Burberry, flung loosely but with great care over his shoulders. It was a style that sophisticated Chinese thought was European but in fact was a distinctive fashion all their own. Dai Choi thought such a stylized image in such a place looked faintly ridiculous. But he masked his opinion behind the deference Kung both expected and deserved. He bobbed his head in a half bow, acknowledging Kung's arrival.

Kung moved his head in a cold, angry jerk signalling Dai Choi to step away from the group for a private conversation.

'I am very disappointed with the way this operation has gone so far,' said Kung, his voice low, the menace clear. 'You arrive in this country and, instead of carrying out a discreet movement of goods from the sea to the shore, you engage in a gun battle with the British and kill their Customs people. If that wasn't bad enough, I hear you were recognized by this man Turnbull.

'And then you appear to have allowed your personal feelings to dictate your actions. To order Turnbull's execution was the act of an inexperienced soldier and not what I would expect from my right hand.

'Finally, to allow the job to be done by such amateurs in a way that does everything to attract attention to us is folly. The whole operation has been put in jeopardy by your stupidity.'

Part of Triad tradition is to bear setbacks and criticism with fortitude. Dai Choi could do nothing but accept

Kung's attack, to explain or complain would be seen as an effort to evade his responsibility. He bowed again. 'I accept what you say. However, this man Turnbull remains a problem. I am concerned that he knows about the operation and that he may have alerted the British authorities. If that is so, they may be waiting for us to make a move.'

'I, too, am concerned about the mission being compromised. But there are ways of dealing with this problem other than gunning down half of the British security forces. You must learn, Dai Choi, that the key to successful leadership is the correct application of force and intelligence. In this case we need information and so we need to use force, but with some subtlety. That way we will get precisely what we want and can then plan accordingly.'

'So what do you want me to do?' Dai Choi asked, eager to recover some face.

'Nothing,' Kung replied. 'The key to situations like this is to find a weak point and then exploit it. I know Turnbull's weak spot and I intend to make use of it. Within two days we will have all the information we want.'

Sally Peters had passed the time since she had first gone into Sean Thomas's bedroom in a haze of lust and excitement that she was sure was true love. After that first morning they had met at night, rendezvoused in the park and stolen secret moments when her parents were out or asleep. The thrill of the danger had propelled her into a relationship that she had convinced herself she wanted to last. She wanted Sean to stay alive, stay around, stay in her life.

At first the secret of their relationship had been part of the excitement. Each time she thought about it, a frisson went through her. She knew something that nobody else knew. But as time passed, the urge to tell somebody became almost irresistible. It wasn't that she wanted to betray Sean; quite the reverse, she would do anything to protect him. But she needed to talk about her feelings, to share the thrill of the sex and the danger. It had become a compulsion that obsessed her but she had managed to restrain herself until this evening.

Her parents had gone to the cinema and she and Sean had been alone. He had gone to take a shower and after he had entered the stall she had taken her clothes off and sneaked in behind him, put her hands over his eyes and then pushed him to his knees. With the water streaming down between them she had circled him, the hair of her pubic mound brushing against his shoulder, his ear, his nose. She watched his nostrils flare as he took in the rich smell of her sex, but each time he tried to bring his hands up to draw her to him, she forced them back down again.

Then she tired of the game and stopped in front of him, her vagina in front of his face, the folds parting in invitation. His tongue bridged the gap to caress her lips, sliding into the valleys and over the ridges. She took her nipples in her hands, squeezing them between thumb and forefinger, sliding her hands over the swelling, amplifying the sensation between her legs. Then she half turned towards the shower, pushing her breasts into the spray, the needles feeling like hundreds of tiny blades against her breasts, the pain absolute pleasure, the excitement intense.

His tongue became more urgent, searching inside her and then moving up to circle her clitoris before flicking gently over its rounded tip. Looking down, she could see his erection straining up towards her, knew that in a moment he could be inside her and she could have her legs wrapped around his driving hips. But she wanted that anticipation, found it exciting to deny herself that final pleasure, wanted to keep him at bay.

He played her game, a hand joining his tongue, one

finger and then two slipping inside her, reaching to touch her innermost walls. Moaning now, she dropped one hand back to the wall to support herself as she pushed her hips forward, thrusting to meet his tongue as it moved faster across her clitoris, his lips coming together to envelop her with his mouth, the inside of his lips contrasting with the roughness of his tongue, driving her to moan encouragement to him.

Unlike their other orgasms together, this one seemed to stretch out on a long plateau of pleasure. She wanted him to go on and on and on but she could sense he was tiring and that brought her down.

Her hand ran through his hair. 'And what about you, my love,' she asked, eyeing his erection.

His hands reached out for her buttocks, drawing her to him, and he rested his cheek on her stomach. 'I'm fine. I don't need to come every time, you know. Sometimes giving you pleasure is enough. We can come back later and start again.'

They had parted, he to do business he refused to describe and she to meet June Douglas, her best friend, for a drink at the Texas Bowl, a bowling alley on the Western Esplanade.

Walking along the street she recalled their lovemaking and Sean's final remark and wanted to cry again. No boy had ever shown her that kindness. It had always been an animal act which she sometimes enjoyed and sometimes did not. But whatever happened, ejaculation always seemed to be part of the bargain. And now here was this man thinking only of her.

The two girls had become friends in part because of an attraction of opposites. Sally was open, enthusiastic and precocious, with little enthusiasm for school and no apparent ambition. June, on the other hand, worked hard, was expected to go to university and was determined to become an environmental biologist. June was still unsure around men and had not welcomed the attentions of the boys who asked her out. The intimate details of Sally's love life both appalled and fascinated her. Sally enjoyed shocking her friend but welcomed her sober advice, though she did not act on it very often.

It had been difficult for her not to tell June about her new adventure. She had always shared her secrets with June, and now as she became more involved with Sean she desperately needed someone to talk to.

June had noticed the change in her friend's behaviour and knew from past experience that it was probably a new lover in her life. But it was unusual that she wouldn't talk about it and June assumed that she was involved with a married man. Over Cokes and a burger, the truth came out.

As the story unfolded, June was at first excited and enthusiastic for her friend, but as the full dimensions of the relationship emerged she was horrified. 'Are you telling me that you're sleeping with a terrorist?'

'It's not like that,' Sally replied. 'He's a kind, gentle man who treats me with respect. He'd never hurt me and I don't believe half the stuff that the papers have been saying about him.'

'But, Sally, this man kills people. He's a member of the IRA. If he gets tired of you he'll kill you too.'

'No. He won't,' Sally said, her voice rising with the frustration of trying to communicate the feelings she had for Sean. 'You don't understand. We love each other. This time it's different, really different.'

Sally had hoped that her friend would appreciate this secret as she had so many others, but she could see that June just didn't understand the beauty of it, the intensity of having a man who took the time to love. Where she had expected the laughter of a shared confidence, she had seen first horror and then revulsion in her friend's face. Tears of disappointment welled and she sprang up from the table.

'God, I hate you, June Douglas. I hate you. You just

don't understand,' she cried, and half ran, half walked out of the building.

Walking home, two conflicting emotions ran through Sally's mind. She was angry at June for not giving her the unstinting support that true friendship demands. She was also furious at herself for giving up the secret that she had held so close to get so little in return. Somehow her relationship with Sean seemed diminished.

June sat in the café, stunned. She couldn't begin to understand what could have made her best friend do such a thing. She had no doubt that whatever happened, Sally would come out of the deal badly. Before, June had been around to help pick up the pieces, but this time she feared that might not be possible. Desperate, she did the only thing she could think of. She went to her mum.

Returning from the north-east, Jonny met with a different reception. The killings in the North Sea and then the attack at the Metrocentre had given impetus to the investigation by New Scotland Yard. He had been embraced into the inquiries, no longer an outsider but a prime source. They all knew the case had moved on from a simple drug bust. It was a race in which, if Jonny lost, he would be dead.

The difficulty was a shortage of information on which to act. Sources in the drug business had been tapped; snitches brought in and questioned; money from the contingency fund spread around liberally, but the net had come back empty. The story everywhere was the same. Sure, the Triads were into drugs, but that had been so for years. The only new supplies coming in were from the former Communist countries in Eastern Europe which the Colombians had infiltrated and were using as a new source of supply and distribution. There was no word on the street of a new drugs shipment from the Far East and prices for heroin, cocaine and crack were stable.

For lack of anywhere to go, the investigation was

essentially spinning on itself. Jonny was spending longer and longer hours in SO9's offices on the fifth floor of the Yard. He trawled through transcripts of interrogations and computer printouts that attempted to discern a pattern where there was none; chatted with the drugs squad specialists in the canteen and in their offices. He was driven not only by his obsession to find Dai Choi but by a growing paranoia about his own security.

Inevitably, he had spent more time away from home and away from Lisu. They had returned to the rented apartment in Sloane Avenue with Lisu swathed in bandages, in some pain but out of danger. The doctors said the wounds would heal within two weeks and there would be no scar tissue. She had been lucky, they said.

For her the trip to England had been a disaster. She had hoped that it would present another opportunity for her and Jonny to start again. He needed something to help him overcome the bitterness she had watched seep into his soul over the past few years. But the image Jonny had conjured up for her was an England stuck in the time warp of his memory. The green and pleasant land she had expected was unfriendly and cold. She did not believe she could make this place her home.

And even here the spectre of Dai Choi hovered over everything, just as it did in Hong Kong. She, too, had been devastated by the death of her son. But in her village in China death had been a part of growing up and she was no stranger to loss. If only Jonny would have more children, she was sure the hurt would heal. Instead, he remained totally focused on revenge. And now the trip to England had turned into another chapter in a saga that seemed to have no end.

To add to her insecurity, Jonny had been spending time with Julie Cohen, the woman who had rescued them from the attack. He had insisted that the relationship was all professional but he was there so much. Jealousy was fuelling her paranoia.

This evening, like so many others since her arrival in England, she was on her own, stuck in the flat in a building that seemed to be filled either with prostitutes, who thought she was one of them, or older couples, who seemed shocked to have a Chinese person as a neighbour. The one advantage to the location of their flat was that Zen, one of London's better Chinese restaurants, was across the road. She had come to an arrangement with the manager and had taken to ordering a dinner which she then carried back to the flat. She was about to take her first bite of the Szechwan spicy ducks' tongues when the doorbell rang.

Peering through the spyglass in the door, Lisu could see the clean-shaven face of a man of Chinese extraction. She could see a striped shirt and a tie which probably placed him outside the class of casual mugger. She opened the door, keeping it on the safety chain.

'Yes?' she queried.

'Lisu Siao-Ling?' the pleasant voice asked.

She sagged against the door, unable to restrain a small moan of horror. It was a name she had not used since leaving China, a name that had not passed her lips for more than twenty years. The mere utterance of it flooded her mind with memories that had been suppressed for years, blocked out in case an inadvertent remark might betray her.

'May I come in?' the voice continued.

Moving slowly as if being dragged unwillingly forward, her hand unlatched the door and it swung open under the pressure of her visitor's hand.

He pushed past her into the hallway and, after a brief pause to absorb his surroundings, turned right and went into the small sitting room. She followed and watched as he sat down, crossed his legs, lit a cigarette and drew deeply. As he exhaled his eyes met hers.

She knew the type, had met them often in China and had seen them enough in Hong Kong. They were the élite, the rich and the powerful. The people to whom people like her were a troublesome detail to be dealt with and disposed of. Under his steady gaze, she could feel all the years of anonymity and confidence-building as the respected wife of a *gweilo* fall away so that she was once again the terrified student she thought she had left behind.

'Lisu, my name is Stanley Kung,' the stranger said. 'Ah, I see you know who I am,' he continued as her eyes widened in recognition of the name. 'That makes things much easier. I won't have to go into the reasons for my presence here as I am sure you already know all about your husband's search for Dai Choi and his colleagues.'

He paused, drawing again on his cigarette. It was a full minute before he spoke again.

'Incidentally, I am sorry about that business in the north of England. I can assure you that was not done on my orders. Indeed, the reason for my little visit is to try and avoid any further unpleasantness.'

'What do you want?' She was ashamed to note that her voice came out as a small whisper, her fear quite apparent.

'I'm looking for just a small piece of information.' He held up his thumb and forefinger and brought them together to show just how little he really wanted.

'But I know nothing! What information could I possibly have that would be of use to you?' she protested.

'Well, we shall see about that. But first, I would just like to make sure we understand one another.'

He picked a black leather briefcase up off the floor and placed it on the table in front of him. There was a brief pause while he worked the combination locks and then he flicked the catches and levered it open. He reached inside and brought out a bunch of papers, held together by a single piece of green string threaded through a hole in the corner of each sheet.

'Ah, I see you still recognise a *ren shi dang an* from the

197

Ministry of Public Security,' he said with a satisfied smile.

The Chinese government runs what is without doubt the most comprehensive system in the world to keep track of every individual in its country. Each person has their own file, known as a *ren shi dang an*, which is kept by the *danwei*, units that keep a record of a citizen's passage through life from cradle to grave. These units report to the Ministry of Public Security who use the files to suppress dissidents and to control the movement of individuals from one job to another, from one town to the next and even a person's right to drive a car.

The Chinese Communists put the system into place after they seized power in 1949 but the government claims it was only formalizing a long Chinese tradition dating back to the Han Dynasty in 206 BC when the first Han emperor based promotions and awards on a person's written record of enemy soldiers killed.

Today, the files pervade all aspects of Chinese life in a way that would be totally unthinkable in any democratic society. It would even have outraged Soviet citizens before the collapse of the Union. The fact that her visitor had her file, a document she had not seen since she had fled China, showed he had immense power and that the Chinese were taking an unhealthily close interest in her.

'I received a call from my old friend Li Chuwen, who, as I am sure you know, heads the Ministry's activities in Hong Kong. He had heard that I might be coming over and he had also heard that his old adversary Lin Yung, the head of the Guojia anquanbu, is taking a close interest in the matter. He seems to think I might be able to be of some assistance to him in giving Lin Yung a bloody nose. He also thought that this file might be of some help to me in that regard. I do believe he is right.'

Kung began to flick through the pages. As he read Lisu's mind went back to those terrible days of Mao Tse Tung's Cultural Revolution in 1968. Never had a period of social change been so badly named. Young men and women had formed into bands, known as Red Guards, and roamed the country destroying books, art treasures and buildings. In the space of a few months China's cultural heritage, stretching back over thousands of years, had been destroyed. A country renowned for its civilization became a byword for barbarism.

But the Revolution was not just about objects. It was the people who suffered. Teachers, doctors, scientists, even humble shopkeepers fell victim to the Red Guards. Thousands were killed, thousands more tortured and yet more thousands banished from the cities to be 're-educated' by working in the fields.

At the time, Lisu had been in her first year at the university, studying to be a doctor. Within three months of arriving at university she had fallen in love with Xie Ming, a third-year student of architecture. It was first love for them both. In long walks through the gardens of the Forbidden City, they talked of their future together, of the children they would have, the life they would build. Then came the Revolution.

The university had been largely destroyed and in the third week of the worst violence, the Red Guards had come for Xie Ming as 'one of the new generation of bourgeois reactionaries dedicated to perpetuating the class myth through the creation of buildings that betray the revolution'. The proclamation was read by a fellow student who had joined the Guards and many of those that cheered him on from the crowd were people they recognized.

Lisu had fought for him with such ferocity that they had arrested her too. They had been left for a week in a cellar of one of the buildings just next to the prison. If anything that time together was what she remembered most vividly. Both had believed they would be killed and so they had nothing left to hide from each other. They shared every intimate thought, watched each other perform every bodily function and managed to make love in the tenderest, gentlest ways imaginable.

Then the Guards had come. They concentrated on Xie Ming, wanting him to renounce his beliefs and denounce his fellow students. He refused and they beat him: the soles of his feet became a bloody mass. They attacked his fingers: his nails were left hanging from knuckles as red and as large as ripe tomatoes. They used pliers to attack his mouth: the torturers shouted the count as his teeth grew in a small pile on the table in front of him.

Then they started on her to force him to give up. They assaulted her, one after the other or in groups, in every orifice and in every position imaginable. Her screams had finally broken his will and he had signed the document repenting his imagined sins. Just after he had signed the paper in front of her, the man who had been leading the interrogation stepped forward and, using a lead weighted baton, clubbed him twice around the head. He had collapsed without a sound, the last thing she heard from him was the solid thunk as his head hit the flagstone floor.

The next day they had come and told her that he had died during the night from head injuries. She was free to go, they said.

Broken with grief, she determined to escape the horror of the Revolution. She fled south and west, joining a nascent underground movement that had sprung up because of the Revolution. Later she had boarded a junk on the east coast and made the journey to British territory, where she and the rest of the passengers had been thrown into the refugee camp.

Now this man had appeared out of the past with her file to awaken the buried memories.

'You seem to have had a rough time at the hands of the Red Guards.' He shuddered theatrically. 'They were a terrible bunch. I'm glad I wasn't around in China then.'

'You were going to explain my position, so why don't you do so?' said Lisu.

'Very well. I see from your file that your lover of the time, a student called Xie Ming, allegedly died under interrogation. Or rather that is what you were told at the time. I would like you to look at this.'

He passed over a black-and-white photograph. The picture showed a man in his forties holding up a copy of the *People's Daily*, China's main newspaper, which she saw was dated a month earlier. She looked closer at the face of the man.

Her heart seemed to stop. Then it felt as if her arteries had expanded to tunnels and her blood was an express train rushing around the tracks of her body. She slumped down into the armchair facing Stanley Kung.

The picture was of Xie Ming. Older, of course; his face was thinner and so was the hair, but the jawline was unmistakable and so was the smile – he was actually laughing, she thought to herself with amazement.

'I can see you recognize the picture,' said Kung laconically.

'How can this be? He's dead. I saw him.'

'No. What you saw was him fall to the ground. He recovered from that and his other injuries. A period of rehabilitation followed and once he had fully renounced all the sins they imagined he had committed he was released. He wasn't allowed back to Beijing, of course. But I believe he has been designing some rather nice buildings in one of the provinces.'

It was all too much to grasp. Xie Ming alive. She felt tears of rage well up in her eyes. 'The bastards. The bastards.' The tears were streaming uncontrollably down her cheeks now. 'To think I have been living like this for all these years when I could have . . .'

'Yes, well, I'm sure that you will want to take all that up with the proper authorities in due course,' he said, smiling slightly at his weak sarcasm. 'The reason for showing you all this is quite simple. My friends in the Chinese government and I want to know what your husband is doing. You are going to tell us. I am offering you a very simple bargain. Tell me what I need to know and your former lover will continue to enjoy the rest of his life. There may even be an opportunity for you to go and visit him – a visit which I am told he would welcome.

'On the other hand, should you refuse to cooperate, then Xie Ming will be killed. I am sure that his death will be particularly painful.'

He paused and then added as an apparent afterthought: 'Oh, and I'm told they'll send you some more happy snaps for the album. Showing the execution. So the first question I have to ask is this: What does your husband know about the Tunnel?'

She had no time to think about loyalty or betrayal. Her instincts were to defend the only man she had ever really loved. There was hardly a heartbeat of hesitation before she answered.

'Tunnel? Tunnel? I don't know anything about a tunnel. He's said nothing to me. He's trying to find the drugs you shipped into the country from a boat in the North Sea.'

She answered almost automatically, her mind still stuck on the stark black-and-white photograph which had raised so many memories and so many possibilities. If she had looked across at Stanley Kung, she would have noticed a brief look of satisfaction flash across his face as she spoke. He had heard what he wanted. Their target was still a secret. No one had discovered their plans. The operation to seize the Channel Tunnel was on.

PART TWO

THE ATTACK

CHAPTER 13

DRIVING A TUNNEL train had given Harry Ritchie a
new status and a new home. For twenty years he had
been driving the Network SouthEast Intercity trains from
Waterloo to Poole and Weymouth. It had been a monoto-
nous job, hours spent with his right arm gripping the
dead man's handle, but he was one of the few British
Rail employees who actually loved their work. Ever since
his childhood spent with notebook and pencil on the
platforms at King's Cross, Charing Cross, St Pancras
and Waterloo he had been in love with trains. He had
experienced the evolution from steam to diesel to electricity and his love affair had never faded. Unlike most
other children, Ritchie had never lost his ambition to be
a train driver, nor had he ever regretted his chosen
profession. While working from Waterloo, he had lived
with his wife Rosie and their two children in a small
house in Amies Street, Battersea. His friends thought he
was mad to buy the place because it backed on to the
main railway line through Clapham Junction, the busiest
rail crossing in the world. But he liked to sit in the back
room listening to the rumble and thunder of the trains
and watching them clatter past, taking people on journeys
of hope or disappointment, love and despair. Trains were
life, and they filled Harry Ritchie with a thrill each time
he drove one.

When the Channel Tunnel was being constructed, he

saw this as the ultimate opportunity. The new Class 373 trains were going to be the most modern trains in the world and they looked wonderful, with their yellow and grey livery and low-drag arrowed nose giving a powerful and elegant aerodynamic shape. The cab, he was sure, would be the last word in high-tech luxury and the idea of driving at 150 m.p.h. under the Channel filled him with excitement.

He had determined to be reassigned and had written both to British Rail and to Alastair Morton, the head of Eurotunnel, the company which was responsible for making the Tunnel a reality. His boldness had been well rewarded. They had been looking for someone to represent the human face of the new train and Harry Ritchie was the answer to any public relations man's prayer. He was a devoted and reliable train driver; he had all the experience any nervous passenger could want; he was an enthusiast for the new system; and he was neither overweight nor divorced. Indeed, he ran most mornings, went to Church and had been married to the same woman for fourteen years. This paragon was paraded before the media as part of the publicity blitz leading up to the Tunnel's opening. Harry had had his fifteen minutes of fame; his picture in every newspaper. The *News of the World*'s *Sunday* magazine had done a profile of him together with a picture of his wife Rosemary and children, eleven-year-old David and nine-year-old Becky.

For a short while the Ritchies were celebrities. It was that publicity which had drawn him to the attention of the researchers from the White Lotus.

The job of driving the passenger trains from Cheriton, the special terminal that had been built just outside Folkestone, to the Calais exit in France, had entailed a move from Amies Street to Folkestone. The money for the Amies Street house had bought a larger one in Wilton Road near the Sports Ground and Radnor Park. There were no trains rattling past the window every few minutes, which pleased the family, Becky could at last learn to ride and Harry had even got used to running through the park without feeling he was breathing poisoned air with every step. Yet it wasn't the fame or Folkestone that made Harry really happy but the pleasure he got from driving his train on a journey that thrilled and frightened every passenger.

Just after he had got his new job, he had been taken with half a dozen other drivers down to Folkestone for the day on a familiarization tour. Harry had followed the development of the project since the signing of the first agreement in 1986. The package of documents given to each of the drivers filled in the history. The idea of a link under the Channel between Britain and France had first been mooted as long ago as 1802 by the French, but it was only as the Cold War drew to a close and there had been no war between the two countries for longer than anyone could remember that the project really took hold. There was still plenty of residual distrust of the French, which was one of the reasons why no British government money was committed, but, with the enthusiastic endorsement of the international financial community, who saw big money to be made from a high-speed freight and passenger link, the scheme went ahead.

Seven thousand men and women had laboured for six years to finish the biggest engineering project in recent times. It had cost around nine billion pounds, a sum which had astonished the public and outraged some of the original half-million shareholders who had to fund repeated cost overruns. But the final price was around the same as the sum Britain had paid for the Trident independent nuclear deterrent, which put the whole deal in perspective.

The result was the longest undersea tunnel ever built – 32.6 miles of which 23.6 miles are underwater – and the journey from London to Paris now takes only 2 hours 45 minutes, half the previous time by rail or road and hovercraft.

The Tunnel is not, in fact, a single tunnel at all but three different ones laid alongside each other and connected by passageways. To the west is the 22-foot-wide tunnel that carries trains from Britain to France every three minutes at an average speed of 130 m.p.h. Seventy-five feet to the east is the tunnel for the French trains. In between is a service tunnel nearly 13 feet wide which in an emergency can be used for evacuation. Every 275 yards, a smaller 6-foot-wide tube links the two main rail tunnels to act as a pressure relief duct. These tubes allow the column of air that a train pushes ahead of it to whoosh into the other train tunnel and dissipate.

In early 1993 when Harry made his first visit, the engineering work had been completed and trains were running through the tunnels to test the complex computer systems that managed the traffic. Their guide had taken them in a single rail car as far as the entrance to the first tunnel and they had all got out and walked in.

That was the one time he had been scared. They had walked into a cutting with concrete banks one hundred feet high on either side. As he walked forward, the holes appeared enormous, black and somehow threatening. He imagined the Tunnel five miles ahead with the whole weight of the Channel above, water seeping through cracks in the walls, the air filled with damp. A tiny fracture could swiftly become a fissure and the whole edifice would come tumbling down, crushing everyone beneath thousands of tons of water.

'There is no danger of leaks and every possible emergency has been evaluated and precautions taken,' said the guide, a pretty young woman in the grey and green uniform of Eurotunnel. She spoke in that confident voice adopted by guides everywhere who know their subject but have given the talk so often they have forgotten what they are saying.

They had walked forward into the hole along a concrete walkway that ran against the left-hand wall. In the well in the centre, the railway track glistened, reflecting the lights overhead. It ran as far as Harry could see, curving gently downwards and to the left. Every few yards bright lights illuminated the grey concrete walls, giving the place a clean, even clinical look. He was pleased to see that no water was visible.

'If you look to the wall on your left you will see two large pipes. These have cold water running through them and will keep the temperatures in the Tunnel at an acceptable level,' the guide explained. 'Above them are the radio antennae which will allow you to keep in touch with your control room at all times. Above us is the electric power supply for your engine and on the far wall you can see the hoses for use in the event of fire.

'Underneath the track is a drainage and pump system to deal with any water that might seep in.'

'What happens if the electrics go down?' one of the other drivers had asked.

'There are three different power sources,' she replied. 'In this tunnel the trains will run on British electricity but if for any reason that is cut then there is an automatic switch to power from the French grid. If that goes down as well then there are back-up generators which will keep the trains running. You shouldn't even notice a cut.'

The doubts had disappeared with the first run through the Tunnel. Used to the vista of the run to the West Country, the claustrophobia of the walls was at first startling but he had quickly got used to it. The speed and power of the train overcame any fear of the dark or being underground. The train was virtually silent, the electricity surging through the transformers in the engine to the tracks and powering the train through at well over a hundred m.p.h. Accelerating up to cruising speed in the Tunnel was extraordinary. He felt like a bullet shooting down the barrel of a gun. The view ahead was a blur of light with the dark hole of the Tunnel at its centre, the digital readouts on the gauges the only mark of his progress.

The whole trip through the Tunnel took under thirty minutes and there were so many checks and waypoints to note or acknowledge that there was little time to worry. Certainly there was no chance to see any water dripping through the roof and after a while he had stopped worrying about it.

Now the Ritchies' world had settled into a comfortable routine. The roster was decided every Monday with one day on and one day off. He tended to drive the same two or three trains (numbers 7, 12 and 16). They were all identical and it made little difference except for the kind of superstitious familiarity which all men seem to develop with particular machines. Each day he did six journeys through the Tunnel, with the first journey beginning at nine a.m. This meant he needed to leave the house at seven-thirty and so the family got up at six-thirty to eat breakfast together. Rosie made him a lunch which he ate in the cab. They had both become rather partial to French pâté and cheeses so he would do some of their shopping on the other side and then ferry the raw materials back home, only to eat the finished product a few yards away from where he had bought the food originally. The gap between the two countries had narrowed to such an extent that they never thought of such intercontinental shopping as being odd.

Breakfast this morning was the usual friendly chaos of stretching arms, shouts for the milk or sugar amid hurried discussion about plans for the day ahead. Rosie had just put her cereal bowl in the dishwasher and was putting bread into the toaster when the doorbell rang.

'Who on earth is that?' Harry asked, amazed and annoyed at the interruption so early in the morning.

'Don't worry, dear, I'll go,' Rosie answered, anxious to keep the peace.

As she left the room, David reached across to steal a piece of apple from Becky's plate, provoking a cry of outrage and a squabble that Harry had just calmed when Rosie returned to the room.

'Who was it?' Harry asked, turning around in his chair to see his wife come back into the room. He had read the expression 'white with fear' but had never actually seen the reality until now. The blood seemed to have drained away entirely from Rosie's face. She looked as if she had daubed herself in white powder.

Concern and instinct pushed Harry half out of his chair before he saw the gun and then the man – a Chinese – who was holding it to Rosie's neck just behind her right ear. He noted vaguely that the gun was an automatic and looked enormous, black and very dangerous. He made to rise until the man spoke, his voice deep and fast.

'Just stay exactly where you are, Mr Ritchie, and make sure your children do the same. Any move by you and I will fire one bullet through the head of your wife. If you still persist in fighting me I will then kill your daughter and, if necessary, your son.'

Ritchie sank back into his chair, unable to grasp what was happening. He saw that David and Becky were looking on with interest at the drama. He saw no fear in their eyes, their imagination too young to make the connections between the words and their possible outcome.

The Chinese pushed Rosie into the room and then put a hand on her shoulder to force her into her chair at the table. He took a step back and put his gun into a holster under his jacket. Just as Harry began to think of opportunities and challenges, two other Chinese stepped quietly into the room. Both had small machine-guns in their hands and took up station, one against the cooker, the other on the opposite side of the room with his back to the fridge.

The leader spoke again. Now that he had established control, his voice was normal, his tone that of a reasonable man preparing for a quiet discussion in the pub over a beer or two.

'That's much better. My name is Vincent Sum and these two gentlemen are my business associates.' He smiled slightly. 'Our business, I'm afraid, involves you, Mr Ritchie. I must apologize for disturbing you in this way but I hope our stay with you will be a short one.'

'What do you want?' Harry asked. 'If it's money, there's nothing except what's in my wallet. Take it, take anything you want but just leave my family alone.'

He could hear the tremor in his voice and was ashamed that he should exhibit fright so easily. Becky could hear it too and began to cry softly. She did not understand what was happening but sensed the fear in her father. He had always been a bastion for her and if he was frightened then so was she.

Vincent gave a humourless chuckle. 'Oh, it's not your money that I want, Mr Ritchie. It's your driving skills.'

Suddenly Harry knew why these men were here. The train. They wanted the train.

When he had been seconded for the two-week familiarization course on the new train, he and the other drivers had spent a morning being lectured about security. One of the sessions had been titled 'Terrorist Attack' and a man from Special Branch had told them about some of the precautions and what they should do in the event of an assault. It had all sounded very impressive and reassuring. Then the SB man had given them a final warning.

'All the precautions are the best but remember the most vulnerable point in any security system is the people operating it. In a bank, it's the bank manager with the combination codes to the safe; in a military base, it's the officer of the watch who knows the password. In your case, you are the people who control the trains. If a terrorist wants in, you might be the key to unlock the door.

'If anyone threatens you, report it. If anyone tries to bribe you or get information from you, report it. If you see or hear anything you think might be threatening, let us know.'

Ha. It was easy to say but Harry was willing to bet that stupid ass had never been stuck in his kitchen with three hoods pointing guns at his family.

Vincent Sum saw the journey from incomprehension to understanding travel across Harry's face. 'I see you understand why we are here. Let me explain further. What we want is for you to leave here to drive your normal train to Calais. Only when you take the nine o'clock we want you to stop in the Tunnel as you pass the ten-mile marker. It should take you 750 yards to stop and then your job will be done.'

'Then what happens?' Harry asked.

'That is no concern of yours. The only two things that matter to you are: One, will you live? The answer to that is yes. Once you have halted the train and remained stationary for three minutes, you will be free to start again and complete your journey.

'The second concern is your family. They will remain here as our security that you will do what we want. Once you have done your job, I can assure you that we will have no reason to hold your wife or children and they will be free to go. Or rather we will be free to go and they can get on with their lives.' The man smiled, in a way that was meant to seem reassuring but which only made him appear more menacing.

Ritchie was calculating, projecting himself forward to Cheriton and then to his cab. At every step there were people he could speak to, people to warn. He could alert the security people, could even press the panic button in his cab. There were so many options, he was sure that rescue was possible, that his family could be saved.

Cooperation was the answer. Buy time. He looked up, trying to put a compliant expression on his face. 'What guarantees do I have that you'll let my family go?'

'You have none, but you have my word. More importantly, perhaps, you also have my word that if you don't cooperate I will personally kill all three of them. So the choice is yours. Trust me that I will let them go because I have no reason to keep them. Or trust me to kill them if you choose to betray us. One way you may win. The other way you will most certainly lose.'

Ritchie nodded, as if accepting the logic of Sum's argument. 'It seems I don't have any choice.'

Sum looked at him, studying his face as if trying to read through the open acceptance to the duplicity that lay beneath. He nodded to himself, the decision taken. He took two steps towards the table.

'I'm afraid, Mr Ritchie, that you still seem to think that you might have a choice in this matter. I think I need to underline for you just how serious your position is.'

He put his right hand underneath his jacket, below where he had holstered the gun. There was a small noise, a cross between a hiss and a sigh, and Harry was horrified to see a huge, silvery knife emerge. The blade must have been at least eight inches long and it curved to a tip that seemed to wink at him in the light reflected from the ceiling.

Moving quickly now, Sum took a single pace forward, snatched Becky's arm from the table top and stretched it out in front of her. He carefully drew back the thumb and the third and fourth fingers.

Harry, understanding and compelled into action, shouted 'No' and lunged across the table. But even as he was moving forward, the knife arced back and then swept forward in one swift, horrible movement.

The two fingers that were lying exposed on the wooden kitchen table jumped as the blade cut through flesh and bone to settle with a 'thock' into the wood. Severed just below the second joint, they landed a foot away. Two screams, one from Rosie and the other from Becky, shattered the silence, and then there was a retching sound as David spewed a trail of half-digested breakfast across the kitchen floor.

214

Blood was pumping steadily from Becky's hand, spreading in a pool across the table. In the pool, the two fingers appeared to have a life of their own, twitching and flexing as the nerves spasmed for the last time.

The screams had subsided to sobs as Rosie focused on stanching the flow of blood from Becky's hand. David appeared to be in shock; and for Harry, rational thought had disappeared with the slash of the knife.

'I am sorry I had to do that,' Sum said, wiping the blade of his knife on a kitchen towel before replacing it in its sheath, 'but it was important for you to understand that I will do whatever is necessary to ensure your cooperation.'

He pointed at Becky. His voice was now almost conversational, the contrast with the scene in front of him giving the words added weight.

'You see that I cut off the first two fingers of her right hand. I read that she loves riding and so I removed the fingers that hold the reins. She is young. She will soon learn to ride with the other hand. But when you leave here, I want you to take that image with you. Your beautiful daughter as she was, as she is now and as she will be if you do anything, anything at all to upset our plans.'

Harry no longer felt defiance. Instead he felt an overpowering guilt that Sum had seen the hint of resistance that had caused the attack. He would do nothing to provoke another assault.

CHAPTER 14

THE OPENING OF the Tunnel has transformed the lives of thousands who live close to any of the stations connecting to the trains heading to France and Brussels. In the same way as the ferries and the hovercrafts broadened the horizons of an island nation used to isolation, so the Tunnel makes the continent easily accessible to a whole new generation of travellers.

The distance between England and France was always short but the sea made it appear long. The journey time had now been so reduced that despite the sea barrier, getting to France from Britain was easier than from almost any other country. The Tunnel facilities were the most modern in Europe and everything was designed for speed and ease of use and thus maximum profitability for the operators.

In the first year of operation, thirteen million people had travelled through the Tunnel and more freight had been moved by rail in that twelve months than in the previous five years.

The southern English counties of Kent, Sussex and Surrey as well as parts of the south London suburbs are often described as the English heartland. They are home to many of those who commute into London to work and there is also a strong agricultural community that has existed virtually unchanged for hundreds of years. When the Tunnel was first mooted, these people were the main objectors. They formed highly organized lobbying groups to object to every proposal for new rail routes and road junctions. Other groups argued that the Tunnel would mean a loss of jobs for Britain as the French flooded the English market with apples, lamb and toys.

While these protests delayed much of the work on the Tunnel so that even today there are still projects uncompleted, none of these fears were realized. The Tunnel has allowed the British quick and cheap access to Continental markets and, now that most of the construction work is finished, most of the local people have not been as badly affected as they feared.

But perhaps the most important change brought by the Tunnel has been in the leisure habits of the people who live in southern England. A day trip to France for shopping, for lunch or just for fun has become a reality for millions of Britons.

The French, with their sound commercial instincts and relaxed planning laws, realized this potential. At the Coquelles Terminal outside Calais, the French have built a vast shopping complex where everything from baguettes to cases of wine and the latest French fashions are available. There is a fun fair for the children, estate agents for the parents wanting to buy a house on the northern coast or inland. Crossing the Channel has become an adventure accessible to all the family.

Kate Carr had been one of those who thought the very idea of a Channel Tunnel a threat to her way of life and that of all residents of Kent. When the project had first been mooted in the mid 1980s she had attended a meeting in Paddlesworth village hall. They had been addressed by a man from the Department of the Environment who had made soothing noises about 'environmental concerns' and 'local sensitivities' but the suspicious locals gave him a frosty reception. Then a circular had come round from a group calling itself the North Downs Rail Concern Pressure Group calling for action to halt the Tunnel and asking for volunteers.

Kate would not consider herself a joiner. When asked what she did she would simply say that she looked after her husband, Tom, who worked as a cost accountant for Touche Ross, and brought up their nine-year-old daughter, Emma. This was true but only told part of the story. Kate was the archetypal English countrywoman. She had married in her late twenties, after many of her friends, but late enough for her to have enjoyed London as a personal assistant to a director of S. J. Warburg. She had left London with little regret and had taken up her country role with an enthusiasm that meant she now blended perfectly into the rural environment. Now thirty-seven, she favoured the country fashions that make Englishwomen look old before their time. Sensible skirts were bought at Marks and Spencer in Folkestone and an occasional foray to the Jaeger or Harvey Nichols sale in London kept her wardrobe respectable for dinner parties and Tom's business functions.

After Emma had been born, she had made a valiant effort to bring her figure back to its pre-pregnancy form. She had invested in some plastic steps and an exercise video, but she had always felt faintly ridiculous and it seemed rather pointless: Tom loved her, they were happy and there were better things to do. So, she was a stone overweight – although she still kept the clothes she once wore at the back of the cupboard in the hope that one day nature might reverse the inevitable.

In her twenties, Kate had been attractive but not beautiful with that round face, clear complexion and dark brown hair that somehow seems so English. Her hair was mostly grey now, which Tom said he found attractive and which she was too self-conscious to dye, although she secretly thought it made her look old. But there were more important things in life. She had friends, a happy family and the village to care about. They were all more important than personal vanity. Stalwart of the local Women's Institute, she was always there when the village needed her and she made sure that it quietly ran as she wanted. She would do whatever she felt was necessary to defend a way of life she had grown up with and intended to pass on intact to the next generation.

The Tunnel had provided a focus for all her considerable organizational abilities. She had become secretary of the pressure group and gathered a network of housewives who wrote letters, lobbied their MPs and generally made the lives of everyone who came up against them completely miserable.

But despite all their objections, the project had gone ahead. When it opened they had declined to go to the ceremony and for the first few months had refused to travel on the trains. But soon, to her disgust, they were among the few in the village who had not been, and she began to feel faintly ridiculous holding out for a point of principle that nobody cared about any longer.

So she had proposed that they break the embargo and try the Tunnel for themselves. This morning was to be their first journey and Kate had determined that the family would enjoy their day across the water.

'Where did you say we are going to lunch?' Tom asked, looking up from the *Daily Telegraph*.

'I've made a reservation at the Château de Montreuil,' she replied. 'It's one of the Roux brothers' places, about an hour from Calais. If we catch the nine o'clock then we should have stacks of time to get there, have a stroll in the grounds and then have lunch.' She turned to Emma. 'And then we can drive to the beach and you can have a swim. So make sure you pack your swimsuit.'

Emma ran from the room to check again that she had swimsuit, passport and the twenty-five francs she had changed at the bank yesterday so that she could buy her friend Harriet a present from France.

The Chinese intelligence service in Britain is known to Directorate K of the Security Service, which is responsible for counter-espionage, as the Hoovers. The term is an apt one because the Chinese, more than any other intelligence service targeting Britain, rely on quantity rather than quality of information.

Sir Patrick Walker, the former head of MI5, had first coined the phrase in a speech he had given to senior staff in the auditorium at the Gower Street headquarters. It was March 1991, the Berlin Wall had come down, the coup against Gorbachev had failed and the Moscow-led branch of Communism was dead.

'The threat of subversion from within is over,' he had told the audience. 'In the new world, we face some new threats from economic espionage and drugs. But we also face old threats such as terrorism which we can attack with renewed vigour with the resources we can now bring to bear. The country that is now the single biggest threat to national security, and, in my view, to the security of the Western world, is China. The gentlemen in Beijing do not understand that the world has changed and are determined to continue with Communism until their rotten regime goes the way of the Soviet Union.

'Today, the Chinese consider themselves at war with the West and they are doing their utmost to gather every scrap of intelligence they can from us. They do not operate like the Soviets and try to suborn or seduce. Instead, they use every agent, every family tie, every fellow traveller they can to gather every scrap of information that might be useful. They are the Hoovers of the espionage business and they are very good at what they do.'

Following that meeting, the K Directorate had been reorganized so that fully twenty per cent of its resources were directed at the Chinese in Britain. There were two principal methods of gathering intelligence about their activities. The first was through electronic interception, which was mostly done by the Government Communications Headquarters in Cheltenham. The second was carried out by the Watchers, as surveillance teams are known, who were divided into Statics and Mobiles.

It was the Watchers who had responsibility for 10 Eton Avenue in South Hampstead, a prosperous suburb in north London. Just off the Finchley Road, Eton Avenue is a street of large Victorian houses which are now mostly divided into flats. At the far end, close to the junction with Primrose Hill Road, is No. 10, the home of the Chinese military mission.

There is nothing to distinguish the house from its neighbours. It is a simple three-storey brick building with bow-fronted windows on either side of the wooden front door. Inside, the ground floor is furnished in what could be politely described as fifties schlock: chintz curtains, green plastic-covered wooden chairs; sofas with the springs gone and the patterns faded. Throughout there is a smell that is a mixture of damp and stale food. It looks and is seedy.

Upstairs, away from the prying eyes of visitors, is where the real work is done. Here Colonel Cheng Wei-yong has his office and the various agents for Chinese intelligence work under diplomatic cover as officers attached to branches of the Chinese armed forces.

Colonel Cheng favours shiny grey and black suits made from polyester, white shirts and single colour ties which are usually black. He is around fifty, short and overweight with the pasty complexion of a man who spends too much time in artificial light. He is known to the Mobiles as The Barber because when he first came to England in August 1990 they were surprised to find that every two weeks he went to get a haircut at a small barber shop in the Edgware Road. A frantic operation was mounted to dissect the barber shop, its owners and customers on the assumption that this was either a pick-up or a dead-letter drop. But they could find nothing and it was finally agreed that simple vanity drove him there twice a month.

Julie had telephoned Jonny before dawn that morning to arrange breakfast at 10 Eton Avenue. He had stumbled out of bed, dressed and taken a cab from Sloane Avenue to Hampstead. As his taxi pulled up at the address, the Statio aoross the road pressed the shutter on his Nikon and the autodrive started to pulse and whirr.

Jonny pushed the bell and a moment later Julie opened the door. This was a different woman to the casual researcher he had known. She was wearing a severely cut two-piece suit with a skirt that stopped just below the knee. She had no make-up on and her hair was tied back with a clip in the shape of a dragon. Julie gestured with her right hand to draw him inside.

'Good morning, Jonny. I'm sorry to drag you out so early but things seem to be developing at this end and Lin Yung thought you should be kept informed.'

'Is he here?' Jonny asked.

'Yes, indeed. He's waiting in the dining room.' A brief smile flitted over her face. 'If you haven't eaten you're in for a surprise,' she whispered. 'British breakfast, Chinese-style.'

He turned right off the hall and into the dining room. Lin Yung stood up from the cheap wooden table. In contrast to Julie's formality, he was in grey trousers and an open-necked white shirt.

'Jonny. How good of you to come at such short notice,' he exclaimed, shaking Jonny's hand as he spoke. Turning to his left he brought Jonny forward to introduce him to a small Chinese dressed in a dark suit, white shirt and black tie. Must be going to a funeral, Jonny thought.

'May I introduce Colonel Cheng Weiyong, the head of our military mission here?' The colonel bowed slightly and muttered a good morning in barely decipherable English. 'The colonel is with my team and so I thought it best that we meet out here away from the prying eyes of the embassy.' He gestured with his right hand. 'Do sit down. Some food will be along in a moment.'

'When did you arrive?' Jonny asked.

'I came in yesterday morning and have been fairly frantic ever since. Julie tells me that you had some difficulty in the north of England and she was able to help.'

Jonny's eyes met Julie's. They smiled at each other, a brief acknowledgement of two friends bound by a common experience of danger.

'If she hadn't turned up both I and Lisu would be dead,' Jonny replied. 'I'm very grateful to you. As Julie has probably told you, it was our old friend Dai Choi.'

'Yes, I know. In fact, that is why I decided to come over. Events appear to be moving rather faster than we expected and in a direction neither of us might have guessed.'

He paused as a white-jacketed servant began bringing in breakfast. From what Julie had muttered in the hall, Jonny was expecting a Chinese meal, but what appeared was indeed a Chinese version of a British breakfast. Instead of bacon and eggs there was fried spam, tinned beans and tinned tomatoes all served with great ceremony out of stainless steel chafing dishes. The food was cold, the coffee lukewarm and he could have sworn that the butter was actually margarine.

Lin Yung laughed. 'I am sorry about the quality of our food. We have tried to tell the kitchen people that they haven't quite got it right. But they insist that in England this is what English people eat. God knows where they got the idea from but they refuse to change.' He pushed his plate aside and continued.

'Shortly after you left, we picked up some intelligence that Stanley Kung was on his way to London. As you know, he rarely comes to Europe, so we thought there might be something more than the simple drugs deal you were talking about.

'Then there was the attack on the British Customs boat which you were involved in.' Jonny nodded. 'That's not the White Lotus style at all. They would not jeopardize good business possibilities with such a brutal killing. Better to dump the drugs overboard and bring in another shipment. Their lawyers would have had Dai Choi and his team out on the streets within twenty-four hours.

'Finally, we have been receiving reports for the last two months of considerable activity among the Chinese community here. At first there was nothing specific, just some rumours about an operation, talk of special training, teams being organized, that kind of thing.'

'Well, if it's not drugs then what is it?' Jonny asked. 'Arms? A robbery?'

'We don't know what it is but we do know what White Lotus wants. As you know they have been worried about the collapse of their business empire after we take Hong Kong over in '97. What they have been trying to do for some time is find a way of relocating abroad.

'From a business point of view they could just do what all the other big Hong Kong businesses have done, which is to move to the Bahamas or the Caymans or some other tax haven. And they expect us to show them respect when they behave like traitors,' Lin Yung exclaimed angrily. 'Anyway, White Lotus has two other considerations that other, more legitimate businesses do not have. First their people are all local and they are their strongest asset. Without them, the business will fall apart. Second, very few of those people have British passports. Kung, Dai Choi and a few others have managed to buy their citizenship but the rest are stuck in Hong Kong.

'So the word on the street in Hong Kong is that White Lotus have got an answer to the problem. Their people are being told not to worry; that the British will be giving them all passports.'

'But that's not going to happen. The government will never go back on such a public commitment and the Chinese government will never allow it,' said Jonny.

'Precisely. So if the gossip is true then all this activity here must be designed to force the British to do what White Lotus wants –'

'That's crazy,' Jonny interrupted. 'The British are never going to concede to that kind of blackmail. What on earth could they do that will apply enough pressure? Kidnap the Queen?'

'I really don't know but we are doing our best to find out.' Lin Yung drew deeply on his fourth cigarette of the breakfast and took another sip of the awful coffee. He looked at the colonel who had been sitting silent throughout the conversation. The glance seemed to Jonny to be conspiratorial, as if the two men had a common secret which Lin Yung was now going to share.

'We have other concerns. My government is not prepared to allow the citizens of Hong Kong to leave in advance of the handover. Hong Kong's value is its people. We are not worried about the Europeans. We can always hire more mercenaries but the local people have a huge amount of experience of operating in a true capitalist system. We cannot afford to allow anything that will take away that resource. The future development of China is tied up with Hong Kong and we need those people.

'At the same time, there are other, more political issues at stake here. As you know the current regime is coming to an end and for some years now different factions in Beijing have been lining up for the power struggle that will follow. There are some who believe that the old Communist ways must continue and they see Hong Kong as a capitalist stake aimed at the heart of China.

'There are others, myself among them, who believe that some change is inevitable, even desirable, now that Communism is discredited everywhere else. China cannot afford to be isolated from the rest of the world and Hong Kong is a useful bridge.

'My organization, the Guojia anquanbu, is in the reformist camp and wants to see Hong Kong work for us. The other intelligence service, the Gonganbu, is in the traditionalist camp. They want the Hong Kong experiment to fail. We have good intelligence that the Gonganbu have been helping White Lotus in their efforts in England and so whatever is planned will be certain to benefit the conservatives in Beijing. I am determined that will not happen.'

'So what are you doing about it?' Jonny asked.

'All our people have been activated. We're calling in every favour, gathering every scrap of information we can and I expect some concrete intelligence in the next couple of days. Also, Stanley Kung is now here in London and we have him under observation. In the end, he may be the key to this. He must know what is happening. Perhaps he might be prepared to let us in on his little secret.'

Colonel Cheng had sat impassively throughout the meal and Jonny assumed he had not understood much of the conversation. Now, he gave a small, grim smile.

Sean knew that Waterloo Road had become a trap. Safety and sex, the twin sirens of all those on the run, had kept him in the house for too long. It was odd, he thought, how the rational side of his brain knew that Sally's protestations of love were not for him but for the person she thought he was, but the irrational human being that still lurked beneath his hardened surface wanted to believe her. He wanted the goodness in her. He needed to be reminded of his other self, the person that had existed long ago before he took this path that he knew now led nowhere.

'I love your body,' she had told him that morning as they lay in bed together. 'I love the shape of your chest, the muscles in your arms and thighs,' she continued, her hand running lightly over his skin. 'I love it that you're a man. All the people I've been with before have been such boys.'

'Sally, you don't understand,' he protested. 'There's no future with me. I'm living on borrowed time here. Either I get out and go back home or they catch me. Whichever, there's no place for you.'

'It doesn't matter,' she replied. 'I just want our time together.'

He knew it was all just childish rubbish. But then he hadn't had anyone to say the right words to him for a long time. It was the innocence that he wasn't used to, couldn't really cope with. She was in love with him and his world without having any real understanding of what that meant. For him, that made their relationship special, a bridge from the darkness to the light. And he had so nearly lost himself in the killing.

He had gone out that morning and made the call to the cutout in the Midlands. This time they had wanted to know his targets.

'You have to understand they're getting concerned at the reaction,' said the woman's voice. 'Condor himself needs to know. They're also worried that you're doing too much; that the Brits are closing in. One more and then you're to come out.'

He had given a name, the man who was next on his list. Since then he had not allowed himself to think of the possibility of getting out of England and going home. Instead he had begun to focus on the next operation, turning over in his mind all the intelligence he had committed to memory weeks ago. It would be easy enough, he thought. A quick kill and then off. But what about Sally?

He looked across the dining table at her, his hands cupped around a coffee, and smiled. She returned his look hesitantly, as if she could read that he was planning their parting.

The buzzing of the doorbell interrupted his thoughts.

In all the time he had been staying in the house, there had been no visitors. Instantly, his senses were alert, instinct telling him that the noise was a threat.

'Is your mother in?' he asked Sally.

'No, she's down the shops and Dad's at work,' she replied.

'Right. Let it ring again and I'll go upstairs and take a look.'

He got up from the table and took the stairs two at a time. He went into Sally's room and stopped by the window. He flattened himself against the wall and eased forward so that he could get a narrow sideways look at the front door.

He saw two men in rumpled suits, one muddy colour, the other dark blue; short hair, tall, big. He moved back from the window to widen his field of view and took in the Vauxhall Carlton parked in the street. He noticed the black plastic aerial on the rear right wing and instantly he knew: police.

He ran back and in a hoarse whisper he shouted down the stairs. 'Sally. It's the law. Answer the door and stall. There's only two of them so they must be fishing.'

He ducked back and into Sally's room, grabbing socks, shirts and driving licence from the dresser and stuffing them into a sports bag. He retrieved the automatic from under the pillow and pushed it into the waistband at the small of his back. He shrugged into a leather bomber jacket, picked up the bag and stood listening at the head of the stairs.

He heard Sally open the door.

'Good morning, miss,' a deep baritone voice began, the Hampshire burr distinct. 'I'm Detective Constable Harris and this is Detective Constable Morrison.' There was a shuffling noise which Sean presumed was the men showing their identification cards. 'We believe that you may have a gentleman staying with you. Is that correct? We are interested in talking to him about some inquiries we have underway.'

'No, there's no one here at all,' Sally replied, her voice clear and firm. 'Dad's out and my mum's at work. I'd ask you in to look around but my mum and dad would kill me if they found I'd allowed strange men into the house.'

There was a pause and then Sean heard the first man speak again.

'Well, miss, I'm afraid our information is quite clear. You told your friend June Douglas, she told her mother and she told her husband who's a part-timer down the station. And so here we are.'

God, that stupid bitch told somebody, Sean screamed to himself. He wanted to leap over the banister and strangle her right now, but escape not revenge was paramount. He thought frantically. Clearly, the fourth-hand story had not been believed; was being treated as a schoolgirl fantasy by lazy coppers who couldn't credit that real drama might actually happen on their patch.

A dash out the back would be pretty pointless. They might have someone there and anyway they'd be after him soon enough. He had to take them out, delay them, buy the time to put some distance between himself and this poxy house. Shoot them? No. That would provoke instant overreaction and anyway killing cops wasn't his job. A tiny part of his mind imagined the effect that would have on Sally. Her illusions shattered, she would never see him again in the same light. Somehow, even though the little idiot had betrayed him, he wanted her to believe in him.

The decision made, he looked around for a weapon, remembering Tony Peters saying to him that he always kept a stick by the side of his bed in case of burglars. He took four large strides into the main bedroom and saw it, a knobby dark brown wood and about three feet long. He picked it up and hefted it, measuring its weight and strength.

The voices at the door were raised now, the policemen

clearly dissatisfied with the answers they were getting from Sally. But he could not hear them any longer, his mind concentrating on the moves ahead, his breathing a rushing noise in his ears. The focus was in hands, feet and eyes. Everything now was coordination and action. There was no time to think, only to do.

He took the stairs three at a time and was at the bottom, in the hallway and pushing past Sally, his arm upraised, while the first policeman was still speaking. As his arm came down in a crashing arc, the man suddenly registered his presence, his mouth open in an O of surprise, then the stick connected with his head.

Sean had seen the arm of the man behind start to move to his jacket and he knew that, sloppy or not, these men were armed. Speed. Speed. He pivoted, not stopping in his headlong charge to measure the effect of the first blow. His arm reached the apex and came down again. This time, the stick hit the elbow of the second cop directly. There was a crack that was much louder than the pistol shots which had killed the commuters on Winchester station.

Elbow joint broken, Sean thought with satisfaction.

The fighter in him was still measuring, calculating the odds. Down but not out, he decided. He was past both men now. He turned back to face them and brought the stick around in a scything motion to connect with the kidneys of the first man, who gave out a choking scream as they were driven into his body. His eyes turned into the back of his head as he folded to the ground, his head cracking on the paving stone of the front path.

His right hand hanging loosely by his side, the second detective knew that he was doomed but also knew that he had no choice but to fight. His left hand groped under his jacket to try and free the pistol that was holstered under his left shoulder. It was an intricate and lengthy manoeuvre that used up the few seconds he had to spare.

Sean brought the stick down again, hitting him along

the side of the neck. For a brief moment, the blood supply flowing through the main artery to the brain was cut off. Starved of blood, the brain shut down and the man collapsed.

He had a few minutes now, Sean thought. A neighbour – there was always a neighbour somewhere – would be phoning the cops right now. He dropped the stick, searched in the second detective's jacket pocket and found the keys to the Ford. He picked up his bag and sprinted down the path to the car. The door was unlocked and he wrenched it open. There was an agonizing delay while he tried to fit the boot key into the ignition and then the engine caught and he drove the gear lever into first and pumped the accelerator.

As the car moved off, the back door opened. He turned, sure that one of the policemen had recovered, and saw Sally, holding on to the door handle and running to keep pace with the accelerating car. Tears were streaming down her face. 'Sean, Sean. Wait for me.'

God, the silly bitch, he thought. I should have shot those bastards. That would have cured her.

He saw her strides lengthen and then she was taking huge, leaping bounds as the car picked up speed.

CHAPTER 15

DAI CHOI HAD long ago rationalized and then controlled his fear. He had understood that fear was a necessary prelude to action. It heightened his senses, sharpened his reactions and produced an awareness of the immediate environment that was not unlike taking a mind-expanding drug. The closer he had got to Cheriton, the more the fear had begun to control his body.

He felt himself evolve through two very distinct phases. The first, shortly after they had left Model Cottages in a three-vehicle convoy, resulted in sweat gathering in pools in his armpits and crotch, so that he had turned the air conditioning in the Granada on to high. The drive gave him the luxury of time to project himself forward into the Tunnel and the action that lay ahead. He imagined not the doing, but the failure that could destroy the mission at every stage.

Then they had turned off the M20 towards the Cheriton terminal and the prospect of the very action he feared forced his body and his senses to switch gears. The sweat on his body dried, his shirt freed itself from his back and he felt calm and confident.

The Cheriton terminal covers 150 hectares and is designed like an enormous horseshoe with the Tunnel entrance and exit at the ends of the shoe's arms. The whole vast complex is designed to speed traffic through, so both French and British Customs work under the same roof. Once through the security checks at the British end, there are no further checks at all at the other side.

Dai Choi led his three cars into the toll booths. Each driver paid the fare and then joined the queue for the Customs and security checks. It was here, Dai Choi knew, that all the research and the dry runs would either pay off or result in their arrest.

When the plan had first been discussed, he had realized that it relied heavily on the fact that all security checks at any airport or port depend on three things: technology, intelligence and luck. He believed their plan took care of the technology; that the British had no advance warning of their plans. And luck? Well, they would just have to wait and see.

The tolls looked just like an Autobahn toll in Germany and Dai Choi led his little convoy towards one of the lanes with a green light suspended above it. He suspected that here the cars might be photographed and the licence numbers checked with a central computer against lists of stolen or suspect vehicles. If so, the checks would reveal nothing as the registration plates all came from identical vehicles owned by Triad front companies in England.

Through the tolls, the vehicles swung round to the left and followed the signs towards immigration and Customs.

From the outset, Dai Choi had debated how to bring fifteen Chinese people into the Tunnel. So many foreign names with the same ethnic background would be certain to set the alarm bells ringing. He had winnowed it down by recruiting the most European-looking of the Triad members so that only the car with himself, Michael Leung and two others had people who were categorically from the Far East.

This solution was facilitated by the hoard of 750 blank British passports White Lotus had bought in 1991. In that year, Her Majesty's Stationery Office's passport printing office in Manchester had printed 3,000 blank

233

passports to test the new maroon European design. The final 1,000 had been so near perfect as to be almost indistinguishable from the real thing. They should have been destroyed, but they had come on the market and fallen to the highest bidder. White Lotus saw the passports as a useful investment for when 1997 loomed larger and the price of such a document would ensure a handsome profit. Dai Choi had the passports finished in Hong Kong by their own forgers and each of his men had British rather than Chinese names.

The result of the compromise between perfect people and those who would pass the immigration checks was a group that was a mix of experienced talent and enthusiastic recent recruits. He and Leung led the fifteen. The best of the rest was the diminutive Kang Sheng, the Sherpa driver, who was travelling under the name of Henry Wallis. He was British born and had a Caucasian mother. He looked English but had been brought up in the Chinese community and was perfectly assimilated into his father's culture. Like many small people, he had the aggression of a man twice his size and all the insecurities of the half-breed.

Kang Sheng had become one of White Lotus's most effective enforcers. He was ruthless and calm in a crisis and Dai Choi was confident in his abilities to help hold the team together. Much of the rehearsals had been organized by Kang Sheng, who had whipped the group into some sort of coherent shape in the past few weeks. What still worried Dai Choi was how these people would react when the killing started.

Dai Choi handed his passport to the immigration official who flicked through it and passed it back. There was no entering of numbers into a central computer, no check beyond the most cursory. He was British, he was one of millions going on holiday or business to Europe. No one had the time or inclination to question such people.

Dai Choi moved slowly off and watched in his mirror as the other vehicles came through the checks.

When the idea of a tunnel had first been considered, the head of G Branch of the Security Service – at the time Stella Rimington – met with Yves Bonnet, her equivalent in France's Direction de la Surveillance du Territoire (DST). At that first meeting in her Curzon Street office overlooking Shepherd Market, the two had agreed on the parameters of the threat. The most likely attackers were terrorists and at the time the obvious suspects were the Red Army Faction in Germany, Action Directe in France and the IRA in Britain. Attacks by Middle East fanatics were also possible. Since then the RAF had given up and AD had been destroyed but the principles of defence against terrorist attack remained.

Following that meeting, the British had set up a committee which seemed to involve just about every branch of government with an interest in either intelligence or security. The Ministry of Defence sent along people from DIS and the Intelligence Corps so that they could give their views about the IRA threat and securing the Tunnel in time of war; the SAS turned up because they loved the idea of breaking into the Tunnel past all the security that everyone else would put in place; SIS sent someone because they always liked to be present at a party to show that they were serious players at home and abroad; the Home Office, the Foreign Office and the Department of the Environment all attended to make sure their views were expressed; and finally the owners and Group 4, the security company hired by Eurotunnel, sent their own people.

It is a function of such a group to look at the worst possible scenarios. They had come up with a series of apocalyptic visions which had frightened even the authors of the reports. Civil servants, and in particular intelligence agents, tend to look at the worst case anyway and then make recommendations based on that.

In 1989, when MI5 had produced its preliminary report, it recommended that all cars and trucks be passed through three different machines to examine them for drugs, weapons and explosives; that every passenger should pass through a dual metal detector and explosives-sniffing machine; and that there should be random searches of both vehicles and passengers. Eurotunnel had gone off and done their sums and were shocked to discover that such checks would cut by fifteen per cent the number of trains that would run every hour, would cost an extra 300 million pounds to install and run each year and would reduce freight and passenger income by twenty-five per cent.

The ensuing fight between the absolutists in the Security Service and the compromisers in Eurotunnel was memorable even by the standards of government bureaucracy. But the Department of Trade had lined up with the commercial side and the result was a half-assed deal that pleased nobody.

The argument took over a year and the contract for the security system was not actually awarded until the beginning of 1992 when Eurotunnel secretly agreed to purchase a new system called Condor, which had just been developed by British Aerospace at their Systems and Equipment division at Filton near Bristol.

Condor includes a Thermal Neutron Activation System which 'fires' neutrons to react with the nitrogen in explosives and produce a gamma radiation that can be sensed by detectors. This is very effective for freight and baggage but cannot be used on food or people as it is banned under the Radiation of Food Act. Therefore passengers and cars are not screened by this system, unless there is some specific intelligence suggesting a real threat.

A second tier of the Condor defence is a Vapour and Particulate Detector. This 'sniffs' an area and gives a visual or audio alarm when target molecules such as those found in explosives or drugs are detected. This works well on specific targets but is not effective for mass searches – rather like an expert wine taster, the sniffer needs to have a clear palate to work perfectly – but the VPD is used for random searches.

There are also sniffer dogs and hand-held detection devices. But the basic defence is the Falcon II X-Ray system which fires X-rays at the vehicles. Different objects and materials absorb varying amounts of the rays and the computer is able to compare each piece of information with its databank and decide which object might be a gun, which a harmless fuel pipe and which a tiny piece of plastic explosive. It was this machine that Dave Leppard was operating that morning.

Like everyone else on site, Dave hated the Monday morning shift. There was always a rush of people trying to get the first train; they were impatient to reach the first business meeting on time or excited about their holiday. Either way, he could feel the resentment flowing in his direction at every second of delay.

Dave was a security operator not because he wanted a career in the business, but because it was where people like him just seemed to end up. He had been in the Household Cavalry and had signed on for what he reckoned would be a life term. Then the Berlin Wall came down, Communism fell apart and the government started cutting defence like there was no tomorrow, which there very probably wasn't for people like Dave. The Cavalry had been chopped in half and asked for volunteers to leave early. Well, this is just the start, he'd thought to himself. Better get out now before civvy street is flooded with people like me.

He hadn't much to offer the outside world except a clean record, a good recommendation from his CO and an ability to follow orders. He was six feet three inches tall and broad-shouldered, which had made him the marker for the rest of the platoon on the parade ground.

It also made him an ideal candidate for security work and so he'd signed up with the Tunnel. It was sod's law that they'd put him behind a computer rather than out in the fresh air frightening people.

At first he'd found the systems fascinating, but now that had evolved into the boredom of routine. In over a year of inspections, he'd never discovered anything, with the single exception of the time the SAS had tried to break through security with Semtex hidden in picnic hampers. It was a childish effort that had not been repeated.

As usual, he was sitting at his console inside the security area and had processed six cars before Dai Choi's Granada came into the view of the camera in the waiting area. Dai Choi and the other passengers exited to go through the X-ray doors to one side while the car moved forward on a continuous conveyor belt.

There were four screens facing Dave. The top two relayed an outside image of the vehicle. The bottom screen to the right displayed a colour image of the X-ray results. As the Granada came into full frame, the X-rays painted the car and within a nanosecond the computer had brought up on the left-hand screen a two-dimensional computer image of the car's design as it left the factory. As the rays flowed back over the car again, the computer defined different areas that varied from the factory blue-print, automatically discarding such commonplace items as radio aerials or cassette players.

On the right-hand screen, the computer was sifting through the contents of the car, bringing in front of Dave a flowing waterfall of orange and reds of different densities that told him here was paper, here a suitcase, here clothing. A flick of the rollerball under his right hand and he could home in on any item.

The machine was not designed to detect the shape of the carefully moulded explosive that had replaced the floor matting and window seals. The density of Demex explosives was so similar to rubber that the computer was unable to discriminate. Only if Dave had been suspicious would a lengthy refinement have produced some minor anomalies.

As the Granada passed through, the Sherpa van came into the frame. Dave laughed to himself. This was the tenth time in two weeks. Same van. Same time and same place. The first time it had come through, every alarm bell in the place had started ringing. The van looked innocent enough from the outside but inside there was enough lead to start a bullet factory. He had ordered the van out of the line and they had bombarded it with all the machines and then searched it thoroughly. All they had found was roll after roll of microfilm and computer tapes.

He remembered the driver because he had been so small and so angry. Furious at missing his train, he couldn't seem to understand that lead containers could cause a problem, even if you were with a company called Security Archives that had offices in Brussels, Paris and London.

The driver had explained that he was driving south to the Massif Central where the copies of financial records from the City of London would be buried in secure vaults deep in the limestone cliffs. The film was transported in lead boxes precisely because X-rays and any other bombardment could damage the material.

That first time, he had been made to unload every film and every tape before driving on to the shuttle. The second time, the Customs people had given a cursory look in the back, and now he was a familiar figure, his little head peering over the steering wheel.

Dave watched the waterfall cascade down his screen, the purples and bright greens indicating the solid lead containers. This time no alarm bells rang and he pressed the button to stop the X-rays and move the vehicle through.

The Volkswagen Kamper, with its two-battery system,

was already in the computer's database and so no alarm was raised as it passed through the scanner.

On his first course as a trainee, Dave had been taught that in his new business there were a few certainties. One was that a gun would always be picked up by the scanners, provided it wasn't dismantled or the shape hidden behind metal screens. The second was that every single explosive charge requires a detonator and every single detonator, big or small, modern or old, has embedded within it a tiny T-shaped object known as an Azide tube. This is made out of lead and produces a completely distinctive image. All security scanning systems are programmed to watch for this shape made out of lead and will automatically sound an alarm if it is detected.

As Dave looked at the profile of the Kamper, the computer sorted through all the original specification and displayed on his screen a bag of tools, clothing and suitcases.

The second battery in the VW had been completely dismantled and the lead plates extracted. Two lead plates had been made, between which were sandwiched the detonators, each measuring only two mm across. The plates had been sandwiched back together and a thin line of lead placed on top. When the X-rays bombarded the battery, all they saw was a battery.

As he watched in his rear-view mirror, Dai Choi saw the Volkswagen emerge from the security check and he breathed a small sigh of relief. They were all through and the forty-eight detonators had passed undetected. Now to the real danger zone.

More confident, he drove around a short one-way system and on to the platform. Each train had an engine at either end and twelve wagons, eight with two decks for cars and four with one deck for light vans. Dai Choi's team had learned that arrival just after eight-thirty a.m. for the nine o'clock train would ensure that they would be close to the front of the queue with all the vehicles going in the front two coaches.

Dai Choi drove directly from the platform into the shuttle wagon, pulling his Granada in behind a green Rover 416 GSi with what appeared to be a husband and wife and their small daughter inside. He steepled his fingers on the steering wheel and for a moment allowed his forehead to drop forward and rest. He came back to the upright position and shook himself, preparing physically and mentally for the next step.

Two hundred feet ahead of him, Harry Ritchie was going through the final checks in his cab. Until today, he had loved this space. Looking around now at the digital dials, the telephone, the computer terminal and the instruments that could tell him everything from the temperature in the Tunnel to the distance travelled to the nearest one-hundredth of a mile, Ritchie saw each one as a threat. Each tiny slug of information would spell out not the progress to journey's end, but the inexorable march to disaster.

He could still see the pain on Becky's face. Unwanted, the image of the blood spurting from her severed fingers had flashed before his eyes a hundred times since that awful moment when his life had been torn to pieces. Even his nostrils seemed full of the smell of her blood. But the instant he remembered most vividly was when the Chinese had drawn out his knife; that awful noise, somewhere between a hiss and a sigh, as the blade parted from its leather sheath, would be with him for ever.

Since he had staggered from the house to the car he had moved like an automaton. He had driven to work, gone to his locker and changed into his driver's uniform. At that hour of the morning there was never much time for banter. Nobody had noticed that Harry Ritchie, the happiest driver of them all, seemed rather down. Nobody had said the kind words that might have unlocked the door to the agonies he was feeling.

Instead, here he was waiting for the Off. He looked to his left and read the words '5 mins to start'. Automatically his hands began to run over the checks, eyes and brain registering the power settings, his left hand gripping the dead man's handle, In fact a horizontal circle which he rotated to make the connection between the power supply and the drive train. His feet moved to the pedals, left for acceleration, right for brake. A final glance around and then the computer cleared and the one word 'Start' flashed up.

In fact, Ritchie had little to do. The signalling centre hidden in the heart of the Cheriton complex controls which trains move where and when. A train is scheduled to leave from either side of the Channel every 2.5 minutes and so several trains were always in the Tunnel at any one time. Sensors tell the computers in the signalling centre that the correct gap is being maintained between trains and can warn the drivers to slow down or speed up.

There was no jolt, just a gentle increase in power that had the train moving out of the station smoothly and almost in silence. There were no side windows in the cab so that Ritchie would not be disorientated by the Tunnel lights flashing by. Instead he had a small window to the front, a narrow vision of the Tunnel ahead. It appeared first as a small black hole between two long grey wafers. Then within seconds the wafers became the concrete side walls and the black hole widened to the yawning mouth of the Tunnel itself. In another moment, Ritchie was swallowed up with a slight lurch as the train broke through the buffer of air at the Tunnel mouth.

Behind Harry Ritchie, Dai Choi and his team were already at work. They had only a few minutes before the train would halt. Leung took charge of the VW and his team lifted out floor mats, ceiling lining and door seals. Dai Choi did the same in the Granada and within seconds there was a pile of Demex explosives sitting in the boot of the Ford.

The second VW battery was out on the floor. A large screwdriver levered off the plastic lid, the water was poured out and then the three lead plates were lifted out. Exposed, the detonators were the size and colour of a thin thimble made of a metal that looked like foil. At one end of the tube, two small copper wires protruded.

In the back of the Ford, one man was cutting the sheets of explosive with a Stanley knife into rectangles six inches by twelve. At the top of each sheet he pushed a screwdriver through to make a small, round hole. On some, he left a small strip at either end so that the rectangle sat on small legs. He then handed them to a second man who attached strips of double sided adhesive tape to them. A third man opened a box of three-mm ball bearings and poured them on to the sticky surface, pushing them down to make sure they had a firm grip.

As each strip was finished, it was carried to the back of the Volkswagen where the detonators now lay next to a small pile of what looked like tiny red plastic top hats, which were in fact holders for the detonators. A small incision in the tape and then a top hat was pushed into each sheet, followed by the detonator.

In the second carriage, the five men in the van had moved into the rear compartment and lifted off the lids to the lead containers. The racks of film and computer tape were discarded to reveal the lead bottom of the chest. A screwdriver scraped along the edge of the bottom revealed a thin layer of plastic sealer which peeled away in strips. When the bottom plate was levered up the armoury was revealed.

The priority now was bomb timers and small arms. The back of the vehicle filled with the slap of flesh on metal, the snicking of safety catches and the slithering sound produced as the magazine slides into the butt of an automatic pistol. With fifteen seconds to go, they were ready.

*

Harry Ritchie had watched the miles tick off on the screen to his right. He had watched each second pass on the digital clock. There was no time now to get out, no opportunity to think again. He was committed.

Suddenly his hand reached out and slapped down on the red emergency button to his left. Instantly the alternating cadence of an alarm bell went off in the cab and the train began to slow down. Even though he was expecting the jolt, Harry was jerked forward in his seat. Each second seemed to elongate into distinct fractions of time as his mind recorded the moments of his betrayal.

Two beads of sweat flew from his forehead, propelled by the sudden jolt, arced through the air and splattered on the screen in front of him, the tiny droplets obscuring his view of the lights ahead. The Tunnel was no longer a blur but had taken on a clear shape as the train slowed down. The lights were distinct now, the joins between the individual concrete blocks lining the wall and roof quite apparent. Then, suddenly, smoothly, the train stopped.

Harry knew that back in Cheriton and at the Coquelles terminal outside Calais the alarm bells would be ringing, or rather the lights on the display boards which show the exact position of every train would be flashing red. The computer system had been designed to deal with any crisis that involved a train breaking down in the Tunnel. Trains travel so close together that there is no time to warn other drivers on the telephone that they all have in their cabs. Instead, the crisis management computer programme overrides all other systems automatically. A signal sent from the British side stops all the trains heading south and an identical message from Coquelles stops the trains heading for England.

Even while the other trains were slowing down, the telephone in Harry's cab began to purr.

'Ritchie? This is Control. What the hell's going on out there?'

But before Harry had a chance to reply, he heard the

sharp crack of explosions and could see in his mirrors bright red flashes illuminating the Tunnel walls.

'Christ Almighty,' he exclaimed. 'The bastards are blowing up the Tunnel.'

As soon as the train began to slow down, Dai Choi's men began to fan out into the carriage, pushing their way through the other passengers who were milling around their vehicles. Each man carried a rifle or machine-gun and had an automatic pistol stuffed into the waistband of his trousers or into a side pocket. There were no military uniforms, just the standard dress of jeans, shirts, gym shoes, the occasional leather jacket and a couple of suits. The very innocence of the clothing combined with the deadly nature of their equipment stunned the other passengers. For thirty seconds there was no move to do anything, not even a question broke the silence.

By then it was too late. As the train halted, a man in each carriage pressed the red emergency release to open the centre doors which immediately slid back on their greased runners. In front was the grey curving wall of the tunnel.

Michael Leung leaped the four feet from the carriage to the ground, his feet crunching on the pebbles that lined the floor of the Tunnel. Looking to his left he saw the tiny form of Kang Sheng follow. They ran towards each other, meeting at the junction of the two carriages. Kang Sheng passed a single E108 incendiary grenade to Leung and wordlessly they ran back past where they had started. Leung was winded by the time he stopped, the exertion and the tension making it difficult for him to breathe.

Reaching into his pocket, he pulled out some grey plumber's tape and, bending over, began to move crab-like along the wall of the Tunnel.

When the Tunnel had originally been designed, the

most serious concern was neither flooding nor terrorism but fire. Eurotunnel knew that unless they had an effective safety system, they would be unable to overcome the public's natural reservations about going underwater in a train for such a long time. The system they came up with was simple but efficient.

On both sides of the Tunnel wall, tiny heat sensors were fixed so that if a fire broke out in any part of the train it would be instantly detected. Once the heat source was picked up, the sensor would activate, sending a message to the control centre. A display board gives the location of every sensor and so the location of the fire can be instantly identified.

There are a number of defences, beginning with the humble fire extinguisher in every carriage, through reservoirs of water and fire hoses, to Halon gas which can be pumped into the carriages to smother the flames.

In theory, all passengers should have time to evacuate to neighbouring rail cars before the final safety system activates. Having detected the source of the fire, the computers automatically uncouple the carriages on either side of the fire and the engines at either end pull the other carriages to the exit, leaving the burning carriages behind.

Kang Sheng found the heat detector, which looked like a small black mine with a perforated lid. Using his tape he bound the grenade to the pipe containing the electrical cables, put his forefinger through the small ring protruding from the side of the grenade and pulled.

The Haley and Weller E108 incendiary grenade is designed for sabotage. It is also often used for agents on a dangerous assignment who might have to destroy documents in a hurry. It is 114 mm long, 50 mm in diameter and weighs just 550 grams. Within a second and a half of Kang Sheng pulling the pin, there was a loud explosion as the bottom of the grenade was blown out and the powder in the body of the grenade was exposed to the air.

Immediately, an intense white light forced Kang Sheng to look away. He shielded his eyes from the reflection off the metal of the train. In an instant, the grenade was burning at 2,700 degrees centigrade. The moment before the heat detector melted, it sent the fire signal back to Cheriton. Looking behind him, Kang Sheng saw the reflected glow as Leung set off his charges. In fact, two signals were received at the same time.

The computer was designed to respond to different messages with a graduated response to a crisis. On this occasion, all the steps were avoided as the fail-safe system leaped up the ladder of response with one mighty bound. Before the operators even had time to assess the seriousness of the situation, the computer had sent instructions to the coupling units at the ends of the two carriages containing the White Lotus attackers. There were two soft clunks as the metal clips parted. There were now two trains and, simultaneously, they restarted their journey, one heading north, the other south, both heading for daylight.

Until they had boarded the train Kate Carr thought the adventure was going exactly as planned. The journey to the train had been easy enough and, much to her relief, there had been minimum delays at Customs. In fact, they had plenty of time to stop off and buy some puzzle books for Emma inside the shopping complex.

They had been directed to carriage A8 and found they were the first to board. A crewman directed them to the front and they parked facing the steel shutters that were designed to isolate one carriage from the next in the event of fire. Just to the right of the shutters, two small glass doors allowed access to the next carriage so that passengers could evacuate in an emergency or simply walk through to the buffet car just behind the front engine.

Kate got out of the car to stretch her legs. She looked

to her left and saw one of those electronic machines that scroll words across a rectangular screen in a series of illuminated red dots.

'THE SHUTTLE WILL LEAVE FOR FRANCE IN ONE MINUTE', she read. 'YOU MAY LEAVE YOUR CAR. COFFEE, TEA AND A HOT BREAKFAST WILL BE SERVED IN THE BUFFET CAR AT THE FRONT OF THE TRAIN.'

'Do you think we should take Emma for some food?' Tom had asked.

'It's hardly worth the trouble. We'll be at the other side by the time the coffee is cool enough to drink,' she replied.

Kate looked around with the unfocused gaze all passengers use to eye each other. Her eyes took in and then dismissed the car behind hers with the four Chinese men in suits. Then the train began to move and she noticed them get out of their car.

'Mummy, what's the answer to "A bug that thinks it is a plane" in three letters?' Emma asked, her mind engrossed in the puzzle book they had bought at the gift shop.

'Fly,' Kate answered distractedly, her mind already moving with the train, imagining the convoy moving towards the sea and then under it. Already they were probably underwater. She felt a shiver run down her spine. This is ridiculous, she reassured herself. Thousands have gone before me and thousands will come after me. There's no reason at all that God will choose my train to collapse the Tunnel on.

She felt a tugging on her hand and looked down to see Emma looking up and pointing with her other hand, the book discarded beside her.

'Look, Mummy. What are those men doing?'

Kate looked behind her and saw that the Chinese men appeared to be tearing their car apart. They were taking great strips of material out of the car roof, lifting out the car mats and even peeling stuff from around the windows and doors and carrying it to the open boot. How extraordinary, she thought. What on earth can they be doing?

She watched for a moment longer and then leaned down and spoke through the passenger door to Tom who was still in the driver's seat.

'Tom, look at those Chinese people behind us. They seem to be taking their car apart.'

As Tom turned to look, Kate felt the train begin to slow down and her pulse raced as all her unspoken fears rushed to the surface. She looked around, seeking reassurance or an explanation to calm her. She saw that the Chinese were now at the entrance door to the carriage. They looked expectant, she thought. They were poised for something, but what?

The digital noticeboard began scrolling a new message. 'EMERGENCY. PLEASE STAY WITH YOUR CAR', she read, the words chattering across the screen with agonizing slowness, her mind racing ahead, trying to anticipate the next words.

Then the train stopped and the action accelerated. The centre doors opened with a hiss and she saw one of the Chinese men jump down to the track. The others turned their backs to the door and faced into the carriage. Their stance seemed an open challenge to the passengers to confront them but nobody did. Everybody seemed stunned, the other passengers' faces reflecting a mixture of fear and curiosity. As yet there was no understanding.

There was a sudden explosion and the carriage was filled with a vicious white light. Kate turned her eyes away from the doorway but still the brightness reflected from the metal walls around her to blind her.

Suddenly the light disappeared. The contrast was so great that for a moment Kate could see nothing. A siren pierced the silence, a high-pitched warbling tone that echoed and re-echoed along the carriage walls. Emma began to cry and Kate felt her heart grow tight in her chest. In a moment of absolute clarity she noticed with astonishment that she could actually feel her heart pumping the blood around her body.

She glanced again at the message screen and knew that she was about to die. 'EMERGENCY. EMERGENCY. PLEASE EVACUATE YOUR CARRIAGE. WALK FORWARD TO THE NEXT CAR. EMERGENCY. EMERGENCY.'

She had hardly digested the instructions when a voice on the loudspeaker system began to intone the same orders.

Kate turned back to the car and opened the rear door, reached in and pulled Emma out. 'Hurry, darling. Hurry. Go through those doors there. Hurry.'

As she spoke, she looked up at the small doorway leading to the next carriage. A man, one of the dark-suited Chinese from the car behind, was standing there. He was holding a small, stubby gun with a long magazine across his chest. He did not speak, but somehow she knew that there was to be no escape.

Kate felt her legs give way beneath her and she put a hand on her daughter's shoulder to prevent herself falling to the metal floor of the carriage.

'No. It's not a fire, you fucking halfwit. It's a hijack.' Harry was shouting into the phone now, all thoughts of his family lost in the anger and the desperate effort to explain. 'There are terrorists aboard. We're being hijacked. Bring the whole train out.'

After his earlier betrayal, duty to family and employer had once again coincided. He knew the only chance for him and his family was to bring the train out intact and to capture the men who were sabotaging the Tunnel behind him. But the voice at the other end of the phone seemed so vacant, so slow.

'Harry, the computer tells us there's a huge fire down there. We've dispatched emergency crews and we'll have you out in a couple of minutes.'

'No. Wait.'

But it was too late. There was a brief trembling through the soles of his feet and he knew that all the procedures had worked perfectly and he was on his way to France.

CHAPTER 16

BRIGADIER JOHN CASSIDY was idly flicking through the latest pile of bumph passed upstairs from the planners on the third floor. The traffic was endless, the options for different scenarios practically infinite. As Commander of the Joint Operations Centre, it was his job to read all the gee-whiz ideas from downstairs and train his guys so that when the shit hit the proverbial his arse would be covered. Even more important, so would the fatter arse of the guy downstairs who wrote the paper in the first place.

A tall, spare man with thin cheeks and a long neck, he appeared permanently coiled with tension that demanded action. In fact he was a calm man, cool in a crisis, with the logical brain much prized by military commanders who want their leaders to think before they act. He was almost completely bald, a handicap he had suffered since his early twenties. His shiny pate tended to go a deep red under stress. One night as a lowly lieutenant in the officers' mess at the Regimental Headquarters in Albany Street overlooking Regent's Park, he had been about to defeat the Regimental snooker champion of many years' standing. The senior officer's friends resented the potent play of the newcomer, sneaked up behind him, lifted him by his legs and used his red, bald head to hit the white ball. Not surprisingly, it was a miscue and the game was lost. It was an early lesson to Cassidy not to get above

himself. But the result was the nickname of Cue, shortened to Q, which had stayed with him through his Army
career.

He had commanded the Queen's Royal Irish Hussars
in the Gulf when the British tanks had fought alongside
the American 7th Armoured Division to liberate Kuwait.
It had been his regiment's finest hour since the battle of
Imjin in the Korean war. Like other veterans of the Gulf,
Cassidy had been able to survive the post-Cold-War
defence cuts.

With a grunt of disgust he dumped a ten-page offering entitled 'Special Forces – Managing or Creating a
Crisis?' into his out tray and turned to his computer
terminal. The white telephone to his left let out its distinctive warble.

There was a time when the ringing of this telephone,
used only for scrambled calls, would have given his heart
a quick flip, but after a year in the JOC, such calls had
become routine.

'Q. Nick.' He did not even have time to respond as he
recognized the voice of Nick Rufford, a captain with the
Special Forces Headquarters in the Duke of York's barracks in Knightsbridge.

'We've had a call from one of our lads. Ex-Hereford,
now with Tunnel security. He says they've got some
trouble down there. It looks like a terrorist attack. I've
got my guys going and I suggest you do the same.'

The low-pitched buzz indicating that the scrambler
was working disappeared as the phone was hung up.

John reflected that as usual the informal intelligence
net had worked far more efficiently than the regular
channels which were supposed to give him early warning
of any crisis. He turned to his OpCon computer system,
inserted the identity card which cleared him to read the
most sensitive traffic classified Cosmic Top Secret and
scrolled through the message board. Nothing. As per
fucking usual, he thought.

With its connotation of roughy-toughy military, the JOC is, in fact, the heart of the British military response to a crisis. It was the JOC that ran Operation Granby, the British response to Iraq's invasion of Kuwait, and it was the JOC which helped fight and win the Falklands War. Within the MoD, the organization gained brief and unwelcome notoriety during the Gulf War when the Commander decided to produce a daily news bulletin on video, which was dubbed by some civil service wag the JOC Jollies.

Situated on the fifth floor of the huge white granite building that is the headquarters of the Ministry of Defence in Whitehall, the JOC is designed only for crisis management. Despite its role, with an obvious requirement for the latest technology and the best in computer software, the JOC suffers from the neglect of years of penny-pinching and an incompetent procurement system. It houses five different units, known as cells, for the Command, Air Force, Navy, Army and Special Forces. The partitions that divide the cells have sprung up like weeds and with as little control. The conduits holding the wires for secure communications run like dozens of miniature railway lines across ceilings and around doorways. The floor is a patchwork muddy carpet with the stains and marks of partitions from previous generations of the JOC.

Even here among the élite, the British class system is at work. The Navy, the Senior Service and proud of it, has filtered coffee and cups with saucers prominently on display. The RAF, always the force with the worst breeding, has a tin of Nescafé and some cracked mugs. In the Ministry of Defence visual status is as important as in any other bureaucracy, so the Navy has stolen the best view out over Whitehall while the Army has been relegated to a vista of the inner court and three other grey walls of the MoD building. By some piece of sleight of hand that is the hallmark of the Special Forces, they, too, have a view of Whitehall, although with the classic perversity of such people, they have boarded over the windows.

The system does actually run on computers. Unfortunately, each service has its own, different, computer system (in fact the MoD actually bought forty-eight different varieties of word processors, one of the great untold procurement scandals which led to all computers in the MoD being referred to as Heinz, after the food company).

Cassidy got up from his desk, turned his back on the hidden inner court of the Main Building and walked out into the corridor. Turning right, he walked down the passage passing the Navy, Army and RAF cells to the last door which, unlike the others, had a special key pad and a peephole. He punched the code and waited for ten seconds, giving the armed guard inside an opportunity to decide that he was friendly, and then turned the handle.

He walked into the Special Forces cell, passed the SAS soldier with his Heckler and Koch MP5 machine-pistol and into the small room from where either the SAS or the Navy equivalent, the SBS, can be despatched. As he expected, Nick had called his own people first and they were now patched through to their former colleague in a public call box at Folkestone. His tinny voice was being broadcast to the eight men and two women in the room.

'I don't know,' the voice replied to a question asked before Cassidy's arrival. 'It's still all very confused. There are reports of a fire. Both trains have come out so that part may be true. But the electrics are out so the computers aren't getting any sensor readings. Some of the passengers talk of shooting but there's no details and there's been no demands from anyone.'

One of the men who had accessed the Press Association wire service through his computer terminal gave a shout. John moved to read the message on the screen over his shoulder.

SNAP. SNAP. SNAP.

Channel Tunnel Seized by Terrorists

By Charles Miller, Defence Correspondent

The Channel Tunnel has been seized by an unknown group of terrorists who are holding a number of passengers hostage.

A message received by the Press Association claimed responsibility for the attack in the name of the Provisional IRA. The caller, who identified himself with the regular IRA codeword, said the hostages would be released when the British government agreed to withdraw all its forces from Northern Ireland and hold a peace conference in which the IRA will participate. The terrorists would begin killing the hostages if the government does not agree to the demands within three days.

More follows

'Shit.' Cassidy turned from the screen and walked rapidly back to his own office. As he pushed open the wooden door his secure phone started to ring. He picked it up.

'Cassidy.'

'Brigadier. This is Paul Fowler in the Cabinet Office. Have you heard about the Tunnel?'

'Yes. It's just come in on PA.'

The voice at the other end coughed slightly. 'Ah. Well. I'm afraid it's not quite as simple as that.'

Cassidy interrupted, annoyed at the silkiness of the civil servant, whose round face, half-moon spectacles and smooth manner came back to him out of the haze of some security conference or other.

'I would hardly call a terrorist assault on the Channel Tunnel by the IRA simple.'

'That's precisely what I mean, Brigadier. It appears that it may not be the IRA at all. We received a call here about ten minutes ago which claimed to be from a group calling itself the Hong Kong Liberation Front. They say it's their people in the Tunnel.'

'You know that the IRA claim was accompanied by the proper codeword?' Cassidy asked.

'J. J. Mulroney? Yes, I'd heard that.'

'Then why do you think it can be this Hong Kong group which I've never heard of?'

'Ah. Well. They explain that,' Fowler replied in a tone which Cassidy thought for a moment might actually have been respect. 'They say they phoned the IRA claim into the PA. That way we can condemn the attack and refuse to negotiate so government policy is maintained. With that kind of cover they clearly hope that we might be prepared to do some kind of private deal ... We won't of course,' he added hastily.

'If true, they must be a pretty smart bunch,' Cassidy acknowledged. 'What exactly do they want?'

'British passports for all the residents in Hong Kong,' Fowler said. 'They want a decision in three days and they say there will be no negotiation. Any military action and they start shooting.'

'So what do you want from me?' Cassidy asked.

'First we need some kind of assessment from the Int people about this group. Who are they and are they for real or is this actually IRA? Second, I want a military appreciation. Can we go in and if so how and when? I need the answers asap. The Prime Minister has called COBRA and they'll be meeting in a few minutes so I'd like something before then.'

There was a click as the phone was hung up. Arrogant little shit, Cassidy thought to himself. Typical fucking Cabinet Office. Sit them close to the Prime Minister and they think they're God.

Despite his reservations, this was a crisis that he was going to have to resolve. The first step was to get the cell commanders in, brief them, task them and then get on the horn to Box. His heart sank. This one was going to involve politicians, intelligence agents and the police. A guaranteed recipe for disaster, he thought glumly.

The Tunnel is an echo chamber filled with silence, sobbing and darkness.

There were seventy-five passengers in carriages A8 and A9 and they had all been shepherded together so that they squatted on the floor in row after row around Kate and Tom Carr's Rover.

The instant the carriages had been uncoupled, Dai Choi had jumped on to the track leaving four of his men behind to guard the terrified passengers with the weapons they had brought forward from the van. They had a formidable arsenal of machine-guns, pistols and rifles and enough night-vision goggles to see them through the darkness that lay ahead.

Dai Choi had attached a strip of Demex 400 no more than half an inch wide and one inch long to the metal tubes carrying the reserve electricity along the wall of the Tunnel. He had inserted the detonator and then trailed the command wire twenty feet away and attached one end to a simple nine-volt battery. Moving behind the protection of the carriage, he touched the other wire to the battery. There was the harsh crack of an explosion which reverberated down the Tunnel, the noise bouncing from the curved ceiling to the floor and back again on and on down until its echoes muted and vanished.

With both the normal supply and the emergency back-up severed, the Tunnel was instantly plunged into total darkness. If there was to be a fight, Dai Choi wanted it to be on his terms.

He turned back and ran down the track alongside the carriage. At the open door to A8 he pulled himself inside and moved to his left. The carriage was lit by the dull, yellow glow of the emergency lighting. Looking at the passengers, he smiled slightly. We're all Chinese now, he thought.

As he moved inside there were more explosions from both ends of the Tunnel. They were followed by a loud rumbling as part of the roof lining fell. His men had just blocked the access tunnels with rubble. Any rescuers would now have to come down his line. If anyone wanted to fight, they would have to walk straight down the barrels of his guns.

He pushed his way through the dozens of men, women and children who were squatting, kneeling or lying on the floor. The whimpers of fear rose around him like a bad smell and he felt himself grow taller as he fed off the fright and terror of these people whom he now controlled.

He turned as he reached the shuttered door and looked out at the upturned faces.

'You are now in the control of the Hong Kong Liberation Front,' he began. 'The explosions you have heard in the past few minutes did two things. First we made the computers in the control centres in France and England think that the tunnel was on fire. To protect the other passengers, the two carriages you were travelling in were separated from the main train and we are now alone in the Tunnel.

'We have also destroyed all the electrics. From now on we will have to live by the light you see around you.'

'How long do you expect us to stay here?'

Kate started, surprised to hear her husband's voice. She reached out a hand to urge him to be quiet, to do nothing that would attract the attention of these awful people.

'That depends on the British government. They have three days to comply with our demands. If they do, then you will all go free. If they do not, then I shall have to think of some way of forcing them to do what we want.'

To Kate's left, a man stood up. In the half-light it was difficult to discern expression but his body was hunched forward, his head leading. His posture spoke of anger and perhaps a willingness to fight. 'This is an outrage. How dare you?' he shouted. Dai Choi watched silently as the man continued. 'My wife is sick. We are on our way to get treatment in Switzerland. She needs help. She won't survive this. You must let us go.'

Kate wanted to shout at the man to shut up and sit down. She knew instinctively that a challenge was not the way to play with their tormentor. He was dangerous. He had prepared the attack and succeeded in carrying it out. There was no chance of persuading him to deviate from his plan. But she kept silent, determined to heed her own advice and do nothing to draw attention to herself or her child.

The man moved towards the Chinese men, determined to pursue the confrontation. Leisurely, almost lazily, Dai Choi reached inside his jacket and drew out a pistol with a long, fat barrel. He raised the gun until it was pointing squarely at the man who was still moving through the crowd towards him. There was no warning, no click of a hammer that always seemed to presage gunfire in the movies. Instead there was a short 'phut' that sounded like a cork being gently pulled from a bottle of fine wine.

The man, whose body had been thrust forward as he forced his way through the prone passengers, was suddenly jerked back so that the upper half of his body reversed itself. In the darkness it looked as if he had changed direction and was now facing back the way he had come. It was an illusion of course. The force of the bullet entering his chest had swivelled his body.

There was a moment when the body was suspended. Kate felt she could actually see the dark of the blood against the yellow of the background as the life drained away. She registered the tinkle of the spent cartridge case hitting the ground. Then the man's body fell on to other bodies and the soft sound was subsumed in the screams of the passengers beneath the dead man. It was so sudden, so shocking that for a moment the vast majority of the passengers had no clear idea what had happened. Then a woman who had been covered with the blood of the victim screamed, her hands slapping her face as she tried to wipe away the sticky, wet substance that only moments before had been coursing through the man's veins.

The cry was taken up by others until the whole carriage was bursting with sound. The fear gripped everyone and soon that would rise, infecting not just the hostages but their captors too.

Dai Choi holstered his silenced automatic and gripped the 9 mm Spectre M-2 sub-machine-gun that was hanging across his chest. His left hand swung the barrel around and his right gripped the trigger and squeezed. There was a long ripping sound and for the blink of an eye the whole carriage was lit by the two-foot-long flame that hung at the end of the barrel. It took only 2.5 seconds for the 30-round magazine to empty into the roof of the carriage.

The effect was exactly what Dai Choi wanted. As he relaxed his trigger finger, there was silence; only the occasional whimper from a child, quickly stifled by a mother or father, broke the stillness.

'Now you all understand what is happening here. My name is Dai Choi and I am in command.' He paused, allowing the seconds to tick by. 'Remember that word, command. Remember it and think about it. What I command, you do. If I say sit, you sit. If I say stand, you stand. If you do anything to annoy me or my men, then you will suffer the same fate as that stupid man now lying in front of you.'

This time no voice was raised in protest. Dai Choi turned away. This was his Tunnel now. And these were his people, to do with what he wished.

CHAPTER 17

THE ATTACK ON the Tunnel had immediately activated COBRA, the acronym for the Cabinet Office Briefing Room, the location of the government's response team to a national emergency. John Major, the Prime Minister, had given the order to Sir Robin Butler, the Cabinet Secretary, and he in turn had ordered his office to call the participants together. The first meeting had taken place an hour earlier when the relevant deputies had got a sense of the problem to report back to their masters. Now it was time for the serious players to get involved.

COBRA is located in the Cabinet Offices, which are in a large nineteenth-century stone building on Whitehall, sandwiched between Downing Street and the magnificent horsemen from the Household Cavalry at the entrance to Horse Guards. Diagonally across the road is the Ministry of Defence and in the other direction is the Cenotaph, a permanent reminder to COBRA members of the potency and price of exercising the military option.

There is no plaque signalling the entrance to the Cabinet Offices, just a set of stone steps leading into a rather gloomy building. Past the security guard, more steps lead down one floor to the COBRA headquarters, a set of modest offices which are unoccupied unless there is a crisis.

Two rooms form the heart of COBRA. The first is a communications centre staffed by military signallers. The room actually looks like the nerve centre of a very rich ham radio operator. Along one wall are secure VHF/HF radio sets that look little different from those of twenty years ago except that most of the dials are digital rather than analogue. There are also two video screens to handle secure communications. To the right of the screens is a modern telephone switchboard that handles secure speech using a system codenamed Chopin (all the government's secure systems for the past ten years have been named after composers. The next update has been codenamed Orff, giving rise to jokes that the current head of Army personnel, Willy Rous, must have chosen it, as that is how he pronounces the word off).

Also in the room are the relay systems which allow officials who are part of COBRA to talk via live video to ministers or the heads of other government departments in a visual conference call.

But the heart of the system is the main conference room which looks as if it was thrown together in a crisis (it was) and has never been equipped properly since (it hasn't). The centrepiece is a long conference table which seats eighteen and is covered with a revolting grey plastic tablecloth. Strategically placed around the table are institutional yellow telephones, each with a warning label which says: 'This is a Secure Telephone. Chopin.'

All the chairs have chrome arms and brown fabric seats and backing. Against the walls are other wooden chairs where aides and personal secretaries sit sandwiched between grey metal filing cabinets which stand like sentries all over the complex. One filing cabinet, just to the left inside the door, is actually a cocktail cabinet. In a classic example of the Foreign Office's concern for maintaining status, only Deputy Under-Secretaries and above have keys to it.

The walls have no pictures. Apart from the two video screens there are a number of maps showing the world and the United Kingdom.

The rooms are used roughly once a month as different parts of the government practise crisis management, which involves everything from handling a mass poisoning of a major British city to a hostage incident abroad to a limited conflict. The way CODRA is structured, there are no permanent staff. Instead, the chairmanship of the group falls to the department most affected by a particular incident, and membership is dependent on the nature of the crisis. None of the strolling players felt any real responsibility for COBRA, only for the successful resolution of a particular crisis. That may explain why the offices have such a depressingly unloved look about them.

It fell to Sir Clive Whitmore to chair that morning's meeting. Strictly speaking the Channel Tunnel fell between the Department of Transport, the Foreign Office, the Department of the Environment and the Home Office. But when the issue of crisis management and the Tunnel had first been raised, memos had flowed thick and fast as each department argued for the cash and resources to cope with the potential problem. It had been seen as a wonderful civil service boondoggle; one of those golden opportunities like a new airport or a nuclear power station that come a Permanent Under-Secretary's way perhaps once in his career. If the plum could be picked it meant money and people, and with both of those came power and influence, the meat and drink of civil servants, one of whose roles in life is to make their ministers seem important.

Whitmore had already handled the battle to bring cruise missiles into Britain in the early 1980s. That had been a relatively small operation but one with high visibility and the MoD had formed committees, established secretariats and generally made the rest of Whitehall jealous of the prize and furious at the amount of extra work it generated. Whitmore was perfectly placed to seize the overseeing of the Tunnel with his background in defence, intelligence and the Cabinet Office, where he served during the Falklands war. He had successfully fought off bids from the Foreign Office and a less serious attempt by the parvenus at the Department of Transport.

His empire had grown as a result and he had relished the increase in power in the corridors of Whitehall and the clubs of St James's. But all this manoeuvring had been predicated on maximizing peacetime advantage and not actually having to justify his role as supremo of Tunnel crisis management. Running exercises and running committees is one thing; chairing COBRA is quite another.

He was in a thoroughly bad mood as he took his seat in the centre of the rectangular table. Looking around, he nodded to Stella Rimington from Box, John Cassidy from the JOC, Sir Robin Butler from the Cabinet Office, Sir John Walsh from the Foreign Office, Geoff Dearth from SIS (Sir Colin McColl was on leave), Mike Williams from SB, John Witherow from SO13 and representatives from Transport, the Environment and Treasury. Whitmore noticed that there was a chap lounging by the door whom he did not recognize. But he knew the type: Special Forces, here to pick up what intelligence he could to relay back to his masters. It always amazed him how they always seemed to hear about these meetings and quietly get a seat.

The room was crowded now, all the seats around the table taken. Whitmore cleared his throat to signal that the meeting was in session.

'Good morning, ladies and gentlemen. I'm sorry you've had to be dragged in at such short notice but as you all will have heard, there is a crisis in the Tunnel.' He turned to his right to address Stella Rimington. 'Perhaps I could ask Stella to open with a résumé of what we know so far.'

Rimington glanced down at her notes which she had carefully written in pen in longhand on a plain white pad. 'The attack took place just after nine this morning. The Tunnel control centre received a report of a fire. Contact was made with the driver who insisted that the train was being hijacked. However, the automatic emergency procedures took over and the trains evacuated the Tunnel leaving two carriages behind.

'A claim of responsibility was made to the PA at nine-fifty. This was in the name of the Provisional IRA and carried the usual code word. PA broadcast the message and that is what will be running in the *Standard* this afternoon and in the other papers in the morning.

'However, at 9.55 a second message was telephoned to the Foreign Office – in fact to the Foreign Secretary's private office – in the name of the Hong Kong Liberation Front. This stated that the IRA claim was a bluff and that they themselves were really responsible for the attack.

'That is what we know. The rest is what we think and what we can guess. First, we have never heard of the Hong Kong Liberation Front, so if it exists, we can assume it is a cover for something or somebody else. Second, we have no information that the IRA were planning an attack of this size. I am inclined to think it's not them. They tend to go for high-value, low-risk targets. This is high value but very high risk and if they fail they would reckon on losing a large number of their best people. It just doesn't seem their style.

'We have some other, incidental, intelligence that may support the Hong Kong theory. In the past few days we have picked up one of the major players in Chinese intelligence coming through Heathrow. We have also photographed Stanley Kung, the head of one of the Triads in Hong Kong, coming out of the Chinese military attaché building in Hampstead.

'The Chinese are here because they suspect that the Triads are going to carry out some kind of operation which will result in the British giving passports to Hong Kong residents, which they obviously want to prevent. It may be that this is the operation they have heard about.'

It is the convention that neither senior civil servants nor government ministers get briefed in detail on operations. They only get told the risks and the rewards, never anything about sources and methods. All those at the table knew the conventions, so there was no further probing. But Whitmore pressed harder.

'Do you have any information on the people in this country who are supposed to be involved?' he asked.

'Well, we do have something which may be of help,' Rimington replied. 'Our Statics picked up some talk of a gentleman called Dai Choi who is apparently in this country in relation to this operation. And a man called Turnbull from the Hong Kong police has been seen going into the Chinese military attaché's offices also. He met there with a senior figure from Chinese intelligence this morning. It's possible he's involved on the wrong side on this one.' She turned to Mike Williams from Special Branch. 'He's been helping you, hasn't he, Mike?'

The question, so innocent in its phrasing, bared all the old wounds. Ever since Box began to take control of counter-terrorist operations in England from the Special Branch, old rivalries had become embarrassing sores. SB saw Box as a bunch of bureaucratic amateurs while MI5 viewed the SB as beer-swilling morons who were too stupid to catch any terrorists. As always in such rows, there was some truth on both sides but this had become lost in the sniping that had been going on since the takeover was announced. SB leaked every mistake by Box, added their own spin and watched the headlines. The Security Service had fewer contacts with the media and were less sophisticated in using them so they lost the public battles while struggling to control the Whitehall war. Now most of the SB Luddites had been fired and overall relations had improved, but still, for Stella, SB's involvement with Turnbull was too good an opportunity to miss.

Mike Williams had always been embarrassed about his Yorkshire accent. Ever since he came to London twenty years earlier he had done his best to disguise what he still thought of as his hick origins. Once he had even toyed with taking elocution lessons but the terror of being exposed had stopped him. Instead he had tried to shorten the long vowels that gave him away. Most of the time he succeeded, but when he was excited, like now, he reverted to type. To these smooth bureaucrats he sounded faintly ridiculous but what he said got their attention.

'Bloody 'ell,' he exclaimed. 'Turnbull. Turnbull. You know,' he said, pointing at Rimington and then at Witherow. 'A few days ago, that Customs boat out in the North Sea. The one that was attacked by those Chinamen. That was Turnbull. And Dai Choi too, now I come to think about it. Turnbull's been working with the Met, not with us, Stella. I've seen a couple of reports. I read that they were intercepting a drugs shipment being brought in by this team from Hong Kong. The Customs people were killed trying to stop the shipment. I messaged Hong Kong about him and they gave him the all-clear. Said he's got good connections on the Chinese side and is their best man on the Triads. Lost a son killed by them, apparently. This chap Dai Choi was involved and Turnbull's become a bit obsessed. He sounds clean to me.'

'Well, maybe the ship he intercepted wasn't drugs at all but something else. Perhaps it was guns or explosives for the Tunnel attack,' said Rimington.

'If I could just bring us back to centre stage for a moment,' interrupted Whitmore. 'It seems we are agreed that the Hong Kong claim may be the right one. Do we know how many people are in the Tunnel? How many hostages or passengers?'

'We're working on that right now, PUS,' said Bill Herman, the PUS at the Department of Transport. He was a florid man with a small pointed beard, not unlike that of Kaiser Wilhelm I. Inevitably he was known in the corridors as Herman the German or just The German. 'All the carriages were full and judging by the average load there will be between 75 and 125 people in the Tunnel right now. We'll have a complete breakdown once the passenger tickets are matched with the vehicles, which should be soon now.'

'Any idea on terrorist numbers?' Whitmore asked.

'Not so far. And it's going to be difficult for us to pin that down as they'll have been travelling on different passports and under different names.'

'We've been doing a little work on that,' said Cassidy. In fact, as soon as the first PA message hit the screen the Special Forces cell had done nothing but model the attack, trying to understand how it might have been done, with how many people, using what equipment. It was the first step towards setting up a counter-terrorist operation. 'By our reckoning they would have needed at least six to take the Tunnel out. Then they have set a deadline of three days so they've got to be prepared to guard the people and control the Tunnel working in shifts. We reckon that will need at least another six, making twelve in all.

'Of course, they might have killed the hostages by now, in which case our calculations might be a little off,' he added helpfully.

'Yes. Well, we'll just have to work on the assumption that they're not completely mad,' said Whitmore.

'There's something else we need to consider, PUS,' said Witherow. 'The French have got the train driver, a chap called Ritchie. The terrorists are holding his wife and kids. Apparently they chopped the finger off his little girl to force him to do what they want. They promised to release the family once the Tunnel was secure but there's no sign of that happening. Kent police have moved some of their quick-reaction people into position and are keeping the house under observation.'

'They have no authority to move in, I hope?' Whitmore asked.

'Not at this stage,' replied Witherow. 'From what the

driver tells us, these are ruthless people and I think we should be prepared to go in and get the family out. I don't think waiting will do much except result in them getting killed. They've already cut up the little girl and once the violence starts, it's almost always a commitment to further bloodshed.'

'Does anyone disagree with that assessment?' Whitmore asked, looking around the table. There were only a few nods of acknowledgement. 'Very well. I'll advise my minister accordingly and let you know the result. Now what about the Tunnel itself,' he continued. 'Do we sit this one out or go in?'

He turned towards Cassidy as the man with the military options. For John, the spotlight was unwelcome. He hated these political meetings where the sub-text was never revealed. Each of the people around this table had fiefdoms to defend, ambitions to satisfy and ministers to protect. Now they wanted a military appreciation where the enemy was unknown and the objective was unclear. It was a soldier's nightmare. Better then to be completely honest.

'As you know, sir, the general policy in these matters is to wait it out,' he began. 'But this one is time sensitive and if these characters are as ruthless as John suggests then we may have to move before the deadline runs out. Before I can do anything for you I need some hard information. Numbers involved, weapons, what counter-measures they might have employed, communications.' He shrugged apologetically. 'Just about everything, really.

'I suggest that we mount a recce into the area and pick up what we can so that we can make a better judgment . . . I suppose there's no chance that we might give these people what they want?'

The ball bounced in front of Walsh from the Foreign Office, who returned it smoothly. 'We have no intention at this time of doing anything that might lead them to think negotiations are possible.'

So, Cassidy thought. The bastards are willing to do a deal if the price is right. Typical fucking FCO, always ready to compromise.

There was a brief lull in the conversation as the group dissected and digested Walsh's statement. Each thought he or she knew exactly what was intended but no one was prepared to break cover and push him further on what exactly 'at this time' meant.

Since Rimington had shifted responsibility for the attack away from the IRA, Whitmore had been mulling over what she had said, thinking about possibilities and opportunities. He remembered the meeting with her and Dickens a few days earlier and the humiliating perform-ance his minister had given in Question Time. The IRA are running rings around us, and not for the bloody first time, he thought bitterly.

'But aren't we missing a trick here?' he suggested tentatively. 'As far as anyone knows, the IRA have claimed responsibility for this attack. That is the story that the press will write and it is the story the public will believe. Surely this is an opportunity for us. We can squeeze Adams and his friends so hard that the pips will squeak and then crack. In fact, we can do what we like and the public will ask us to do more.'

'This could be the opportunity to apply the kind of pressure that's needed to find the team operating here and put it out of business,' he added, warming to his theme. 'With the gloves off, we can begin to make life pretty rough for our friends in the Provisional IRA.'

'I like it,' said Rimington, her enthusiasm clear. 'We know that Adams has been having a tough time recently. The loss of his seat at Westminster has reduced his credibility. The fact that the team operating here has stayed at large for so long has strengthened the hand of the militants and Adams is getting worried that he's going to be pushed aside. If we do this right, we might be able to drive a wedge between the politicos and the gunmen so that they'll be too busy tearing each other's throats out to worry about us.'

'Aren't we getting a little ahead of ourselves?' Mike Williams's brogue cut through the civilized discussions, 'Two points. First, how can we be sure this is not PIRA? We have some pretty scanty information from Box, some intelligence from Hong Kong and not much else. All the security systems in the Tunnel were designed with the IRA in mind and now when something actually happens we just dismiss the possibility. For all we know the Hong Kong people could have done a deal with them so we could have not one but two problems on our hands.'

'We are, of course, still gathering our information and we continue to look at PIRA as a possibility,' Rimington interrupted. 'But even if you're right, doing what PUS suggests should not affect our policy towards the terrorists. If we find out more then we can change our emphasis as we go along.'

'What happens if the public find out they've been misled?' Mike Williams asked with the policeman's concern for form and procedure.

'They won't,' replied Whitmore. 'But even if they do, the minutes will show that we have no clear idea who is carrying out the hijack. We are being prudent by pursuing all leads. Nobody could expect us to do any different.'

His hands spread open in front of him in a gesture of benediction and innocence which everyone understood and the minutes would never reflect.

'So, to sum up. I will consult about a rescue operation for the family of the train driver. We will do what we can to find out about what is going on in the Tunnel. We will explore the IRA angle.'

A sudden thought occurred to him.

'Surely we should bring this man Turnbull into the operation. He knows the Chinese, knows Hong Kong and apparently knows some of the people involved. Is there anyone else from outside who might help?'

Aside from the return volley, Walsh had been silent but now he saw a chance to make a modest contribution.

'Dame Mary Cheong is in town. She visited the Foreign Secretary yesterday and I know she plans to stay a few days. She would be invaluable with her contacts both in London and Hong Kong among the Chinese community.'

'Very well,' said Whitmore. 'We have a plan. Let's get to it.'

The Provisional IRA has no equivalent of COBRA. In one sense the organization is in a permanent state of crisis, so there is no need for a special management tool to deal with particular problems. There is also no real bureaucracy, thus the coordination is relatively simple even if on occasion the politics are labyrinthine in their complexity.

Adams heard about the attack on the Tunnel in his holiday caravan on the Cooley peninsula just over the border in the Irish Republic. Adams used to holiday in a supporter's cottage in the glens of Antrim north of Belfast but a death threat from the Protestants had sent him south.

He had installed ˙a modest caravan near Dundalk, between Greenore and Carlingford. After the IRA shot a local farmer, Tom Oliver, Adams and all other Sinn Fein/IRA supporters were banned from the local pub. Despite the local enmity, Adams still enjoyed his private refuge. This was IRA country. They controlled it; even owned large chunks of it. Little happened around here without them knowing about it and the communities were sufficiently remote that strangers were always seen and reported. Adams was well defended and it was one of the few places in the world where he felt he could truly relax.

The caravan is in the yard of a farmer called Josie Donnelly and its side windows look out over the peninsula towards the Irish Sea. It is a beautiful spot with that lovely soft green behind, the sea immediately ahead and the Mountains of Mourne rising in the distance. Adams would spend hours walking along the beach, kicking the pebbles, occasionally spinning one into the sea and just thinking and reading.

He had come down with Eamon McCaughley and Frank Hartley, his two bodyguards, to get away from the pressure cooker of Belfast. The conversation with Gerry Kelly had depressed him. In fact, he had been depressed a great deal lately as he felt the struggle slipping away from him. He could recall with vivid resolution the late seventies when he was in control, the bullet and the ballot seemed to be working, the Sinn Fein vote was rising and he actually believed they could force the Brits out.

Oh, they still listened to what he said. They still deferred to him, but he could tell that his message was no longer getting through. With men like Kelly in the wings waiting with their guns and bombs it was only a matter of time before a showdown. And he thought that this time Adams, the great survivor, might actually lose.

He always listened to BBC Radio Ulster and this morning was no exception. The regular programming had been interrupted by the announcer relaying the PA report about the seizure of the Tunnel. He heard the news with astonishment that swiftly turned to anger.

'The rebellion has begun,' he told himself.

He toyed with going back to Belfast but decided against it. That would be seen as a sign of weakness and a clear indication he did not know what was going on. His priority was to establish control of the situation. To do that he needed to meet with whomever of the Northern Command he could get down here at short notice.

By the time Clive Whitmore was sitting down in the Cabinet Office Briefing Room, the first of the Northern Command had arrived at the caravan. First through the door was Gerry Kelly, dressed, Adams was disgusted to see, as if he were on holiday in the South of France, in baggy white trousers, linen shirt and a sweater tied around his neck.

Next came Michael McDonald, the man in charge of the IRA in South Armagh. South Armagh is a traditional centre of Irish entrepreneurial activity and McDonald has gained respect in the Movement for his innovative ideas. In particular, he obtained a growth-promoting steroid for cattle, known locally as Angel Dust, which he imported in the south and then illegally exported to the north. He is a rich man, but like everyone in the area he dresses and smells as if he is a pauper.

McDonald is small, not unlike the little Irishman who had escorted John Wayne in *The Quiet Man*. His face is round with the healthy rosiness of a man who spends his time outdoors. At first glance his eyes appear merry, the crinkles suggesting a man who smiles often. But a second glance reveals that his real business is killing people. His brown eyes are flat, almost opaque, and seem to show no emotion, neither happiness nor sorrow. He has killed a lot of men.

There was no doubting his value as smuggler, fund-raiser, organizer and killer, but Adams just wished he would take a bath more often. When McDonald sat down in the caravan, Kelly pointedly shuffled his chair further away as the smell of sweat and the farmyard filled the small room. Adams lit his pipe and drew deeply so that the room was filled with the perfumed smoke of the Condor tobacco.

It was a perfect moment for the Quartermaster to enter. The man is a legend, his identity a closely guarded secret. He is responsible for the delivery of weapons and explosives to the IRA units operating in the north and on the mainland and he is the best the Boys have ever had. It was he who fixed the Libyan shipments, the largest of which had been landed just down the road at Clogher Head.

In a group of individuals, the Quartermaster has taken eccentricity to a new art form. He takes incredible steps to conceal his identity and in fact no one inside PIRA is quite sure who knows who he really is. He always arrives late for meetings and always in disguise. Today, he was wearing a heavy dark overcoat, a fedora and a patently false beard. 'Anonymity,' he had once said, 'is the cloak that disguises success.' As long as he continues to deliver, his little diversions are tolerated.

'Right. Now that we're all here, what the fucking hell is going on?' Adams asked, determined to dominate the meeting from the start.

'Don't look at me, Gerry,' Kelly protested. 'This has nothing to do with me.'

'What about you, Quartermaster,' Adams said, turning to the muffled figure. 'Have you delivered anything special to the mainland to set this up?'

'Nothing.' The answer was flat and final. 'Everything this campaign needs was delivered between three and five years ago. And all of it is the standard packs. Nothing special and not enough to mount something like this.'

'Well, what the fuck is happening!' Adams shouted.

'Perhaps it's the Prods,' suggested McDonald.

'Oh, come on, Michael,' protested Kelly. 'They couldn't coordinate a farting competition let alone something like this. The best they can do is kill people a few at a time. Taking the Tunnel would have required real planning, a proper logistics tail and well-trained people. They couldn't manage any of that.'

'Well, if it's not us and it's not the Prods, who the hell is it?' Adams asked. 'We'd better find out because you can be sure that whatever happens we're going to get blamed. If people start to die in that bloody Tunnel, the Brits are going to be down on us like there's no tomorrow. And there well might not be.'

As Adams ushered the three men from the caravan, he felt slightly relieved. He took some satisfaction from the fact that there was no open revolt under way. Whatever was going on he would have time to find out the truth and orchestrate a response. That was the reality of politics, he knew, and he was very good at it.

CHAPTER 18

IT HAD BEEN six hours since Vincent Sum invaded the Ritchie household and he should have been gone long ago. Once Harry Ritchie had left, the house had settled into a routine: Rosemary, Becky and David stayed in the kitchen with Vincent while one Chinese watched from the front and the other from the back. Sum had turned on the kitchen radio to listen for the news. When the first broadcast about the successful takeover of the Tunnel came he was elated, certain now that White Lotus would triumph.

But the expected message from the leadership had not appeared. He had been told to expect a message as soon as the Tunnel was taken and then they could make their escape. As the minutes had slipped into hours, he became increasingly worried. Doubt was eating away at his self-confidence and he knew with an awful certainty that he had become an inconvenient loose end, too costly to save and too easy to sacrifice.

He could imagine Harry Ritchie sitting in some French police station telling the cops about the Chinese who had invaded his home, tortured his daughter and blackmailed him. He knew well enough how these things worked. Even as he was stuck in this kitchen, the cops would be preparing to do something to take them out. There had been no sign of any activity so far, but it was only a matter of time. And he knew that time was short.

His imagination and the constant whining of the little girl were beginning to get on his nerves. He could almost feel the police outside creeping up on the house, hear them getting into position, sense the first few seconds of the attack. He knew the story Harry Ritchie would have told meant that there would be little quarter given. The focus of the police would be on rescuing the family and anyone who got in the way would be shot. He knew his men would fight; they would obey orders and die if necessary. But he had no intention of dying or even being captured.

His thoughts were interrupted by another cry from Becky. Since she had lost her fingers, Rosemary had tied a tourniquet around her arm to stanch the flow of blood and wrapped a dishcloth over the stumps as a crude bandage. But the little girl was in agony, the hand a huge, throbbing mass of pain from which there was no relief. She was crying almost continuously now, her pale cheeks streaked with tears, her eyes withdrawn into her skull.

'Can't you shut the kid up?' Vincent Sum asked again.

'No, I can't,' Rosemary replied. 'Can't you see she needs treatment? Much more of this and she's going to die. You've got what you want. You've taken the Tunnel. Why don't you just leave?'

'That may be the best idea I've heard all day,' Sum replied.

Her words had made the decision for him. But leaving meant leaving no witnesses. First he'd deal with that whining bitch who'd made his life a misery for the past few hours. He got up from the table and moved four paces to his right until he was standing behind Becky. His left hand grabbed her blonde hair and pulled it back so that her head was stretched back and their eyes met. Her neck was perfectly white and perfectly smooth. With a swift motion, Vincent Sum drew his long-bladed knife from its sheath and brought it round to slip the point in

278

underneath Becky's left ear and draw the blade across her throat.

Rosemary saw the movement and acted instinctively to protect her child. She lunged across the table trying to grab the knife arm and stop it in mid-swing. Surprised by the attack, Vincent Sum drew back slightly. It was enough for Rosemary's hand to miss his forearm and grab the blade of the knife.

She watched in horror as her hand slid smoothly along the knife's length, cutting her palm open like a piece of raw steak on a butcher's block. She felt no pain, just the absolute revulsion of something alien invading her flesh, a paper cut magnified ten thousand times.

The blood poured out and she recoiled in disgust from the sight of her hand sliced open before her like a ripe tomato, the white of her sinews the seeds, her blood the juice. Her eyes flicked back up and she saw the knife coming around again. The Chinese had been only momentarily diverted by her intervention and the knife was arcing back towards Becky's throat.

The child's eyes were looking at her, wide with terror, the plea for a mother's help not to be denied.

Rosie's left hand reached out and this time there was no surprise or reflexive withdrawal. Her hand clamped on his wrists, just as the knife pierced Becky's neck, drawing a thin string of bright red blood that trickled down the white skin. Her hand was around his wrist and she pulled with a strength she didn't know she possessed, her bloodied right hand clamping on her left wrist, adding to the force. She grunted with the pain and effort, pulling the man away from her daughter.

Vincent Sum reared back, pulling Rosemary across the kitchen table.

'Butcher. Butcher, butcher.' The muttered chant was squeezed out between gasps as Rosemary struggled to maintain a hold on his arm and a grip on reality. She knew that death was only moments away as the Chinese forced her wrists around so that the knife was pointing straight at her. Sliding along the table-top she could see the knife waiting for her at the other side, ready to impale her.

Desperate now, she knew that her own death would mean the killing of her children. As if in the distance, she heard the screams of Becky and David, their terror exaggerated by the sight of their mother bleeding. Their cries pushed her to one last act of sacrifice. She used the only thing she had left that could be fashioned into a weapon – her body.

Twisting on the table-top, she spun around, using Sum's arm as a lever, and dragged her body straight at him. Taken by surprise, the Chinese lurched backwards, the knife moving slightly to one side. As their bodies collided, Rosemary felt the weapon slide into her body the way a gutting knife enters the stomach of a dead fish. But there was no time to think of the pain.

The two fell backwards towards the sink in an embrace sealed by the knife jutting from Rosemary's side. Vincent Sum reached behind him to steady his fall and his fingers closed on the drying-up rack which tumbled down as they fell to the floor in a tangle of limbs and shattered china. The Chinese was trapped underneath, his knife stuck inside the body which was collapsed on top of him. With her left hand, Rosemary scrabbled in the wreckage around her for a weapon and her hand closed around a Sabatier knife – a present from Harry.

Without thinking, she began the execution of the man who had tried to kill her children.

For a right-handed person, doing anything precise with the left hand is difficult. But Rosemary was making no attempt at accuracy. There was no intent to aim, only to maim. The first blow sank through the fleshy part of his cheek and she drew the blade out with a sucking sound that made her want to vomit. A second blow sliced off the fleshy part of his nose before bouncing off his cheekbone and into the linoleum.

Vincent Sum was screaming now, all thoughts of killing anyone banished by the immediacy of the pain. His body was being torn by the violence of the attack, the determination of his attacker. His body arched on the floor, bucking to unseat his unwelcome rider, trying to free his hands so that he could stop the agony.

He heard a crashing sound and out of the corner of his eye he saw a small grey egg land on the floor, bounce once and roll towards him. His mind shouted 'grenade' but no words came out. There was a blinding flash of light and a massive shock wave. A nanosecond later both Sum and his attacker were. unconscious. The rescuers had arrived.

Brigadier John Cassidy moved to the podium in the briefing room of the JOC at the Ministry of Defence. The different cells had been working continuously since the beginning of the crisis and it was time to update the decision-makers on the current status of the hijack.

The room contained around thirty people. Looking around, Cassidy could see the brown, dark blue and light blue uniforms of the services with a sprinkling of civilians from the Defence Intelligence Staff and one or two genuine civilians looking out for the interests of their political masters. To his right, the five directors of the JOC cells were sitting, ready to answer specific questions if any should be asked. Behind and to Cassidy's left was a large screen that could be used to display slides or videos while behind his right shoulder a television screen linked this room to COBRA and to the Prime Minister's office at No. 10. Cassidy was facing a small camera mounted on the wall. He knew this would be a command performance.

'Prime Minister, ladies and gentlemen,' he began. 'This briefing includes all information up to 1500 hours today. The attack on the Channel Tunnel, which took place at 0903 this morning, was carried out by terrorists linked to the Triads in Hong Kong. We are now satisfied that the IRA has no involvement in this matter although, as you know, inquiries are proceeding in this area.

'The family of the train driver was successfully released in an operation carried out by a special unit from Kent police. The wife was badly injured but is well enough to speak. The daughter is currently in surgery but it is certain that she has lost two fingers and will be in hospital for some time. Their son is in shock but is otherwise unhurt.

'Interrogation of the family has revealed very little. One of the Chinese was badly injured in a fight with Mrs Ritchie. He will lose the sight of one eye, has lost most of his nose and a great deal of blood. He is not in a position to speak at this time. His two followers appear to speak no English and we are organizing an interpreter to question them now. I doubt we will learn much from them.

'Passenger records suggest that there are 90 people inside the Tunnel. As you know, we have a photographic record of all passports checked through the Tunnel security system and passports are now being matched against the records in Petty France. We have turned up 10 false passports so far and there may be more.

'That means a maximum of 80 hostages, although it is likely we will end up with a slightly smaller figure. Of those, we have identified 18 children under the age of 15, 27 women and 35 men.

'So far we have insufficient intelligence on the terrorists and their weapons to determine their strength or the nature of any defence they might be able to mount.

'Given what they have already done to the train driver's child – two fingers cut off simply as a warning – I think we can assume they are ruthless and will kill hostages if we do not meet their deadline.

'Our military assessment is that an assault on the Tunnel at this stage would result in high casualties on both sides and a probable high loss of life among the hostages.'

The Prime Minister had sat patiently through the briefing, making notes in the painstaking longhand which had become the bane of his civil servants. They were used to briefing a minister, getting an answer and then taking the brief away for action. Major always insisted on making his own notes, thinking about the subject, seeking other advice (an unheard-of insult to his civil servants) and then dictating a memo with his decision. His predecessor, Margaret Thatcher, had tended to listen without making notes at all and then reach her own decision without consulting anybody. This made for fast and firm government but a lot of unhappy colleagues. The Major style might be a bit slower but it had reintroduced the idea of government by consensus.

'Thank you for that, Brigadier,' he said. 'I have to tell you that after their recent success in the rescue of the driver's family, the police are keen to go into the Tunnel and try again. What do you think about that?'

'I'll defer to Captain Daria from the SAS if I may, Prime Minister.'

Despite his name, Daria came not from Sicily but from Scunthorpe. Like many in the SAS he was a quiet man, whose thoughtful caution had kept him alive in Northern Ireland and in the wars in the Falklands and the Gulf. Like most of his colleagues, he had prospered not because of an enthusiasm for shooting people but through an obsessive attention to the detail of planning each operation, which ensured that only rarely were shots fired and, if they were, he and his men were fully prepared.

It was hardly surprising therefore that Daria gave a cautious response to the Prime Minister. 'We have looked at the problem and so far we simply do not have enough information to launch any kind of rescue effort. We could go in now and we could certainly get the hostages out but some, perhaps many, would be killed. We would lose some of our men and I have no idea what the damage to the Tunnel might be. I strongly recommend that we do nothing for the moment. If you can, Prime Minister, buy us some time.'

'I'm afraid, Captain, that may not be possible.' Major paused and appeared to be consulting with someone off camera. 'What we need is information and we need it as fast as possible. I understand your reservations, Captain, but I must have something on which to base decisions. I am prepared to allow a police tactical unit to go into the Tunnel to try and find out something about the terrorists. They will be authorized to look but not to attack.'

Cassidy realized that Major had made the classic politician's compromise: the short-term gain of placating an anxious police and a panic-stricken business community against the longer-term needs of the operation itself. The police always made a cock of this kind of thing, Cassidy thought gloomily. This is going to be another one.

'Meanwhile, is there nothing else we can be doing to prepare for action against these people?' Major asked. 'I'm told that some allowance for this kind of attack was made in the building of the Tunnel. What do you have on that, Brigadier?'

Captain David Mills RN had watched the byplay between the JOC and COBRA with fascination and frustration. Mills was a seasoned MoD warrior in the guerrilla warfare that was constantly waged in the corridors of Whitehall. He had watched and listened and understood that there were two very distinct games being played here. The first was the release of the hostages, and that could probably be accomplished by the SAS, the police or some other group who had the guts and wanted the glory. At the same time, this was a fight for visibility, a game that everyone had to play. If you were in, then the payoffs afterwards in funding and positioning at the high table could be enormous. If you got left out of an operation of this size then awkward questions would be asked about roles which could lead to cuts – and no one wanted that. So the Prime Minister's question was perfectly timed.

'I can take that one if you like, John,' Mills said smoothly, rising to stand at the podium. 'You are quite right, Prime Minister. During the building of the Tunnel a number of small vertical pipes were inserted in the roof that led out to the sea. Officially these are ventilation shafts, but in fact they can provide access from underwater.'

'Are the Navy in a position to exploit this opportunity?' Major asked.

'Unfortunately, Prime Minister, the Tunnel was designed when the Navy was planning to build two Mermaid class submersible rescue vessels and these were cancelled by the previous government.' (Get that in the minutes for after this is all over, Mills thought to himself.) 'The only vessels that can access the shafts are in the United States and we are making inquiries to see if we can get one of them over here. Meanwhile, we do have HMS *Campbeltown* on station in the Irish Sea as the Fleet Contingency Ship and we can bring her down to the Channel just in case the vessel arrives from the States.'

'Excellent, captain,' Major replied, some enthusiasm in his voice now that he felt something was happening. 'Have *Campbeltown* make all speed to the Channel and tell the Americans we need their help immediately. Let me know if you need me to call President Clinton to move things along. Thank you, gentlemen.'

The screen in the JOC went blank.

CHAPTER 19

ACROSS WHITEHALL, MAJOR turned away from the screen and asked his ministers for their comments. There was a brief silence and then Douglas Hurd spoke, the distinctive voice sounding even more nasal in the confines of the briefing room.

'I had a call half an hour ago from Mr Ma Yuzhen, the Chinese ambassador in London. He told me that he understands that there are some terrorists from Hong Kong holding hostages inside the Tunnel.'

'Bloody hell, how did the little bastard know that?' exclaimed Sir Robin Butler, the Cabinet Secretary.

'We don't know, Robin,' Hurd responded, sarcasm evident in his voice. 'We assume that he has sources that are about as good as ours. Anyway, he made it crystal clear that his government would take very strong exception indeed to any deal that we might do with the terrorists. He explained that Beijing would consider any effort to give passports to more Hong Kong residents a breach of the spirit and the letter of the 1984 agreement. He said that the people are what makes Hong Kong strong, that he relies on us not to negotiate.' His voice tailed off as his right hand made a dismissive gesture. 'You get the general idea. He's not happy and he wants to make sure that we're well aware of that fact.'

'Do you think there is any room for compromise,

Douglas?' Major asked. 'For that matter, do you think we should seek to negotiate?'

'Our experience of the Chinese over the past few years has been marked by their absolute determination to get as much of Hong Kong as possible, and that certainly includes the people. I think they see it as their lifeline to the future and they will do their damnedest to make sure nothing interferes with that. So I think compromise with the Chinese government is unlikely and that makes the question of whether the terrorists will negotiate a fairly moot point. Of course, we could defy the Chinese and do a deal anyway. But if we did that I can guarantee that the Chinese would leak the story and we could find ourselves in serious trouble both at home and abroad.'

'But if we don't negotiate we face the danger of the Channel Tunnel being blown up,' pointed out the Chancellor of the Exchequer. 'I don't want to be too doom and gloom but my advisers tell me that could have a catastrophic effect on the stock market. There's about fifteen billion pounds tied up in the Tunnel if you include all the infrastructure and if it goes down the pan – if you'll forgive the pun – it will be the biggest single loss the City has ever experienced. Lloyd's is only just beginning to recover from the asbestos business and I doubt they could absorb another loss like this.

'I imagine Eurotunnel will go bust and there won't be anybody around to pick up the pieces. I cannot believe that the public will use the Tunnel after this, even if it can be repaired.'

'Well, if that's the case we'd better prepare for a rescue operation,' said Malcolm Rifkind, the Secretary of State for Defence. 'But if we're going down that road, I really think the Army and the Navy are better equipped to work in the Tunnel than the police.'

'That's as may be,' replied Major. 'But you heard what I said to the JOC. The police are going in to do a preliminary reconnaissance and then we'll see.' He leaned back in his chair to stretch an aching back and continued in a more soothing tone. 'Look, Malcolm, you and I both know that when it comes to this kind of thing, the military are probably the best we've got. But we've poured millions into the police in recent years to give them an effective counter-terrorist capability. The Kent police are specifically trained for just this kind of operation. If we don't use them now, then it will send a very clear signal to the police that I think they're not up to it. It will also raise serious questions about why we invested the money in them in the first place.

'We have two days left before the deadline runs out so we need to move without delay on a number of fronts. So, Malcolm, you will make sure the Navy ship is heading for the Channel and that it takes up position above the Tunnel. You may need to speed up things on the American side as well. A call to Les Aspin might help.'

Rifkind nodded and Major turned towards the paunchy figure of the Home Secretary, Kenneth Clarke. 'Kenneth, you will make sure the police go in without delay and get a report back to the JOC and to COBRA as soon as possible.

'Finally, what is the position with the IRA? Are we making any progress on that front? Time is very short and so if we are to exploit that opportunity, we must do so immediately.'

'It's in hand, Prime Minister. As we speak the Army and the police are moving into Belfast and Derry on a sweep of the Republican areas. We are putting out that it is related to the Tunnel and so far there has been no comeback either from the Labour Party or the SDLP over there. We are also seeing what else we can do as a matter of urgency.'

Major had no wish to find out what the 'else' might be. Better that he shouldn't know and then later, if it all went wrong, he could truthfully say he did not know about it. He was sure that both Kenneth and Malcolm had taken the same precaution. All of us politicians clearing the decks for action, he reflected ruefully.

'Very well. Thank you for your time. We will reconvene in the morning or sooner if there are developments to discuss.'

There was the usual shuffling of paper as the ministers gathered their documents. Major left the room first and went straight up the stairs towards No. 10 and his own office. Hurd followed but instead of going up the stairs, he turned to the right and entered one of the secondary conference rooms that form part of COBRA.

Both Dame Mary Cheong and Jonny Turnbull were seated at a rectangular wooden table surrounded by officials from the Cabinet Office, uniformed and plain-clothes policemen and other men and women who were presumably from the intelligence community.

Hurd strode across the room briefly to embrace Dame Mary. 'Mary. Good to see you again. I'm so pleased you have been able to help in this terrible situation.'

'Thank you, Douglas. Obviously, I'm happy to do what I can.'

She turned towards Turnbull and stretched out an arm, bringing him forward into their little group.

'Foreign Secretary, this is Jonny Turnbull from the Royal Hong Kong Police. He first alerted us to the Triad problem and he has been passing on his extraordinary knowledge of the people involved in the attack to the police and others here. I've not been of much use, I'm afraid.'

The two men shook hands as Hurd muttered formal bromides about 'gratitude' and 'significant help'.

Mary Cheong steered Hurd away from the crowd and into a corner of the room. Leaning closer to him so that he could smell a distinctive, expensive perfume, she spoke in a tone low enough so that people a few feet away could hear nothing. 'I warned you something like this would happen, Douglas. I told you the people of Hong Kong are so angry that they would be bound to take action. But you refused to listen and now we have a really serious problem.'

Hurd held up a hand in protest. 'Now just a minute, Mary. Certainly, you warned me but I didn't ignore what you had to say. On the contrary, I considered it very carefully but decided that there was nothing to be done. We simply can't change our policy at this very late stage.'

'But surely you are not going to let those hostages die and the Tunnel be blown up?'

'No, of course not. We hope that it won't come to that.'

'Well, why not give the people of Hong Kong what they deserve by right? Then you solve the problem.'

'First, that's not in my gift,' Hurd replied. 'And even if it were, I would never agree to changing government policy under such circumstances.'

'But you must. You must,' Mary repeated, her right hand gripping his upper arm and squeezing to underline her emotion. 'The people in the Tunnel will die unless you do something. And if they die, they'll take the Tunnel down with them.'

'That's as may be, Mary.' Hurd turned back to the room. 'If I can have your attention for a moment, ladies and gentlemen. The Prime Minister has decided that we will send in a reconnaissance team tonight to see what intelligence we can gather from inside the Tunnel. Then a decision will be taken on whether or not to mount a rescue operation. There will be no concessions.'

The whispered asides and even the two tentative claps that broke out in the tension-filled room showed Hurd that he had struck the right note with his audience. He knew from past war-gaming in COBRA that after a few hours all the participants tended to become entrenched with a collective determination not to give in. This was clearly the case here.

*

An hour later, Jonny pushed open the door to the flat in Sloane Avenue. He glanced towards the sitting room and saw that Lisu was in exactly the same position as she had been when he left her nearly twelve hours earlier. She was sitting staring into the fireplace where there was nothing to see except an unlit fake gas fire.

He moved around in front of her. 'Hey. Hey. Wake up.' He snapped his fingers in front of her face and felt a momentary frisson of panic as she did not move. Then she started out of the trance and looked up at him. Her eyes were red-rimmed and sunken into their sockets. Her cheeks were streaked with the lines of tears which must have been falling for hours.

'Christ, Lisu, what's the matter? You look terrible.'

She felt so fragile that it would have made little difference what he said. But the fact that his voice reflected the misery and self-loathing she felt caused her to begin a fresh outbreak of weeping.

'I'm so sorry, Jonny,' she cried, the words coming out syllable by syllable as the sobs prevented her from drawing a full breath. 'You shouldn't see me like this.'

Like most men confronted with a woman crying, Jonny wanted to pat her head as he would a nervous dog. Instead, he awkwardly got down on his knees by her and took her hands in his.

'What on earth has brought this on?' he asked, forcing her eyes to meet his. 'You've been really upset for a couple of days. Why don't you tell me about it? A burden shared is a burden halved, you know,' he added with a half smile which received no acknowledgement except another bout of sobbing.

'Oh, Jonny, I'm just so miserable. It's all so depressing.'

'But what's making you so miserable? Just tell me and I'll see what I can do to help.'

'It's being here,' she cried. Her small hands formed into fists to beat her frustration into the arm of the chair.

'I want to be back in Hong Kong. I want to be back in a world I understand, I want to be with people I can trust. I want to be away from here.'

Her hand swept around to encompass the room, its contents and, Jonny thought, London as well.

'But I thought we had discussed all this,' Jonny replied. 'You know that I've got a job to do here. That will be over soon and then we'll be going home. Surely that's not too long to wait?'

Lisu shook her head. 'But that was before.'

'Before what?' Jonny asked.

'Oh, Jonny, you just don't understand. You get attacked, you see people die and you just charge on. Well, I'm not like that. I don't care if Dai Choi lives or dies. All I care about is my life and I don't have one here.'

He wanted to shake her, to force the self pity out of her. He wanted to tell her that he still loved her, that they could build a new life together. But somehow the words just wouldn't come. Instead he was furious that she couldn't understand how after all these years the man who killed their son was finally in his sights. This time, he was certain he would triumph.

'Look, Lisu. I know you're depressed but things will look much better in the morning. I've got to go out for a meeting about the damn Tunnel. The police are planning to move in tonight and I need to be around to help coordinate it.'

He pulled his hands from hers and stood up. His right hand gave her shoulder a small squeeze and then he walked out of the room. He left behind the fragments of his marriage and the vital intelligence on the planned operation that night.

Jonny drove the two miles to Julie Cohen's flat in Regent's Bridge Gardens, just over Vauxhall Bridge. The image of Lisu's face, streaked with tears, the lips puffing and blowing with her sobs, floated before him. He felt sympathy, certainly. He even felt concern. But he remembered how he used to feel if she got upset: a constricted chest, an absolute and overwhelming determination to help; a concern so intense that he often felt like crying himself. He felt none of these things and the realization was another confirmation of just how wide the gulf between them had grown.

He pulled up at the double gates leading to the private complex formed out of an old vinegar factory. It lies behind Fentiman Road, the most burgled street in London because of the number of MPs and rich city businessmen who live there. He pressed the button for No. 36 and the small light came on over the surveillance camera. There was a slight pause and then the buzz of the gates opening.

He drove through, parked and walked the one flight up to Julie's flat. From the outside the block looked just like one of thousands in the city: red brick outside, anonymous corridor inside and plain wooden door with a spyhole in the centre. He pressed the buzzer and could hear steps walking towards him. There was a pause as he was assessed through the spyhole and then the door opened.

'Jonny, come on in. I was just getting a drink. Like one?'

He walked into a stunning black-and-white sitting room. Two leather sofas dominated the furniture and sat on a white rug with an intricate geometric design woven into it. One wall had five Chinese *wenrenhua* ink paintings and facing them were three magnificent Georgia O'Keeffe prints done in her black-and-white period. The curtains, which were drawn, were heavy black moiré silk.

Julie was different too. When they had met before, she had been either formal or in a work environment. Now, on her own territory, she allowed herself a very much more relaxed image. She was wearing a simple white silk blouse with a choker of white pearls at the neck and a pair of black and purple striped Girbaud trousers.

The whole effect of the apartment and the casual clothes was intimate and pleasing, giving the impression of a woman with both taste and money. The only jarring note was the slight smell of ammonia which he assumed meant there was a cat hiding somewhere. Julie noticed his surprise and laughed.

'Just because I work for Beijing doesn't mean that I have to dress in polyester suits and live in a hovel in deepest Romford,' she said. 'I was lucky that Grandfather left some of his ill-gotten gains from arms dealing to me, and I earn a decent salary – enough to buy this place and furnish it, anyway.'

She finished pouring herself a glass of white wine from a newly opened bottle of Cloudy Bay. She waved the bottle in his direction and he nodded.

'So,' she continued, 'what's going on at the Tunnel?'

'A nightmare. I've spent the day being squeezed dry by a bunch of people who seem to think Hong Kong is on another planet. I've told them about Triads, the economy, weapons, tactics and people. I've told them just about everything I know about everything.' He slumped down into the sofa nearest the fireplace and took a deep drink of his wine.

'Ah, that's better.' He exhaled noisily. 'God, I'm wiped out. I don't seem to have had any sleep or any rest since we came back from Newcastle.'

'And what's new from the front?' Julie asked.

'Not a lot really,' he replied. 'We're satisfied that it's White Lotus and not the IRA. But the police and everyone else are continuing on both fronts just in case. There's an operation planned for tonight to try and gather some intelligence from inside the Tunnel but God knows how much that will produce. What about you? Has Lin Yung turned up anything?'

'No. He's trawled everywhere but so far it's all just superficial stuff. Our intelligence people in Hong Kong say the word was out in the Chinese community for days that something was happening but there's been no details. Anyway, that might be just backfilling analysis. People know about the Tunnel, know that they may get passports as a result but that's pretty much as far as it goes. There are no names, no details on who's doing what.

'Lin Yung is getting pretty frustrated,' she continued. 'He thinks the British may cave in once the deadline gets a bit closer. He's sure they'll seek some kind of compromise and he's determined to prevent that.'

Jonny felt overwhelmed by it all: the pressure of the past few days, the questioning by the COBRA team and the tension with Lisu. He rubbed his left hand across his forehead, over his eyes and down his face, squeezing his nose and compressing his mouth. He hesitated, finger tugging at his right ear. Then, before he had time to make a conscious decision, he found himself confiding in Julie.

'I've also got problems with Lisu. She is really upset; wants to go home. I left her a few minutes ago in tears. She's so miserable and there doesn't seem to be anything I can do.'

'What's the problem?' Julie asked.

'Oh, she says she hates England, hates being away from home. But there's more to it than that. She thinks I should stop chasing Dai Choi, get on with my life. But now she's in really bad shape. She won't tell me what it is but something or someone is giving her a real hard time.'

He took another swallow and then crossed the boundary from information to intimacy.

'At the end of the day, I think it's us.' He saw Julie's eyebrows rise and laughed ruefully. 'No, I don't mean you and me. I mean us, our marriage. I think that after all this time, there may be nothing left for us.'

Now that the confession had begun, he wanted to tell her everything. It seemed somehow right that he should confide in her; they had already shared so much together: the chase, the hunt and now, perhaps, the kill. The extremes of human endeavour had stripped away the normal conventions.

Her hand reached out to take his glass and their fingers touched briefly. 'I'm so sorry, Jonny. This must be a tough time for you both. I can understand some of what you both feel. I've lived two lives for as long as I can remember. I live here but I suppose my spiritual home will always be China.'

'Do you still believe in their system?' he asked.

She paused, sipping her wine and buying time to phrase the answer. 'That's a very tough question. You have to remember that I was around after the Cultural Revolution and so I never really saw China in those times. I've seen the corruption of the old Communist system, the senility of much of the leadership and the struggle to balance Communism with capitalism. I suppose the answer is that I believe in the ideal but not in the reality. What I want is a government in Beijing that is really egalitarian, that does share the wealth, that embraces capitalism but controls it well enough so that it doesn't destroy us. That is what Lin Yung wants and I think he's right.

'I certainly believe in Beijing more than I believe in what I see around me here. There, the government takes care of all the people and there really is opportunity for all. Here you have an underclass that is forced to beg on the streets and sleep in doorways. You talk of justice for all when in reality it is for the few with money to pay for the good lawyers.'

'Huh,' Jonny grunted dismissively. 'At least we don't have a police state that arrests any dissident who raises a voice in protest against the government and then has a show trial to try and convince the world that we have justice.'

'That's hardly fair, Jonny,' she replied. 'Whatever the shortcomings of the system, and I admit that there are many, China is one country with one set of values which have come a long way in the last twenty years. In the next twenty we might see real progress for everybody. Maybe China will be the first country to have democratic socialism that actually means something, and be the first country to achieve it peacefully.'

'Yeah, and it's just as likely to tear itself apart in another of your "cultural revolutions",' Jonny replied sarcastically.

His cynicism infuriated Julie. 'Well, at least I actually have something to believe in. What exactly do you have? A marriage that's going down the drain or maybe is already there; a life in Hong Kong you appear to have come to despise; a country which you can no longer call home. What exactly do you believe in, Jonny? What is it you want? What are you working for?'

Jonny stared at her, silenced. Each of the statements and each of the questions crystallized the emptiness for him. She was right, he thought. There really is nothing left. It was all so hopeless, the struggle so senseless, such a waste of energy.

Seeing the despair in his face, she was instantly contrite, annoyed with herself for hurting this man who seemed so vulnerable. She moved across to sit by his side. Her hands reached out to touch his.

'Look, Jonny. This is a rough time. You're operating in a strange country under great stress and you are bound to feel isolated. But this is as much a time of opportunity as change and you should look at the positive things in all this.'

'Well, I would like to know what they are.'

'First of all, if we pull this off, then you'll have settled accounts with Dai Choi and maybe with Stanley Kung also, which should make up for some of the frustration back in Hong Kong. And second, you see the changeover in Hong Kong as a time of destruction. You think the Chinese are going to come in and wreck everything. Well, I'm sure you're right – up to a point. Beijing won't allow the corruption to continue, and they'll change or destroy many of the traditions that have kept Hong Kong, made Hong Kong, such an anachronism all these years. But you're not going to object to any of that, are you?'

'No,' he admitted reluctantly.

'Precisely. Then there's the business side of things. I've no doubt that Beijing will put its oar in. What government can resist filling a regulation vacuum with new rules? But the essential work ethic will remain. In fact, Beijing is relying on Hong Kong to be the engine room for the capitalist revolution that has already begun in China.'

She looked into Jonny's eyes, willing him to share her enthusiasm. 'This is not a time for you to run away. It's an opportunity for you to use your experience for the good of Hong Kong. Stay, Jonny. Stay on and use everything you've learned in your years there. Help Hong Kong make the transition. You can be a real force for change, for good. It is a chance for you to do something you can believe in.'

Her words began to beat back the tide of loneliness and depression with which he had lived for so long. Perhaps there was a chance of making a different kind of new life in the colony, of sweeping the place clean of the scum who had corrupted it for so long. It would be a vindication of everything he had tried to do during his police career. Perhaps he really could make a difference.

CHAPTER 20

AS HIS DRIVER negotiated the sleeping policemen under the watchful eye of the security cameras and the heavily armed guards, Bryan reflected how much Gough Barracks had changed in forty years.

On June 17, 1954, the British were made to look like the amateurs they were at the time. That morning twenty men rendezvoused in the Republican town of Dundalk for the journey over the border to Armagh and the headquarters of the Royal Irish Fusiliers in Gough Barracks in Armagh City.

The IRA had done their planning well. A week earlier two volunteers had gone to the barracks for a dance in the sergeants' mess. During what everyone thought was a passion break, the couple made a detailed tour of the barracks sketching and noting sentries and guard posts as they strolled through the grounds.

The truck arrived at the barracks just after lunch and an IRA man approached the single sentry to ask about enlisting in the British Army. Once he was close enough, the IRA man drew his pistol and ushered the startled sentry into the guardhouse where he was tied up. The truck then drove into the barracks and, using the guardhouse keys, the men broke into the armoury. Over the next half-hour, they loaded 250 rifles, 37 Sten guns, 9 Bren machine-guns and 40 training rifles. Others of the unit left on duty at the gate – complete with British

Army uniforms – escorted soldiers and visitors into the guardhouse where they, too, were tied up. By the time the IRA men left, there were eighteen soldiers and one civilian under guard.

After cutting the telephone lines, the IRA men drove unhindered to the border and then into the Republic. The British had been completely unprepared for such a brazen assault. The single sentry on guard duty had no ammunition for his gun; there was no effective method of raising the alarm; relations between north and south were such that it was several hours before news of the raid reached the border and by that time the IRA unit had made good its escape. It was also striking that rather than killing the British soldiers, the IRA men had simply tied them up. Nowadays such a humanitarian approach would be unthinkable.

Today Gough Barracks is a major base for the British Army in South Armagh but the lessons of that IRA raid have been well learned. The perimeter of the barracks is a six-foot-high grey stone wall which has been topped by brown ten-foot-high metal screens. A watch tower is incorporated into the wall, giving the whole place the feeling and atmosphere of a prison camp. It helps make Northern Ireland look like the colony of an occupying power.

After parking the car behind the barracks' social club, Bryan left his driver and walked the fifty yards to a single-storey, redbrick building which until 1991 was the headquarters for special operations in the Armagh area. Known as the Task Coordination Group, the different branches of Special Forces and Intelligence would be briefed in this building before going out on an operation. Then the TCG was moved to the Mahon Road Barracks in Portadown where most of the day-to-day business is run. But some operations are still organized at Gough, partly because it is closer to the border and partly because all the equipment is there and most of the people involved are familiar with the place.

Bryan moved through a plain wooden door which was propped open by an old copy of the *Belfast Telegraph* jammed under it. He moved forward and stopped in front of a camera that peered down at him from the wall to his right. So many of these precautions were ridiculous, he thought. He had spent many long hours running operations from this building and he knew that if the outer door was shut then there was insufficient light for the security camera to work. The people inside always let you in anyway.

He pressed the buzzer by the door and a moment later heard the click that released the door handle. He walked in, turned right through a swing door and walked into the general office.

As always he was struck by how seedy the place looked. The door to the room is painted the colour of Newcastle Brown ale, a different shade of brown marks the coloured tiles on the floor, a third shade of lighter brown is painted on the bottom half of the wall with a beige colouring the top half. There are seven brown desks surrounded by dark green or grey filing cabinets. It's a sour and depressing place which the transient occupiers treat as a way station from the comfort of a proper base to the discomfort of action and back again.

The only bright spot in the room is a huge map of Northern Ireland, eight feet high and fifteen feet long. The map is covered in a plastic skin with perhaps two dozen little red boxes marked on with a chinagraph pencil. These denote out-of-bounds areas where either a covert operation is going on or a suspicious object has been spotted. The grid reference is marked on orange sticky tape which is then pinned above or below each box. A line of tape strips hangs from the bottom of the map ready for use. The red boxes are imitated on every Army map in every command post around the province to ensure that no ordinary foot patrol blunders into a covert operation or, even more important, that the two sides don't start shooting at each other.

On the right-hand side of the map, the plastic covering had torn and was hanging slightly away from the main body. Bryan was reminded of a snake he had come across once shedding its skin. The difference here was that this skin was permanent and would probably get much worse before anything was done.

A television monitor, which acts as a relay from the camera by the entrance door, is mounted on the wall to the left of the map. Along the next wall is a green pinboard which contains a photographic display of the latest terrorists sighted in the area and a calendar showing a bare-breasted woman leaning back against a saddled horse. This artwork is supplied courtesy of Detective Steve Potts of the Special Branch who has an account with the A1 betting shop downtown.

As Bryan walked in, a young captain, whose shoulder patch showed him to be from the Royal Green Jackets, finished speaking and hung up the telephone which dominated the desk. This was a Goliath, a coded telephone which is secure from IRA penetration for up to twelve hours. The man stood up and saluted. 'Afternoon, Colonel. You've set us an interesting challenge this time.'

Bryan knew Richard Ellis from previous incarnations, first in the Intelligence Corps and then on detachment to Army headquarters in Lisburn where Ellis had been on the staff of Commander Land Forces with special responsibility for liaising with the RUC on covert operations. Today, Ellis was in command of the second detachment of the 14th Intelligence and Security Group, a unit of twenty men who would be handling the security for tonight's mission. Bryan liked the man. He was enthusiastic without being gung ho and had a sense of humour which after a while became a requirement for continued sanity.

'I thought you might enjoy it, Richard. Must make a change from selling houses in the Derry,' he added with a smile.

As the conflict in Northern Ireland had expanded in the 1970s, so the British Army had developed ever more complex methods of fighting the underground war. There had been an initial deployment of the SAS by Harold Wilson in 1974 but, even before then, Brigadier Frank Kitson, fresh from Kenya and Malaya and eager to apply the lessons he had learned in other insurgencies, had established the Mobile Reconnaissance Force. This small group of soldiers used IRA informers, known as Freds, to point out other terrorists, their safe houses and their ammunition dumps. The MRF also set up a massage parlour, a laundry and a taxi service. They had some success until one of the Freds became a triple agent and betrayed the existence of the organization and some of its operations.

The Army changed its name to the 14th Intelligence Company and this evolved into the 14th Intelligence and Security Group, which is about a hundred strong and carries out the vast majority of the Army's covert operations in Northern Ireland today. Its speciality is surveillance. The SAS tend to be used only if some extreme violence is likely.

The week before the Tunnel had been seized, a major undercover operation by the Group had resulted in the arrest of forty-five IRA supporters working in Derry, Belfast and Armagh. The Army had established Brennan's Estate Agency to draw in the IRA who had been blackmailing such businesses to launder their money through fake mortgages and illegal property sales. For two years, it had been one of the most successful 14th Int and Sy Group's operations ever and Ellis was understandably pleased.

'My men could do with a bit of fresh air, Colonel. Although with the forecast I've seen, they may get a bit wet.'

Bryan made himself a cup of instant coffee and stood sipping it, grateful for the warmth and the comfort of the

hot cup in his hands. He could sense the tension beginning to mount. For some reason he had never been able
to fathom, he felt it in his right lower eyelid first. Now he
was conscious of it flickering and, as always, he worried
that everyone could see this sign of nerves. But he knew
that the eye would settle down once he was out of here
and on the road.

A door at the far end of the room opened and a head
with a shock of bright red hair peered round the edge,
spotted Ellis and shouted, 'We're all set, Richard. Whenever you're ready.'

'Be right with you,' he replied and turned to Bryan.
'Well, Colonel, we'd better go and see what they have
planned for us.'

The two men walked through the door into a narrow
corridor and then through a second door to the briefing
room. This is smaller than the general office and is
known to everyone in the building as the sergeant's
office. Next door is the superintendent's office which is
where operational briefings are usually given.

Bryan could see that today the sergeant's office was
needed as the five bright orange plastic chairs were
already occupied and other men perched on the edge of
four of the desks. The briefer, a lieutenant from the
Black Watch, was sitting behind a desk in the far corner
facing the room. To his right was another large map of
the Province alongside an aerial photograph of Crossmaglen. To the left of the briefer was the office dart
board, which has been so well used that pieces of wood
and felt hang from the surface. Next to it was a line of
plaques presented by men from different regiments who
have passed through. The only clue to the real purpose
of the room was a hand-drawn picture of three SAS
soldiers in black assault gear and a limited edition print
of the painting of the SAS siege of the Iranian embassy.

Bryan knew there would be no introductions here. But
he had been around long enough to be able to identify

everyone in the room, if not by name, certainly by affili-
ation. Over the years, each of the groups working for the
security forces had developed clear dress codes and everyone tended to conform, consciously or unconsciously.

Box's representative was sitting against the left-hand
wall smoking a cigarette. His dark grey suit and white
shirt meant little but the striped tie and the black half-
brogues were distinctive marks, as was the more expensive
cut and material of the suit. Next to him was another
civilian, also in a suit but with the type of soft grey shoes
that Bryan always associated with state school teachers.
He would be a Special Branch officer. The liaison officer
from Military Intelligence headquarters at Lisburn was
perched on the edge of the desk to Bryan's left, the check
of the Viyella shirt, the round-necked blue wool jumper
and the olive green corduroy trousers his required civilian
uniform. Despite the civilian 'disguise', he still wore his
army issue watch.

The four members of 14th Int and Sy Group each
wore black or brown bomber jackets, jeans and running
shoes, and they were all smoking. Lung cancer had
become a hazard of the posting as the men always carry
packs of cigarettes to offer to any local they meet. To
cement the relationship they have to light up as well.

One man seated in an orange chair off to one side
wore a green duvet jacket, black jeans and a pair of
Timberland walking shoes. He had replaced his army
watch with a black plastic-strapped shock-proof diving
watch (good to four atmospheres, tells the time in three
zones and will remember the wife's birthday). That was
SAS uniform.

Bryan was amused to note that he himself was wearing
the senior officer's civilian uniform of twill trousers,
wool shirt, plain tie, tweed jacket and Barbour jacket. Ah
well, he thought, you have to expect soldiers to conform
to something.

'Right, gentlemen,' Ellis began. 'Most of you know

each other so I won't bother with introductions. We're here to be briefed for Operation Zinc and I'll hand you over to Lieutenant David Hughes for the details.'

There was a shuffling as each of the men in the room positioned pens and pencils over their notepads. Hughes was a spare, dark-jawed man of around thirty with dark curly hair and enormous jug ears. He was dressed in a rugby shirt, jeans and scruffy Reebok running shoes. He stood up, extracted an expanding metal pointer from his trouser pocket and moved closer to the map.

'As we speak, the Army and RUC are beginning Operation Scorpion, which is a sweep through the Republican areas of Belfast, Derry and Crossmaglen. This is in direct response to the seizing of the Channel Tunnel this morning by the IRA. The intention of Scorpion is to lift as many Republicans as we can find and to apply maximum pressure in the shortest amount of time to try and encourage the Boys to sue for peace. At the same time, a number of separate operations are under way to lift known IRA terrorists in the sticks.

'Operation Zinc is not part of either of these but is nonetheless related to the IRA's activities in the Tunnel. The objective is to insert Colonel Dickens here.' His baton pointed to a small red box that had been drawn around an area between Warrenpoint and Rostrevor on the shore of Carlingford Lough, south-east of Newry.

There is no real manual written for handling briefings and styles vary from officer to officer. Some will tell the men only the most limited information on a strict 'need to know' criterion. The actual operators are told 'what' the operation is, 'who' is involved directly affecting them and 'how' they will carry out the mission. They are rarely told 'why' an operation is required. In this way, all the operators are protected by only being able to react to a situation as they see it on the ground. There is then less room for confusion, personal agendas and judgments based on out-of-date information.

'The colonel will be in the area for approximately forty minutes and he will be meeting with one individual and then returning alone. Our job is to make sure that the colonel is well protected both going in and coming out. At the same time, we want to make sure that we hear and record everything that is said at the meet.'

'Are we going in ahead to fix that?' one of the men in the orange seats asked.

'No. As you will have gathered this is a short notice op and there's no time to do anything other than scout the area. Also, we are not sure of the precise location so sensors probably won't do the job.

'We've fixed the colonel up with a mike and we will establish a scrape overlooking the beach with a laser mike. That way we have a back-up.

'We will drive to the area in three cars. The lead car will go thirty minutes early, followed by the colonel and the trail car five minutes behind. We'll be in radio contact on the portables which should stop the Boys listening in, but keep the chatter to a minimum.

'The forecast is for rain and it could be bloody out there. I want you in as close as you can get so that if anything goes wrong we can pull the colonel out. There'll be two helos a couple of minutes away if things go badly wrong. ETD will be thirty minutes from now.

'Any questions?'

Bryan had just arrived home at his house in Ballymullen Road in the village of Crawfordsburn south of Belfast when the telephone had rung.

'Colonel Dickens?' a voice with a strong Northern Ireland accent had asked.

'Speaking.'

'This is Gerry Adams. I would like a meeting.'

He had been astonished to hear the voice of a man whom he knew better than his own wife but whom he had never actually met. The fact that Adams had his phone number was not such a surprise – the IRA have had informants in British Telecom for years and regularly tap both the military and civilian lines. But that Adams should risk direct contact was extraordinary.

'Just why should I agree to that?'

There was a small chuckle at the other end. 'Oh, I think you'll agree just out of curiosity. But I want to meet because we have matters of mutual interest to discuss regarding the Tunnel. I suggest you come to me as I'm out of town at present.'

'Very well. But we'll have to agree some ground rules,' said Dickens. 'We both come alone. We must both meet in the open outside the city. There must be no record of the conversation.'

'Agreed. I am at my holiday home which I am sure you know about. I have a little boat down here and can row across the lough to meet you in the north.'

He had given the location of a pebble beach west of Rostrevor and agreed a rendezvous for that evening.

There was no question of Dickens going to the meeting without cover and without making sure that all the powers had signed off on such a politically sensitive confrontation. He had no qualms about lying to Adams. After all, the IRA leader was hardly going to be shot by the Brits, while there was every possibility that he, Dickens, could be gunned down in a trap set by Adams or by his comrades.

There had been an hour of frantic meetings at Lisburn, first with the Commander Land Forces' Chief of Staff, then with CLF himself. Northern Ireland Office had been brought in and then there had been checks to London. To Bryan's surprise, there was great enthusiasm for the meeting.

'We've flushed them out early in the game,' CLF had exclaimed. 'Now's the chance to go in for the kill.'

Six hours later, after the briefing in Gough Barracks, he

was standing on the beach on the edge of Carlingford
Lough. His feet were soaked. The rain was driving in a
classic Northern Ireland downpour almost horizontally
across the lake so that the Barbour jacket, which only
came down just below his buttocks, gave no protection
to his legs which were also soaked. Visibility was cut to
fifty yards.

On his head Bryan had one of those waterproof hats
that look like a fisherman's sou'wester. They may look
good, he thought miserably, but they never stop the drips
from sliding down your neck. He shuddered as another
dribble coursed down his spine.

He had been peering around nervously for fifteen
minutes waiting for Adams to appear but there had been
neither sight nor sound of him. Then, suddenly, Dickens
saw a dark shape loom out of the rain and a moment
later Adams was clearly recognizable, his beard and rain-
spotted glasses quite distinctive.

Neither man offered to shake hands. There was too
much blood under the bridge for years of enmity to be
overcome in one meeting.

'So, Colonel, I'm sorry if I'm a little late but the
weather's bloody and rowing is no fun in the rain,'
Adams began. 'You're here alone, I trust?

Dickens nodded.

'And no recordings, no fancy infra-red video recordings to embarrass me later?'

'None at all. I gave you my word.' Dickens thought
the lie sounded both pompous and implausible and
doubted whether Adams, whose distrust of the Brits was
almost pathological, really believed him.

'Very well.' Adams seemed to take a deep breath,
steeling himself. 'I asked you here because of this bloody
business in the Channel Tunnel –'

'I know that, Gerry,' Dickens interrupted. 'But you
don't normally ask us to discuss your operations. What
makes this one different?'

'The difference is that this one is nothing to do with us.'

'Oh come on, Gerry,' Dickens scoffed. 'You guys claimed responsibility. The right code word, the right timing, everything. Just because it's getting a little warm in the kitchen, you can't expect me to buy that kind of line.'

'But it's true,' Adams replied, his voice rising to make himself heard above the wind and rain. 'It's nothing to do with us. It's not our people; not our idea; not our operation. We didn't plan it. We didn't do it. In fact, even if we had wanted to – and we may have looked at it once – I'm telling you we haven't got enough people to pull something like that off.'

'Gerry, Gerry,' Dickens exclaimed, his head moving from side to side in dismissal of Adams's words. 'Why on earth should I believe you? We are in the middle of the biggest sweep against your people since Motorman in the seventies. Your lot are on the ropes and if what I hear is right, you've even got some troubles inside your own high command. I hear that the militants may be winning, Gerry. That you're about to be sidelined.'

'Look, Colonel. I don't know what's going on here. All I know is that some bastards have done this in our name and we're being given a hard time for something we didn't do.'

'Well, Gerry, I hear what you say but what am I supposed to do about it?' Dickens asked, his tone still mocking.

Adams drew a deep breath to control his temper and began to take small paces back and forth along the beach in front of Bryan, his feet making small crunching noises. 'You may be right that there is some concern inside the Movement that we have not been active enough. You and I both know that there are those who want more emphasis on the military struggle. That is not in your interests and it's not in mine either.

'What you're doing in the Six Counties tonight – the arrests, the searches, all of that – will strengthen the hand of those who want to use the bullet and not the ballot. The killing will escalate, more people will die both here and on the mainland . . .'

The greatest challenge and the greatest satisfaction for any intelligence officer is that critical moment between seduction and consummation. It is the time when the slightest error can break the delicate thread that binds two people together and it requires experience and great skill to handle properly. Dickens could feel his pulse race and the dryness of his mouth contrasted with his dripping wet face. This was the moment.

'We certainly have no interest in seeing the violence get any worse,' Dickens admitted. 'But on the other hand, whatever you or I may think, the politicians have to respond to public pressure and there is outrage over the Tunnel. That's probably going to get worse if there isn't a peaceful resolution, which I have to say doesn't look very likely at the moment. If I'm to placate my political masters, I'll have to give them something, some gesture of goodwill that will show them you mean what you say; that this whole Tunnel affair is not your fault.'

'What exactly do you have in mind?' Adams asked warily.

Dickens paused as if seeking inspiration. 'One thing that might convince them would be details about some of your people in the field. I'm sure they wouldn't need much,' he continued persuasively. 'We are particularly anxious to find Sean Thomas who has been active in England recently. Perhaps if you could point us in his direction, or give us some idea of his next target . . .?'

Adams's mouth opened for an immediate denial as he began calculating the options and weighing up the political considerations. He cast his mind back to the conversation in his caravan with Gerry Kelly. The choice for him was clear. Silence would mean his eclipse but the

Movement would probably survive. If he provided the information, it would mean that the single most important reason for Kelly's current influence – the success of the campaign in England – would be removed. At the same time, his position at the top of the Movement would be secure once again.

'I'll let you have a decision in two hours,' Adams replied.

Dickens had watched Adams think it through. He knew that for a politician like Adams there was really no choice at all. Once he had made it, Adams was a lost soul. The microphone hidden in the top button of his shirt was ensuring a record of the conversation for posterity. There would be no need to expose Adams's duplicity. Instead, the IRA leader would work for him. It would take years, but in the end the organization would be destroyed from within.

There were no farewells as the two men turned and crunched their way off the beach.

CHAPTER 21

TWENTY MINUTES EARLIER Dai Choi had received the message on his radio receiver that an attack was imminent. There had been no details, just the few words that were enough to alert him and his men to the approaching threat.

He had laid his trap with care. His men were dispersed either side of the two carriages, lying flat against the tracks or hunched behind small piles of pebbles that had been carefully scraped off the Tunnel floor. They would offer scant protection against shrapnel or bullets but they gave an illusion of a defence and so were an important psychological asset for his men.

When the attack came, Dai Choi hoped that none of those approaching would get close enough to fire at anything, let alone hit his team. He had prepared his ground and he hoped this would not be a fight but an execution.

He heard the light crackle of shoes treading softly on the gravel and then the shadowy form of Kang Sheng loomed in front of him. He leaned down from the doorway of the carriage so that his head was on the same level as his lieutenant's. The whisper was so soft as to be almost imagined and he could feel the man's hot breath, sense his excitement. 'They're coming. We've picked them up on the night sights. About twenty so far, maybe more.'

313

'Good,' Dai Choi replied. 'Make sure there is no shooting.' He grinned wolfishly, his teeth making a brief flash of white in the darkness. 'Let them come.' His head bobbed, a small gesture of appreciation to himself for his forethought and planning. 'Let them come.'

Stewart Lawrence was terrified. This was not the simple fear of a darkened room or a high building. It was not even the fear of reprimand or retribution. This was the gut-wrenching, nerve-tightening panic that turns bowels to water. With every step he had to remember to clamp his buttocks together in case he soiled himself.

He could feel and smell the acrid, pungent aroma of sweat, his body working overtime to keep pace with his free-floating imagination which had already reached journey's end in the black hole that stretched ahead of him.

To left and right he could see the others from the Special Patrol Unit. They appeared a ghostly green through his night-vision goggles, each a distinct and bulky shape who walked as if through treacle. Each foot rose and fell in slow motion in an attempt to keep the noise to a minimum. It would have been funny if it wasn't so frightening.

He should have been reassured by the familiarity of the Kevlar helmet and the Armourshield GPV 25 body armour that can stop a .357 magnum at ten feet. His face was covered with an SF10 Respirator which had an inbuilt Davies CT100 communications system. By pressing a large button on his chest he could speak to others in the unit while his earpiece received a constant stream of messages from the team leader.

At his waist in a quick-snap release holster was a 9 mm Browning automatic pistol and across his chest a Steyr Aug 5.56 mm semi-automatic rifle hung from a harness. Lawrence had his right hand around the trigger and backsight while his left gripped the barrel. That way, if anything happened, he could swivel the gun into action.

Others in the group carried all the paraphernalia of a

modern counter-terrorist unit: pump-action shotguns for close-quarter work, which could fire pellets, solid shot or gas; flash-bang grenades to stun and blind the terrorists. But this was a recce and so a few special items had been added. One of the guys carried an infra-red video camera that would record everything inside the Tunnel for later analysis; another carried a still camera with superfast film; yet another carried a long tube which was in fact a directional microphone that would relay all conversations picked up inside the Tunnel back to the teams waiting outside.

Much of this should have had the familiarity of routine but nothing had prepared Stewart for the present situation. Their training had been for a fast assault against a known target: grenades through windows followed by the blowing off of doors and the rescue of hostages. The good would triumph over the bad in a few seconds of exhilarating action. This was very different: a slow stalk through the darkness where every step was threatened by unseen eyes and every limb a potential target for the hidden sniper.

'Why me, why me,' he muttered over and over again as his toes delicately searched for the next noiseless step. He knew there was no answer to the question but his mind cried out the litany, hoping for a reprieve.

He had joined the SPU because his mate John had and it seemed like a pretty good idea at the time: lots of high-tech kit, a bit of travel, the challenge of something new and the opportunity to be part of an élite.

When the Tunnel was under construction, the Kent police had quietly begun the formation of a special team to deal with any crises that might arise. There were already hostage rescue units and groups trained to respond to armed attacks of one kind or another. But the Tunnel was seen as a particular problem requiring dedicated, specially trained people. John was his great mate on the force. He was the leader; Stewart tended to follow.

At his prodding, Stewart had signed up as well and the two men had gone through the six weeks of intensive training together.

There had been plenty of walk-throughs in the Tunnel and endless discussions about different scenarios, most of which had revolved around hostage-taking by an individual or a gang. Then they had gone off for a week to put some of the theory into practice with the SAS.

He had read about the Regiment and accorded it the kind of status that politicians reserve for Churchill or strategists for Liddell Hart. But he had been surprised to find that they didn't go to the SAS headquarters at Sterling Lines in Hereford at all. Instead, the coach had taken them through the town and then south-west on to the A465 Abergavenny road. Just after Kenderchurch, about ten miles outside Hereford, the bus turned left and into the small village of Pontrilas.

The camp lies just outside the village and is spread over about a hundred acres, surrounded by a wire fence topped with razor wire. The whole perimeter is regularly patrolled by armed Military Police who interrogate anybody who stops anywhere near the camp. Such security is something of a farce, however, as a village road runs straight through the middle of the camp. At various times, the SAS have tried to get the road closed on security grounds, but each time the local farmers have protested and the road has stayed open.

Inside the camp there are buildings, bunkers, firing ranges and an extremely difficult obstacle course which the SAS training sergeants love to tell outsiders takes the Regiment's men eight minutes to complete. Stewart staggered around in twenty-five minutes and felt completely wiped out at the end.

The week they spent was continually humiliating for the SPU men. The SAS trainers tried to build up their confidence but it was clear that they wanted standards of which the policemen were incapable. Where reaction times of seconds were required, they often took minutes; where initiative was needed, the police simply could not solve the problems.

Still, Stewart had been reassured by the emphasis that all the instructors both at Pontrilas and at police headquarters had placed on the security systems outside the Tunnel. It would be impossible, they were assured, to penetrate the security screen. So, the most likely target of all their training would be the lone madman with a knife.

That was one of the reasons why the briefing this afternoon had come as such a shock.

'The Tunnel has been taken over by a group of men who we assume are well armed,' the inspector had begun. 'Numbers are unclear but we think at least ten men are holding more than seventy hostages inside two train carriages past the ten-mile mark.' He had pointed to the map of the Tunnel to his left and indicated the spot. 'Your job is to go in there and gather intelligence on numbers, arms and the location and nature of any defences.

'I want to stress that this is a reconnaissance mission. You are to avoid contact with the terrorists and you will only use your weapons if you are fired upon. We are making this a unit-strength operation so that if anything does go wrong, you will be able to get out again without difficulty.'

'Fucking hell,' John had muttered to Stewart. 'No numbers, no weapons and no location. This sounds like a right fucking disaster waiting to happen.'

Stewart had nodded, the band of fear already tightening across his chest.

Now he could hear the rasping of his breath inside the respirator grow in volume and frequency the further down the Tunnel he walked.

He was about halfway down the small group that was spread out over about thirty yards of the Tunnel, with men moving along either side, some on the walkway along the right wall and others moving either side of the tracks.

'Blue unit, I can see the carriages ahead,' Stewart heard in his headphones. The point man, moving forty yards ahead of the rest, had picked up the heat from the people inside the carriage through his night-vision goggles. Stewart narrowed his eyes, trying to see something in the darkness. He wanted the reassurance of a hot spot, some kind of target that would reduce the fear from the unknown to the known.

It was the point man's body that broke the photo-electric beam that ran across the Tunnel. By breaking the beam, an electrical relay in a tiny integrated circuit tripped, allowing the current to flow to the electric detonator. It was the final connection in the circuit, which heated the element inside the device and in turn set off a chemical reaction within the explosive compound.

The first flat package of Demex exploded with a shattering blast of heat and light. The ball bearings that had been so carefully stuck to its surface sprayed out with a noise like the hum of a swarm of bees. There was no room for the ball bearings to spread into a wide arc and they struck the scout's body with tremendous force.

A single ball bearing pressed into the flesh makes a small indentation, pushing the skin into a tiny hollow made by the circle of metal. Fifty ball bearings hitting flesh at 5,000 feet per second behave very differently.

The man was struck in the chest and staggered under the impact. His Kevlar vest protected his heart and lungs from the worst of the blast, but the cover stopped at his waist and it was his abdomen that bore the brunt of the assault. Each ball bearing forced its way through the skin with devastating power. Unlike a bullet which has a point to drill a hole, a ball just punches a hole through the body mass. Flesh, blood vessels and bone were literally torn apart as twenty of the little metal spheres bludgeoned into his frame. In fractions of a second, his legs were severed from his torso and the man collapsed on the ground. His lungs and heart, which had been so well protected by the Kevlar vest, continued to pump his life away into the pebbles on the Tunnel floor.

Dai Choi had prepared his trap well. The single Claymore with the photo-electric cell was connected by wire to the other mines that led back down the Tunnel towards the entrance. He had positioned them high and low and on both sides so that anyone coming behind the first man to break through the light beam would be caught in a withering crossfire.

Stewart neither saw nor heard the lead man die. He saw the first explosion and felt the shock wave. Immediately there was a series of ear-rupturing explosions that seemed to compress and pulverize his body. There was the sound of angry hornets and then the screaming began. He could hear the cries of men all around him; horrifying and invisible. He looked around frantically but could see nothing, his night-vision goggles turned into a white fog by the blaze of the explosions. Instinctively, his hand reached up to his respirator and tore at the straps. He tossed it aside and looked around searching for John, for answers, help, a target, anything that would explain what had happened.

He saw fires where some of the men had been caught directly by the blast of the explosives and their clothing had been set alight. He looked again for John and saw his friend lying by the track. Black blood was fountaining out of a gaping wound in his throat like oil from a gusher. He could see the whites of his friend's eyes and heard him try to say something but the effort was too much and the eyes closed. He watched a moment longer as pumping blood ebbed and then died.

He turned to run, his only thought now one of escape, the light of the Tunnel mouth a tiny imagined window beckoning in the far distance.

At the first step, his leg collapsed beneath him and he

fell to the ground. He looked down and saw a hole the size of his fist in his right thigh. He could feel no pain and at first it was as if the terrible wound belonged to somebody else. Then his mind made the connection from what he saw to his own flesh and sinew. He turned to one side and heaved vomit on to the track.

He could feel the wetness of the blood soaking his leg and he tried to stuff his fist into the wound to stanch the flow, but it made no difference. He tried to raise himself but again his leg collapsed beneath him. He tried to cry out but he seemed to have no strength left. Suddenly a quick, deep chill swept the length of his body. He laid his head back against the ground, feeling the sharpness of the pebbles against his skull. The last sounds he heard were the tortured screams of the wounded and the dying echoing and re-echoing down through the darkness of the Tunnel.

In the train carriage, Kate Carr had been woken by the explosions and the screams. She had been dozing in the darkness. Although they had only been underground for around twelve hours, she had lost all sense of time. Her watch had marked the passage of the minutes and the hours but those facts seemed somehow unrelated to the reality of her position. The tension had exhausted her and the lack of communication with her captors or with her fellow passengers had given her no relief from the strange mixture of boredom and terror which is the experience of all hostages.

She had been sleeping with Emma's head in her lap and her husband Tom beside her in the aisle seat. Their captors had banned all conversation so there had been no opportunity for reassurance or plotting. Nor had they been allowed to leave their seats, despite the pleas of the elderly and the parents on behalf of their children. The result was that the carriage was filled with the pungent stench of sweat and the sickly aroma of faeces and urine.

They had all woken up with the explosions and for a moment they had hoped that rescue was imminent. Then when the sounds grew no nearer and there appeared to be no sign of alarm among their captors, they knew that whatever had happened it meant nothing good for them.

Kate watched as Dai Choi came into the carriage, his body dark and ominous in the yellow emergency lighting. He was shining a torch ahead of him, letting the beam run across the faces of the passengers to left and right. As he came level with their seats, the beam caught Tom square in the face and, to her horror, stopped.

She saw the Chinese's hand reach into the beam and then grip Tom's arm to pull him up. She pushed Emma aside and tried to get out of the seat to help her husband. Dai Choi let go of Tom's arm and, with an almost casual gesture, flicked his hand across the middle seat and into her face. She was tossed back against the carriage wall, her head a flaring mass of agony.

By the time she had recovered her wits, Tom was halfway down the aisle, struggling in the grip of Dai Choi and another of the guards. Emma was sobbing, her child's instinct making her keep her distress as quiet as possible to avoid attracting any further unwanted attention. Kate put an arm around her daughter's shoulders to provide a reassurance she did not feel. She tried to follow her husband through the window but could only see a very narrow angle of the track. The dark shadows came briefly into her line of sight and then moved away. A moment later she heard a bang and saw the flash of an explosion reflected against the Tunnel wall.

She knew it had been a gunshot, had known from the moment the gunmen had come to their seat what the end was going to be. She imagined his body falling to the ground and lying there crumpled, lifeless and alone. Crying silently, she brought Emma to her and rocked her gently back and forth against her breast.

*

Dai Choi ordered two of his soldiers to pick up the body and they dragged it to the back of the first carriage, the shoes of the dead man making small clicking sounds as they bounced over the gravel.

At the end of the second carriage, the Chinese had opened the rolling steel shutters and put two of the escape ladders that are provided with every carriage on to the track. A white Vauxhall Cavalier had been rolled down the improvized ramp and on to the track. Kang Sheng hotwired the ignition to start the engine. Then Tom Carr's body was dumped in the driver's seat, strapped upright and his hands laced through the steering wheel and tied.

One of the terrorists got into the passenger seat and steered the car down to the carnage that marked the spot where the assault team had been destroyed.

Strolling behind the car, Dai Choi reflected that his men had indeed set the perfect trap. Bodies littered the track and his nose wrinkled as his nostrils took in the powerful stench of fresh blood mixed with the sweetness of burned flesh and the sour smell of cordite. The occasional scream or groan broke the silence as the wounded looked in vain to their visitors for succour.

His men poked among the bodies, turning some over to inspect for signs of life, moving others out of the way of the moving car. Once the vehicle was through the trap, it stopped and the terrorists opened the back doors. Four of the wounded men were piled into the back seat, their bodies flung into the car so that limbs dangled outside the open doors. Dead bodies were piled on top until the car looked like a twentieth-century version of a wagon used to carry away the dead during the Black Death.

Dai Choi stepped forward, slid a piece of paper over the end of a knife blade and then plunged the weapon into the chest of the unfeeling Tom Carr. There was a sighing sound as trapped air escaped from the dead man's lungs.

Dai Choi put the car in second gear, jammed Carr's foot on the accelerator and took off the handbrake. Uncertainly at first, and then more smoothly as it picked up speed, the car with its awful cargo began its journey out of the Tunnel.

Twelve hours earlier the scene that Harry Ritchie had seen as he entered the Tunnel was familiar and dull. Two enormous circular holes let into a concrete embankment marked the entrance to the British Tunnel and the exit of the French line. For 200 yards back from the entrance, concrete walls lined both sides, to control rock slides and to help draw off rainwater from running directly on to the tracks and then into the Tunnel.

Now, the scene was very different. The tracks were covered with all the equipment that the Army and police find they need in a crisis. Furthest away from the Tunnel mouths, several Army and police trucks were parked. Inside, men played cards, drank tea and listened to directional microphones aimed at the Tunnel or watched infra-red cameras to spot any movement. Closer to the Tunnel, barriers had been set up to stop the terrorists in the unlikely event that they found a way of driving the train out and making their escape. Behind the barriers, snipers rested their rifles and other men watched anxiously through thermal imagers, infra-red systems and even, for those lower down the totem, simple binoculars.

The site was filled with people. There were the Army in green camouflage, the police response units with their distinctive blue berets, the Special Forces dressed all in black, ordinary coppers in their blue uniforms and ambulance men who had moved forward as the first explosions came echoing out of the Tunnel.

The whole area was flooded with harsh white light from the portable floodlights set up as darkness fell.

Half an hour earlier, there had been the noise of organized chaos as people ran back and forth with messages, the chatter of portable radios and the revving of car engines. Now there was silence as everyone waited for news from inside

When the first explosions had been picked up by the microphones, there had been a hurried conference among the commanders. Attempts to raise the men on their radios had failed but that was not unexpected as their communications system would not work out of line of sight. The police inspector who had briefed his men wanted to go in immediately, but wiser counsel prevailed and they decided to wait and see what had happened before taking a decision on what to do next.

Then, suddenly, the door to one of the Army radio vans opened and a head appeared around the door. 'There's a car coming,' the voice shouted and then the head ducked back inside.

There was a flurry of activity as police and Army took the positions they had been assigned in the event of an attack. There was a brief clatter as weapons were cocked and launchers primed.

The front line could hear the noise of a revving engine interspersed with a crashing, grating noise as a car lurched from side to side against the Tunnel walls. Out of the darkness a white shape appeared, first a blur and then defined as a small saloon car. Then it was out of the Tunnel, engine still revving, careering straight for the first crash barrier. A popping sound echoed through the air as the car tyres hit the spikes in the road and punctured. There was a crash as the car hit the concrete block.

For a moment there was silence apart from the hissing of the car radiator spurting water on to the engine block. A strangled cry from inside the car broke the spell and there was a rush for the vehicle.

Constable Frankie Ward of the Blue Berets was the first man to reach the driver's door. He wrenched it open and then jerked back as the carnage inside the car was revealed. The ride had thrown the bodies around so that blood now covered the roof and the seats and the windows.

There was no honour for the dead. The men who minutes earlier were husbands and sons were now just brutalized objects. The act of opening the door had freed Tom Carr's body from its bindings and it slid gracelessly out of the vehicle so that the waist and chest hung down, the head just touching the ground.

Constable Ward had to bend in what might in different circumstances have been thought a gesture of respect for the dead. But the note pinned to Carr's chest was now upside down and he wanted to see what it said. It read simply: 'Keep Out. You were warned.'

CHAPTER 22

THE DEBRIEFING FROM the Adams meeting had taken two hours and Dickens did not get home until nearly midnight. His wife was already in bed and he walked through to the sitting room to pour a whisky and try to wind down.

Sitting in the armchair staring at the empty fireplace, he thought back over the meeting. He had listened to the tapes at the barracks. Aside from the background hiss of the rain and the occasional crackle as a drop hit the mike, the recording had been perfectly clear.

Now he replayed the conversation in his head, searching for subtleties and nuances that he might have missed. He decided it had gone well. Adams had no idea that the British had listened to the conversation in the caravan between himself and Kelly, had no idea that all those conversations had been recorded for months from a small hide in the hillside directly behind the caravan. From there, a micro-transmitter beamed the information to Army headquarters at Knock where it was pored over by the intelligence analysts and then disseminated, with the sourcing suitably disguised, to Box, the RUC and others who might be interested.

That intelligence meant that Dickens had gone into the meeting well prepared but not necessarily with a winning hand. It all depended on how Adams would respond to pressure. It would depend too on how much he wanted to cling to power and how much he felt threatened by the current ascendancy of the militants in the Movement.

Dickens sipped at his whisky, allowing the liquid to do its work, the burning in his throat the prelude to the relaxing effect it would have once it reached his stomach.

What mattered now, he reflected, was the act of betrayal itself. He needed Adams to cross that line between complicity and duplicity, where he moved from merely talking of subverting his own organization to actually doing it.

Dickens had spent much of his adult life analysing the IRA and exploring the motives of its leaders. He understood and even sympathized with the flame of Republicanism which some leaders like Adams had inherited from the previous generation. He had no doubt that Republicanism would win out in the end. The British would leave Northern Ireland with some kind of fudged compromise that would allow the south a say in the north's politics and with some guarantee for the Protestants to stop them rising in revolt against the deal. It would be a good thing too, he thought: nobody really gave a damn about Northern Ireland. It was a suppurating boil on the rump of Britain and everyone knew it. The British public didn't care if the whole of Ireland sank beneath the sea. In fact they would be rather pleased to see it go. But no politician could afford to be seen to give in to the terrorists and until the IRA were a total irrelevance the Army would stay and terrorism would continue.

Where he parted company with Adams was over the use of terrorism. There could be no justification for the kind of violence Adams encouraged. The murdering of innocent civilians was never right, whatever the cause. And expanding the killings to civil servants or to men and women who worked for the British government was just an excuse to widen the terrorist net as more 'legitimate' targets became increasingly difficult to hit.

If this little ploy worked, then terrorism in England

could be stopped until the IRA inserted another team to carry out the bombings and the killings. But, by then, he could have his hooks in Adams. It would have to be played with consummate delicacy. Too much pressure and Adams would fall, too little and he would continue to run the show and be of little use. The balance would be a delicate one, but then, wasn't it always? The important thing was to create the opportunity and then manoeuvre for maximum exploitation.

The front door bell rang – God he hated the tasteless ding-dong note that seemed to accompany all government housing. Rising from his chair, he walked out of the sitting room to the front door, turned on the porch light and peered through the spyhole.

Rita stood looking directly at the tiny glass circle and her eyes met his. He took a step back, astonishment vying with concern for her safety.

He flung open the door and dragged her inside. 'Rita, for God's sake, you're mad to come here,' he whispered as his head darted to left and right to check that no one had observed her arrival. 'What the hell do you think you're doing?'

He shut the door and moved towards the sitting room. There was no sound from upstairs. His wife was used to the late-night visitors and knew enough to keep out of the way while the secret business was done.

'I've brought you a message, Bryan,' Rita replied.

There was a flatness to her voice, a hesitancy in her movements that set Bryan's antennae twitching. 'A message? What message? Who from?'

Rita turned to look at him. He noticed that her face looked terribly sad, her eyes watery with unshed tears. He had an awful premonition of what she was going to say.

'It's from Gerry Adams, Bryan,' she said.

And then he knew. All these years that bastard had been toying with him. All these years while he was being so clever, Adams had known about his relationship with Rita. He had used her just as Bryan now wanted to use him. But Adams had turned defeat not into victory but into another shabby episode in British–IRA relations. The clever British scheme designed to entrap Adams into betrayal had succeeded – but only at the price of Bryan realizing he had been fatally compromised. Now there were trades Adams could demand as a price for his silence. The choice of messenger was a signal that there were no winners in this war, only victims.

He felt the bitter taste of betrayal in his own mouth. He recalled that delicate seduction in the prison cell, the physical relationship that came later, the pride he had taken in the recruiting and running of this, his best agent. Ah, what a fool he had been.

But there was business to be done. She had come to deliver two messages: the first the knowledge that her presence alone would supply, the second the information that was worth the compromise of Rita – the price Adams would pay for continued political power. It was an expensive bargain for both sides. Now he wanted to know its full dimensions.

'So, do you have a name and a time?' he asked, his voice hard, dismissing the past and setting the tone for the future.

'The name I have been given is Sir Robert Sanford and the time is tomorrow.'

The deal made, he suddenly wanted to ask her why she had done what she had. What had led her to betray him. But then he realized he would only sound as foolish as he must appear. She hadn't betrayed anything at all. It was she who was true to her faith and he who had been courted and then seduced.

With the truth came an understanding that they had nothing between them. All those years of careful meetings in safe houses, the afternoons spent making love, the information exchanges, they had no substance. The new relationship was that of betrayer and betrayed but he was no longer sure what role he was supposed to be playing.

Bryan moved to the door, opened it and allowed her to pass out into the night.

CHAPTER 23

JONNY WALKED DOWN Whitehall, past Admiralty
House and Horse Guards, turned into the Cabinet Office
and then down to COBRA. He had listened to the news
before coming in and had heard nothing but speculation
and updates so assumed that the reconnaissance had
gone smoothly. The offices told a different story.

The main conference room was filled with the detritus
of crisis: ashtrays filled with cigarettes smoked down to
the filter; coffee cups with the overflow congealed in the
saucer, binding the cup to the base; above all, the stench
of frying. Jonny had been warned about the food at
COBRA and in particular about the breakfasts. Apparently they are delivered the night before from the canteen
at New Scotland Yard and after sitting all night are
heated in the microwave in the morning. The result is
what is supposed to be the most disgusting breakfast in
London. Judging by the smell, the reputation was well
justified, Jonny thought.

There appeared to be a lull in the activities of the
centre. There was no meeting in progress, just individuals
in and out of uniform walking around with the glazed
look that real exhaustion brings.

Jonny ducked into the communications room to ask a
soldier on duty for an update.

'Christ, it's a fucking disaster, mate,' the corporal said.
Seeing the question in Jonny's face the man continued

331

with the relish of the depressed embracing a newcomer into the brotherhood. 'Yeah, they went in last night all right. But they walked right into a fucking ambush. Cut to pieces, they were. Seventeen dead by the latest count, three in hospital. Oh, and one civilian bought it too.'

'What's happening at this end?' Jonny asked.

'Everyone's been running round with fires up their bums all night,' the soldier replied caustically. 'But nothing's actually been done. They can't decide what to do. Go in and you die. Stay out and the hostages die. Give in and its curtains for the politicians. Mug's game if you ask me.' The soldier turned back to his radio and replaced his headphones.

Jonny walked through the main room into the smaller conference area where he had met Hurd the day before. He saw John Witherow of SO13 sitting in a corner, nursing a steaming cup of coffee. The dark pouches under his eyes and the growth of stubble were mute testament to the man's exhaustion. Jonny walked over.

'I've heard the news,' he began. 'What a mess.'

Witherow only nodded, too tired to indulge in small talk.

'There must be something we can do,' Jonny persisted.

'Well, if you've got any bright ideas, do let us know. The fact is those policemen walked straight into a trap. The terrorists had laid mines in the Tunnel and the men just walked straight into them. They'd even primed them with ball bearings.' Witherow shook his head in anger and sorrow. 'It was carnage. The lads never stood a chance. Well, I'm off for a wash and brush up,' he said, levering himself out of the seat with a small groan as unwilling limbs were forced into action yet again. 'I'd better look my best for the PM and his mob. It's their party now. Poor bastards.'

Jonny glanced at his watch. There was nothing for him here and it was time to head for his rendezvous with Julie and Lin Yung.

*

Stanley Kung had taken a comfortable apartment in Clarges Street in Mayfair. It was perfectly situated within walking distance of the gambling at Les Ambassadeurs, the spinach soufflé with anchovy sauce at Langan's, and his shirtmaker in Jermyn Street, across Piccadilly. He might be running a terrorist operation but there was no need to slum it. After all, he had operated as the head of White Lotus for years in Hong Kong. Everyone who needed to know knew what he did, from the police commissioner through to the Governor, and there was never any difficulty. He did not see why a trip to London should alter his pleasure patterns at all. The police would probably not know of his existence but even if they did, there would be no evidence linking him to any of the criminals involved. And even if there were, nobody would speak out against him for fear of retribution, which would be swiftly enacted back in Hong Kong. So it was a relaxed and confident Stanley Kung who stepped out from his flat to walk across to Cork Street. He had an appointment at Waddington's to see some Nicholson sculptures.

As he left the doorway and turned left towards the junction with Curzon Street, his bodyguard fell in behind him. He might be confident but there was no point in behaving like an idiot. Anyway, Chang had been his shadow for ten years now and he would feel only half clothed without him.

He ambled along, taking in the atmosphere and admiring the attractive women who seemed to have a unique and very expensive style that was all Mayfair's own. As he came level with the junction with Fitzmaurice Place and Curzon Street, he heard a soft 'plop' behind him and then the sound of a falling body. He turned in time to see Chang's body hit the pavement and the bloody exit wound of a bullet that had torn a hole in the back of his jacket. He turned to run but already the three men had rushed past the dead bodyguard and had his arms pinned by his side. Then his arms were forced behind him and a pair of plastic handcuffs slid over his wrists. He winced as they were tightened hard enough to bite into the flesh. He opened his mouth to shout. A car pulled up next to the pavement, the rear door opened and he was half led, half pushed into the back seat. As his brain completed the instruction to his vocal chords, the car pulled away from the kerb. Any noise he might have made was drowned by the car stereo playing some unrecognizable rock music.

The car headed back down Curzon Street, crossed over Park Lane and headed north up the Edgware Road into the anonymity of North London. At the start of the journey, he tried to ask questions of his captors but they simply ignored him. All the men were Chinese so he knew this was not a matter of 'helping with inquiries' or 'taken in for questioning'. These were people like him. He was about to pay a heavy price for his over-confidence.

Twenty minutes later, after passing Lord's Cricket Ground, the car turned into Charles Lane and then turned again into the small driveway of a large Victorian house. The man in the front passenger seat pressed a small plastic box and the garage door opened in time for them to drive straight in. The door closed behind them and Stanley Kung knew that his fate was sealed.

Kung was helped out of the car with a gentleness that reflected his captors' confidence in the strength of their position. Kung knew there was little point in struggling. Instead, he tried to prepare himself mentally for the real test which he knew lay ahead.

He was taken through a white door and directly into the kitchen of the house. He looked around and simply saw rather average wooden cabinets, an oven, fridge, freezer, gas hob. He was made to sit at the wooden table and his handcuffs were removed. Just as he began to draw breath, the door opposite opened and another

Chinese walked in. Kung sensed from the movement around him that this man was a leader.

'Stanley Kung. I have wanted to meet you for a long time. My name is Lin Yung. I am head of the Guojia anquanbu in Hong Kong.'

Kung watched as the newcomer bowed slightly. So this was Lin Yung. He knew of him, of course, but their paths had never crossed before. Frantically, Kung searched his memory banks for what he knew of Lin Yung, to see if there was anything that might give him a lever into the man's mind.

He kept files on all these people, in some cases very detailed files, and as 1997 approached, he had been laying out very large sums in China itself to make sure that his files were the best. That way he could find weakness among the men soon to be his masters and position himself early to exploit it. But hc could recall nothing about Lin Yung and that fact alone told him something. If he could remember nothing that meant there was nothing that made him attractive to the White Lotus. He was clean, which meant commitment, and that meant trouble today.

'I can't say this is a pleasure,' Kung replied sarcastically. 'I assume because of the way I was brought here that you have some questions to ask – questions which, I may say, I am very probably not going to be able to answer.'

Lin Yung had been taught by his masters in Beijing that there are two different methods of interrogation. The first is the slow erosion of a man's will, its gradual corruption until the mind disintegrates and can be bent and twisted into any shape the torturer wants. The second method is the rapid application of intense psychological and physical pressure. Most men, he had been told, believe they can stand pain because they imagine only what they know and they believe in civilized bounds of behaviour. Show a man that there are no such bounds and the will breaks quickly. Lin Yung had always adopted the second method and he had found it to be most successful.

He picked up the Moulinex food processor from the kitchen counter and brought it over to the table.

'You know, Stanley, this is a very interesting device,' he began conversationally. 'It has revolutionized cooking for millions all over the world. It even brings mousses and soufflés into the range of idiots like me.' He pointed at the metal blade in the base of the clear plastic container. 'This turns at 500 revolutions a minute. It chops almost anything: steaks, carrots, lobster shells.'

Lin Yung walked back to the sink, picked up a knife and returned to the table. He gave the top of the Moulinex bowl a half-turn and lifted it off. He then pressed the knife point down to bypass the safety device that is supposed to prevent the machine working without the lid. Immediately, the two steel blades at the bottom of the bowl began spinning with a soft humming sound.

One of the guards reached forward, picked up Kung's arm and plunged it into the bottom of the bowl.

Without even a momentary pause, the blades chopped and cut through skin, tissue, veins and bone. Kung's hand was shredded by the machine. In an instant the bowl was covered with bright red blood and then there was a horrible splatting sound as larger pieces of flesh and bone were cut from his fingers.

The pain was unimaginable. Stanley Kung screamed, his mouth wide open as if the noise could somehow diminish the agony that began at the end of his right arm but spread to cover every single part of his body. It was as if every nerve had touched a red-hot flame at the same instant.

Then, just as suddenly, it was over. Lin Yung lifted the knife, the connection was broken and the blades stopped.

The guard lifted Stanley Kung's arm out of the bowl. When he saw what was left of his hand, Kung turned away with a half-cry, half-sob and vomited all over the shoes of the guard standing on his left.

His fingers looked as if they had been chewed by some ravenous beast. Three of his fingers had been cut back to the knuckle, the fourth was just a long piece of white bone with no flesh remaining. He had lost the top joint of his thumb although by some quirk the nail still hung from the flesh. Blood spurted from the ends of all the fingers in a steady stream, covering the table and the white base of the dreadful machine.

'So, now that we understand each other, I have one or two questions I would like you to answer,' Yung continued in the same reasonable tone with which he had begun the conversation. 'I need hardly add that if you fail to answer them, then we shall begin again. I can assure you that this little machine has a voracious appetite.'

Lin Yung paused for a moment to allow his words to be absorbed into the agonized mind of the man in front of him.

'I want to know what instructions the terrorists in the Tunnel have. I want to know how you communicate with them and I want to know who is supplying information on police movements to you.'

There was a moment when it looked as if Stanley Kung might be going to resist. But then his eyes fell on the bloody stump of his hand and he knew that resistance was pointless. There would simply be more torture and then more and in the end he would talk. He had seen it often enough to know that there were no heroes in such circumstances.

'Dai Choi has been ordered to kill half the hostages tonight in advance of the deadline as a final push to get what we want. If that fails, then the rest will die. But he will spread it out so that we can keep the pressure up for another few days.'

'He's surely not going to decide when to do that,' Lin Yung interrupted. 'How are you going to tell him?'

'We have agreed a stand-by watch for radio messages every odd hour on the hour,' Kung replied, his voice now so low that Lin Yung had to lean forward to hear him.

'And your informant outside?' he prompted.

'Lisu, the wife of Turnbull, the Hong Kong policeman,' Kung replied, his voice almost inaudible.

Lin Yung leaned further forward so that the two men's faces were almost touching. 'What radio frequency?' he shouted, desperate to keep his victim conscious.

Suddenly, Stanley Kung jerked upright, his left hand thrust out. He grabbed Lin Yung's right wrist which had been resting on the table and pulled it back towards him. At the same time, he drove his head forward. The knife pierced his neck just below the ear and a huge fountain of blood spurted four feet across the room as the blade cut his jugular.

'Shit, the bastard,' Lin Yung exclaimed, pushing away from the stream of blood.

He watched for a moment and then, realizing that there was nothing to be done, he moved to the sink, washed his hands and left the room.

Jonny had listened to the torture of Stanley Kung with growing horror. He had arrived at the house half an hour earlier and been shown into the sitting room, where he was asked to wait. He had expected Julie to be there but had been told by one of the guards that she was delayed.

One cup of coffee later, he had heard the car turn into the driveway and the garage door opening and closing. Then he had heard Lin Yung introduce himself and he realized that there must be a microphone in the kitchen relaying the conversation to him.

He had no idea what was going to happen until he heard the motor of the food processor whirr into action. Suspicions were confirmed by the rending scream which seemed to go on and on and on. He tried to go through to the kitchen to stop the torture but two Chinese with drawn guns were standing just outside the door and they thrust him back inside.

Revulsion at the brutality had been subsumed by the stunning revelation that Lisu had betrayed him. God, what could she have passed on? he thought, as he frantically reviewed their conversations of the last few days. He remembered his remark about the planned move into the Tunnel the previous evening. It must have been she who betrayed them. Oh God.

Lin Yung came into the room and sat down opposite Jonny. 'I'm sorry you had to listen to that but, as you heard, I got the information we need.'

'Not enough though,' Jonny replied. 'We still don't know where the radio transmissions were coming from or who was making them. Even without Kung, this operation will be running on autopilot. To stop it we need to find the messenger before the next signal gets through.'

The door opened and Julie walked in. He noticed that she had changed back into a more formal skirt and blouse. Lin Yung turned to her and continued speaking.

'We have some information that the terrorists plan to kill half the hostages in advance of the deadline and that they will get their orders via radio from outside the Tunnel. Unfortunately we don't know where those orders will come from or when.'

'But at least it's something,' Jonny interrupted. 'We should go to the authorities with what we have. We can at least make them move.'

'I don't think that's a very good idea, Jonny,' Lin Yung said quietly.

'Why the hell not?' Jonny asked. 'We've got a chance to save some lives. We should take it.'

'I think you're being a little bit simplistic,' Lin Yung contradicted. 'Of course we should tell the police about the radio. They'll be able to block the transmissions and so Dai Choi won't know when to start the killing.

'But we don't want to encourage an assault on the Tunnel. If you tell them the terrorists are going to start killing before the deadline, then they're bound to move in. On the other hand, if we let this play out a little longer, we may all get what we want.'

'And just what exactly is that?' Jonny asked.

'Well, for a start, you'll probably get Dai Choi. But more importantly, the longer this goes on, the more discredited the Triads become. The British are not going to give in and they will have to go and clean out the Triads once this is over. The British government has been held to ransom by a bunch of crooks who have been tolerated for years. Once the media hears about all the cosy relationships that exist back home – and I can assure you they will hear about it – then the government will have no choice.'

Jonny felt Julie's hand on his arm. 'It's true what he says, Jonny,' she said. 'The longer it runs, the higher the price the Triads will have to pay. And that's what we all want.'

Jonny's mind had been racing ahead, seeing the opportunities that the information gave him. He needed time to get his man and for now that is what the Chinese were prepared to give.

'For the moment, you can have my silence,' he told them. 'We both want Dai Choi and the Triads to suffer so at least we have a common goal.' He got up to leave. 'I'd better go and see Lisu. She's done enough damage. What about you, Julie?'

'I'm heading back to the flat so you'll be able to get me there for the next couple of hours.'

The drive to Chelsea took thirty-five minutes, the cab weaving in and out of the snarled traffic in a semblance of forward progress that seemed to do little but make the meter tick faster. The journey gave Jonny time to think. Lin Yung was right when he said that the defeat of the Triads was a reasonable excuse for his silence and Julie's promises for the future mattered little against the opportunities today. But what really mattered was that today, and for the first time, Dai Choi was trapped where neither money nor influence could buy his escape. It was the chance that he had been waiting for all these years and he would not allow it to slip through his fingers because of some spurious deal. Instead, the information he now had could ensure him a place at Dai Choi's final party. It was madness, of course. He could see with an awful clarity the dangers of the course he had chosen. Once the detail of his role was uncovered – and it surely would be – there would be little sympathy for his actions. He had sold his job and his soul for the price of a shot at Dai Choi. But after years of frustration, this was his first real opportunity to get his man. He shrugged, the small movement of his shoulders a visible sign of his mentally dismissing the risks. He was tired of the hunt and wanted to end it, to have the chance to start a new life free of the burden. Perhaps Dai Choi's head would buy him personal freedom and the forgiveness of his masters.

The cab pulled up outside the block of flats and Jonny walked swiftly through the doors to the banks of lifts. As the lift wheezed its way to the eleventh floor, he steeled himself for the confrontation. Letting himself in, he walked through to the sitting room. Lisu was in the seat she had taken as her own in the past few days. Now Jonny understood the reasons for the tears and the despair. He felt a rush of sympathy for the woman who had once been so much to him.

She looked up and somehow seemed to sense his knowledge. She flinched as if he had slapped her. He saw her reaction and knew with absolute certainty that Stanley Kung had spoken the truth.

'Yes, I'm afraid we know,' Jonny said. 'Stanley Kung told us.'

At the mention of the name she shuddered, her

revulsion for Kung and for her own role clear in the expression of disgust. 'Evil. That man is evil.'

'Well, you don't have to worry about him any more. He's dead.'

'Thank God. Thank God.' Her hands covered her eyes and she began sobbing.

'But why did you do it, Lisu? Did they force you? Did you volunteer? What?'

'They blackmailed me, Jonny. I had no choice. If I had refused, someone in China would have been killed. I had to do it. I had to.' She looked up, a new fear in her eyes. 'What will happen to me?'

'God knows,' he replied. 'The intelligence people will already be investigating how information on the attack leaked and they'll get to you in the end. Better to say something now and be seen to cooperate. That way you can maybe limit the damage.'

Before she had time to argue or think through the consequences of Stanley Kung's death and the effect that might have back in Beijing, Jonny moved to the telephone, dialled New Scotland Yard and asked for Mike Williams. After the head of Special Branch came on the line Jonny identified himself and explained the circumstances.

'I think it would be best if you got a couple of your people round here to talk to Lisu,' he advised. 'She's happy to tell everything she knows and you may get some leads into both Chinese intelligence and what they know about the Tunnel. Also, they may be in touch with her again so you might catch some of their people in the act.'

'I'll fix that right now,' Williams agreed. 'Look, Jonny. You'd better get down here. I'm about to go to a meeting of COBRA and you should be there.'

But Jonny needed more than just a deal for Lisu and another meeting. 'Mike, it's vital that I talk to you before the meeting. I have some information that you might want to use at the meeting. I also want something from you. Can you be outside the Whitehall Theatre in fifteen minutes?'

That arranged, Jonny hung up and was about to leave when Lisu reached for his arm.

'There is something else you should know,' she began nervously. 'These past few days, you've spent so much time with that Cohen woman I was sure there was something between you. Kung has been obsessed with you and what you might have found out. They see you as the real threat to their plans and want to stop you. Their people have been trying to kill you but you've been moving around too much. They asked me what might make you stop and I told them about the woman. I said that if they threatened her, you might be forced to stop. I'm sorry, Jonny.'

Jonny stared at her, appalled. 'There was never anything between Julie and me,' he said finally, anger cutting through his sympathy. 'You've not only killed the policemen in the Tunnel but placed an innocent woman's life at risk.'

He turned away, leaving a broken Lisu behind him. He paused briefly by the phone, debating whether to call Julie. He was already late for the meeting with Williams and if he delayed any further he would miss him altogether. She was a pro. She could take care of herself. He went out of the door, slamming it behind him.

Regent's Bridge Gardens was supposed to be a secure area. The double gates into the complex of townhouses and luxury flats could only be opened with a remote control or by someone already inside. It reassured the occupants but to anyone other than the casual amateur teenage burglar, the defences were a joke. When the gates opened, they stayed open long enough for two or more cars to pass through. By parking on Rita Road and waiting for a resident to turn into the entrance, it was possible to get instant and unobtrusive access.

When Julie returned to her flat from Lin Yung's house, she was exhausted. The interrogation had been shocking. It had revealed a dark side to her business that she had never experienced before. They taught you how to kill, to live a shadow life and to exploit human weakness. But there was a difference between manipulation and the brutal extraction of information.

She parked her car and walked up to her flat, looking forward to a quiet evening with a glass of wine and her cat for company. The door had two locks and she carefully undid both and pushed open the door. She had not left talcum powder in the hall to betray an intruder's footsteps, or hairs stuck between the door jambs to show they had been opened in her absence. But still, the flat seemed different, smelled different. She controlled the shudder down her spine as instinct prevailed.

Cautiously she opened the door to her sitting room and flicked on the lights. At first she could see nothing. Then her hand flew to her mouth to stifle a scream of horror.

The body of her cat lay on the glass table in the centre of the room. It had been disembowelled with a single knife cut from anus to throat. The guts were spilled out on the table like bloody spaghetti and blood had dribbled off the edges of the table to form wide red pools in the carpet.

She could feel her stomach begin to heave. Then the bedroom door swung open and two Chinese men stepped out. Despite the darkness, both wore large dark glasses, plain grey suits and white turtlenecks. They looked like mutants modelling clothes bought in a church bazaar. They also looked very frightening.

'Good evening, Julie,' the larger of the two men said. 'Catch.'

Julie's hands rose in reflex in front of her to catch the ball he threw at her. As her hands caught it, she felt how wet it was, glanced down and threw the cat's head to the floor with a cry of disgust.

The first man produced a gun while the second brought a long-bladed knife from an armpit sheath.

'That is to show you we are serious, Julie,' he continued, his voice soft.

'What do you want with me?'

'You are a little insurance that the person we work for thinks might be useful. So we'd like you to come on a short drive with us. We don't wish you any harm but I can assure you you will suffer much more than your cat if you try to escape or attract attention in any way.'

The two men moved into the room to stand on either side of her. She thought for a moment of resisting and then dismissed it. She had no wish to end up eviscerated beside her cat on the floor.

'Oh, and one other thing,' the leader of the two men continued. 'I've been told to tell you that if all goes well, then you will be released unharmed.' He laughed lightly. 'I always think that's such a bad line. After all, what choice do you have?'

CHAPTER 24

FOR TWO HOURS now Captain Jeremy Greaves had been on the bridge of HMS *Campbeltown*, his gut taut with the solid overwhelming tension that in the end will break a man. His Type 22 frigate had been powering up the Channel at its full speed of twenty-nine knots through driving rain and visibility down to half a mile. In any other circumstances barrelling like that down the world's busiest waterway would be considered suicidal and terminally damaging to a promising naval career.

But the orders he had received from CINCFLEET North-wood two hours earlier had been quite clear: He was to make 'all possible speed' to take up station midway between Folkestone and Dover, over the Channel Tunnel.

The only way to carry out that order was to rely not on precision navigation but on the integrated radar and detection systems that would normally be used to control and fire Harpoon and Sea Wolf missiles as well as the Goalkeeper gun, which can fire 4,200 30 mm rounds a minute as a final defence against incoming missiles.

Perched on top of the bridge, three feet above Greaves's head, were two huge white metal spheres which looked like giant bowling balls. The similarity was emphasized by the three black holes in each of the balls, which are in fact different eyes. One is for thermal imaging, the second has a TV camera and the third is a laser range-finder adapted from the Challenger tank. The system is known as G-PODS for General Purpose Electro-Optical Directors and relays a series of images to screens on the bridge and in the operations room.

At that moment the TV camera was showing only the opacity of the mist and the rain but the thermal imager could pierce the murk to hunt out all sources of heat and show them in green outline to the G-PODS operator. By lightly touching the rollerball under his right hand, the operator moved the cursor over the image and fired the laser at the target. Instantly, the distance and direction of the vessel in relation to *Campbeltown*'s heading appeared on the screen.

Greaves felt like a racing car speeding through the night with the lights off. There was a difference though. The massive power of the Rolls-Royce Spey engines combined with the Tyne gas turbines meant that the 440-foot-long ship could be brought to a halt from 29 knots in under 700 feet, the equivalent of bringing a Volvo from 30 m.p.h. to a stop in 12 inches.

Looking out of the bridge he could see nothing except the huge foaming mass of the bow wave as each thrust of the bows into the sea drove 200 tons of water out to either side.

He sat erect in the Captain's leather swivel chair looking straight ahead. Listening intently to the radar operator's constant stream of information, he related it to the moving map display he was keeping in his head and then issued instructions to the helmsman standing to his left.

Bobbing and jinking, the frigate sped down the Channel. Looking around the bridge, Greaves felt the pride of all commanders when men and machine work to their maximum. It was magnificent, fantastically exciting, and mad. But there was no emotion in his face apart from heavy dark eyebrows drawn close together to hood his eyes. The two vertical lines in the centre of his forehead were the only real outward signs of tension. He had learned during the campaign in the South Atlantic the value of leadership in a crisis. If they survived this, it would be the stuff of legend, but until then he would remain exactly where he was for as long as it took.

As a much younger lieutenant serving under David Hart-Dyke, the skipper of the *Coventry*, he had first experienced what the Navy doctors call FUF or Fear Under Fire. It had been brought about by a recognition of two things: his vulnerability and the fickle nature of technology.

HMS *Coventry* had been sunk after her 909 Sea Dart radars had been unable to distinguish between the land mass of the Falklands and the low-flying Argentine Skyhawk jets. The Sea Wolf on her sister ship, HMS *Broadsword*, saw two aircraft flying wingtip to wingtip and hesitated, unable to decide which aircraft to aim at. Rather than make a mistake, the computer decided to do nothing and turned itself off. Three thousand-pound bombs had hit *Coventry*, causing mortal damage.

Greaves had been knocked unconscious by the blast and when he came to it was to see a scene straight from hell. The bridge had been destroyed and men all around him were on fire, flaming like burning candles, their screams adding to the horror. He looked down and saw that his white fireproof gloves had been literally burned off and the skin underneath appeared to be boiling in the heat, blisters rising and then popping like some miniature sulphur spring.

Greaves had jumped from the canting deck into the sea, swimming to one of the liferafts with the salt turning his hands into agonizing balls of fire. Ironically, it was that short swim which had saved his hands from permanent damage. The plastic surgery gave them a mottled appearance, his own red badge of courage, although every time he looked at his scars he was reminded not of his heroism but of his fear. The hard-won lesson ensured he never again relied on technology to save him, his men or his ship.

Like many of the Falklands veterans, Greaves had moved swiftly up the promotion ladder. *Campbeltown* was his first command and at forty-three he was clearly still on the fast track. He wanted to make sure it stayed that way.

The routine patrol in the Irish Sea had been interrupted twelve hours earlier with the order to head south for Plymouth to take on cargo and men. As usual with such signals there were orders but no explanation, and so he had arrived in Plymouth certain that the task had to do with the Tunnel assault but with no idea of exactly what was required.

When the ship arrived at No. 5 Wharf, the 'cargo' was already sitting on its pallet alongside. It was an Avalon submersible. Known officially as a Deep Submergence Rescue Vehicle or DSRV, the Avalon is forty-nine feet long and can dive to 5,000 feet with ease. The vessel is shaped like a fat cigar and is divided into three self-contained spheres. The front houses the captain and two crew, the middle can hold twenty-four rescued submariners and the fourth crew member. The third sphere holds the engine and the enormous batteries used to drive the single propeller. It has a range of twenty-four miles at three knots.

The most important part of the ship lies below the centre sphere. It is a circular set of watertight doors with a ring seal at the bottom. By delicate manoeuvring, the vessel can be brought over a submarine's escape hatch, the ring dropped on top of it, air pumped out to form a seal and then men transferred from one ship to the other.

A small man, Greaves had to do a little hop to get out of his seat and on to the deck. He moved to the back of the bridge to look at the TV monitor that relayed the image from the rear flight deck. There he could see the squat shape of the Avalon where he was used to seeing a Lynx or EH101 helicopter. The fact that the Avalon was there at all was little short of a miracle.

When they had tied up alongside in Plymouth after the mad dash down the Irish Sea, he had looked curiously down at the dock and the little knot of men standing by what looked like a very long and very fat torpedo. As soon as the gangplank hit the dock, two of the men came aboard.

He met them in the security of his cabin. The first man wore the three stripes of a commander on his dark blue uniform. Even without the short cropped hair cut close to the skull, Greaves would have known him as an American. He had that tall, confident air that Americans of a certain type seem to carry with them. But he also had a rounded stomach that looked as if he had stuffed a football up his shirt. It was extraordinary, Greaves thought, what odd shapes Americans are, as if they are in perpetual training for the Fat People's Olympics.

The man saluted and then grinned. 'Hi, Captain. My name is Frank Rostenkowski. I'm the skipper of the Avalon, the little baby you see on the dock.'

'A pleasure to meet you, Commander. Welcome aboard.'

Greaves turned towards the second man who had been standing behind the American. The man saluted and stepped forward. 'Lieutenant Mike Hodder, sir. SBS.'

Greaves nodded and considered the younger man. He had trained with the Special Boat Service and seen them operate in the South Atlantic, so the type, if not the individual, was familiar. The SBS is the élite unit within the Royal Marines responsible for carrying out beach reconnaissance and some counter-terrorism work at sea. There are many similarities with the SAS and a great deal of duplication in both training and roles.

During the Second World War, when both organizations were founded, the divisions were easier, with the SAS working mostly on land and the SBS at sea. Peacetime had brought different problems and different solutions. The SAS found that sometimes they needed to get to their targets by sea or river and the SBS learned that parachuting was an essential requirement to get within striking distance of a harbour or installation near the sea. But without merging the two, there was little to be done to avoid the competition and the duplication. Some specializations have evolved so that the SAS will deal with most counter-terrorism on land and the SBS, through Comacchio Group, looks after the security of North Sea oil installations, the Trident submarine base, and guards convoys carrying nuclear materials.

In an effort to streamline, a joint Special Forces Group headquarters was set up in 1989 based at the Duke of York's Barracks in London under a brigadier who is always drawn from the SAS.

Beyond those basic facts, Greaves knew little about the black arts practised by the SBS. The man standing before him looked like a fairly normal Marine in beret and brown uniform. He was around five feet eight inches tall, clean-shaven, with sandy hair slightly longer than regulation cut, dark brown eyes and a very large nose that could have been unattractive but actually gave an ordinary face some character. Only two visible things distinguished Hodder: an enormous neck which must have been seventeen inches round, which Greaves presumed was caused by all those hours spent swimming and paddling canoes; and a shoulder patch with the winged oars and blue parachute and the motto 'Not By Strength By Guile'.

'I understand you're going to give me a lift up the Channel,' the American continued.

'That is certainly the plan, although I am still not clear just how we are going to get you and your vessel to our destination,' Greaves replied.

'Well, we gave some thought to that back in the States and reckon that we have come up with a pretty good solution.' The American walked out on to the starboard flying bridge and pointed out what looked like a pair of large steel railings lying alongside the submersible.

'What is it?' Greaves asked.

'Our problem was not so much getting here – we routinely deploy using one of the C5 transports – but once here getting from your deck into the water. So I had a word with some of the boys at Norfolk.'

Greaves nodded. He had once visited the vast headquarters of the Supreme Allied Commander Atlantic on America's east coast.

'There's an old Nike Hercules air defence system on the base. You remember the type? Brackets, trailer, rocket and a hydraulic system to get it to the vertical for firing.' He smiled with the satisfaction of the creator showing off his invention. 'We took the rocket off, left the trailer behind and brought the mountings and the hydraulics. The way we figured it, we can mount it on your helicopter deck, put the Avalon on top and then instead of levering up to the vertical, we'll pump the tail up and slide off into the sea.'

So far, it had worked exactly as planned. While the mountings were bolted into the deck, Hodder had brought his men and their kit aboard. Ten men dressed as Marines with bag after bag of equipment which he didn't see and really didn't want to know about. Greaves had the serving officer's obsessive concern with 'need to know'. Know what you need to do your job, know any more and it just causes trouble.

The men had stayed below since they had come aboard and the chief petty officer had brought him regular reports of their progress. 'They've changed out of their uniforms, sir,' he had confided earlier. 'Got up in some all-black suit of some kind. They're laying out all their kit in the chopper hangar. I've never seen so much stuff: guns, grenades, grappling irons, ladders. They must be going to start a war. And finish it too.'

Greaves pulled himself back into the captain's chair and tried to peer through the rain and mist. There was nothing to be seen in the dull, grey afternoon, just the sound of the radar operators calling out the sightings of other ships in their path. The rolling map display inside his head continued to scroll through the Channel towards the target.

The damp and the cold had seeped through Kate's bones so that she was shivering all the time now. Once the electricity had been cut off and there were no trains passing through the Tunnel generating heat, the temperature had dropped rapidly. It was now only a few degrees above freezing.

The explosions earlier had not caused any massive rupture, but she could hear the steady drip drip drip of water from all around. There were no pumps working in the Tunnel so there was no way for the water to be extracted. It was a subtle and modern refinement of the old Chinese water torture. The way the ancients did it was to tie their prisoner under a steadily dripping pipe. At the beginning each drop felt soothing but after a short time the drops felt like lead weights and then as if they were drilling a hole into the centre of the skull. The prisoner either talked or went mad. It was simple and effective.

For Kate the torture was more subtle than that. She felt trapped by the mass of water above and the drips that were forming pools below. She knew she wasn't going to drown. That was the logic of her position. But her imagination kept taking her on a short and horrible journey where the Tunnel flooded, the water rose up and up into the carriage and, as she struggled to swim, she sucked in a mouthful of water, then another, and another ... Hours after the first nightmare, she felt she could actually taste the water and could imagine her stomach filling, her throat constricting and her lungs, starved of oxygen, collapsing.

Tom's execution had made it worse. She imagined that Emma would be taken next and was frantic to avoid making Tom's mistake and attracting attention to herself or to Emma.

All around her people were shivering in the cold. The passengers had moved closer together, shuffling their bottoms along the cold metal. But their bodies were generating so little heat now that there was no comfort, only the chattering of their teeth breaking the silence.

For three hours she had been desperate to pee. Each drip of water piled on the agony until she could stand it no longer.

Others had been faced with the same dilemma and had simply let go into their underwear. The stench of urine was almost intolerable. Kate had heard some of the passengers vomiting and was sure that it was only a matter of time before she did so too. The only reason she had held on this long was because she was near the sliding door and so got some breaths of moderately fresh air.

But wetting herself would be the final humiliation. She did not want to give the Chinese the satisfaction of seeing her debased in front of them. Of course, they probably couldn't see anything in the dark and wouldn't be interested even if they could. It was the principle of the thing.

Kate had been quietly transferring items from her handbag into the pockets of her skirt and jacket and now the bag was empty. She opened it wide and slid it between her legs. She unrolled her pants until they were below her knees and then slid one half of the open bag under her buttocks. With a sigh of relief and explosion of urine she began to fill it, fearful now that it would overflow and wet her neighbours.

The mission successfully completed, she lifted herself up slightly, brought the handbag out from underneath her and stood it carefully upright.

The relief was wonderful. Now she could concentrate on what she had been thinking about ever since Tom's death: revenge and escape – in that order.

Kate felt her pockets, touching each of the items, assessing their value. Keys, lipstick, comb, old sweetie paper, a stale toffee, wallet were all discarded. It was when she picked up her copy of that morning's *Daily Mail* that an idea came to her. Far-fetched, idiotic even. But at least it was an idea. She pulled the newspaper out and carefully, quietly, began to roll it into a tube.

Like the situation in the Tunnel itself, COBRA was now in a state of permanent crisis. As the hours had gone by and plans were made, hopes raised and dashed, the tempers and the tensions inside the windowless and seemingly airless offices had become stretched, twisted and torn.

The news of the failed mission inside the Tunnel had acted as a catalyst for most of the people. The story had leaked to the press and the media hounds were looking for political victims to pillory. At the same time, the IRA cover was peeling away as the Chinese community in Hong Kong learned on their own accurate and astonishingly fast bush telegraph that the fate of the terrorists in the Tunnel would directly affect their welfare. There had been riots which were turning increasingly ugly.

Few now in COBRA were arguing for conciliation and peace. Those who were used to negotiation as a way of sustaining life recognized they were not dealing with reasonable men. Everyone knew that it was capitulation or conflict. There was no middle ground.

Few of the people in the room were used to such stark choices. Diplomats, policemen and intelligence agents are all used to fudging issues, to taking political decisions that inevitably involve a measure of give and take. Now there was no room for manoeuvre, there seemed to be a collective inertia that prevented the group from taking the next – and toughest – decision: actually to commit troops for an assault.

As Jonny looked around, he saw the same people he

had first seen and met just the day before. They all looked different now. This was not a war game where everyone knew that they could leave at the end of the day and forget the winners and the losers. This was real life. The choices they made here might kill hostages, would almost certainly kill terrorists. It would, of course, make or break careers as well, depending on the wisdom of the decision.

'I think you should all be aware of a message I received from General John Foley, the Commander of British Forces in Hong Kong,' said Sir Clive Whitmore.

Jonny knew Foley, a tall, thin, balding man with a very long jaw and an easy smile. He had been Director of Special Forces after a long career in the SAS and then head of Defence Intelligence. He was a tough, experienced operator, the best type to have in charge at this time. Whitmore read the communication:

> The situation here has deteriorated rapidly in the past 24 hours. News of the assault on the Tunnel has leaked or been deliberately fed to the local Chinese community. The result has been huge demonstrations in favour of the terrorists and against the Chinese take-over.
>
> Two hours ago a march involving around one million people began in Sheung and is heading for Causeway Bay. The scale of this protest exceeds that which followed Tiananmen Square. There is a similar demonstration planned for Tsim Sha Tsui on Kowloon. The uncertainty seems to be creating panic in the local community. There has been a run on the banks and they have been advised by the Governor to close their doors.
>
> There have been sporadic outbreaks of violence as the police try and control the crowds and the armed robbers who are taking advantage of the unstable situation to carry out a wave of attacks across Hong Kong.

I have placed my troops on full alert and expect to deploy them within hours. I do not believe that in the present circumstances my forces will be enough to contain the crisis. We are therefore faced with a complete breakdown of law and order.

We have three choices:

1. Send reinforcements
2. Call for help from the PRC
3. Resolve the crisis in the Tunnel in the next few hours

Unless 3 is achieved, you must do 2 without delay and 1 may be necessary to avoid very heavy loss of life in Hong Kong among both expatriates and the local community.'

Whitmore took off his spectacles and laid them on the table in front of him. His expression was bleak and, as he looked around, Jonny thought there was little left of the urbane civil servant of a few hours ago. The suit was still well cut but the face looked pinched and the bags under his eyes huge.

'As you can see, the Commander is pretty pessimistic and I have to concur with his judgment,' said Whitmore. 'I spoke with the Prime Minister a few minutes ago and he remains resolute that we must not give in to the terrorists. But he is also determined that this matter must be resolved without delay. That seems to leave us with little choice but to go in and get the hostages out.'

'That's easy to say but difficult to do,' said Williams of the Special Branch. He had been badly burned both personally and professionally by the débâcle of the reconnaissance mission, which had been partly his idea. He knew it was not the police's fault that they had walked into a trap but he also knew that the knives would be out yet again. 'But I believe we have no choice,' he continued. 'I have received some intelligence that the terrorists in the Tunnel are receiving instructions by radio from an outside controller.'

Jonny's deal had taken only minutes. Williams was desperate for information and Jonny desperate for access to the Tunnel. Williams was bruised by the failure of the police action in the Tunnel and needed to restore his credibility and that of SB. Jonny wanted Dai Choi and Williams was happy to help him kill himself if that was what he wanted to do. So, the price of knowledge was Jonny's participation in the rescue mission and Williams had paid it. Now he passed on the rest of his intelligence.

'We also know they will receive instructions to begin killing the hostages some time before the deadline runs out.'

The men and women around the table seemed to collapse as one. The knowledge that the one benchmark which had given a solid foundation to all their plans – the deadline – was being taken away was another blow on the backs of already exhausted people.

'For God's sake, why?' Whitmore asked.

'Apparently there is a feeling that a few more bodies will help concentrate our minds as the deadline comes up,' Williams replied. 'It's interesting psychology, actually. We've always worked to deadlines in these situations. By moving them, the terrorists are piling on the pressure, forcing us on to the defensive.'

'It's not psychology that matters, it's doing something to stop them,' Witherow interrupted. 'First, we must make sure the signals people down at the Tunnel are jamming everything going in there. Second, we'll have to send our people in to rescue the hostages. As Mike says, we've really no choice.'

'I agree,' Whitmore said. 'I will advise the Prime Minister accordingly and we can expect a decision within the hour.'

Mary Cheong had listened to the exchange with growing despair. Before the crisis had begun and since the terrorists had taken the Tunnel, she had done everything in her power to try and persuade the British government to negotiate and honour its obligations. At every step she had been rebuffed, first by Hurd and then by the COBRA committee. She knew, knew with complete certainty, that the terrorists' demands were legitimate. Their methods might be questionable, but the goals were not.

The whole build-up to the transfer of power to the Chinese had made her cynical about the British, a nation she had admired from afar when she was still in China. There the missionaries had spread the word about honesty and integrity and the British had been held up as the finest examples of such qualities. She had believed it, which was one of the reasons why she had fixed on Hong Kong as her goal when she escaped from the Communist yoke.

Freedom had brought with it the successes she had dreamed of. But then the British had done their deal with the Chinese and it had all suddenly gone very sour. Her belief in British justice had been destroyed and her confidence that she could rely on British honour to stick to promises already made had been cruelly undermined.

At the start of the Tunnel crisis, she had actually believed that the British might finally be persuaded to do what was right and just. But each successive meeting she had attended had depressed her further. After the first few hours, the participants had taken up positions which were supposed to be flexible but which were in fact set in stone. No one wanted to argue for negotiation, for it would be seen as weakness amongst a group that had trained in and practised a policy of never giving in to terrorism. Instead the focus had shifted to turning the crisis against the IRA, and as that sideshow had played out, there had been considerable satisfaction around the table that something had been salvaged from the mess.

But Mary knew that if the assault on the Tunnel went ahead, there would be a bloodbath. She knew the Triads, understood how they trained and how they worked. She knew that lives – both among the terrorists and the hostages – would be lost and nothing gained. The apparent satisfaction that men got from the prospect of action she thought childish. Unable to contain her anger she spoke directly to Whitmore.

'I don't think you understand just what you are planning to do,' she began.

Whitmore turned to her, his spectacles glinting in the fluorescent light, eyebrows raised in interrogation. She saw his lips move in that half-smile which the British reserve for foreigners when they think they are being welcoming but are, in fact, merely being supercilious.

'I know these people. I understand how they think and how they work. It was Sun Tzu who told us that "The art of war teaches us to rely not on the likelihood of the enemy's not coming, but on our own readiness to receive him; not on the chance of his not attacking, but rather on the fact that we have made our position unassailable." In other words, the people in the Tunnel will have prepared for this, be expecting you as they were last time. You go into the Tunnel and the people holding the hostages will kill as many of them as they can. There will be carnage in there.'

'Oh, I think you underestimate the capabilities of our forces, Dame Mary,' Whitmore said, his tone dismissive of her remarks.

Mary brought a small fist down on the table, her anger now clear to everyone. The noise the blow made was small but its effect was to still her audience. They were shocked. All those who had played the COBRA war games had learned to think and do without outward display of emotion. This outsider clearly didn't understand.

'No. I understand what your SAS can do. But I also know that the terrorists will be dedicated people. They will give their lives for a cause they believe in and I can assure you they believe in what they are doing. And you choose to believe that if you take the Tunnel, this will be over. These are Chinese people; they deal in subtlety, in move and counter-move. You recapture the Tunnel and what then? Perhaps you will simply expose the next move in the game, a move that could be far worse than anything we have seen so far.'

Jonny had listened to Dame Mary with growing respect. She believed passionately in her people but equally believed in trying to avoid unnecessary bloodshed. It was clear where her sympathies lay but, even so, what she said made sense.

'I agree with Dame Mary,' Jonny interrupted. 'These men are tough. They will have fought dozens of battles for their masters in the Triad and will be used to the idea of violence and its consequences. Once they know you arc attacking, they will kill the hostages and then fight to the end. It's going to be very messy whatever we do. The key is to keep surprise on our side and that means stopping any orders reaching Dai Choi and his men.'

'And what happens if you attack, free the hostages and kill the Chinese in the Tunnel?' Mary Cheong asked. 'You have demonstrations in Hong Kong today, you'll have riots tomorrow. General Foley has told you – and you know he's right – that he will be unable to keep control of the situation. You won't be able to get reinforcements there fast enough and the Chinese will move in rather than have their crown jewel destroyed.'

Whitmore took off his glasses and squeezed the bridge of his nose between thumb and forefinger. 'I think you are being over-alarmist, Dame Mary. If we send the Gurkhas from Brunei today then they should be there in time to help keep the security situation under control. The alternative is negotiation, which will only be fruitful if we actually plan to concede anything, and I'm afraid that remains out of the question. However, if you have any alternative suggestions, I would be happy to hear them.'

It was clear to her that the course for confrontation was set, that there was no further point in hoping that those in the Tunnel could provoke a change in policy. It was time to try and extract some dignity from a lost cause.

'There is one solution we haven't thought of,' Jonny began, thinking out loud. 'The one person the terrorists might listen to is Dame Mary. She is the one person all the Chinese in Hong Kong respect and her commitment to the cause they are fighting for is well known. Perhaps if Mary spoke to them directly and at the same time we stop any other instructions getting through?' He left the thought hanging in the air. It was Whitmore, still smarting from her attacks, who picked it up.

'That's a splendid idea,' he said warmly, his voice picking up speed as the thoughts gelled. 'We could fly you down in a helicopter, rig up some system so that you could talk through a microphone straight into the Tunnel. Great idea.' And it would play well on the news tomorrow morning, he thought to himself: 'GOVERNMENT'S OLIVE BRANCH'. He could see the headlines now. He turned expectantly to Dame Mary.

'Actually, PUS, there's a chopper leaving from the Horse Guards parade ground in ten minutes,' said Williams. He had kept to his part of the deal. 'The helicopter will take Jonny down to *Campbeltown* and it could take Dame Mary as well.'

There was a pause. Then, realizing that she had been cleverly boxed in by her own concerns, Mary spoke, scepticism clear in her voice. 'Well, I suppose I could give it a try. I can't believe that I could do anything to persuade such dedicated people to surrender. But if you think I can, of course I'll try.'

'Good. Good,' Whitmore was almost rubbing his hands together in satisfaction. 'I knew we could rely on you.'

'Right. John,' he said, turning to Witherow. 'You make

the arrangements to fly Dame Mary down there. I'll go upstairs and give them the current state of play. We should reconvene in three hours by which time we'll have the result of Dame Mary's peacemaking.'

Jonny thought that Dame Mary's expedition would almost certainly be futile. He simply could not imagine that some of Hong Kong's most hardened hoods would give themselves up on the basis of some sweet words from anybody, let alone a woman, and particularly after they knew that they would all be charged with murder. It was a futile gesture.

Whitmore got up to leave the table and the others followed suit. As Jonny and Williams left the room, a police officer came up to Williams and muttered in his ear. Williams turned to Jonny. 'Our men are with your wife. She got a call a few minutes ago and needs to speak to you.'

Jonny called the number and a moment later a frantic Lisu was on the line. 'They've taken her, Jonny. They've taken her.'

'Taken who?' he responded automatically, although he already knew the answer.

'Julie. They've taken Julie. A man rang a few minutes ago to say that they had her. You're to go back to Hong Kong tonight or they'll kill her.'

He put the phone down. He felt the anger course through his veins. Again, White Lotus had moved against him. But this time the pressure point was badly chosen. He owed Julie his life but theirs was a relationship between professionals and she knew the risks. Flying back to Hong Kong was unthinkable. That way lay the certainty of defeat. In the Tunnel was Dai Choi. It was a simple decision.

CHAPTER 25

MIKE HODDER AND his team needed to know precisely where the train was in the Tunnel. That would tell them which access hatch to approach with the mini submarine. The task should have been easy enough but the destruction of the electrics in the Tunnel had taken away the eyes and ears of the Tunnel controllers. They knew to within a mile where the train was but that was not good enough. One hatch removed from the right location and Hodder would drop not on the train but into a trap.

Since the end of the Second World War, the focus of all submarine development work has been on either the detection or suppression of sound. Sonar, which detects sound emissions, has become more sensitive, while all parts of a submarine have been made quieter until the limits of what is scientifically possible have almost been reached.

It was an ex-Royal Navy able seaman sonar operator called Jeff Sims who provided the Nato navies with the answer. After leaving the Navy he had joined the Liverpool Fire Brigade and was one of those called to fight the spectacular blaze that engulfed much of the city's undeveloped old docks in 1985. Searching for bodies in the rubble he had used a new piece of equipment recently purchased by the Brigade. It was a hand-held infra-red detector that could send out an invisible beam through the rubble to detect heat spots. It was astonishingly effective and solved the age-old problem both of finding the dead and injured and seeing the heart of a fire in the middle of a large blaze.

Fireman Sims mentioned the equipment to a submariner friend and idly wondered if such a system would work underwater to detect submarines. His friend mentioned it to the weapons engineering officer and he in turn talked to a friend at Marconi Underwater Systems. A little idea became a stunning technological breakthrough.

The result of that development is the Tentacle, a new system for detecting submarines that has only just started being installed in British anti-submarine frigates. It is so new and so secret that few in the Royal Navy have even heard of it and it was only in 1993 that the US Navy was given a demonstration of its capabilities.

The technology is simple yet revolutionary. A ship tows behind it a small robot which has a number of highly sensitive infra-red sensors on board which can detect heat sources at up to 11,000 metres. At a stroke, the ocean, which had become at best opaque, and more usually pitch black, was transparent once again. All submarines give off large amounts of heat and wherever that signature is, Tentacle can detect it.

Tentacle had never been used to try and detect heat through rock. But after a hurried meeting in his cabin with the principal warfare officer and an equally hurried conversation with Marconi Underwater Systems at their headquarters in Waterlooville, Greaves thought he had a solution to Hodder's problem that was worth trying.

The Batch 3 of the Broadsword Class had been back-fitted with Tentacle beginning in 1992. *Campbeltown* had received the system at the beginning of 1993. It was stowed aft on the port side, opposite the more conventional towed array sonar which was also used to detect submarines.

Since taking up position over the Tunnel, Jeremy

Greaves had ordered action stations and moved down from the bridge to the operations room one deck below. Looking around the square room from his small stool in the centre, Greaves could understand why it was known as the gloom room to officers and men alike.

The light was dim, the only illumination coming from the reflected glow of the screens and the red lights recessed into the metal ceiling. Behind Greaves eight screens provided the picture for the tactical and surface plot and for the control of the helicopter and its dipping sonar. To his right, a flat table recorded the general operations plot and three screens provided different sonar images for the surface and subsurface.

In front of him there were four larger screens. The two in the centre drew information from all the different systems for the two principal warfare officers (PWOs) who coordinated the response to threat from the sea surface, the air and the subsurface. The left-hand screen controls the Harpoon anti-ship missile and the right-hand screen handles Tentacle.

To Greaves's left there were six screens for the weapons systems, including Sea Wolf, Goalkeeper and the 4.5-inch gun. There were also two seats for the electronic warfare director and his deputy. In a modern ship, the EW is critical to a ship's survival and it is his response, often measured in seconds, which really matters. Ironically, in such a high technology environment, the PWO carries a whistle around his neck which he blows to attract attention. This not only works but avoids blocking the communications channels.

Each man in the room wore headphones and had a small boom microphone in front of his mouth. Through his own headphones Greaves could hear the low-level chatter as his men constantly updated the data appearing on the screens before them. It was a whispered Babel of sound.

Greaves levered himself out of the leather chair and

walked the five paces to the Tentacle operator's console. Looking over the man's shoulder, he made out the bushy white beard and knew that Petty Officer Bob Pleming was manning the Tentacle. Good, he thought with relief, the most experienced hand for the job.

'What sort of picture are we getting, PO?' he asked.

'It's not bad, sir,' Pleming replied, 'but it's taking a long time. The Tentacle's working at the limit of its range and we are having to go very slowly just to get the returns.'

Greaves looked at the screen in front of Pleming and watched as the image unfolded. One mile astern of *Campbeltown*, the heart of the Tentacle, a sphere-shaped object four feet long, was being towed through the water twenty-five feet above the sea bed. The Tentacle has a hundred small saucer-shaped blisters attached to its body which look very like the suction pads on an octopus's tentacle. In fact each blister is a highly sensitive infra-red detector. The images picked up by the sensors are relayed down the command wire and then converted by a Logica 3020 computer into pulses of electricity.

The screen in front of Greaves had a black background with a white overlay which showed the ambient temperature of the sea. As the temperatures picked up by the sensors became colder so the white turned progressively more blue; as it picked up sources of heat, the white turned red.

'You can see that we have found the Tunnel.' Pleming pointed to the pink oblong within the dark blue of the cold chalk and rock of the sea bed. 'Our problem has been pinning down the train and the people. So far we've got the outline of what looks like the two train carriages.'

His hands flickered over the keyboard, delving back into the computer's memory. The screen cleared and a new set of images appeared.

'This was the third pass; the clearest so far. You can

see the carriages and there are two concentrated heat sources within that which could be the terrorists and the hostages.'

Greaves looked at the screen and could see the changes in colour but little else. As always, he was astonished at the detail a good operator could prise from the merest hint of information appearing on the waterfall in front of him.

'Well done, PO,' Greaves congratulated him. 'We've got enough for a Go. Keep at it and see if you can extract some more details.'

Greaves walked out of the ops room, turned right down a flight of metal stairs and walked 200 feet to the helicopter hangar at the stern of the ship. Inside the hangar, the outer doors were shut, blocking the view of the Avalon secure on her missile mountings. The SBS team were there, their equipment spread out on the deck. Each of the men was bent over a small pile of gear going through the meticulous checks that all Special Forces do as a matter of routine before trusting their lives to the machinery that is supposed to give them the edge against the opposition.

Seeing the captain enter the hangar, Hodder put down a gas mask and moved towards him.

'Well, Mike, we've found your bandits,' Greaves said.

'Great. Great,' Hodder replied. 'Are they near one of the access points?'

'As far as we can tell, it looks like you should be able to drop among them. But what they'll have waiting for you we can't tell.'

'That's my problem, Captain,' Hodder replied. There was a grimness about the man, Greaves noted. His men had changed out of their Royal Marine uniforms into all-black neoprene diving suits and now they were busy festooning their smooth bodies with all the accoutrements of war. They looked sinister and chilling, Greaves thought. He was glad he wasn't going with them to see their bloody work at first hand. He preferred the remote and clinical war decided by missile or torpedo. These men were trained in the arcane skills of close-quarter killing.

'Do we have a Go from Northwood?' Hodder continued.

'I'm just going to send them a signal that we have located the terrorists. We should get a response pretty quickly provided they can get the politicians to make a decision for a change. I suggest we meet in my cabin in twenty minutes.'

Hodder saluted and turned away, anxious to return to the comfort of the weapons and systems he understood.

The IRA are patient observers of the foibles of men. Their intelligence cell that operates under the direct control of the Army Council is extraordinarily methodical. The small staff of seven work from an anonymous terraced house in Clonard Gardens in the Falls area of Belfast, just down the road from the St Vincent's Convent School. They cut and paste from magazines, reference books and newspapers, piecing together pictures and articles on potential targets.

Curiously, one of the most useful sources of information is parish newsletters. Many of their targets tend to be churchgoers and newsletters frequently recount their activities around their home. To manage this resource, the IRA established a small Dublin-based church charity in the early 1980s which claimed to carry out missionary work in Africa. A letter to all the parishes in England including a modest donation to church funds and asking for copies of parish newsletters as examples to the struggling Christians in Africa had proved remarkably productive.

The files are stored in conventional grey filing cabinets that occupy three rooms of the six in the house. In 1991, the team bought an Apple Macintosh and now the files are cross-indexed with each other and with a new video library that was started in 1989.

Of its kind, it is probably the most comprehensive terrorist resource in the world. Like most libraries, the vast majority of the material is never used, never even looked at once the initial entry is made. But what the cell looks for are the aberration or the signs of routine. They want the regular visit to get a haircut, the call on the tart, the Friday lunch at a club. It is those little flags that elevate an individual from the humdrum to the particular.

Once the team brings the file forward, the reconnaissance cells operating in England and Northern Ireland get their instructions. Once again, this is a very general order for intermittent surveillance. The requirement is still information, not action, and this phase can also last several years. Often, no action is taken, but occasionally the target, the timing and the opportunity coincide and then the killers are unleashed.

Sir Robert Sanford had been a civil servant all his life. He was a man of routine who valued the structure it provided. His career had begun in the Ministry of Agriculture, Fisheries and Food but an early promotion to the Ministry of Defence found him in his element. He had become well known not for his understanding of conventional war but for his devout Catholicism which made a strange marriage with his deep intellectual knowledge of the theory of nuclear deterrence.

He might have remained a minor player in the conferences and corridors of the nuclear capitals had he not written a paper entitled 'The Deployment of Cruise Missiles and Their Impact on the USSR'. He had argued that if the Americans deployed cruise missiles in Europe, this would force the Soviet Union into a new arms race which they would be unable to afford. The paper had been drawn to the attention of Margaret Thatcher, then Britain's Prime Minister, and she had been convinced that Sanford had articulated a policy that held potential promise for the West. She persuaded Reagan and Cruise was deployed in the early 1980s in spite of a massive propaganda campaign by Moscow. There were many in London and Washington who believed the collapse of Communism could be directly attributed to that single decision which in the end was to bankrupt the Soviet economy.

During the 1980s, the Thatcher star shone on Sanford. A period in the Cabinet Office was followed by promotion to Deputy Under-Secretary at the MoD and then the coveted post of Permanent Under-Secretary.

There were few apart from his immediate family who thought Sanford a warm man – and even the MoD wags said that was unlikely. He wore dark suits, dark shoes and dark socks. His grey hair lay flat against his skull, his heavy black spectacles putting a barrier between his dark brown eyes and the rest of the world. He had a small mouth which appeared to be pursed in a perpetual moue of disapproval.

He had been repeatedly briefed by the Security Service on the nature of the threat posed by the IRA and had learned to live with the consequences of high office. When Operation Octavian was at its height in 1989, he had an armed team of undercover police hidden in his garden shed twenty-four hours a day, seven days a week. A police patrol car was within sixty seconds of his house at all times and a helicopter within a few minutes' flying. He had been lucky. Another PUS on the hit list had no garden shed and the police had lived in his dining room.

Sanford resented the constant intrusion in his life but had accepted the routine of checking under his car every day (his wife had even made a flat version of a church kneeler to keep his trousers clean). But the end of Octavian meant some relaxation of the rules. He still checked under his car and varied his route to and from work. But he always went to the Bath and Racquets Club in Brook's

Mews behind Claridge's twice a week, on Tuesdays and Thursdays. On good days he would walk back to the Ministry of Defence, but when it was raining his driver would both drop him off and take him back to work.

That morning one of the anonymous figures from the Security Service had turned up at his house just as he was settling down with his copy of the *Daily Telegraph* and a bowl of All Bran.

'I'm sorry to disturb you at such an unearthly hour, Sir Robert,' the man had begun. 'I'm afraid that we have reason to believe that you are going to be a target of the IRA sometime in the next few days.'

He had heard this before many times and each time it had proved to be a false alarm. He continued eating and asked, between mouthfuls, 'How reliable is this information?'

'Very. We are as certain as we can be that you are the target and that the attack is imminent. What we don't know is the precise where or when.' The man paused as if embarrassed. 'As you know, Sir Robert, our policy on these occasions is to protect the prospective victim and move him or her out of sight for a while.' He coughed slightly. 'However, in this case, we would like you to continue working as usual, stick to all your normal routines in the hope that we can draw the gunmen out.'

'And just why should I agree to be the sacrificial lamb in this instance?' Sanford asked, dabbing softly at the corners of his mouth with a linen napkin.

'We believe that the gunmen are part of the IRA unit that carried out the shootings in Winchester and who murdered Bill Royce and his family.'

Royce had been Sanford's man, his protégé at the MoD. He had also been a friend. His brutal murder had been a terrible blow and had brought home once again just how vulnerable they all were.

'In fact, Sir Robert, we believe that one man was responsible for those two attacks and we think that he will be coming after you. We have a chance to get him and at the same time stop the IRA in England for a while. Will you help?'

There had been no choice. He had volunteered in part because he owed it to Royce and in part because if he had not done so, he would have been a laughing stock in the Ministry of Defence.

So, as usual this Thursday lunchtime, he was being driven to his club. Looking out of the window, he could see no sign of the team that he knew must be surrounding him. They were good, he thought. But then they needed to be if the bait was going to work and live to talk about it.

He glanced up. It looked like it was going to turn out fine after all. He could enjoy the walk back.

CHAPTER 26

DAME MARY CHEONG walked forward into the dark, cavernous mouth of the Tunnel. A crowd of civilians and soldiers watched her small figure until it was swallowed up in the darkness. Behind, her progress was being watched by a battery of infra-red and thermal sensors. Each of them registered when she stopped precisely at the 500-yard mark.

At the briefing earlier, the young army colonel had told her the limits of her mission. 'We are obviously grateful for the effort you are making to resolve this peacefully, Dame Mary,' he had said. 'But there is no point you going in there and becoming yet another victim. We have done our sums and reckon that if you go in 500 yards, up to the first bend, then they should be able to hear you well enough.'

She had accepted the portable loudspeaker and set off. As the darkness closed around her, she was sure that the people inside the Tunnel would have picked up the movement and be wondering just what a single person could do against so many. She quickly became cold. The temperature was little above freezing as with each step she moved further into the Tunnel. The walls were running with water and the atmosphere was unpleasantly dank. It reminded her of some sea-water caves she had visited years ago on the east coast of Hong Kong Island. They had been beautiful, but she had hated the claustrophobia.

Now there was neither the warmth of the sea nor the beauty of the surroundings to compensate for the feeling of being trapped.

She knew she should turn and leave. But somehow she kept putting one foot in front of the other, her shoes making small grating sounds as the rubber soles ground down on the grit of the Tunnel floor. She knew this was a mission doomed to failure. She had agreed with those in the COBRA meeting who said that these men would never give up. But she had to be here. She had to attend this last rite in the same way that a mother returns to the grave of a favourite son.

This would be the grave of the people inside the Tunnel, both aggressors and victims. But this disaster would also bury many of her own dreams. In the past few days, she had seen so many of her hopes dashed. All the years of work, of climbing up the ladder had counted for nought. In the end, she was just another foreigner trying to persuade the British to change their ways. Looking back now, she couldn't understand why she had ever thought in terms of success. The arrogance of the just, she thought to herself. And what a price I've paid.

So now it was time for this one final, futile gesture to salve a conscience burdened by the thought that she should have done more.

She lifted the loudspeaker, clicked the switch and heard the nervous smacking of her lips echo and re-echo down the Tunnel. She began to speak.

The helicopter had dropped them both off. Jonny knew nothing would happen until Dame Mary's mission was over and he wanted to watch the drama. He had been escorted into the green command truck which controlled all the police and military operations in the area.

The colonel who had briefed Dame Mary greeted him. 'Colonel Simon Douglas,' he said, shaking Jonny's hand. 'You must be Jonny Turnbull from the Hong Kong Police.'

While they waited for Dame Mary to get into position, Jonny asked Douglas if they'd picked up any messages.

'Ten minutes ago the signals people got a short burst transmission. They're trying to unscramble it now.'

'Was there a bearing?' Jonny queried. 'Any indication where it was coming from?'

'All we have is the single bearing and it looks like the broadcast came from a ship in the Channel,' said Douglas. 'We need the cross-bearing when they transmit again to get a proper fix and the best way to do that is from a ship at sea. That way we'll get the widest angle. *Campbeltown*'s well placed and their boys are on the job. You can see for yourself when you get out there.'

From a loudspeaker in the corner of the room came the high sing-song tones of Cantonese spoken with the slight overlay of the Hong Kong dialect. Jonny listened to Mary's voice, trying to pick out the words. The voice sounded tinny and ill-defined as if the Tunnel and the transmission had filtered out all the emotion.

'The British government will not negotiate,' he heard her saying. 'I have fought long and hard to persuade them that your cause is just. You know that I believe in what you are doing but your struggle has become pointless. All that is left is the loss of your lives and those of the innocent people you are holding. You should give yourselves up. The struggle is lost.'

Jonny heard the click of the loudspeaker being turned off. It was impossible to imagine that the terrorists were just going to lay down their weapons and walk out of the Tunnel. There was only going to be one way to resolve this.

The captain's cabin on HMS *Campbeltown* is one of those miracles of design that makes the maximum use of the minimum amount of space. When the ship was being built at the Cammell Laird shipyard, designers had been called in from the manufacturers of Avon caravans. They were able to show the shipbuilders how to squeeze the extra bit of comfort out of the very small amount of space available. On a good day, Jeremy Greaves had a desk and chair to himself, a folding dining table, a private bathroom and a couch that converted into a decent-sized bed. This lunchtime was one of those occasions where the real limitations became apparent, irrespective of the caravan-makers' contribution.

Packed into the cabin were Mike Hodder, his number two, a saturnine and untalkative second lieutenant called Jake Ellis, the PWO, the navigator and anyone else who felt they should be in on the act. The result was a crush and a meeting which should have been short and well directed by Greaves, but which had in fact kept them stuck in the stuffy cabin for forty-five minutes waiting for a reply from Northwood to his last signal. As usual, he thought, Their Lordships at the Admiralty were taking their time.

The telephone on his desk rang. He reached behind him and picked it up. 'Captain.'

'Comms here, sir. There's a message coming over from Northwood for you. You'd better come down.'

'On my way.'

He left the cabin and went to the communications centre one deck below. Like many of the work spaces on the ship, this was crammed with equipment and the four people working in the small space appeared to be almost an afterthought. Along one wall there was a bank of data processors, along the other three were receiving systems and transmitters for fighting the electronic war. In the centre of the room where the four men sat were word processors and teleprinters.

All messages are encrypted using different codes depending on the level of classification. Only three people, the captain, the operations officer and the petty officer in charge of communications are cleared to handle traffic marked Top Secret, the highest level of coding. During the Gulf War, Top Secret messages had arrived at the rate of one or two a day, but in more normal circumstances, such a message might appear once a week. Since the Walker spy case, the whole system of coding messages has been changed. Top Secret codes are changed at random but usually every day.

As soon as Greaves entered the room, the petty officer moved to a rank of BID word processors and plugged in what is known as a Fill Gun, which is in fact a small transmitter. From the safe on the floor behind him he pulled out a six-inch-long strip of yellow paper with a series of holes punched through it. He inserted the paper in the Fill Gun and in a single smooth motion slid it through. The Gun instantly read the dots and converted them to a digitized code which was then registered by the processor. All outgoing Top Secret messages would now be encrypted by means of that code.

Greaves moved to a small cubicle on the far side of the room. The petty officer slid into his seat and Greaves watched over his shoulder as the BAe Aroflex receiving system stood silent and watchful.

'We got the alert about five minutes ago, sir, so the message should be coming through any time now.' The petty officer had just finished speaking when the first of the five-letter groups appeared on the screen. Ten groups filled each line and after four lines had been completed, the cursor bobbed to the bottom of the screen and a message flashed up which read: 'Enciphered Message Received'.

The petty officer inserted another Fill Gun and hit the 'Execute' button. Immediately, the cursor started to convert the groups of five letters into a complete and clear signal, a process which takes about ten seconds.

Greaves watched the first line appear. It was the usual string of letters and numbers that indicated the routing of the message. It was incomprehensible to anyone but the petty officer but it provided additional verification, if any were needed, that this was a genuine message. Then the first word appeared and with it he knew that this was the call to arms he had been waiting for. It read 'Immediate', the word that commanded instant obedience and action to carry out the order that followed. His brain absorbed the message:

IMMEDIATE
FM CINCFLEET
TO CAMPBELTOWN
   TOP SECRET   YOU ARE TO TAKE WHATEVER
STEPS ARE NECESSARY TO EFFECT THE RESCUE OF
THE HOSTAGES INSIDE THE CHANNEL TUNNEL
   ACKNOWLEDGE

'Send the acknowledgement back to CINCFLEET,' he instructed the petty officer. As the man's fingers flew across the keyboard, Greaves left the room and took the ladder up to his cabin, where he was met with the silent and expectant faces of the men on whom the success of this mission would depend.

'Well, gentlemen, that was CINCFLEET. We have a Go.'

There was a collective sigh, part relief and part the beginning of a deeper breath as each man drew in the oxygen to help adjust to the instant heightening of tension that the captain's words produced.

For each man, the waiting, the endless refining of ideas, the discussion of options, the worry about the unknown was over. Now there was only commitment and action.

Colonel Douglas picked up his peaked hat and headed for the door. Jonny trailed in his wake, nervous now that the action was imminent.

They walked out towards the Tunnel mouth and the Sea King helicopter that stood off to one side silent and still on an open patch of plain white concrete.

They had only walked a few yards when ahead of them

a single figure emerged from the right-hand tunnel. Jonny stopped and watched Mary Cheong as she walked towards him, the loudspeaker dangling limply from her right hand. He noticed the scuffs on her court shoes, the water stains on the silk suit. Two strands of her dark hair had come loose from the chignon at the back of her neck. They waved and bobbed as she walked, two small signs of life in an otherwise empty and lonely traverse from the darkness to the light.

The despair in Dame Mary's form was obvious. Her shoulders were hunched, her step slow. It was clear that her mission had failed and that no terrorists would be following her out of the Tunnel. It was clear too that her failure, which everyone else had expected, had come as a cruel blow to the woman who had believed until the end that right would be served. As she came level with Jonny, she looked up. He expected to see tears of frustration but was surprised to see her face was perfectly clear. As their eyes met, he saw not despair, but determination, even triumph.

She walked past Jonny without stopping and passed out of his sight. There was no time to speak to her. He felt the colonel's hand on his arm, pulling him towards the helicopter.

Jonny had never really understood how it was he loved helicopters yet hated normal flying. He knew it was completely illogical. After all, if a helicopter stops working a crash landing is virtually certain, while the fixed-wing pilot can glide his way to safety. He spent the ten minutes from Cheriton to the frigate enjoying the sensation and admiring the view. It seemed remarkably bereft of shipping for what some said was the busiest waterway in the world. Maybe the crisis had scared everyone off, he thought.

They came in over the Navy ship in a wide looping turn and then hovered above the rear deck. He moved to the belly of the Sea King and allowed the winchman to put the collar around his body. The last time he had done this had been in Hong Kong when he had been taken ashore after the Mas' escape all those years ago. How strange that it should begin and end in the same way.

This time he felt no terror but could not help an involuntary spasm as he was pushed out of the door and left hanging in mid-air for a moment before the winch-man began to lower him to the ship. As his feet touched the deck, he was grabbed around the waist and drawn to one side. A seaman unlocked the collar and it was pulled back up.

He looked around curiously, surprised to see what looked like a huge ski ramp taking up much of the stern of the helicopter deck.

Three minutes later, they were escorted into the gloom room. A figure approached out of the darkness, hand outstretched. 'I'm Jeremy Greaves. Welcome aboard,' he said. 'We have a few minutes before you need to go below. Let me show you what we are doing to track down the signal to the hijackers.' Greaves drew Jonny towards the general operations plot, the large table located next to the sonar screens.

'This is Lieutenant Jeff Randall. He's plotted the bearing Colonel Douglas passed along,' he said, his finger following a line on the map that headed out to sea east both of Cheriton and of where they were holding station above the Tunnel. 'When do you expect the next signal?'

'Well, if the information is right, then their system calls for a watch every odd hour on the hour,' Jonny replied.

Greaves glanced at the digital clock above the chart table. 'That gives us a little over an hour and a half.' He looked pensive for a moment, thinking of Hodder and his men down below. It was going to be close.

CHAPTER 27

HODDER HAD LED his men inside the central sphere of the Avalon where they were now sitting, waiting. Half my bloody life is spent sitting and waiting for some other bugger to do his job, Hodder reflected sourly.

He looked around, mentally checking his men. When he had first seen the Avalon, he thought there would be room to spare inside the central sphere, but now, with all his men surrounded by their personal equipment, there was barely enough room for the ten of them and, despite the vessel's air-conditioning system, it was already unpleasantly hot.

Each man wore the black neoprene body suit that fitted like a second skin. It was indeed a second skin, something they had lived in, swum in, slept in and killed in over the hundreds of hours of training and action that had led the team to this place on this day.

It was fortunate that this time they had none of the flippers, goggles and oxygen rebreathing systems that they usually carried as a matter of routine. This would be a dry operation or it wouldn't work at all. The suits would protect them from the cold they expected inside the Tunnel. All of them had learned the hard way that the diver's first and worst enemy is cold.

Each man carried a pistol and had a black diver's knife strapped to his calf. Beyond that, there was a bewildering array of personal equipment. Two men carried the Heckler and Koch Close Assault Weapon System (CAWS) with a large box cartridge containing thirty shotgun rounds. These could be fired at great speed and with devastating effect at close range. Three other men carried the silenced version of the Heckler MP5 9 mm automatic rifle. They would be first in, their job to take out the sentries as quickly and quietly as possible. After that, Hodder knew, it would quickly develop into a free-for-all where darkness made everyone equal and only the superior training and discipline of his men would make the difference between survival and death.

Other men carried the normal H. and K. with the folding stock. Attached to the underside of the barrel was a powerful Maglite torch which could be turned on with the left hand. Its beam could blind as well as illuminate a target. Each man carried grenades that would release brilliant white light, a concussive bang or hundreds of flechettes that would kill anything within a thirty-yard radius.

'It's going to be very fast once we get down there,' Hodder said to Jake Ellis, his second-in-command.

'Isn't it always?' Ellis grunted.

Hodder smiled a short, grim smile. Ellis never talked much and before an operation hardly at all. But once the shooting started he was quick and reliable, a careful operator who would cover your back and expect you to do the same for him. The right man for this operation.

Hodder turned to his other side. Jonny stood out not just because he moved awkwardly and was clearly uncomfortable in his black body suit but because he was much taller than everyone else. SBS men tend to be squat, a useful characteristic when you spend hours crawling and swimming in confined spaces. They also tend to be very broad-shouldered from all the swimming. Even with most of his face covered by the black hood of the suit, Jonny seemed out of place, a stick insect fallen among killer bees.

'OK?' Hodder asked. He resented the presence of this stranger in their midst. Amateurs not only got themselves killed but they put the professionals at risk. He had protested to London but apparently promises had been made. He had given Turnbull none of the exotica that festooned his men. At least he knew how to fire a pistol and a sub-machine-gun, and he couldn't do much damage to Hodder's men or himself with the knife strapped to his calf.

Jonny had been on plenty of undercover operations before. Usually, surveillance was followed by the raid. There was plenty of information and plenty of people so the unknown and the uncertainty were kept to a sensible minimum. This time was very different. It had been clear from the briefing just how little they knew about the terrorists. The Tentacle had given a general location but no numbers; there was no intelligence about their arms, apart from what had already been gleaned in the abortive police raid; and the condition and location of the hostages could only be guessed. Without information, the men around him would have to rely on instinct and training to keep them alive. That was fine if you had honed your night-fighting skills and made a virtue of living on your wits. As it was, Jonny was more frightened than he could have thought possible. He had played over the first few minutes in the darkness of the Tunnel below and each scene was more terrifying than the last. Each one had his body writhing on the end of Dai Choi's knives and guns. Added to the fear was the heat and claustrophobia inside the mini submarine. The incredibly constricting neoprene suit was not only hot but seemed to pinch his skin every time he moved. Worst of all, his bowels really had turned to water and there was nothing he could do about it except pray for the journey to end.

Rationally, he knew the team had rehearsed the general operation of a Tunnel rescue often enough. They had even rehearsed getting into the Tunnel through the access hatches, so there would be nothing strange about the environment. But there were always unknowns that lay in wait.

They were up against men who were willing to die, which would make them reckless. That in turn required Hodder's men to be equally prepared to kill – and kill quickly. There would be no opportunity for such old-fashioned ideas as quarter or surrender. Once this started the only ending would be the deaths of the terrorists. No doubt some of the men around him would die along with some of the hostages. But this was no zero sum game. For now, thoughts of killing Dai Choi had vanished. He would be happy to get out of the Tunnel alive.

'Thirty seconds to lift off, gentlemen.' The voice of Frank Rostenkowski emerged from the small speaker over Hodder's head. He sounded very American, very professional, and also very tinny.

Hodder felt the deck begin to cant as the missile launcher elevated. There was a moment when everything seemed suspended in movement and time and then suddenly the vessel was sliding with an agonized groan down the launcher. There was a jarring crash as the Avalon hit the sea and then silence. It lasted a few seconds before the electric engines cut in. The deck remained at around fifteen degrees as the ship moved beneath the surface and headed for the safety hatch below.

Hodder would have preferred the journey to last long enough for him to review the operation just one more time. But within four minutes, the deck levelled. Looking up, Hodder watched the TV monitor which was slaved to a camera in the Avalon's nose. The dark screen flashed white as Rostenkowski turned on the floodlight. The sensors self-adjusted and then he could see the Channel bottom and just ahead the grey metal of the escape hatch.

This was the moment when all Rostenkowski's confident skill would be needed. He had to drop the rubber skirt of the pressure chamber below Hodder's sphere right on to the escape chamber. A knock against the metal would reverberate inside the Tunnel and warn the terrorists that an assault was under way.

Hodder could almost feel the delicate touch of the skipper's fingers as the tiny thrusters moved the Avalon to left and right until the two chambers were positioned exactly one on top of the other. There was an almost imperceptible settling.

'As promised, delivery right to the door,' came the voice over the speaker.

Air hissed as the pressure equalized around the collar of the escape hatch. In the centre of the floor, recessed into what looked like a manhole cover, a red light turned green. Hodder spun the small wheel that opened the hatch and pulled it towards him. He looked down the hole and saw the concave weed-and-mollusc-encrusted shape of the hatch that led directly into the Tunnel.

He beckoned his men forward.

Sean Thomas had watched Robert Sanford enter his club from the security of Three Kings Yard on the other side of Davies Street. He was seventy yards away, far enough not to be spotted and close enough for quick access. The plan was simple enough. He would walk to the other end of Brook's Mews and wait until Sanford appeared. Sanford would turn left, away from Sean and towards Davies Street. Sean would follow. At the same time Sally would start the Suzuki up and head towards them both. Once the job was done, he would hop on to the pillion, continue down the Mews, turn right into Avery Row and away.

He had hesitated about bringing Sally. Back at Waterloo Road there had been no time to negotiate as she forced herself into the car. There had been no convenient way to dump her without drawing attention to himself and now he had reconciled himself to her presence, her company and even her love. After all, he had justified to himself, women were no strangers to the Movement. On the contrary, they had played a valuable role in this campaign and had often proved more dedicated and ruthless than their male counterparts. When this was all over and they were back in Ireland, he would make sure that she got a proper grounding in the tactics and techniques of the Movement. A Brit used to living in England could be a useful asset for the future.

The journey up to town had been simple enough. He had stolen the bike in Southampton and they had simply driven up the A31, keeping off the high-profile and well-patrolled M3. He knew another, more focused manhunt would be following his wake after their escape from the safe house. But he was no stranger to that and knew the steps he would have to take to keep ahead of the hounds. It was another reason why Sally should stay with him. Alone, she would quickly be found. Together they had a chance.

In South London the IRA has a strong network of supporters founded originally among the workers who travelled the London building sites as brickies, plumbers and plasterers. Today, many of them have settled down but still remember old loyalties. Sean normally stayed clear of such people as they had been widely penetrated by Special Branch, but he reckoned a couple of nights would be safe enough. It would take that long for an informer to do his dirty business and the police to respond.

He had walked past the building three times on both sides of the street, strolling nonchalantly, a casual window shopper looking for something to buy. With each journey he could feel the tension mounting. He had to control the impulse to reach under his jacket for the reassurance of the cold metal of the gun. He wanted to take it out, check it over just one more time, make sure the magazine was full, the first bullet in the breech. He knew he had done all this already not once but three times. He knew that he was the most professional gunman he knew. But even so, the waiting brought the doubts and with the doubts came the tension.

Then suddenly there he was. Sanford walked down the steps to the street and turned away exactly as expected. The suddenness of his appearance after so long spent waiting had taken Sean by surprise and he hurried to catch up with his target, his long legs striding out.

He watched Sanford's shoulders move, imagining the impact of the bullets, his killer instinct taking over, measuring angles, judging timings, assuring success. A few more feet and at last it was time. His hand swept behind his jacket to feel the confidence-building coolness of the pistol butt. A slight jerk and the spring clip gave up its gift and the gun moved down. His thumb flicked off the safety as the whole hand brought the weapon into the firing position.

He stopped, the retreating back just five feet away. His right arm extended in front of him, his left hand moved over to grip the right wrist.

His finger had just begun to take up the first pressure when his faithful watchdog, instinct, made him look across the street. A fleeting glance was enough; the recognition of the enemy instant. His professional's subconscious weighed the odds and judged the risk. In a macrosecond he recognized that this was The One, the time that he'd always known would one day be his. But he had no time now to think of escape or shout for mercy. It was the mission that mattered, the final gesture for the Cause for which he was about to die.

He focused again on the back in front of him and squeezed the trigger.

Time telescoped. Thomas heard the beginnings of a shout even as he saw Sanford start to fall to the ground. His gun tracked him down, his finger squeezing the trigger for the first time. He saw the impact, the puffing of the charcoal suit in the right shoulder, the entrance hole, the fountain of blood as the bullet exited, even the white scar on the pavement as it ricocheted down the street.

He caught a glimpse of Sally on the bike coming towards him, her mouth opened in an enormous O of horror. But there was no time for distractions.

The slide of the automatic was forced back by the exploding gases from the spent cartridge and the shell case sparkled in the sunlight as it arced out into the street. As another round chambered, his finger flexed to take up the pressure once again. He fired again, saw the impact and the power of the bullet propel Sanford's body along the pavement. But the image was wrong. Vest, the bastard's got a vest. His gun moved towards the unprotected head, his finger once again pulling the trigger.

But now that shout – clearly a warning – was translated into action. He heard and felt the shot simultaneously, his body buffeted as if by a giant wind. His feet left the ground and he was momentarily weightless, as if he were actually flying. He crashed to the ground, gun hand on top of his body. Training and instinct still forced him to concentrate on the target.

On the pavement together, the killer and his victim. Sean could see the frightened face of the enemy lying opposite him. Their eyes met, a brief communion of unspoken fear.

His trigger finger jerked and he felt the recoil and saw the bullet go home. The body in front of him was pushed up the pavement like a leaf in a storm.

But then the pain began. Agony in his groin. He looked down and saw blood fountaining from his stomach. In almost clinical fashion he watched as his body disintegrated in front of him as shot after shot hit his flesh and tore it apart. He had always imagined that when it came he would go with fist raised and a defiant 'Up the IRA.' But now there was just the final revolution of death.

CHAPTER 28

HODDER AND HIS men had slid down the ropes to the Tunnel floor, landing silently and secretly. His team formed a small rectangle of firepower around him, their weapons facing out, the barrels nosing through the darkness for targets.

Looking through his night-vision goggles, Hodder saw that their positioning had been almost perfect. They had emerged about halfway down the second carriage and the ropes dropped through the hatch had landed on the walkway that ran alongside the tracks. There had been no crunch of gravel as they landed, just the silent flexing of the neoprene suits.

The stench from the carriage was unbelievable. Faeces and urine combined to grab at the throat. Jonny felt himself swallowing, trying to contain the retching. If he vomited now he would never live it down – if he lived at all after losing the element of surprise.

The green image of the hot spots around him showed clearly that there were two groups of terrorists at either end of the train, but there was nothing moving and it was impossible to pick out individuals. There was another large hot spot in the carriages themselves. The hostages, he thought to himself. At least that's clear.

'A squad head down the Tunnel and secure that perimeter,' Hodder whispered into his throat microphone. He heard the double click in his headphones as the squad leader acknowledged. 'B squad head up the Tunnel. Go under the train and up the far side. That way, you'll stay clear of the open doors. C Squad stay with me and we'll take the hostages. Move out.'

The rectangle splintered and the men moved off. Each squad was led by one of the men with the silenced rifles so that if a threat emerged there was still a chance of a silent kill before the alarm was raised.

Doubled over, Jonny followed Hodder as they advanced towards the carriage nearest the French end of the Tunnel. Now that they were actually moving, he felt better, the focus of his fear shifting from his body to his weapon. His hands, slippery with sweat, gripped the stock and barrel tightly, finger alongside the trigger guard. They passed the first open door and it was clear that this car had nobody inside. At the next carriage, Hodder paused just before the gaping hole of the open doorway. Peering over his shoulder, it was clear to Jonny that this was where the hostages were. The whole floor of the carriage appeared as one solid green glow of bodies. He raised his goggles and by the faint yellow illumination of the emergency lights could distinguish faces in the crowd. He looked carefully but the terrorists must be concealed by the carriage walls.

Whispering into his mike, Hodder ordered his men off the walkway and on to the track. Creeping softly forward, he wanted to bracket the doorway so that when the assault came it would be from all sides and at the same time.

Jonny could feel the pebbles move as he brought each foot down carefully towards the ground, his toes feeling for the gravel, ensuring that no stone was dislodged. He saw the shape of Hodder ahead of him duck even lower as he came to the doorway. Suddenly, Jonny's foot slipped. It was just a tiny movement, a slight hesitation in his step but it was enough.

There was the rattle of rock on rock. In normal

circumstances, the sound would have passed unnoticed. But this was terrorism and nothing was normal. If these people were half as good as they were supposed to be, Jonny thought, the rescuers were about to be in deep shit.

Inside the carriage, Kate Carr had been waiting for an opportunity to strike back. She neither expected one nor knew exactly what she would do if one presented itself to her. All she knew was that she wanted revenge for the death of the man she loved, for the destruction of her family, for the frightening of her daughter and for the humiliation they had all suffered.

For two hours now she had been rolling and unrolling her *Daily Mail*. She had done it so often that she had almost forgotten just why it was she had begun to do so. The twisting of her hands around the newsprint had become a nervous twitch, an excuse for movement where no greater gesture was allowed.

Then she had heard the rattle of rock just outside the carriage door. She had heard enough noises in the past hours to inure her to such sounds. But there was something about this that pricked her senses. It seemed stealthy. She listened, but there was no other sound. Then she saw the bulk of a shadow move past the doorway. Her eyes had become extraordinarily attuned to the half-light created by the yellow lamps. She could see that the man was all in black and appeared to have his head sheathed in some kind of helmet. This was not one of their guards. They were all wearing ordinary clothes.

She thought she could actually feel her heart leap. Rescuers. Help had come at last.

Her peripheral vision picked up one of the Chinese moving quietly towards her. He came level with her and she saw that it was the one she had nicknamed the Poison Dwarf, the little one, whom their leader called Kang Sheng. His machine-gun nosed out ahead of him, probing the doorway for the source of the noise that had disturbed him. He leaned over her, trying to get a view of the track outside without exposing himself.

Without pause for thought, Kate struck upwards. The rolled-up newspaper had the strength and composition of an iron bar. With all Kate's fury and frustration behind it, the newspaper struck deep into the man's throat. The blow jarred her arm and she felt the paper thrust against flesh of his neck, forcing it inwards. There was a cracking sound as the larynx was crushed and then the man jerked upward, gasping, unable to draw breath for the scream that his body demanded to be released.

Searching for air, Kang Sheng jerked forward again. Kate drew back and stabbed once more. The man's downward momentum met the upward thrust of the paper. With a horrible squelching noise, his left eyeball was crushed as the paper drove into the eye socket. Still there was no sound, just a strangled gasp as his body tried to respond to this new level of pain.

Blinded and starved of oxygen, his body continued its downward fall and hit the steel floor of the carriage. He was dying now and Kate turned away, the frenzy over, revolted at the results of her handiwork.

Kang Sheng's body twisted and jerked off the floor, arching so that his body bowed and only his toes and the crown of his head remained in touch with the ground. He spun away from Kate and fell through the doorway to land with a clatter on the track below.

The sound of the falling body told Hodder that surprise had been lost. Now seconds were everything and there was no time for hesitation.

'Go. Go. Go,' he shouted into his microphone. He rolled through the doorway of the carriage, turning over and over until with a bone-jarring crash he hit the far wall. Jonny followed, his elegant parachute roll turning into a jumble of limbs as he tried to reduce his body to a tiny ball while holding on to his gun. He peered around frantically, eyes darting first left and then right as he searched for the microseconds of warning that would tell him he was a target.

Outside, one of the men was shouting, 'Stay down. Stay down,' in the hope that the hostages would remain still while the terrorists would be forced to expose themselves.

There was the ripping sound of a machine-pistol on full automatic and the carriage was lit briefly by the red and yellow flame sprouting from a gun barrel. The image of the carriage was seared on to his brain: the cowering passengers, bodies huddled together, old and young, male and female, all merged into an uneven bumpy mass of fear.

Then his eyes locked on to a terrorist, the one who had fired his gun. Jonny swung the barrel round and let out a short burst of four rounds. The man was lifted off his feet and fell back on top of some of the hostages.

There was screaming in the carriage now, the confined space magnifying the noise, expanding the terror. Each of the hostages felt that every bullet was aimed at them, each gun pointed at their heads.

There was more firing from the far end of the carriage. This time, Michael Leung was not bothering to attack his attackers but was doing what he had been ordered to do if attacked: kill the hostages. Like a gardener with his hose, he was spraying the bodies around him. As each bullet struck, there was a visible reaction as nerves were cut, muscles torn and limbs broken. Arms, legs and torsos flailed in the air as if massive jolts of electricity were being sent through the carriage floor.

Jonny felt the adrenalin of raw rage spurt through him. Disregarding training and caution, he leaped to his feet and charged the man, firing as he went. The terrorist was concentrating too hard on the easy targets and his reactions were slow. As he looked up and his gun changed direction, the first bullet struck him in the groin. Jonny allowed his barrel to move upwards with the recoil so that the bullets formed an upward pattern, following the body as it was lifted up and back. Each bullet drove the man further back until he smashed into the rear wall of the carriage, hung for a moment and then slumped to the floor.

If inside the carriage was raw power and mayhem, outside it was a stealthier battle. Dai Choi had heard the first shots and knew that the attack they feared had begun. He wanted to run but wanted, too, a chance to make the attackers pay a heavy price. Killing the hostages was his goal; killing the attackers a matter of survival.

He was hidden under the rear of the carriage and watched as a small group of men walked quietly by him heading for the guard post twenty yards in front.

Reaching into his pocket he drew out the cheese wire with the wooden stakes at either end and hefted it in his right hand. As the last man moved past, Dai Choi pounced, his right hand releasing one end of the wire and throwing it around the man's neck. His left hand caught the wooden stake and with a single fluid motion he brought the wire of the garotte into the flesh of the neck.

The garotte is the deadliest of silent weapons. It is simple but, when applied correctly, absolutely lethal. Dai Choi hoisted his knee into the small of his victim's back and then brought his fists together until they were touching behind the man's neck. He pushed with his knee and pulled with his hands. The wire cut through flesh and sinew, only stopped by the bone of the vertebrae.

Jake Ellis felt a moment of agony, the hot dampness of blood, and then he died.

Dai Choi lowered the body to the ground and slunk back underneath the carriage. The sounds of the dead and dying were all around. He could see the probing torchlights of the enemy as they searched for the living among the dead and wounded. Escape was impossible, a deal inconceivable. He knew that he was going to die and was ready to accept his fate. But if he was going down, he would take all these bastards with him – if he could. The controls to the explosive charges were just ahead. He began a slow, sinewy crawl up the track, his body hugging the ground. He could feel the pebbles grate against his chest and stomach but the discomfort meant nothing to him. He was going to make it. He could already imagine the fire storm that the explosion would unleash inside the Tunnel, the burning human flesh, the cordite.

The carriage was secure and Jonny jumped down on to the track. Now that he was still alive, his real purpose had resurfaced and he wanted Dai Choi, even if it was only to stand over his corpse. He looked underneath the train and then began walking slowly towards the British end of the Tunnel. The firing had died down now but he knew that this was often the moment when the unwary dropped their guard and paid a heavy price for their stupidity. He came to the end of the carriage and peered around. He saw a body lying in the track and recognized the dark suit of one of his own team.

He risked a quick flash of the Maglite that was fixed underneath the barrel of his gun. In its white glare he saw the crumpled shape of Jake Ellis. His head was almost severed from his trunk and there was blood everywhere. But then Jonny's brain registered the trail of blood leading away from the carcase. Holding his gun away from his body, he turned the light back on and saw that the killer had crawled through Jake's blood to make his escape. The trail was wide and distinct. A flick of the wrist and the killer was trapped in the white of the light.

He had imagined this scene so often; not the setting but the time when he could become this man's nemesis. He had played the conversation over dozens, perhaps hundreds of times. But now the moment had come, he found he really had nothing to say. They both knew the whys of this final confrontation. All that needed to be decided was exactly how it would be resolved.

'So, Mr Turnbull,' Dai Choi began, the old confidence returning as he saw Jonny's finger relax slightly on the trigger. 'Finally you have an opportunity to make an arrest for which I will have no alibi.'

'Wrong, Dai Choi. No arrests, no lawyers, no alibis. This is where it all ends.' He spoke with such absolute finality that Dai Choi realized that Turnbull intended to kill him. He began to edge backwards, moving a fraction of an inch at a time. His right hand was just outside the pool of light and his fingers were searching, groping through the pebbles for the small black box and the detonator button.

Jonny saw the movement and pivoted the Maglite a few inches to his left. Dai Choi's fingers were inches away from the box. There was no hesitation. Jonny moved the gun fractionally and squeezed the trigger. The bullet struck Dai Choi in the shoulder, shattering the bone and leaving the arm hanging limp and useless. Dai Choi was flung backwards and skittered two feet along the gravel. As the pain hit him, he screamed, a taut, high-pitched cry of agony.

Jonny moved forward to stand at his feet, his torch now flooding his enemy's body with white light. The blood from the shoulder wound glowed bright red in the reflection from the torch. Jonny wanted to fire again, to end it all, but paused for a moment to take in the fear that he saw cross like a cloud over Dai Choi's face.

'So how does it feel?' he asked. 'After so long giving out pain, what is it like to suffer a little yourself? Can you understand just some of what I felt when Sam died?'

Dai Choi grimaced, struggling to maintain his composure. He wanted to regain the ascendancy in a relationship he had controlled for so long. But the levers were gone. 'You think you've won.' He squeezed the words out between teeth clenched with pain. 'Well, you're about to discover just how ignorant you really are.'

'Cut the crap, Dai Choi,' Jonny replied. 'It's over. You lost. We won. Simple.'

Dai Choi let out a long sigh of pain and his head fell back. For a brief moment the whites of his eyes showed and then he struggled back to consciousness.

'Simple?' he asked. 'It was never as simple as you thought. Our Leader planned for just this moment. Negotiate and there was a chance. Attack and whatever happens we all die.'

'But there's nothing you can do,' Jonny insisted. You're finished. Your men are all dead or taken.'

'No, you stupid man. I do not matter. I never did. White Lotus controls me and now controls you. It's too late for us both.'

Jonny squeezed the trigger twice. The first bullet hit Dai Choi's kneecap squarely in the centre, the second missed the right knee, hit the ground then ricocheted off the stones into his thigh and exited leaving a gaping hole about two inches across. Another scream was torn from him, the agony transparent. Jonny moved over and knelt by Dai Choi's head.

'Now that's control,' he breathed into his ear. 'Can you feel that blood on your leg? That's an artery. Another few minutes and you're a dead man unless I do something about it. So, what's this great plan?'

Dai Choi had seen too many men die at his own hand not to be frightened of death himself. Now that the reality was moments away, he wanted desperately to live, wanted the pain to stop, wanted to assert himself over Turnbull just one last time.

'On the bottom of the sea above our heads there is a nuclear bomb. If the radio message isn't answered, then it will be detonated. You, me, everyone in here will die. So, Turnbull, another game you've lost.'

Jonny jerked upright, stepped over Dai Choi's body and kicked the detonator out of reach. He looked down at Dai Choi. Then he turned and walked away from the dying man, leaving the blood to pump out the last few minutes of his life into the gravel of the Tunnel floor.

As he hurried off into the darkness, searching for Hodder, he shone his torch on his watch: 14.35, just twenty-five minutes to go before the next radio message. It was going to be damn close.

He saw Hodder in the distance, herding some of the hostages out of the train carriage and on to the track. He shouted to attract his attention.

'Mike. Mike,' he called. Hodder broke away from the group and came towards him. 'Mike, there's a nuclear bomb on the sea bed. It will go off on the hour unless we can warn *Campbeltown*.'

'Christ Almighty,' Hodder swore. A moment and then he had made his decisions. 'Right, I'll have to stay and get the hostages out. You go with my sergeant in the submersible. You should be on the surface in ten minutes or so. Alert *Campbeltown* and then it's up to them.'

He turned away and began shouting at his men to gather the hostages together for the journey out of the Tunnel.

Jonny felt his arm gripped and was propelled back the way they had come to the ropes and the escape hatch.

'Able Seaman Williams here is the man you want to watch,' Greaves explained helpfully. 'The console in front of him is the UAA1 Electronic Warfare system. He can detect any vessel by its radar emission. By comparing that emission with our computerized data base he can give me course, speed and ship type within a few seconds.'

Jonny peered at the screen, amazed at the number of small green dots that seemed to pepper the circle.

Williams spun the roller ball under his right palm and brought the cursor over a green dot that appeared to be about two miles astern of *Campbeltown*. His left hand pressed some keys of what looked like a small typewriter keyboard.

'That tells the system to interrogate the target, identify all known characteristics and report back,' Greaves said.

A moment later a short line of letters and numbers appeared on the screen.

'That tells us she is a French destroyer of the F70 class. Probably the *Jean Bart*. She's been with us almost since this began.'

'So what happens if we pick up a message?' Jonny asked.

'Comms will pick up the signal and give us the cross-bearing. Williams here will identify the target and then we decide on what action needs to be taken. If we pick up a signal, I want you to translate it as it comes in so that I can keep my options open.'

Greaves glanced to his left and saw the digital clock change from 14.52 to 14.53. Jonny had made it just in time. The most difficult part of the journey had been climbing back up the damn rope to the escape hatch. It had been agonizingly slow and he had only managed it in the end because the sergeant had gone first and pulled him up most of the way. The Avalon had taken them smoothly to the surface and they had climbed up a scaling ladder lowered over the side of *Campbeltown*.

The crew were already at action stations, alerted by a radio message from Avalon. He had been escorted directly to the gloom room where Captain Greaves sat perched on his leather fighting chair.

'Do you have any idea of the type of weapon it is?' Jonny asked him.

'It could be all sorts. I assume it's one of those that are supposed to have reached the market from the former Soviet Union. The Soviets had a portable nuclear weapon, known as the backpack nuke, for use by their Special Forces. They had plenty of nuclear mines which are small and are easy to transport. We just have no idea. In a sense the type doesn't matter, it's how it's set off we care about. If your chum down below is right and it detonates on a radio command then we might just be able to do something about it.

'The trouble with radio these days is that there are just no certainties. With frequency hopping in use everywhere, we can jam one signal and the radio hops somewhere else and it always takes us a moment or two to catch up. It's that moment when we could all be blown out of the water. If you'll forgive the pun,' he added sarcastically.

Having survived the terror of the Tunnel, Jonny found the tension in the gloom room almost an anticlimax. There was none of the shouting and shooting of the Tunnel. Instead, the machinery was noisier than the operators speaking quietly into their small boom mikes. But it was all an illusion. If the next few minutes went wrong, he and everyone here would be at the heart of the explosion. They would all be melted by the heat, the water in their bodies instantly vaporized. It would indeed be Dai Choi's final triumph.

Jonny's headphones chattered with a message from Comms. 'Signal just came in, sir,' the voice announced. 'We're tracking now.'

It was for this moment that the officers and men of HMS *Campbeltown* had trained. It was for now that the hours, the days and weeks had been spent practising again and again the coordination required to make an operations room run effectively.

'PWO Air, target type and range? CHOPS, Sea Wolf status.'

The principal warfare officer responsible for the air battle receives all the information from the sonar operators and any other data that might help analyse the threat. In his coordinating role, he has the total picture and it is his responsibility to produce timely and accurate information for the captain. His response was immediate.

'Small cruiser, sir. Range 7,000 yards. Speed fifteen knots. Course 280, bearing 120.'

The chief petty officer, operations (missiles) runs the Sea Wolf missile system from two television screens situated to the left of the captain's chair. Jonny looked over and saw him hunched over his keyboard, his fingers flying furiously. 'Sea Wolf B radar scanning, sir. Missiles on line. All systems in the green.' As he spoke a line of fifteen green lights above the two television screens came on.

'Fire when ready.'

'Fire when ready. Aye, sir.'

The Sea Wolf radar conducts a ninety-degree vertical sweep every second. Once the target coordinates are fed into its computer, a second sweep narrows the arc to forty degrees. A second later the missile radar locks on to the target. Ten seconds after Greaves gave his final order the first missile fired out of its launcher with a massive cloud of white smoke and a roar that could be heard in the operations room. A fraction of a second later, the second missile launched.

'Fail safe,' Greaves muttered.

The two TV monitors in front of the missile controller lit up. A small television camera in each of the Sea Wolfs' nose cones relayed an image back to the controller who could then direct the first stages of the missile's flight by means of a tiny joystick to the left of his console. Once the seeker in the missile nose cone locked on, then the course was set, the target certain and all the operator could do was watch the final moments before impact.

'Another message, sir,' Jonny heard in his headphones. But it was too late.

For a few seconds the screen was blank and then suddenly a white power cruiser appeared on the TV monitor. At first a tiny speck, it grew and grew as the operator homed the six-foot missile to its target. The operator focused the nose camera and for a brief moment the image was frozen on the screen. Jonny clearly saw the faces of the two women. Julie Cohen, the hostage of last resort, was looking directly at the camera, the terror clear on her face. Then the second woman looked up from the microphone. With a frisson of horror, Jonny recognized Dame Mary Cheong. Their eyes seemed to meet across the chasm of water. The memory of that moment outside the Tunnel, when he had seen determination on her face instead of despair after her failed mission to persuade the terrorists to surrender, crystallized in his mind. Now it made sense. She – not Stanley Kung – was the Leader, the mastermind behind all this horror. It was her ruthless control that had created Dai Choi. With her consummate understanding of corruption and manipulation of power she had worked from within the establishment to undermine a system she despised.

Dame Mary Cheong stopped speaking and then her face fixed in horror as she understood in her final moments that death was arcing towards her at 3,000 miles an hour.

Long after the explosion had obliterated the small ship, the image of Dame Mary Cheong, despairing and defeated, remained.

The shuffling, shambling crowd of passengers and their escorts looked like refugees rescued after a long sentence in a concentration camp. A dreadful toll had been taken on the seventy-five passengers who had embarked on the journey to France. Fifteen were dead, twenty wounded, all showed the scars of their incarceration.

Hodder wanted to shout at them, to urge them forward, to tell them that time was rapidly running out. But the vacant stares, the frightened eyes and the sheer exhaustion were eloquent testimony that these people had suffered enough. Any suggestion of an even more horrible fate lurking above would, he suspected, simply cause what little life was left in them to fizzle out. Already his men were supporting one or two of the wounded. They had run out of painkillers from the meagre supply they had been able to bring with them. Each step along the track brought a shriek of agony from one of the wounded. But each step was a few feet further towards the safety of the dry land.

The attack on the train had left Kate Carr purged of her anger and sorrow. She had replayed the killing of the Poison Dwarf in her mind, had heard again the sickening impact of the tube sinking into his throat and then his dying gasps as he struggled for breath. She felt no revulsion now. With every step, she knew she was heading back to a life she understood. With every step she felt the security of Emma's small hand in hers. Looking down at her daughter now, she marvelled at the resilience of small children. She was filthy, but there was a spring in her step and some of the old ebullience was returning. Kate wanted to stop and put her arms around her daughter. She was her family now. This time, Tom would not be there to welcome them home. She felt the tears course down her cheeks.

Then suddenly she heard a shout and looked up from the tracks. Ahead the circle of light that was the Tunnel mouth beckoned to them. Those in front started to run in the short, drunken steps of the exhausted. Caught up in the excitement, she felt her own pace quicken. The circle got wider, the light sharper, and then they were out into the glorious bright summer afternoon.